T0195921

Also by Stone Spicer:

Deep Green

First Kensington Stone novel, featuring Teri White and Viane Koa

Viane Koa finds two artifacts dating back to AD 1269 brought by the first Polynesians arriving in Hawaii. The treasures are hidden deep in the bowels of a lava tube together with mysterious human bones lying close by. Her discovery brings black marketers like flies to a fresh kill, initiating a series of dramatic events. The artifacts are taken from her, and she is thrown from a yacht miles from shore and left to die.

Her rescuer, Kensington Stone, and her best friend, Teri White, begin the odyssey to locate Viane after she's later kidnapped. Together they all set out to discover the whereabouts of the artifacts so they can be returned to their original resting place in the lava tube.

Within the pages of *Deep Green*, you will travel deep into the bowels of a lava tube, get caught in a brutal storm at sea, spend a terrifying night off the coast of Kailua-Kona, and find serenity in the moonlight on the sands of Waikiki Beach.

MYSTERY – INTRIQUE – HUMOR – ROMANCE
Find it at StoneSpicer-Author.com

HIDDEN SO DEEP

A novel

STONE SPICER

Order this book online at www.trafford.com
or email orders@trafford.com

Most Trafford titles are also available at major online book retailers.

Print information available on the last page.

ISBN: 978-1-4907-7132-8 (sc)
ISBN: 978-1-4907-7131-1 (hc)
ISBN: 978-1-4907-7133-5 (e)

Library of Congress Control Number: 2016903843

Trafford rev. 03/19/2016

 www.trafford.com

North America & international
toll-free: 1 888 232 4444 (USA & Canada)
fax: 812 355 4082

StoneSpicer-Author.com

Acknowledgments

I'd like to thank my dear friend Ms. Colleen Randle for her phenomenal editing support. Without her, there may have been mass confusion as you, my dear readers, crashed into some very long and confusing sentences, which, thanks to Colleen, are no longer present—except perhaps for this one.

Also my appreciation to my Envisioning Group for continual encouragement as well as support: Dr. Rhonda Hull, Rev. Pamela Douglas-Smith, Ms. Colleen Randle, and Jacques Thiry.

To my readers, a heartfelt *mahalo*. Thank you for your interest in my writing.

If you would like to make a comment or suggestion, please go to StoneSpicer-Author.com

I am eager to receive any observations you wish to make, good or not good (the latter, hopefully, not too numerous).

Dictionary of Uncommon Words

There may be many unfamiliar words used throughout my story, both Hawaiian and Pidgin. To talk of Hawaii and tell a story of the people and places in the Islands, it would be a challenge not to use the commonly known words—the flavor of the Islands and the story would surely be lost.

Words used in my story also offer you, my reader, a glimpse into how I view and love the islands, a place I will always consider home.

If you choose to expand your knowledge, refer to the list in the back of the book.

For my Hawaii family and friends, there's nothing more to say—you live these words every day.

Author's Note

*Lunar lava tubes have been discovered and
have been studied as possible human habitats,
providing natural shielding from radiation.*

—NASA

Throughout this story, there are references to a phenomenon in nature appropriately named lava tubes. If one was to know nothing about them, parts of this story would undoubtedly be confusing. The last thing I wish to accomplish would be to confuse you, my readers. I'd much rather you are amused and hold me in high acclaim, so please allow me to explain.

Lava tubes are a common feature associated with the type of volcanoes and lava flows that make up Hawaii, especially so on the Island of Hawaii, better known as the Big Island, where this story begins. Visitors to the Big Island usually visit the famous Thurston Lava Tube, which makes up a part of the tourist experience when visiting Hawaii Volcanoes National Park.

As a type of lava called *pahoe'hoe* flows from its source deep in the earth, the newly exposed surface of the liquid rock touches cool air and moisture, causing the outer surface to cool and harden, thus creating a *roof.* The coolness has little effect on the scorching-hot molten rock beneath this hardening surface, so it continues its flow, moving through its newly formed *straw*.

When the eruption ceases and the pressure behind the flow abates, the molten rock drains out of its straw, leaving behind a long, virtually empty tunnel. These tunnels can be fifteen to thirty feet or more in diameter and several miles long. The longest documented lava tube on the Big Island is the Kazumura Cave situated 3,614 feet below the surface and measuring 40.7 miles in length. Centuries of time and numerous lava flows later, a series of tubes have been created, built over older lava flows. The result is a deep swiss cheese–like surface covering the island.

Early Polynesian settlers looking for places to secretly bury the bones of their chiefs and high priests discovered the ideal location within old lava tubes. Most of those would be extremely difficult to relocate as time has eroded and collapsed many of their openings.

A few fortunate property owners have discovered an opening to a lava tube on their property. They usually then go about finding suitable uses for them. Lights have been strung into the darkness, carpeting and furniture added to create additional living space; social gatherings have found their way into these depths; and some resourceful owners have gone so far as to use the dark, cool interiors for growing mushrooms and other not-so-legal produce, the latter often assuming precedence over mushrooms.

The woods are lovely, dark and deep,

But I have promises to keep,

And miles to go before I sleep,

And miles to go before I sleep.

—Robert Frost

One

Far below ground on the slopes of Mauna Loa, Big Island of Hawaii

A SMALL BEAM OF light, that's all. There was nothing else.

It inched its way down the wall of rock with painstaking slowness, finding its way across her face. The intense burning sensation caught her left eyelid as her hand took a reactive swing to bat whatever it was away. It felt like a recently extinguished match head still smoldering hot being held a breath's distance from her skin, which made no sense as her swatting hand connected with nothing but air.

She'd been unconscious, totally out, for several hours; but the penetrating ray of sunlight brought her back to the surface of consciousness. She instinctively shifted her head, the movement of her hand creating a slight breeze across her face. The resulting pain from moving her head was excruciating. She screamed involuntarily, the echo rebounding as if she were in the bowels of a cave. The agony radiated out from the back left side of her head and continued to pulse throughout her body as nerve endings felt compelled to respond. Her foggy brain registered the action, *lesson learned.* Viane Koa shielded her face from the sun with her hand and tentatively opened her eyes, but there was nothing to see but the darkness.

Struggling to comprehend the best her mind would allow, she found she had absolutely no recollection of where she was or how she had come to be wherever that was. Her mind was blank—painful and blank.

Her body felt as though it had been rolled over by a cane-haul truck; everything hurt all the way to her toes. All she could be certain of was that she was lying on a very hard, uneven surface, and propped slightly askew by a large lump under her left shoulder. Her right arm was pinned beneath her hip, and she was cold, and her pinned arm was numb—but she still dared not move. There was nothing to see except a hole far above that allowed a ray of sunlight to enter. She watched the strand of light penetrating the darkness, marveling at all the tiny particles of dust dancing in the air in a silent slow-motion waltz in and out of the ray of light. The display was actually beneficial, encouraging her to relax and let go of as much pain as she could find the will to do.

There was a thread of memory floating around in her mind trying to come to life, like the name of an old acquaintance just beyond the mind's reach. Try as she might, she found it impossible to bring that thread to light.

She slowly lifted her left arm, the least painful part of her body, sideways, feeling a rocky edge to the surface she was lying on. It seemed to drop away less than a foot distance from her. Reaching as far over the edge as she could without stretching muscles to the pain threshold, she felt nothing but chilly air and space—and emptiness. A foreboding sensation rippled through her in response.

Unconsciously, she moved her hand to her head and, as she suspected from the sharpness of pain, felt the sticky mess in her hair that had run down into her ear. Unexpectedly, a high level of delayed pain followed after her hand touched the raw scalp wound, and she screamed again; but this time her scream was flooded by a deep level of fear that had been absent moments before. Her nose picked up the coppery scent of blood.

Intentionally, virtually forced, she laughed aloud at the seemingly hopelessness of her situation. *At least my humor is not hurting*, she kidded herself and then proceeded to force out more laughter. The jiggling of her body, though, hurt too much, so she quickly stopped. Laughter was a strange but learned response to help her think beyond most fears. It was something her father had taught her to do whenever she was in a frightening situation—it wasn't an easy habit to acquire. *Do it with as much humor as you can muster*, was what he said to her whenever such a situation arose, *and your fear will trade places with understanding*. An image of Pops, his face displaying a profound concern, tracked across her thoughts. Along with his teaching, he'd also instilled a warning: Keep fear at bay by whatever means you can devise. Unchecked, he'd warned her and her brothers, fear becomes terror, then panic; and at that point, you've lost the battle. Strong advice or not, she felt like crying as his image evaporated into the air.

Her right hip was becoming more and more sensitive to the hard rock beneath her. Attempting a slow-motion move into a more comfortable position, she found it wasn't going to happen without her pushing her system into grave response. Besides the torrent of pain rushing through her with each muscle shift, she again became aware of the soft lump beneath her that wedged her upper back to the side and kept her arm pinned. She ultimately decided it was her backpack to blame as she felt the pull of the straps on her shoulders.

Continuing her blind investigation, she reached in the direction she faced and discovered a wall of rock rising less than an arm's distance away. *I'm lying on a ledge of rock encircled by dark, chilled air.* She shivered.

Her backpack became a conscious catalyst for her, symbolic of hiking. Her surroundings began to take on clarity as memory began flooding back. It was like opening a bottle of liquid understanding upside down above her head. It was good having clear thoughts return, but those thoughts led to the horrifying reality of where she was; and her disbelief heightened with the memory of how she had gotten there.

She remembered rappelling through a small cave opening on the remote slope of Mauna Loa. She realized it was the very cave she discovered years before and had always wanted to return to explore ever since. Her mind replayed the sudden and frightening sound of her rope breaking far above her head. As a kaleidoscope morphed its patterns, she relived the fantastic cavalcade of thoughts that flooded her thinking during the brief, split-second fall to the rocky shelf. Even in the fleeting moments of her fall, she had time to pray she'd land on the ledge instead of falling beyond into the bottomless abyss below.

As her returning memory began clouding over from loss of blood, the startling impact of her situation slammed into her: she was trapped, on a narrow rock ledge, in the shaft of an old, vertical lava tube thirty feet below the ground. And the worst part? *No one knows where I am.*

Just as the sheer horror of her situation became agonizingly clear, her thoughts began segmenting and slipping away, pulling her toward a muted state of nothingness.

A peaceful euphoria, a warm breeze, and swaying palms swept over her as her eyelids relaxed and closed, closing out the hurt and closing out the dancing display in the sunlight. A loving presence and brilliant light began cradling her damaged body, gently pulling her deeper into a loving, unseen embrace . . .

And all her conscious thought was simply gone.

Gone?

There's more to being simply *hidden* from sight.
There's . . . *gone!*

There's gone . . . but then there's also gone for good;
good and gone. *Gone forever!*

But then there's the sweetness of finding, of rediscovering
the *hidden*
and all the unexpected good that rides with that . . .

The realization of how our lives would
change, though, becomes crystal clear
when
gone is *forever!*

Early Saturday morning
Kapapa Island, Kaneohe Bay, Oahu, Hawaii

D AWN HELD THE PROMISE OF being the picture-perfect day to be on an island—that's a very promising statement.

Sunrise was still thirty minutes away but had already staked its claim over the sky for a picturesque pre-sunrise dawn. It was the kind of morning you sense with each breath you take, knowing full well it couldn't be anything *but* a really good day.

The ocean was *malie*, flat, not a ripple creasing its surface—liquid mercury at rest in the partially light foreground of a lush landscape. Dawn's coming light over the water's surface began to resemble a huge shiny mirror reflecting the adjacent Koolau Mountains, creating a near-touchable reproduction. The reflection offered an impression of an artist's finished canvas adorning the wall of a fine art gallery—the mountain's face rising into the sky, its identical face reaching down toward the very same sky. A gentle trade wind caressed the air with its softness. The sky, devoid of clouds, silently waited for the sun's first rays to appear above the far horizon, edging the water of the Pacific.

It was, unfortunately, all just a grand illusion. The seemingly picturesque morning was long on promises, but mostly smoke and mirrors—an illusion built on nothing more than learned hopes and desires. That's the way a small band of people on this island would come to see it. Early in life, we learn as children to accept as gospel the camouflage of a day hidden in a sunrise and a calm breeze.

Things had already been set in motion that would have great significance, not only for the six people camping on the island but would soon expand, engulfing several of their friends and loved ones and still continue to magnify.

No one had yet discovered the chaos and uncertainty that the day and the days following would bring into their lives. In fact, no one on the island had as yet stirred from their dream-filled sleep, except for one.

STONE, AWAKE AHEAD OF the sun, crawled on hands and knees from the tent and then stood up, the residue of sleep still thick in his eyes as he gazed out over the ocean appraising the early morning in the dim predawn light. He filled his lungs with the fresh, sweet, salt-laden air, then did it again. His daily routine of rising early was a habit he'd always had and always enjoyed. If, on odd days, he lingered in bed, he would invariably develop a strange sense that he was missing out on something important—something that would compel him to get out of bed, an elusive draw he could never put a name to. He loved this time of the morning with its peace-giving serenity of unspoken promises.

His name was Kensington Stone, though he preferred to be called Stone. When he first *officially* adapted an abbreviated identity, something friends had been using for years, he discovered, to his wonderment, that he was occasionally asked to explain his one-word name when introduced for the first time. An elderly couple once questioned why his parents, *obviously* old hippies as they alluded to but didn't specifically say, would choose an unusual name like *Stone* for a small child. Their observation was followed by a snicker as they travelled off into their own tangled past.

Kensington Stone was the legal listing on his marriage license and divorce decree, as well as on his birth certificate and sundry other such everyday things like the rare—thank God—speeding ticket. The most amusing and amazing incident having to do with his name happened one day when information had to be provided to a customer service representative of the company printing his new order of business checks. The person on the other end of the phone sounded suspiciously like she was, and later confirmed, sitting at a desk in Bangladesh and was having a difficult time spelling *Stone*, much less *Kensington*. For simplicity, he preferred his abbreviated identity—it was simple and people were more readily inclined to remember it and, at times, make pleasant comments.

He'd been fortunate in his two-decades-long, now-past marriage to have brought two sons into the world, sons that he was extremely proud of. They, in turn, were raising six children—his grandchildren—and he thanked God each day for that blessing. He didn't get to see them very often because of distance and his wandering spirit; but it never failed to produce a smile whenever any of them crossed his thoughts.

He was a man who loved the outdoors regardless of where he was or what activity he was engaged in. If given a choice, he would lay claim to a mountain trail, enjoy a swim in the ocean or a picnic beside the water, or take a lengthy walk on a deserted beach simply to feel the softness of the sand beneath his bare feet. With the exception of a short time when he was quite young living in Australia, his life had revolved around the waters of Kaneohe Bay.

When not out enjoying nature, he could be found buried in financial charts and company profit and loss statements. He was a financial planner, managing his own company, FSI. He had started Financial Security and Investments after a decade of working as a patrolman with the Honolulu Police Department. His company boasted of a small clientele of very wealthy individuals and had grown quickly by word of mouth after an incident while he was still with HPD. That incident would become a defining moment in his future working career. He'd saved a wealthy politician from drowning at Makapuu Beach, and the man remained a close friend ever since, continually encouraging him as well as endorsing him to many of his equally wealthy friends.

Although he spent his working hours cooped up in an office on Bishop Street, the great outdoors was never distant. Twenty-three stories below his office in the Office Towers building, the waterfront of downtown Honolulu spread out in a panorama of incredible beauty. His view encompassed Diamond Head to the east and Pearl Harbor and beyond to the west. The iconic Aloha Tower and Honolulu Harbor with Sand Island Park farther beyond were centered in his picturesque view. Even the belching steam of the boilers rising from the stacks of the Hawaiian Electric power plant directly below helped to provide a calming ambiance.

When he originally moved into this office, he discovered that he had to keep the huge window shades drawn in order to get any work done. A constant stream of cars ran in both directions on Nimitz Highway, flowing around Hawaiian Electric's yard that straddled the divide of the highway. Tourist buses loaded to overflowing with people from all parts of the world with flashing cameras as they recorded as much of their surroundings as possible paraded past in a nonstop procession. The most distracting was the ever-popular and numerous pink-striped Kaiser Willys Jeeps that tourists, outfitted in brilliantly colored and matching aloha shirts and muumuus, rented in order to find their Hawaiian dream. On work-intensive days, he would admit that if he couldn't be hiking a trail or cruising in his yacht, then at least he was in the position to appreciate all the splendor surrounding him just outside his windows—whenever he dared open the shades to look.

His was a one-man, one-secretary office, so he could shorten the hours he spent working if he chose to; but he took his work quite seriously and was very successful, as he would cautiously admit. He knew in the visceral innards of his heart that he owed all his considerable success to the many clients that trusted him and placed their financial futures in his hands. He wasn't going to let any of them down if he could manage it.

Now, standing a short distance from his tent in the middle of an island, he smiled at nothing in particular other than being present with the day and surrounded on all sides by calm, clear-blue water. A tangible grogginess, the residue perhaps of having enjoyed too much wine the night before, clouded any clear thinking he might have had; but he knew that would soon pass. He couldn't help but wonder when Teri, the love of his life, would wake up and join him. Since meeting Teri White, he found he never felt totally complete without her standing beside him. He was hooked, and he knew it.

As he looked out over the ocean, a troubling awareness suddenly began to overshadow his mood as he raised his arms overhead to stretch the stiffness from his back. The euphoric smile he awoke with faded in response. He began to sense something at odds with the beauty of the day: he intuited that things weren't as they appeared to be—but that was as far as his early-morning wakefulness would allow him to travel. He drew in several more deep breaths, feeling the stretch radiate energy out to his sore muscles.

As much as he loved camping, the ground held a hardness his body was finding reason to fight against. *It wasn't like this just yesterday when I was twenty, was it?* At fifty-seven, his body was beginning to protest such things as not having a blow-up air cushion to soften the ground. He readily accepted aging as inevitable and had decided long ago that he wouldn't spend time dwelling on it. *What was that old saying about changing the things you can and accepting the things you can't?* He knew and easily accepted the difference.

He continued pushing his arms overhead into the emerging morning light, one then the other, hoping the surge of blood brought on by his stretch would also diffuse some of the uneasiness he was feeling; but it alleviated nothing and actually seemed to sharpen it. *What could possibly be wrong on a day like this?* He looked around as if the culprit of his emotional disturbance was lurking close by but on seeing nothing out of the ordinary decided to chalk it up to having had one too many glasses of wine the evening before. And by all appearances, that might be the case. All he had to do was count the number of empty wine bottles stacked against a large outcropping of coral situated in the middle of the grassy area. *It's not that big a pile, is it?* But regardless of the size of the pile or the number of bottles, he wasn't wholly convinced that the wine was affecting this gut reaction he was experiencing to something unexplainable. The wine fog only served to make him a little slower than normal in his attempts to find a logical answer.

Three

THE WEEKEND ADVENTURE TO Kapapa Island started on Friday afternoon. The six individuals were intent on opening the door to a greater depth of friendship among them, and all were excited at prospects of enjoying two days of unplanned companionship and fun. Each couple had talked of little else during the past week. It would provide time away from the demands of everyday life spent in the company of trusted friendships on a small island. What could be better? They selfishly hoped there wouldn't be any others on the island that would require sharing the limited space, but they would do so, and without complaint if others showed up.

It was midafternoon when their two boats pulled in close to the island. Both skippers had kept vigilant watch as they made their way through the shallow water over the coral-strewn ocean floor. The hazards lay silently in wait for any hapless captain not paying attention or not too sure where he or she needed to be—or perhaps both.

The smaller of the two boats pulled in several yards closer to shore since it drew much less water. By the time they had prepared their anchors and were paying out the chain attached to them, the sun had already dipped into the shadow cast by the Koolau Mountains.

Both skippers placed bow and stern anchors, a precaution against the wind and wave action, either of which would shift the boats' position when the tide changed or the squall passed through. The double anchoring would also keep the boats from drifting dangerously close to one another.

Teri White, along with Lloyd Moniz and his wife, Pam, had ridden out to the island on *Wailana Sunrise*, Stone's recently purchased and still-gleaming fifty-two-foot Sea Ray-Sundancer, a sleek, white and blue trimmed fiberglass, twin-engine power boat—a yacht, not a boat, as Stone adamantly insisted.

Besides, all the adventure and fun the weekend promised, Guy Montana and Deborah, his wife of eight years, saw it as an ideal opportunity to initiate their aged but newly purchased and refurbished boat. They had used most of their leisure time over the past year making it seaworthy and making it shine.

Guy had launched *Lehua* at Heeia Kea boat ramp, a small marina on the west edge of Kaneohe Bay, and met up with Stone and the others outside the marina's entrance for the short journey to Kapapa Island.

After making the rendezvous, he'd followed close in the wake of *Wailana Sunrise*, relying on Stone's knowledge of the water and location of coral hazards. Both captains managed to guide their crafts to the lee side of the small island without mishap.

The water surrounding the island was quite shallow during low tides and was an obstacle course of nightmarish proportions at any level of tide because of the helter-skelter array of coral extending out from the island. A brush with one of these scalpel-sharp hunks could cut into the fiberglass of a boat's hull like a razor blade cutting through a paper bag. Stone knew his way in and around them from his many years of camping and fishing in the bay. Guy had confidence in Stone and felt he was a fitting guide for a novice boater like himself—at least that's what Stone had told him on several occasions.

Instead of making several trips back and forth from their boats to the island, attempting to carry their possessions high out of water's reach, they commandeered Stone's inflatable Zodiac dinghy, packing it high with clothing, food, tents, and all the other necessary gear too heavy to carry. The ice chest was filled with beer, wine, water, and requisite ice was the main culprit, adding to the bulk, but was, of course, considered crucial. They pulled the dingy behind them, managing to bring it ashore with nothing spilled overboard, though they did struggle twice to keep the overloaded, top-heavy inflatable from tipping in the small swells.

All was going good up until the last five feet from the beach when Deborah, pushed off-balance by a small swell, took a fast step to regain balance and came down hard on a piece of coral, puncturing her skin just above the ankle. Blood quickly began snaking through the water, a wisp of red weaving among the coral. Guy took her arm and helped her to the beach, where she could sit and allow everyone to examine the wound and offer advice. With serious concern and as straight a face as he could muster, Guy explained that from his long experience with coral cuts, urine was called for to kill any chips of coral that may still remain imbedded under her skin. He told her he was ready to help with the procedure, but the amused expression that claimed his features gave it all away. This and a few similar remedies carried the conversation and fun well into the evening. At her insistence, though, her not-very-serious cut got only a bandage.

STONE HAD MET GUY purely by chance a few months prior, and a bond of friendship had grown quickly as both discovered common ground in their lives. Stone had been in the process of finding a reliable printer for a presentation brochure and had walked into Rainbow Lithographers, a small shop in Kakaako, an industrial area close to downtown Honolulu and close to his office, where he met Guy, the shop manager. Guy was an ex-firefighter who had been seriously injured when a building collapsed during a fire, severing a tendon in his right knee. He had taken early disability retirement, found work in the print shop, and quickly became the shop's key person.

Stone discovered that Guy was an easy person to come to know. His gentle Hawaiian nature and openness blended well with his large stature, unshakable good nature, and ruggedly handsome face.

It was during the course of several follow-up meetings that both men began to develop their close bond. It wasn't long before their meetings moved from Guy's office to the more relaxed setting at the Landing, a sports bar located on the second floor of the building where Stone had his office. The Landing was Stone's chosen watering hole and was easily accessible from his office. At times, he acknowledged that it was much too accessible. His *calabash* sister also bartended there, so he could count on a welcoming atmosphere for himself as well as clients he often took there.

Their meetings—they insisted on calling them business meetings—soon included Teri and Deborah, along with dinners at Canoes, Royal Lanai, the Chart House, or one of many other nightspots in Waikiki and vicinity. All four enjoyed each other's company and the good food, and all of them delighted in trying out new restaurants. It was agreed that the seared ahi at Irifune Restaurant on Kapahulu Avenue was to die for.

Stone was looking for an opportunity to bring his friendship with Lloyd and Pam into the fold, and a weekend campout being discussed opened that opportunity. The only hang-up was that neither Lloyd nor Pam was very crazy about roughing it in tents, but everyone promised to make it as cozy as possible.

Lloyd Moniz hailed from Honokaa, an old plantation town on the Hamakua coast along the north edge of the Big Island of Hawaii. His father had been the town's dentist, and as such was also the local confidant to his patients, so Lloyd grew up knowing most of the people in the small community along with a host of secrets his father had been remiss in keeping to himself. The ocean around Honokaa was also prime fishing grounds and offered the young Lloyd an opportunity to develop a lifelong love and respect for the ocean and the huge diversity of life it contained. The stories of his exploits in and around the coastal water could be quite humorous as well as endless.

Stone and Lloyd's history went back to their freshmen college days at the University of Hawaii. They had met on the first day of classes, and their friendship grew rapidly over conversations about cars, cold beer, and ukuleles; and they both harbored a similar outlook on inept college professors they were forced to endure for fifty-five minutes three times a week. Stone was without a car in those days, but Lloyd had an old 1940 Mercury Coupe that had undergone a major engine upgrade and could boast of having a 312–cubic inch overhead valve V-8. Sitting at stop lights, it would emit a distinctive rumble, and the car would vibrate with it like there was a nervous twitch under the hood. Both of them found immense pleasure leaving would-be challengers sitting dead at a traffic light bathed in exhaust fumes and tire smoke and wondering how an old car like that could leave them so utterly in the dust.

KAPAPA ISLAND WAS ONE of Stone's favorite places to go to when he needed a bit of solitude and could engineer time off work to do so. It offered a welcome pause from the hectic demands of business. The island of Molokai was his second refuge, but that took much more planning to get to. He would kayak to Kapapa if his schedule and the weather permitted, although the distance from his house bordered on the edge of being too far, the fun dissipating proportionally with the miles. When his energy tank was less than half full or he had too much on his mind, he would have serious doubts about the sanity of kayaking so far, knowing all along he would have to paddle back at the very moment he was most relaxed. It wasn't unusual for him to turn back toward home at that point, but not before making a loop around Coconut Island halfway in the journey. His rationalization for shortening the ride could be comforting, fortunately, since the water around Coconut Island was mostly shallow reef with masses of beautiful corals and sea life.

Kapapa Island was not much more than a three-acre coral head that rose a few feet above the water's surface on the outer edge of Kaneohe Bay. There was just enough ground cover over the old coral outcropping to support a patch of grass, lending space for tents to anchor and still leave ample room for a few *kiawe* trees and *haole koa* bushes to thrive and soften the otherwise-harsh landscape.

The island boasted of having an ancient *heiau* and canoe repair platform constructed from nearby pieces of coral and lava rock. It was a tribute to the ancient builders that both relics still retained their recognizable shapes so many centuries later.

The island also served as a nesting place for a sea bird called the *Ua'u Kani*, a wedge-tailed shearwater. It was often considered a menace, as many unsuspecting individuals came to discover after inadvertently anchoring their tent over an unnoticed opening in the soil leading to a below ground nest. The feisty birds had little hesitation in forcing anything in its way to move if the obstruction happened to block the opening to their nest, or even worse if the adult birds themselves became trapped beneath the floor of a tent. Many innocent souls, as stories travel, have awakened in the dead of night to a real-life nightmare feeling something unknown relentlessly moving and forcefully puncturing a hole through the canvas floor with sharp beaks. And God forbid the ensuing chaos if the bird made it through the floor of the tent but couldn't find an opening to get out.

THE FIRST AFTERNOON, FRIDAY, on the island couldn't have been better. It was the sort of afternoon they would all look back on with fondness and laughter: the trade winds soft and warm, the ocean waves gentle and the sound caressing, and the laughter spontaneous and continuous.

Once all their gear, food, and supplies were safely ashore and the three tents erected and made comfortable for the two nights' stay, a fire was started in a fire ring left behind by a previous camper. Jokes were quick, and stories and laughter abounded. Each of the six had made a conscious decision that the weekend was their time to unwind and have fun.

Steamed rice, spam *musubi*, poi, *aku poke*, green salads, kimchee, and lots of chips and dips had been brought from home; and now a small hibachi was set up to grill some teriyaki chicken and pork. They ate well. It was agreed that, although wonderfully delicious, the meal was incidental to the camaraderie being created. A few glasses of wine— many—contributed to stories being conveyed that may have been best kept untold. There was little doubt that some of the stories carried the potential of coming back later to haunt them, but they'd worry about that some other time. As the night settled, each drifted away to the comfort of their tents.

Stone and Teri had crawled into their two-person sleeping bag feeling a little tipsy from the wine but warmed in heart. They wrapped themselves around each other in a gentle embrace and quickly fell asleep.

Early Saturday, Kapapa Island

THE STRETCHING WAS WORKING. Stone could feel blood rushing to the parts of his body that had gone numb from sleeping on the hard ground beneath his tent, but the uneasy feeling that had begun when he first emerged from his tent persisted. He looked around, hoping to identify anything that might be out of place but saw nothing and willed the troublesome sensation to lessen.

If only he had looked out over the water toward Heeia Kea he wouldn't have been so casual in dismissing it . . . If only.

Twisting to his right, he gazed at the other two tents crowded together in the small grassy area, scanning for signs of life stirring within them. Teri, her eyes not fully opened, still in the throes of sleep, slowly crawled out from their tent. She stood beside him, instantly folding into his arms. She wasn't an early-morning individual by nature, preferring instead to remain in bed beyond seven whenever she had a choice and could easily push that envelope to eight o'clock and beyond with little encouragement. This morning, she'd had that choice but instead felt the need for Stone's bodily warmth to that of a blanket, tent, and hard ground. She swore it wasn't softened in the least by the inch-thick blow-up ground cover supposedly designed for such purposes.

Since first meeting Teri, Stone had witnessed some of the most caring, loving times he'd yet experienced. They'd met when Teri's friend Viane Koa was in trouble having had two artifacts she'd found stolen from her and subsequently had her life threatened as a result. Stone stepped in to help her recover her treasures and met Teri as a result.

The attraction between Stone and Teri had been instantaneous the moment she opened her front door and stood there facing a complete stranger. He proceeded to tell her a bizarre tale of having saved a drowning woman who had disappeared before reaching shore. She thought it an interesting coincidence having talked to the victim who happened to be her best friend, Viane, just an hour earlier.

The man she saw standing in her doorway was tall and handsome, in his fifties, in great physical shape with a magnetic boyish charm that instantly began to tug at desires she'd tucked away long ago; so she stood and listened.

Stone, equally startled when the door opened, saw a stunningly beautiful woman in her midforties with an enticing hint of Italian in her appearance. She had dark blonde hair and the most mesmerizing green eyes he'd ever known to exist. She wore a colorful muumuu that teasingly concealed any detailed shape beneath, adding to the allure of her eyes. All the other details fell into an irresistible package.

So entranced by this vision, he was suddenly unable to recall why he was even standing at her door. He'd been attempting to find the woman he had rescued and who had vanished when he wasn't looking. The search by him and his friend Lloyd ended at this house.

The entire reason why Stone was stepping in to help Viane, the near-drowned woman, when she was in trouble was cloudy at best. Maybe he was destined to make this appearance at Teri's door. He had been on the maiden voyage of his new yacht, *Wailana Sunrise*, navigating toward Kaneohe Bay when, without warning, he came very close to running over a woman floating, seemingly lifeless, several miles from shore. As luck and God would have it, a barnacle-encrusted cargo net that she'd become entangled in also snared his starboard propeller, causing the engine to stall, starting the sequence of events that led him up Laimi Road, a narrow old street in Nuuanu Valley on the leeward side of Oahu, to Teri's door.

Early during their eleven-month relationship, they had grown to believe they had found their soul partners in one another. The bond was still fresh, and neither was yet willing to rock the other's boat by suggesting they move in together. There was a right time for everything, and both knew that time had not yet arrived. They liked having their own space too much to willingly give it up so quickly. They had talked of marriage but agreed that second marriages were not to be embraced too quickly. Time alone would dictate the natural course of events. For now, they were quite content with how things were.

Teri had an underlying motive besides the timing for not wanting to move in with Stone, and reluctantly decided it bordered on selfishness. She had spent the better part of a year looking for a house she'd had visions of in a dream, and she had finally found it. It was a small, quaint older house, and she'd spent considerable time and effort since buying it, long before Stone showed up in her life, repairing and modernizing it; and she wasn't anywhere near being ready to leave it behind. She had named it Halepuanani, her house of flowers. She probably could have named it the Pagoda just as easily since a previous owner had remade the unfinished basement into an indoor koi pond and stocked it with twelve fish. A few were even quite large. She suspected it was the result of a leak through the aging foundation that the owner couldn't find, but so be it. She loved it and fed the fish regularly.

She was equally certain that Stone would choose not to leave his beach house in Kaneohe and move to her house of flowers for similar self-motivated reasons. For the time being, they were both content with their unspoken arrangement.

AS THEY STOOD OUTSIDE their tent in the early-morning light, they felt complete in each other's embrace. Stone loved having her join him early in the mornings like this. Teri was innately a very happy person, and claimed to have always been so. It hadn't taken Stone very long to see this quality in her, and he finally figured out something that a lot of men never got—how very beautiful, how very attractive happy people were.

Standing beside him, sleepy thoughts rambling through her mind, she immediately picked up on tension radiating from his body, but chose not to comment on it until she knew more. She had learned over the months that he would share his concerns with her as soon as he himself understood them. It did little good to question him since half the time, he wasn't sure what the root cause was of odd intuitive concerns that occasionally popped up. As a perpetual optimist, Stone rarely looked to see if there was a negative side to his world; and when something unexpected or disastrous happened, it could throw him temporarily but hopelessly off course.

NOW, IN THE GLOW of the rising sun, the island feeling the first rays of the day's heat, they stood in silence, arms wrapped around each other's waists, holding tight. The uneasy notion Stone woke up with had almost faded in her presence. He was able to let it slip away and instead look forward to a day of relaxation and fun with their still-sleeping group of friends.

When the idea of camping together first came up in conversation a few days before, Stone had had some minor difficulty convincing Teri to join in. Had she not agreed to come, he probably would not have followed through with the idea since he was finding his life becoming increasingly connected to her.

As Stone's camping plans were materializing, Teri was planning to accept an invitation from Viane to fly to the Big Island to spend time with her, exploring the higher reaches of Mauna Kea, the tallest volcano in the islands. Moments before agreeing to go with Viane, Teri had glanced at Stone and saw his puppy dog expression of pending disappointment and immediately gave in to his plans and told Viane no. In truth, the idea of spending the weekend with Stone and their small group of friends enjoying the island and the surrounding water was much too tempting to refuse. There would be many opportunities in the future to go hiking with Viane.

Teri was pleased at having made the decision she did as she stood in Stone's embrace, breathing in the sweet scent of fresh ocean air. She had just discovered that waking on the quiet island, with a group of dear souls nearby, felt wonderful; and with Stone's arms enveloping her, accompanied by a good-morning kiss, her world as it existed on the island was complete. At that very moment, at least, she didn't think she had any concerns. Some of Stone's apprehension was regrettably casting its shadow, and she was finding it difficult to rid herself of the sensation. In an unconscious response, she tightened her hold around his waist.

Five

"CAN I INTEREST YOU in a fresh fire-brewed cup of coffee?" Stone asked, disengaging his arms from Teri and giving her a quick peck on her cheek. As delightful as the morning was, he decided he had absorbed as much of it as he could without a cup of coffee in his hand.

"If I can get more than a brush of your lips on my cheek, you could interest me in a lot more than a cup of your special fire-brewed coffee back in the tent," she teased and let her hand drop, coming to rest on his butt. She proceeded to give it a decidedly suggestive and lingering squeeze.

His grin answered her. "Does that mean *no* to the question of coffee?" He bent over and offered a lingering kiss, which she willingly accepted. Her hand remained fixed in place. "I hope you'll hold on to that train of thought a bit longer, though. I'm too restless at the moment to be of much use to you." It was an apologetic look he gave her.

Her warning smile answered him. "Be careful what you turn down, fella." But she knew the moment had passed and was inwardly pleased it was. If they were to crawl back into the tent, it would be a few hours before they surfaced again, and a portion of the day would have escaped them.

She gave his butt a slight tap but still didn't pull her hand away. "What made you think I was going to make any use of you anyway? I wanted you to crawl back into the tent and fix the bed so I wouldn't have to, that's all." Her eyes were laughing as she turned toward the water. She just wanted to taunt him and was actually glad he hadn't taken her up on the offer. She was feeling some of his restlessness, and it was very unsettling.

He started a fire and began heating a pot of water while she wandered off to check life in one of the tidal ponds close by. Whenever time and circumstance permitted, she loved to sit beside tide ponds and watch the intricate community of marine life, interrupted by her arrival, slowly return to normal as the inhabitants of the pond cautiously became accustomed to her presence. It was a fascinating universe within itself. Stone took two mugs of coffee and walked down beside the water to sit before the others awoke. Teri came over and joined him.

"See anything of interest in the ponds this morning, *kuuipo*?"

She loved his *sweetheart* endearment. That and *angel*, the other name he frequently used, went straight to the butterfly depths of her heart. She'd never known a man who said such things with any level of conviction, much less even a hint of love. The last person she had been in a relationship with couldn't get much beyond calling her babe and a few other names that mostly related to various parts of her body. That particular relationship was short-lived and tended to embarrass her whenever she thought too long on how stupid she'd been at having ever allowed such a person into her life. She tended not to talk much about that portion of her past.

Not bringing up her past was fine with Stone since he didn't really want to hear any of it anyway. He'd told her when they were just getting to know each other that he was quite happy being totally ignorant of other relationships she'd had unless they held special meaning to her, in which case he might possibly make an exception. She admired him for this viewpoint. She wasn't sure she shared the sentiment, though. She wanted to know everything about his past conquests that he thought were serious and how she compared. It was self-flagellation, and she was working hard at letting go of it. He wasn't about to volunteer any of it anyway.

"The intricacies of life in those ponds never cease to amaze me", she relayed. "You walk slowly up to the edge, look in, and it appears to be entirely devoid of life except for the flash of action moments before you arrive as everything living there seeks a safe haven. Yet sit beside it and remain motionless for a few moments, and a whole hierarchy of marine life slowly melt from the surrounding rock and coral to resume their lives within their mini cosmos.

"While I sat there, I was listening to the song of the waves, as small and gentle as they are, breaking against the beach."

Stone never tired of listening to her romantic view of life, expressing the sights and sounds of her experiences. He loved her ability to blend all of life and knew it was having a positive impact on his own outlook.

"Scientific types claim that sounds create vibrations in the air, and those vibrations keep going, forever expanding out into the universe. Since the sound of waves are so soothing, that would mean everyone on earth is continually being bathed in a myriad of soothing ocean sounds without ever realizing it. Isn't that an amazing thought, honey? If that's true, then why is there so much strife everywhere? Maybe big cities and crowded areas have too much counternoise surrounding them, drowning out all the good that ocean sounds create. I think that's a plausible answer, right?" she said with finality in her voice.

Stone figured it was a redundant question, so he felt no need to respond. Instead, he was listening to expressed thoughts and marveling at the depth to which her imagination could go. He figured his own imagination had disappeared somewhere around the age of five. She'd once made a comment after they had sat eating popcorn and watching *Titanic*, tears streaming down their cheeks, that if that movie were played backward, it'd be a story of a magical ship rising from the floor of the ocean and saving people. He couldn't have thought up that scenario if he sat and watched the movie for a year.

As he shifted his rear end into a comfortable spot on the rock, finally feeling totally relaxed, he casually looked out toward his yacht. It was an unconscious sort of thing all boat owners were in the habit of—visually checking their boats at anchor to satisfy themselves that all was well.

It took less than the next instant, though, for the shockwave of awareness to wash over him, overshadowing anything Teri might have been saying. Why hadn't he noticed it earlier when he was so certain that something was wrong?

His yacht was fine, riding on her bow and stern anchor lines just as he'd set them the evening before, but Guy's boat was nowhere in sight. He searched his memory, replaying exactly where Guy had anchored in relation to his own yacht. His being a much smaller boat, Guy had come in about fifty feet closer to the island, so it should have been quite visible even in the early morning light.

This awareness crystallized in less than a second.

He hurriedly slammed his coffee mug to the ground as he jumped to his feet, the mug tipping over as it settled unevenly onto a small piece of coral, spilling its contents; but he failed to notice. Teri sensed the boat's absence as well as she simultaneously sprang to her feet in hesitant disbelief.

Stone briefly toyed with the idea that Guy may have gotten up earlier and taken it somewhere on his own, but Stone had witnessed the apprehensive tension on Guy's face the evening before as they maneuvered through the coral and quickly put that thought aside. Guy was too protective of his new boat to attempt anything like that, unless it had been an emergency; and he knew he wouldn't have slept through any loud commotion any emergency would have caused.

Pointing off to his left, he spoke hurriedly. "Teri, run over to that side of the island and see if you can spot it anywhere. It may have drifted away. I'll head the other way."

They both rushed off in different directions to see if they could spot the boat adrift someplace close by. Stone searched the water at the eastern edge of the island, but the boat was nowhere in sight. Two other boats were faintly visible as fishermen headed to their favorite deep-water spots, but he could tell neither were Guy's—Guy's boat had a very distinctive profile. He moved to the open ocean side of the island but still saw nothing. As he ran back toward the grassy tent area, he met up with Teri, who exclaimed that she hadn't seen any boats on that side of their small island.

They both began yelling loudly as they approached the tents.

"GUY, WAKE UP, wake up," Stone and Teri were calling out in unison through the closed tent flaps to the sleeping couple. They heard the ruffling of sleeping bags in response to their shouting, indicating its occupants were at least moving, albeit, from the muffled sound, not too quickly. Stone called Guy's name again, his voice carrying an elevated urgency. The dual groans emanating from the tent were clearly audible as its inhabitants pushed aside their dreams or whatever they may have been involved in and surrendered to the shouting.

"*Auwe!* What do you mean 'wake up, wake up'? Guy's voice carried the telltale sound of someone still walking on the edge of sleep and wakefulness and not at all appreciative of having been jarred awake. (Hangovers could be brutal.)

"What's the matter with you two? One of those *u'au kani* birds bite your toes, or are you just anxious to have our delightful company this morning?" Humor was there, but it was noticeably a grappled attempt.

"Guy, for God's sake, we're not fooling around. Get out here. Your boat apparently drifted away during the night. Hurry up, we've got to go looking for it."

Stone could hear Deborah in hushed tones urging her husband. "Go see what they're so worked up about—they sound anxious. If it's a joke, we can both strangle them later." Her voice grew louder, intent on its being heard. An audible moan escaped through the tent flap, and then more shuffling of a sleeping bag, and then a moment's hesitation before the flap flew open and Guy emerged wearing only his boxer shorts. It would have been humorous were it some other occasion. His shorts were adorned with an assortment of palm trees of various sizes and colors, some with ukulele strummers sitting leaning against their trunks. He would definitely be the focus of kidding at some point later in the day. His thick black hair stood out at odd angles, sleep creases cascading down his left cheek. There was wild wonderment in his eyes.

"Stone, this better be a joke." His eyes momentarily lit up with a warning before he turned his gaze to the water where he'd anchored his boat the night before. He saw the silhouette of Stone's yacht in the dim morning light, just as it had been the night before, riding effortlessly in the mirror-flat water—but not his own.

Stone and Teri trailed along behind Guy as he ran the twenty feet to the water's edge for a closer look. It wasn't yet 5:30 a.m., and the light was not much more than a warm glow coming from the distant lights of Kaneohe. The glimmer of the approaching sunrise made everything, lost boats included, difficult to see. Guy wadded out up to his knees in the shallow water, ostensibly to get closer to the empty spot and gain a sharper view, hoping to see his boat materialize where there was nothing.

"Ahhh...this is not possible, Stone," he groaned. "It was riding on a thirty-pound Danforth anchor and brand-new chain. I double-anchored it just as you suggested...." His voice trailed off. It carried resignation, no accusations. He walked back to the shore, taking long glances in both directions, not trusting his eyes, expecting to see it someplace on the horizon. "If it somehow started to drag both anchors, wouldn't it have snagged a coral head within a few feet? I don't understand this. It wasn't even windy last night." Deborah joined him and put her arms around his waist from behind, having overheard what the excitement was about as they both continued to study the horizon. Her expression was full of wonder, frustration, even anger—all the emotions that cycle through when something precious is lost.

The boat had been a shared experience between them, one they'd put their labor and love into; and the boat in turn had brought them closer together. It was a child they raised, only to have it taken away when their backs were turned.

"Teri and I have circled the island, Guy, and your boat is nowhere to be seen. Obviously, it's difficult to see anything in this light, but I think we would have spotted its silhouette if it was there. Let's do this," Stone suggested. "Get some clothes on and we'll take my boat out for a better look. I think we need to search the entire bay as well as a few miles out."

Stone was about to go and wake Lloyd, knowing his friend would want to be a part of the search, when he felt Teri's arms slip around his waist. She had circled the small island a second time, scrutinizing the horizon as best she could. Shuffling of feet on the loose coral along the water made them all turn to see Lloyd and his wife, Pam, walking toward the small gathering, a cup of coffee being carefully cradled in their hands as they walked. Lloyd, also not an early-morning person by nature or desire, sported an expression of sleepy concern that creased his forehead as he drew close. Pam was a few steps behind him, looking back at the campsite, subconsciously not wanting to be up yet.

"What's going on with everyone? All of you look like fish that got dunked in olive oil and suddenly had a premonition of a new murky future. And how come all this yelling so early, and how come Guy's almost naked? You'll end up ruining my beauty sleep." His taunting smile in Stone's direction was an open invitation to an inevitable response. Stone didn't disappoint him. "Lloyd, my friend, you'd better get lots more sleep tonight if that's the case." He briefly returned a smile before his expression became serious once again. "Guy's boat's gone. Somehow it drifted away during the night."

"That's impossible. I saw the anchors and chain he used. There's no way that could break, unless..."

"Unless what?" Guy was quick to hook into Lloyd's unfinished thought.

"Unless one of the shackles between the anchor and the chain wasn't screwed in tight and worked itself loose."

"Not possible, Lloyd. I checked everything before pulling the boat off the trailer at Heeia Kea, and I specifically checked the shackles on both ends of the chains. They were as tight as they could get, and it's all new five-eighths-inch link chain, so it couldn't have broken."

Guy, as a brand-new boat owner, had done his homework on knowing the size of anchor and chain needed. He'd learned a volume's worth over the past year since buying his treasure. For the paltry sum of two hundred dollars, which included an old, nonworking Johnson outboard, he had bought a fifteen-year-old wooden-framed teakwood- decked Chris Craft with a small bow cabin, the kind that sold as a self-build kit years ago. The entire boat had been in dire need of repair, so he and Deborah spent the past year restoring it. They did a beautiful job, giving a lot of love and attention to every detail. His last act in restoration was to add two brand-new Johnson 55 horsepower motors and hooked them onto its stern. It could figuratively, and almost literally, fly across the water. It was christened *Lehua*, in honor of Deborah's much-loved but deceased younger sister, Dessa. As a small girl, Dessa happened to see a picture of an *ohia lehua* tree in a *National Geographic Magazine* and immediately identified with the beautiful red *lehua* blossom as being the most wonderful thing Nature had ever come up with. She always told Deborah that she'd someday caress a living *lehua* flower—and she did.

Her sister was actually a contributing reason to why Deborah was now married to Guy. Deborah had come to the islands during summer break from the University of North Texas where she was studying creative design. She had held a dream of learning to surf since she first saw a documentary on a handsome Olympic swimmer from Hawaii named Duke Kahanamoku and had developed a crush on the man who had traveled Down Under to introduce surfing in Australia. She was ten years old at the time.

On the first day she was in the islands, she walked onto Waikiki Beach, wandering past the well-known and much-photographed Pink Palace, the Royal Hawaiian Hotel, and past the eminent Moana Surfrider. Just beyond that, she came to a tall bronze statue of the Duke himself watching out over Kuhio Beach and immediately knew she was in the right spot.

In front of the statue was a row of surfboards standing erect, planted in the sand like strange monuments waiting patiently for a rider. A handsome young Hawaiian boy was sitting in the sand beneath the statue, and when she approached and asked him who she could talk to about surfing lessons, he jumped to his feet, displaying what Deborah could only describe as a dazzling and wonderful smile, took hold of a board with one arm and Deborah's hand with the other, and together they spent the day in the water—and the next day, and the next, and...

She had learned to surf, and had also fallen in love with the Islands, with Waikiki, and with Guy Montana, her teacher. She hadn't wanted to go back to Texas; but too many responsibilities demanded her return, including her younger sister, Dessa, so she reluctantly went home.

A few years after graduating, she happened to find an ad for a service representative posted by a phone company in Hawaii in a copy of the *Honolulu Advertiser* newspaper in the library in Denton, Texas. She'd been displeased with the job she'd taken after graduating and thought the newspaper ad was an omen. She quit her job, and applied for and got the job with the Hawaiian Telephone Company. She was returning to the islands she'd fallen in love with carrying a prayer that she could find Guy once again.

Since her sister wasn't about to be left behind, the two of them moved to Oahu; found a small apartment on Royal Hawaiian Avenue off Kalakaua Avenue, the main street through Waikiki; and settled in. She found the surfboards still standing in the sand; Duke's statue still maintained its vigil, but no Guy. Some of the beach boys there remembered his name, but no one could say where he had gone.

As destiny often dictates, the day that Dessa went to Chinatown to shop was the day a small apothecary store on Hotel Street caught fire, and she got trapped in the crowded maze of the store's aisles. The fire department arrived quickly and went to work. The man directed them to go inside to see if anyone there was Guy Montana, and the one person he found overcome with smoke lying on the floor was Dessa. Guy and Deborah found each other at the hospital and married a few months later—seven years after walking into the water carrying a surfboard in front of the Moana Surfrider Hotel.

Dessa survived her injuries and stayed in Honolulu as long as she could but finally gave in to a common mental block often referred to as rock fever, a malady that many mainland transplants to the Islands suffer from. She couldn't adjust to the notion she was living on a speck of land in the middle of a huge ocean—much like claustrophobia with no escape. She moved back to Texas with her sister's and Guy's blessing but died in a horrific car accident a short time later.

STONE GENTLY PULLED TERI into a hug and in a hurried explanation, said, "Lloyd, Guy and I are going to take my boat and search the bay. Why don't you, Pam, and Deborah stay here and start packing our gear. Unless we find the boat, I don't think anyone's going to want to stay out here any longer than necessary, and if we do find it"—he raised his hands together in fashion of prayer—"we'll all gladly set up camp again. We'll be back as soon as possible."

Teri leaned in close to Stone, still holding him tightly around the waist. He thought a kiss was coming, but instead, she whispered, "Did I just hear you actually refer to your yacht as a boat—twice? Didn't you tell me on more than a few occasions that anyone who calls your big yacht a boat would be forced to stand on a pier, in the hot sunshine, and admire it for a minimum of two hours?" She loved teasing him.

He brought his lips close to her ear and then kissed it, and, with a sheepish grin and a mock scowl creasing his forehead, turned and headed for the water's edge. Looking back over his shoulder, he placed a finger over his smiling lips and said, "Shhh."

With their T-shirts held above the water to keep them dry, the men waded out to Stone's waiting yacht.

A SEARCH OF THE ENTIRE SHORELINE of the bay around Mokolii Island, better known as Chinaman's Hat, around Coconut Island, along the shoreline of Kaneohe Marine Corps Air Station, as well as a few miles seaward of Kapapa Island, gave no sign of Guy's missing boat. Feeling dejected and unsure of what to do next, they went back to Kapapa to collect the women and their camping gear.

The mood of the weekend had definitely vanished along with the boat. Guy had called the Coast Guard and alerted them to what happened so they could put out a Hazard to Shipping warning in the bizarre chance that his boat actually drifted out into Kaiwi Channel and was floating in the path of one of the cruise ships or freighters that frequently passed through. Now there was nothing else to do but clear off the island, go home, and figure out what needed to be done and where else they needed to look. Guy was very thankful he'd had the forethought to buy insurance but was questioning the uncertainty of negligence on his part that may have contributed to the loss.

Stone called his friend Mike Kalama but had to leave a message asking that he call back since his friend was not available right at that moment. Mike, actually Sergeant Michael Kalama, was a police sergeant with the Honolulu Police Department currently assigned to the Maunakea Street station in downtown Honolulu. Stone knew Mike would help in any way possible, or at least be able to discover what may have happened to the boat. Stone and Mike had been friends for thirty years, both members of Hui O'Kainalu, a group of guys living on the windward side of Oahu who got together to play poker and horseshoes or to prepare the occasional fundraising luau for local groups—they were all pretty decent cooks and a close-knit group always willing to pitch in and help one another. Stone's close friendship with Mike would be a significant asset.

With everything on board Stone's yacht, he took Guy and Deborah to the Heeia Kea boat ramp so they could retrieve their car and empty boat trailer. Then he headed for the yacht club and *Wailana Sunrise*'s waiting slip.

With the various authorities notified, there was nothing any of them could do but to cruise the shoreline of Kaneohe Bay by car and check the numerous small marinas in hopes of spotting it. Lloyd and Guy agreed to meet at Stone's house within an hour. They'd divide the bay into three segments so they could complete their search quicker. If they failed to find the boat, they weren't sure what they would do next. They weren't ready to consider that option.

Stone also advised Guy to call the state boat registration office and let them know his HA registration number needed an alert flag attached in case someone had actually stolen it and tried to change the registration.

"If we don't find your boat during our search, then..."

Stone didn't finish. They had all been thinking along the same line: someone had come during the night and stolen it and was doing a great job of hiding it. They all agreed it would have taken a very stealthy and daring person, or persons, to pull something like this off.

Seven

University of Hawaii, Manoa campus, Honolulu

VIANE KOA WAS ECSTATIC with the prospect of having a pair of hiking boots back on her feet. They had already been set aside too long because of all-consuming hours spent in completing her doctorate program in geology. She was so excited she pulled her dusty hiking boots from the closet and began to polish them. When they were as shiny as they were going to get and her enthusiasm began waning, she placed them on the has-to-be-done shelf, toes protruding from the wall at eye level above her desk. The shelf had been the holy grail of her study program. She'd even named the shelf Holy Grail right after moving into the dorm on her first day there. In doing so, she had laid down a challenge to herself that whatever was placed on that shelf became time sensitive and had to be cleared off—completed—before she allowed herself to rest for the night: critical homework and notes on papers to be written constituted most of her evenings. Now the shelf no longer carried that duty; it had done its job well. In place of research to be done, her boots occupied its center presiding like a welcoming star on a clear night.

During breaks from studying, she had often daydreamed about the direction her life was assiduously moving. She was thrilled by the prospect of being a geologist working deep in the cracks and crevices of the planet and would half-jokingly tell anyone who asked, mostly family, that she could even become an astronaut if she chose to be one. Wasn't being a geologist a background requirement of NASA's astronaut program? If not, it should be, she proclaimed.

Never distant from her thoughts were the many treasured memories of times spent hiking her favorite trails, especially those on the Big Island. They were continually beckoning her back and often provided the seeds for many daydreams.

For the past year, she'd been immersed in the critical, all-consuming requirements of completing her PhD program, but now she was finally there. It was over: Dr. Koa had emerged. That long thought about the next phase of her life was about to begin.

Her plan for the next few days, starting first thing in the morning, was to fly home to Hilo. She would spend some time with her father and then head out into the crisp, high mountain air of Mauna Kea. She longed to be bathed once again in the intoxicating scent of *kiawe* trees, *haole koa* bushes and wild grasses that grew in profusion at mid elevation.

As she leaned back in her chair gazing at the toes of her boots, she became aware of a deep exhaustion, a magnitude of tiredness she'd never experienced before and could only attribute it to the culmination of nearly twenty intense, very long years of schooling that had defined her life. Tomorrow, with degree in hand and a visit with her father, she'd drive to Mauna Kea State Park on the slopes of Mauna Kea and step out onto a trail.

Most of the trails around the state park, sixty-five hundred feet above sea level, aimed toward its famous summit. The few that went laterally from the park took hikers around to the opposite side of the mountain to a place that overlooked the Hamakua coastline. Instead of picking out a trail now, she decided to wait and choose when she got there. Any of them or all of them would be perfect. *Maybe I'll just start walking and see where I end up,* she thought. She couldn't keep a lighthearted smile from rinsing through her heart at the prospect.

During her twenty-eight years of life, she spent the first twenty living on the Big Island. Her father had often taken her and her brothers up onto the slopes of Mauna Kea for no other reason than to just be there and absorb its energy. When she was old enough to drive and could beg her father to allow her use of his pickup, she'd spend hours upon hours hiking the trails. She knew the mountain well and could close her eyes and still visualize the contour of the land. Her mind's eye could see the Hamakua coastline and Hilo on the east side of the mountain and the boat harbor of Kawaihae Bay, the Kohala Mountains and the town of Waimea on the west. She could see the tell-tale white bumps housing the astrological observation telescopes studded across its famous often-snow-covered, peak; and smell the aroma of the small lake resting below the summit. She considered Mauna Kea hers and liked to think she knew every square inch of it.

The next few days of adventure were her reward before returning to campus to pack her belongings and move from her Freardon Hall dorm room. It was customary for the university to give graduating doctoral students at least two weeks after receiving their degree before requiring them to vacate their dormitory rooms. It was their gift in exchange for their extensive efforts. She hadn't the faintest idea where she was going to move all her possessions to, possessions that consisted primarily of books, most of which she'd never refer to again. She hadn't crossed that bridge yet but knew the right place would show up and at the right time; it was the way she'd been taught the universe worked and didn't expect that universal law to change in the next few days. She didn't own any furniture to speak of other than the desk chair she sat in. It was a godsend having so little when she considered the logistics of moving. Everything in the room had been there when she arrived, including an old armless chair with a cushion that had witnessed way too many hours of being sat on. Knowing the number of endless hours she would have to occupy that chair, it hadn't taken much convincing to replace it with a new one that had arms and plenty of thick padding.

She had talked to her dearest friend, Teri White, in an attempt to persuade her to join in on the hiking adventure. They enjoyed each other's company and could, and usually did, end up talking for hours whenever they were together. Despite the almost two decades that separated their ages, they had very similar curiosities in geology, as well as an insightful compatibility into nature that had naturally evolved into a deep-rooted friendship. But Teri turned down the opportunity, saying she wanted to spend time with Stone and some of their friends on a camping adventure.

The prospect of going by herself, usually her preferred way to hike, made her think about cancelling plans and staying put in order to concentrate on moving; but she had promised her father, Pops as she fondly called him, that she would be there before lunch; and she didn't want to disappoint him by not showing up. She realized it would actually be a double disappointment for him if she didn't go. He had mentioned wanting to introduce someone to her and by the sound of his voice when he'd told her this, she could only guess it was a woman, a very special woman from the sound of it. *Imagine, my father getting romantic again.* Her mother had been gone for over twenty-four years. *He's sixty-nine. Maybe it's about time.*

Two days ago, she'd called her father to let him know she was coming and to ask if he would let her borrow his beat-up but beloved old pickup truck, his aging powder-blue Ford that he'd been navigating around the Island for the past forty years. He'd responded that there would be no problem and repeated how anxious he was to see her. He'd told her that as far as he was concerned the newly licensed Dr. Viane Koa could do anything she pleased and whenever she pleased. He also reminded her that it had been too long since she had been home.

With renewed energy, she reached for her large backpack that doubled as her carry-on suitcase and threw her shiny hiking boots into the bottom of it. It felt marvelous to have all those years of study behind her. The thought of beginning a job search and finding the right avenue to best use all her hard-earned knowledge was a daunting shadow hovering overhead, and one she'd soon face with excitement—but not right now. She also didn't want to think of the massive pile of student loans heaped all over her desk waiting for payments to begin. She'd also consider those later—much later.

Eight

Hilo, Big Island of Hawaii

ALOHA AIRLINES FLIGHT 582 set down smoothly on the tarmac at Hilo airport, right on schedule. As Viane stepped from the ramp into the open-air terminal, she couldn't help hesitating for a moment before going on. Eyes closed, she drew in a deep breath of Big Island air. It was an involuntary reaction every time she stepped off an airplane in Hilo. The energy in the air on the Big Island was so alive it was palpable, compelling anyone the least bit mindful of their surroundings to do the same without really being aware of what they were doing. It didn't take much understanding on the part of anyone arriving on the island to know the ground beneath their feet was very much alive, still growing—liquid rock hunting for a means of release.

As she descended the escalator to the terminal floor and the baggage claim area, she saw Pops standing off by himself, as usual, a broad, beaming smile as he watched her approach. He had always harbored an aversion to crowds, especially airport crowds, with people jockeying to reach their luggage-burdened loved ones, their arms laden with flower leis primed to be draped around a waiting neck.

Her father was holding two full strands of plumeria flowers, their white and yellow petals dazzling with freshness. Knowing Pops, she was certain he had picked them from his trees that very morning and probably just finished stringing them into leis moments before leaving for the airport. In typical old style, as was his way, he wouldn't think to stop at one of the lei sellers that were in abundance throughout the terminal with their wealth of leis of every island flower imaginable to choose from. His pleasure came from picking his own flowers and creating what he would claim was "a much better quality lei, made with love." She had to laugh when she noticed the small hand-lettered greeter's sign he held high over his head: "Dr. Koa" was all it said.

Pops was a single parent, having raised Viane and her two brothers, Sonny and John, after her mother died giving birth to John, the younger of the two. Viane felt a deep obligation to repay him by being a loving daughter and responsible adult. It came naturally for her, especially where her father was concerned. When she finally reached him, her hug was especially long and warm.

Viane Koa was a cosmopolitan by Hawaiian standards. Her father, Pops, Rudy Ian Koa, carried the genealogical lines of Caucasian, Japanese, Filipino, and Hawaiian. His thin, wiry frame exuded an inner strength and fearlessness that would, unknowingly or otherwise, cause a comparatively bigger man to concede space on a crowded sidewalk; and he was still young enough in spirit, and in spite of being sixty-nine, to do something about it if that bigger man ever decided to take offense to this wiry older man.

Pops had become known around the island when he was still a teenager for a culinary talent he had acquired from his father. He'd learned how to create what was considered the best *patis* anyone had ever enjoyed. A sauce made by combining his own concoction of spices with fermented fish innards, it is a verbal horror but a gastronomic masterpiece, dubious in description but waiting to be appreciated.

Pops began his career selling his *patis* from the back of a horse-drawn wagon in order to earn extra money for his struggling family. He would travel from plantation to plantation, arriving home late each night with nothing left, having sold it all. At age fifteen, he made the decision to quit school and devote all his time to growing his small business. Plantation laborers had long since learned that a bland lunch of rice, a piece or two of Spam, and some kimchee, their normal fare, could come alive with a little of Rudy's *patis* sprinkled over top. His business quickly flourished. Even now, with all the plantations gone into history, people who knew about Pops's *patis* would seek him out in order to take a bottle or two home no matter what island they had to travel home to.

Viane's mother, Etta Makanani Koa, carried a blood mixture consisting of a small percentage of Portuguese and a large portion of Hawaiian. If one was to ever ask Etta about her genealogical lines, she'd often tell them, straightfaced and proudly, "I'm Hawaiian, with papers." And then invariably laugh at her own humor. She had grown up as a *hanai* child of an elderly couple on a Hawaiian homestead land in Keaukaha, the beautiful oceanside community east of the town of Hilo.

Etta and Pops, not yet twenty years old, had married at Malia Puka o'Kalani, the small Catholic church in Keaukaha with Etta's adopted parents, Rudy's grandparents, and two visiting nuns as their witnesses. Viane's older brother, Sonny, wasn't too long in arriving after that.

Viane's varied cosmopolitan ethnicity was responsible, if that can be said, for her striking looks. She had flawless olive skin and long, thick jet-black hair that hung like a flowing waterfall to her waist. It was the envy of every professional hula dancer that met her. Dark, captivating eyes accenting

her athletically trim five-feet-two 120-pound frame. It all
came together in a classic sense of island beauty.

BESIDES GETTING AWAY FROM the university and
her completed couldn't-have-been-too-soon doctoral papers
to enjoy the trails on Mauna Kea, Viane had a secondary
objective that carried almost as much excitement as being
out on a mountain trail. When she'd talked with her father
two weeks prior, he'd mentioned that her brother John had
recently purchased a fifteen-acre property in Hawaiian Acres,
a large subdivided tract of land fourteen miles south of
Hilo, in the middle of the island's rainforest. According to
Pops, John had met a woman one Sunday when he'd driven
to Kamuela to attend service at the Unity Church. Their
relationship had fast-tracked into his proposing to her with
plans to build a home for them both. Viane was ecstatic. She
had always felt her brother needed and deserved someone
special in his life.

Of the two brothers, Viane had always enjoyed a soft
spot for John. Her older brother, Sonny, had been forced to
mature early and carry a large portion of the responsibility
of the family after their mom passed away. Their father had
struggled emotionally while working long hours to bring
in the needed income. She respected Sonny immensely
and loved him dearly; but her younger brother, John, had
captured her heart. She knew he always bore an underlying
responsibility for their mother's death and she did her best to
smooth that rough surface for him. Having found someone
to share love with, together with a piece of land to build
their future on, it was the beginning of a new chapter of life
for him.

Pops had told Viane that along with bulldozing a house
pad in the rainforest land and excavating a hole for a future
fish pond, John was also planning to clear the entire property
sometime in the future with plans to plant ten acres of

bamboo and another two acres of bird-of-paradise flowers for the tourist trade. He'd heard that construction bamboo was quickly becoming a rewarding and renewable fast-cash crop, a venture requiring little effort. The flowers were a different story labor-wise but equally rewarding. He'd told Pops, who told Viane, that the acreage would give him a decent income once the initial seven-years-to-harvest-time span needed for the bamboo was bridged and the flowers began producing. Everyone agreed it was a well-thought-out plan.

It's common practice for landowners, mostly new landowners like John, to hire someone with a D-9 Caterpillar to clear a house pad and driveway in their overgrown property. The ancient lava flows that covered the island beneath thin soil were uneven and so jagged that walking on it, much less building a home, were close to impossible. The large bulldozer with its yards-wide steel blade in front and monstrous iron teeth in back took care of that, doing blatant carnage in leveling it all.

John's friend who owned a D-9 had just started clearing the ground for the house pad on the front part of the property, according to the story John had relayed, when he ran into trouble. Perhaps *trouble* is too soft a word describing the situation. The rear claws of the machine broke through a shallow unseen ceiling of a lava tube stretching out beneath the surface, crashing through and landing thirty feet below on its tail end. Pops assured his daughter when he heard the concern edge into her voice that the driver had not been injured. Neighbors, who'd been idly watching the bulldozer knock trees down and rake the ancient lava into a flat surface, said the driver eventually climbed out of the gaping hole on his own, brushed himself off with visibly shaky hands, and supposedly announced that he'd be back soon, that he had to go home to reset his nerves and change pants.

It was unfortunate that John's friend had been unaware of the gargantuan hollow space that existed hidden beneath him, but it was an accepted hazard of his job, one that rarely became a reality. It was going to take enormous effort and expense to pull the D-9 free from its trap.

Since lava tubes are so common in the islands, Viane knew a great deal about them, and they continued to hold a fascination for her ever since Pops took her to see one when she was barely four years old. The one he took her and her brothers to, although a well-lit and often-visited tourist attraction in the Hawaii Volcanoes National Park, the Thurston Lava Tube was responsible for creating that interest that had stayed with her and became fodder for many of her dreams and her eventual doctorate studies.

The cave-in on John's property offered Viane a rare opportunity to explore something that had never felt the weight of a human foot. It gave her an opportunity to find a type of stalagmite or stalactite made from the cooling lava. They were not common, but they did exist, and she really wanted to find and photograph one. She knew such a find would help propel her deeper into the reaches of her chosen geological field. The prospect was mostly wishful thinking, but she wasn't about to pass it up.

POPS WAS SMILING AS they drove home from the airport. Watching his face, Viane couldn't help but wonder about the smile on his lips. It carried more meaning than simply having his daughter sitting beside him. She also noticed he'd bought new floor mats for the old truck and that the interior was unusually spotless—not what he would do with the prospect of his daughter bringing in trail dirt and mud from a few days of hiking. She quickly surmised the changes she was noticing had to do with whoever it was he mentioned wanting to introduce her to.

"What's her name, Pops?" she finally asked. Her guess was confirmed when his smile widened in response.

"Until you meet her, *kuuipo*, I'll only tell you this much. All else will wait till we're all sitting together over a meal. Her name is Leilani Davis. She's hapa Hawaiian and lives on Oahu with her dog, Ichi."

The name was familiar. Viane was sure she'd heard it before but couldn't place the circumstances. "I'm guessing you met her around Hilo since you haven't been to Oahu for over a year." It was really a question, not a guess, until suddenly, in the recesses of her mind, the name fell into place. She couldn't remember meeting the woman, but remembered hearing her name, along with the circumstances surrounding her appearance.

She was about to say more about the woman who'd helped lead rescuers to her kidnappers when her father reached over and lovingly patted her leg but remained silent. It was a signal she knew well—he could be very frustrating. She knew from years of past experience that further information would have to wait—it would be wasted breath to pursue anything further so she let go of it for the moment and sat back.

Viane loved the new feeling of returning home with no thoughts of pending homework or books waiting to be read. It was the first deeply felt awareness of her achievement she'd had since leaving campus. It was a good feeling.

Her home had always been such a nurturing place for her, simply because of Pops' dedication to make it a loving home for her and her brothers. There was an unconfirmed rumor that Mrs. Takata, the woman responsible for bringing Reiki to Hawaii, had rented the house from Pops's father for a period of time when she first arrived from Japan. If that story was true, it explained the unique spiritual energy that still remained within its walls, a kind of energy Viane had thrived on while growing up.

As they pulled into the driveway, Pops' new relationship was pushed aside. Her adventure was about to begin, and she was thrilled.

WITHOUT POWER STEERING, VIANE struggled to turn left off the Belt Highway onto South Kulani Road, which led into Hawaiian Acres. She drove the ten miles through the bushes and odd homesteads and, thanks to Pops's directions, was able to find what she was looking for. A small piece of wood nailed to an *ohia* tree at a crossroad proclaimed it to be "G Road," the last crossroad in the subdivision. The specific property wasn't hard to recognize either as she slowly drove along the rutted cinder road: it was the only one anywhere close that had been partially cleared fifty feet back from the roadway and came to an abrupt halt where the impressive steel blade of a bulldozer stood sentinel a few feet aboveground. There were no longer any onlookers hovering over the gaping breach in the ground and its captured machine. The air all around was eerily quiet; the neighborhood's interest and excitement was obviously gone. The area deserted.

As she surveyed Nature's beauty that abounded all around, she could easily understand why John chose this spot. She recognized how perfectly it fit her brother's character: no neighbors, absolute quiet, and with no electricity or running water, she could see her brother's return to nature that he'd talked about since childhood. She had yet to meet the woman he had fallen for, but Viane knew she must be a cut from the same cloth as her brother for her to be his partner in this remote area. Water catchment was not much of a problem, especially in a rainforest; but collecting solar power had its challenges, for exactly the same reason. She couldn't guess how close the nearest neighbor was, she hadn't seen a house for the previous mile or more; but she knew there must be some fairly close by, somewhere.

With ease, she climbed down into the lava tube using the vertically standing tractor as a ladder. Her excitement was riding at such a high she easily overlooked the black grease covering the skin of her palms by the time she set foot on the lava tube's surface.

It turned out to be a huge disappointment. She walked several hundred feet in both directions, directing her flashlight into the void of light with accustomed proficiency but saw nothing new or astonishing. It was much like most other lava tubes she'd been in—dark, damp, and featureless, but she was pleased she'd taken the time to look nonetheless, as the prospect of finding something unique had been its own reward beyond the pleasure of seeing where her brother would be living.

She used her cell phone and took several photos to document the space before climbing back up to ground level. She cleaned the grease off her hands with rags that Pops always had shoved behind the bench seat in the truck's cab along with a little gasoline she managed to wick out of the gas tank. She climbed behind the steering wheel and headed back to the highway and the waiting trails on Mauna Kea.

On the floor of the lava tube under the wheel of the D-9 but in plain view if one was to look, was Viane's cell phone that had missed her pocket when she put it away before climbing out. Its absence and eventual discovery would be both catastrophic as well as foretelling.

Nine

DRIVING OUT OF HAWAIIAN ACRES Viane, let her thoughts dwell on John's property and the opportunity it had given her to explore. She considered her brother very fortunate to have a unique feature like a lava tube suddenly open up to him: it brought the potential of creating something unusual right in his front yard. John was a creative individual by nature, so she had little doubt he'd end up making some bizarre use of it that no one else had yet thought of. *What if he built his house over top of it,* she thought with amusement as she drove the narrow road leading out of the subdivision. *He'd gain a natural, exclusive and virtually endless basement in the process.*

Her mind was so absorbed in thought that when she reached the Belt Highway she mistakenly turned south instead of north. She had intended to drive into Hilo and head up the Saddle Road to Mauna Kea State Park. The air at that elevation was magnificent. Unfortunately, along with John's property, she had allowed her thoughts to drift to the land beneath her—land that was still so alive, vibrant, and mysterious; land that was still pushing it's boundary into the ocean as it belched molten rock from deep recesses along the Kilauea fault-line. It had been doing so virtually nonstop for over thirty years, longer than she'd been alive and didn't appear ready to stop any time soon. The Island's natural volatility became a centerpoint of her passion for geology.

Her intention when she originally drove away in Pops's truck earlier that morning had been to see John's property and then drive up Saddle Road, the road that winds its way between Mauna Loa and Mauna Kea, and end up at the state park to begin some hiking. Now, driving south, she had to laugh at her seemingly unconscious turn of the wheel. Without the need to think very seriously, she knew what her unconsciously chosen destination was. Hawaii Volcanoes National Park lay straight ahead on the slopes of Mauna Loa above the Kilauea crater. The trail head at Bird Park was the gateway to Mauna Loa's summit trail. It was a trail she'd always known she would return to, having climbed it many times in the past few years. She hadn't figured on doing so on this particular trip, though.

The last time she was here, she'd been an undergraduate student struggling though her sophomore year. Her geology class had been studying the Mauna Ulu lava flow from 1969. During that trip, she had spotted an opening to what she thought was a cave or, more likely, an exposed lava tube. She made a promise to herself to return someday to explore it. Interestingly enough, with no conscious intention, this cave opening had crossed her thoughts several days ago while preparing for the trip but she had brushed that aside, intent on saving it for a future time. *Apparently that time has arrived.*

As she reached the Bird Park parking lot, she pulled in next to a park warning sign. It listed the usual assortment of dangers involved in hiking on this remote trail. The sign warned hikers to carry plenty of water and be certain to take time to acclimate to the altitude as they hiked—fourteen thousand feet was high altitude and could cause a hiker severe physical distress. It was also strongly suggested that if you placed significance on words boldly printed, that no one should hike solo, but if you chose to do so, be sure someone knew your plans and when they could expect you to return. Above all, it declared, let the park office know what your plans are. She had hiked alone so often and had read so many similar warning signs they no longer gave her pause to question her own sanity in solo hiking. She knew all the hazards and was comfortable shifting them off to the side and out of thought.

As she began to assemble her gear she reached for her cell phone to call her father. He would want to know of her plan change. In his mind, he still thought of her as his *little girl*, and she still enjoyed his attentiveness. His children had been and would always remain his life's purpose, but she couldn't find her phone. She searched her clothing and backpack, the cab of the truck, even the crease between the seat cushions, but it was nowhere to be found, and she had to accept the idea that it probably fell from her pocket as she was climbing out of the hole at John's place. Somewhere in her mind, she heard the sound of something glancing off the D-9 but had paid no attention to exactly what had made the sound but instead assumed it was just a loose rock. She decided this journey up the trail would therefore be quick and planned to stop on the way north to retrieve it.

As she got her backpack ready she paid particular attention to pack her fleece warm-up suit: it could get bone-chilling cold if she just happened to stay in the lava tube too long, even in the general warmth of her island. She packed her flashlight, a small rock hammer, some collection bags, a liter of water, two nutrition bars, a sturdy thirty-foot length of half-inch, lightweight climbing rope, belay equipment, and a piece of leather she used as a rope protector against sharp surfaces. She figured her pack weighed over thirty pounds but didn't think much more about it: she was accustomed to carrying this kind of weight on trails. She wouldn't need everything she packed, but experience had taught her to opt on the side of being oversupplied. She had backtracked too many times in the past after discovering that something intentionally left behind—like cleaning out an overcrowded kitchen drawer—was often the very item she ended up needing most.

She was uncomfortable about her change of plans and not being able to let Pops know. As a compromise—she was talented at finding compromise when one was needed—she made herself a promise to stay only long enough to get a *feel* for the cave and no longer. If she felt it warranted more intensive exploration, she'd return, perhaps even tomorrow, since she was not on any sort of rigid time schedule. Clearing out of the dorm would wait; what Pops didn't know would certainly not cause additional worry.

After locking the pickup, leaving the windows partially open, she made her way onto the trail. In such remote parking areas, she'd learned long ago that an open window told would-be thieves there was nothing inside worth their effort of stealing—and she really didn't want Pops's windows getting broken if it could be helped.

With her favorite well-worn floppy, purple—yes, purple—hiking hat plopped on her head, she walked to the trailhead and immediately felt the familiar exhilaration accompanying the first few steps on a trail. *It's been way too long*, she thought as she made her way up the first of many steep inclines.

The day was perfect, her spirit was soaring. She had noticed an unusual lightheadedness earlier in the day while driving to John's property but had been trying her best to ignore it. She was determined not to allow anything to interfere and figured she'd just take extra vitamin C tonight before she went to sleep.

Progressing upward on the moonscape, rock-strewn trail, she remained focused on looking for the cave opening. The trail was easy to follow since numerous hikers before her had been busy building rock cairns along the trail, and they provided an easy visual marking to follow. It was something a lot of hikers did while taking short rest stops and water breaks. She actually didn't like them. They carried an implied touch with civilization that she hiked specifically to get away from—much like seeing candy bar and trail mix wrappers discarded along the way. She preferred hiking in a natural untouched environment if at all possible, something that was becoming more difficult to find, especially on the relatively small confines of her islands.

She remembered the lava tube opening being about halfway between the trailhead and the Red Hill cabin, which sat at 9,000 feet elevation; but she wasn't planning to hike to Red Hill. The cabin was a place intended primarily for hikers heading for the summit. It offered a place to rest or to sleep overnight to help diminish the possibility of altitude sickness from climbing too high too quickly. It was a sterile, strictly function-oriented cabin equipped with eight bunks; thin mattresses flopped over old stretched-out springs, and one wooden chair sitting by the door. There was a small kitchen area—if a wood counter and sink, minus a faucet, could be considered a kitchen—and a broom and a dust pan leaning in one corner. It covered the basics for through hikers: it was shelter from the elements, it was dry, and there was a gravity-filled water tank close by for refilling water bottles. Bathroom facilities were located in a tiny woodshed a short distance from the cabin with an iconic half-moon cut in the door.

The lava tube opening was about a hundred feet off the trail on the north side. She had a mental image of an unusually shaped lobe of *pahoehoe* lava a few feet upslope from the opening. Her initial impression of it was that it appeared to be an amazing likeness to a masculine face, a Hawaiian warrior seemingly looking off into the distance. It had taken shape when a lava flow in centuries past had piled up and slowly cooled. She kept a watchful eye for the telltale landmark.

Viane had always been a strong and fast-paced hiker used to strenuous climbs without the need to slow her pace; but today she didn't feel as strong as she normally did, and it took her longer than she thought it would to locate the cave opening. She finally saw the familiar rock formation off to the right of the trail. It was much farther off the trail and a lot closer to the Red Hill cabin than her memory had placed it, but at least she'd found it. Her problem now, she realized, was that it was getting late, and the air was cooling rapidly as the sun slid behind the slope of the mountain. Her lightheadedness had slowed her pace significantly. *The day is certainly not shaping up as I had originally hoped it would.* She was very conscious of that fact as she stepped over some large rocks in the trail.

In a hastily made judgment call, she decided to continue up to the cabin. It was another hour's hike, but she knew she had to. To ease her mind, she would spend the night there but then get an early-morning start down to the cave opening. The thought of lying down, albeit on an old tired mattress, made her want to hurry. She knew her body needed a good rest. In the morning, she could take a quick look at what she now considered *her* cave and decide whether it was worth coming back to another day. After that, she'd head north to Mauna Kea State Park—back on track. *It's a good plan*, she thought, pleased with having the forethought to pack her fleece warm-up clothes.

She took a few moments to build her own rock cairn, situating it dead center in the middle of the trail, laughing all the while she built it at her own personal sarcasm of doing so. Its benefit, though, was important in giving her a quick location fix when she came back down the trail. She'd be sure to break it apart in the morning.

Ten

VIANE STRETCHED AND YAWNED as daybreak peeked through the sole window in Red Hill cabin. She sat up, swung her legs off the bunk onto the cold wood-plank floor, and immediately began to shiver from the cold air. She dug her fleece warm-up jacket out of her backpack, grateful to have brought it with her. She also silently thanked whoever it was that had left a blanket behind, either intentionally or simply forgotten. It had provided a lot of needed warmth during the night.

She didn't think she could ever become accustomed to cold temperatures. The dozens of times she'd hiked to the higher reaches on her two mountains, enjoying the sensation of snow on top of Mauna Kea, she had always looked forward to getting back down to lower elevation and warm air. She still felt cold even with her fleece jacket.

As she sat on the bunk, drawing energy for the day, she realized the dullness in her head still lingered and knew her equilibrium was not quite what it should be even after a fairly decent night's sleep.

Looking around at the other seven bunks in the small room, she wasn't surprised to see them empty. She knew that any late-arriving hikers during the night would have woken her up—in the small confines of the wood-floored cabin, there was no way the resulting noise wouldn't have.

Dull feeling or not, she was anxious to start her day. She did all the necessities required on waking up, even taking an unpleasant but necessary journey to the outhouse close by. She was out the door with her backpack within fifteen minutes of waking, and within another thirty had found the cairn she'd built the night before. She broke it apart and then walked over to the rock formation, her anticipation running high on what she would see down the unusual opening in the ground.

Placing her backpack on the ground, she peered down the vertical shaft of the cave, using her flashlight to illuminate its dark interior. Her breath caught in her throat momentarily at the dazzling display of light reflecting back from the walls, like gazing at a faraway city whose lights were all turned on, except here all of them were glowing with a rich gem-green-colored light. She knew it was olivine: the wall of the cave was impregnated with a profusion of the semiprecious, albeit tiny, gem stones, in far more abundance than she had ever seen or believed possible.

Olivine crystals are abundant in lava rock in the islands and very recognizable to anyone growing up here that was sufficiently curious. One need only look down upon Papakolea Beach at Mahana Bay close to South Point on the Big Island to see a shoreline the color of limes because of the volume of olivine chips intermixed with the black sand of the beach. The small inlet was commonly referred to as Green Sand Beach because of it.

From what she could determine, the cave appeared to be an old lava tube that she suspected had been countermanded by other underground flows that closed off the distant end, forming a vertical cavern. A ledge thirty or forty feet down blocked a clear view of its depth, so she dropped a small rock and waited for it to hit bottom, curious to know how far down the cave reached. From the rebounding sound it made glancing several times off the walls before the faint *thud* from the impact with the unseen floor, she estimated it to be about three or four hundred feet deep—a great distance. She lay on the lip of the opening, mesmerized by its sheer brilliant beauty before becoming aware of a sharp piece of a'a lava digging uncomfortably into her pelvic bone. She turned her flashlight off, sat up rubbing the sore spot into submission, and pondered her next move. It was still early enough in the day that she felt no need to rush to get to Mauna Kea State Park; there was time to do it all. She just wished she could call her father, though, and tell him what she was up to.

She knew she should leave well enough alone and be satisfied with having found the cave again and make plans to return tomorrow, or even the day after that, but she disliked putting things off. Besides, she knew returning was dependent on using Pops pickup. If he needed to use it, she was unsure when the next opportunity would present itself. On close inspection, she decided the opening was just big enough to accommodate her body and, hopefully, her backpack, but not much more. She finally concluded that she could make it all fit—she was very adept at rationalization and really wanted to go down and look.

Viane figured she could drop down inside the cave, take a quick look, and, hopefully, spend no more than an hour seeing everything she wanted to see.

She began by looping the climbing rope around a large boulder that was close by. The boulder looked big enough to suspend twenty people if the need ever arose for that large a crowd to suspend into the abyss, so she felt safe. She secured the line and looped a portion around herself and attached the rope climbing pulleys and cleats, and with a final tug on the line to satisfy herself of its sturdiness, she slung her backpack and scooted on her rear end over the lip of the cave and managed to squeeze through.

At the last second before her head submerged below the rim, she remembered that she was wearing her favorite hiking hat. Not wanting to chance having it accidentally knocked off and have to watch it fall to impossible reaches, she took it off and tossed it at the base of the boulder. Satisfied all was well, she began lowering herself into the void.

She dropped down fifteen feet and locked the climbing devise to keep from dropping further. Retrieving the flashlight from her backpack, awkwardly since it was behind her, she maneuvered to face the closest wall. It was even more astounding viewed up close than she had first thought, and the olivine even more abundant with larger pieces than one would normally find. A small rock hammer in one hand and the flashlight securely wedged between the taut rope and her chest, she began to chip at a piece of rock protruding from the wall, wishing she'd thought to put her headlamp in her backpack.

She worked diligently for fifteen minutes and was finally rewarded when she felt the rock loosening to her touch. She also felt a sudden jarring as her body unexpectedly dropped a fraction of an inch. Panic, the likes of which she'd never experienced, flooded through her as every muscle reflexively tightened. She felt all her innards shrivel and retreat to the center of her body. She'd always been taught that panic served no purpose, but up close and personal, she decidedly found it wasn't something that was as easy to shrug off as words implied.

Her mind traveled the length of rope above her to the loop secured around the boulder. As she dangled freely with all her weight born by the rope, something she'd done countless times in the past, her fear and initial panic eased and she relaxed a little. She attributed the slight drop to the loop tightening its hold around the large boulder holding the strain of her weight.

As she returned to her task, her thoughts kept revisiting the rope and the knot far above. She was unable to completely rid herself of the initial panic; it persisted to hang on like an unwanted piece of debris. She was experienced in tying knots and had never had one slip like that. She instinctively knew there was something else happening but couldn't pinpoint what that something else was. Her mind, she knew, was still not thinking clearly; she hoped she wasn't getting the flu.

Her continued, albeit less enthusiastic, chipping finally showed success as the rock loosened sufficiently to be pulled free of the wall. She twisted around and returned the hammer to a loop in her utility belt, no longer needing it. Facing back to the rock, she jiggled it as much as she could but decided two hands were essential to pull it totally free of the wall. With the flashlight back in her pack, she grabbed the rock with both hands and yanked. It came loose in her hand in a sudden motion, sending an unintended vibration travelling up the rope.

Experience brought an abrupt realization with heart-chilling clarity, to what had bothered her so much a short time before when the rope had cinched tighter: she'd forgotten to place the leather rope-guard over the rim of the opening to protect it from being damaged. Remembering the sharp poking she'd felt in her stomach while initially lying on the ground looking down, together with all the jiggling she'd been doing chipping at the piece of rock, she immediately understood that the slight drop wasn't the rope tightening at all but was instead a strand of the rope being cut through by the sharp a'a lava. In her haste to explore, combined with the lightheadedness she'd been experiencing, she had unthinkingly over-ridden all the precautions she'd ever learned.

She carefully secured the piece of rock, which had suddenly become meaningless, to her belt and began a slow, steady climb toward the opening, trying her best not to cause any uneven strain. She had gained five feet when she heard and simultaneously felt what she knew for certain was a second rope strand breaking apart. Her body dropped a few inches more, and her heart began palpating wildly like an old woman beating the dust from a dirty rug. It was a five-strand rope but the three remaining strands were not sufficiently strong to bear her weight for very long.

She involuntarily stopped breathing, as if even a breath would shake the line and cut her remaining attachment to the world. She remained still for a moment and began to pray, not sure what else to do. She resumed climbing with as little unnecessary motion as she possibly could, but deep in her gut, she knew what was coming—and it came. *Snap . . . snap . . . snap . . .* The sound was instantaneous, shattering in the silence of the cavern, bringing a halt to her next heartbeat as the remaining three strands broke in rapid succession. She felt her body plummet through the darkness, the cave opening rapidly growing smaller, her thoughts running rampant, instantaneous understanding all too clear.

She landed hard, and a severe pain immediately radiated up her leg and into her back as her head struck rock and began swimming in bright light. The severed end of the rope fell with a hard smack, glancing off her face—a humiliating slap as if in payment for her stupidity. She knew she wasn't on the cavern floor; the fall was much too short and too quick—and she was still alive. She could only guess she'd landed on the ledge she'd noticed earlier. She remembered that it wasn't very big, so she lay as still as she could, afraid to move, not daring the slightest shift for fear of continuing her fall. She sensed a wet-warmth traveling down the right side of her head and knew it was blood even before reaching up to feel the massive stickiness that had already accumulated.

She had landed on her back and right side. Looking upward, she could see the opening above, but it didn't look right. A thirty- or forty-foot distance wasn't that far; it should have appeared bigger and closer, but it didn't. It was blurred and growing smaller and more distant as she watched.

Mere moments before blacking out, she sensed an excruciating pain suddenly radiate from the back of her head like the stab of a knife.

Eleven

As VIANE LAPSED INTO unconsciousness, two teenage boys, twins from the neighboring town of Volcano Village, happened to be walking past the parking lot leading to the Mauna Loa Summit trailhead. They had nothing to do, like most of their days, so they were hanging around the golf course adjacent to Bird Park Road chasing Nene geese simply because they knew they shouldn't. There was a very restrictive state law designed to protect this endangered state bird. They wouldn't harm any of them even if they could manage to catch up to one.

The boys shared an unspoken agreement; one derived from lengthy experiences of beatings and verbal assaults administered by addiction-claimed, often-inebriated parents. It was an agreement to spend their time anywhere—it didn't matter—other than at home. Their parents weren't concerned about them unless a police officer knocked on their door asking where they were. It was a regular occurrence. The parents weren't particularly concerned about their offspring, but they certainly disliked the disruption when they were zoning out on drugs or booze. It was never really clear whether the police showed up because of something the boys may have done or as an excuse just to check on the parents to make certain the boys were still OK. Police or not, for the boys it didn't matter. If their mother wasn't yelling at them because of some assumed mischief she suspected them of, she was yelling at them for whatever reason that was annoyingly rattling her cage from the time she and their father crawled out of bed, usually around midday.

"Eh, Raymond, try, look the old truck sitting there all by itself," Pidgin English was prevalent in Vince's speech as he elbowed his brother to draw his attention. He was pointing at Pops's old blue Ford, the only vehicle in the parking lot. "Let's go check, see if we get anything good inside."

Vince and Raymond were known by neighbors, park rangers and the police as being mischievous and usually involved in some sort of trouble, though generally quite harmless—pranks, really. Most neighbors and local elected as well as non-elected officials of the town knew their parents, and everyone mistakenly took the clichéd assumption that coconuts never fell very far from the tree, never really wondering if that pearl of wisdom actually applied to the boys—everyone just assumed it did.

In reality, they were basically decent kids if included mischief could be overlooked and, like many young people in today's society, they just had too much time on their hands with no parental supervision and no constructive activity other than amusing themselves by roaming up and down the east side of the island. Raymond was the leader of the two, and always had been since they were old enough to know the difference.

Vince was different. His mind was absent to many things that took place around him. He walked with a list to his right like he might be off-balance most of the time. When their mother's wrath reached the necessary degree of boiling, which was most of the time she was sober, she'd claim he must have absorbed too much of the pot she smoked when the twins were still in her womb. When she got really angry at both of them as well as their father, which was commensurate with her current level of sobriety, she'd swear Vince suffered from being in the wrong place in her womb and got bonked in the head too many times when she and hubby got on a roll and had too-rough sex during the last few weeks of her pregnancy.

When the boy started their morning, they had planned to walk to the Belt Highway and catch a bus or hitchhike downhill to the town of Keaau some twenty miles north toward Hilo, but they could be easily sidetracked, which was why they ended up by the Mauna Loa Summit parking lot. It didn't matter to either of them that their direction had changed. At least they weren't home waiting for their parents to wake up and start to either drink or fight—one usually leading to the other in rapid succession.

They quickly noticed that the windows in the old pickup were only partially closed and reasoned that the driver didn't know what he or she were doing. As they stood looking into the truck after having reached in through the window and opened the door by the handle, a similar thought coursed through both their heads—these old pickups were very easy to hotwire. They were sure their neighbor's three-year-old sister could do it.

"You know, Vince"—Raymond was looking at his brother with a knowing smile—"we no need hitchhike to town. We go drive in style and be in Keaau quick. *Bumby* when these hikers come back, we'll be long gone."

Vince could always rely on his brother to think up potential trouble, and he admitted the situations Raymond got them into always gave him a thrill. He knew it was never easy for the two of them to hitch a ride on the highway, and waiting for a bus to come could mean hours of listless standing. This idea made total sense.

Twenty minutes later, they pulled off the highway into the parking lot of Shipman Park across the highway from the main part of Keaau—a short two-minute walk away.

"Eh, Raymond, there's a mountain ball game today, lots of cars. We can park an' walk across da road. Nobody going find dis truck for hours. Maybe can even drive up the hill when we stay *pau* an' leave it in da bushes close to home. Den we can use 'em again sometime." Vince tended not to think too far into the future. Raymond didn't comment. Chances were good that his brother wouldn't give the pickup another thought.

As they walked across the highway and into Keaau, Pops's pickup virtually disappeared from sight among the other cars and pickup trucks overflowing the parking lot.

Twelve

Kaneohe, Stone's backyard

STONE SAT IN THE glow of sunrise absent-mindedly watching a large twin-mast schooner exit the yacht club across the bay. Kaneohe Yacht Club was a little more than two miles away, which made guessing the size of anything difficult, but he made a guess anyway.

Being in such a remote position in the Pacific, Hawaii is a necessary, as well as a desirable, port of call. Numerous long-distance yachts pull into the various harbor facilities throughout the year, their crews wanting to touch land and feel a surface that didn't constantly move under their feet,and the yachts usually needed re-provisioning, repair work and a good scrubbing to rid the encasement of salt and dampness that had invaded everything. The laundry machines at the club received a lot of action.

During the time he was an assistant port captain there, Stone had the opportunity to meet many such people passing through the islands.

One particular family often came to mind when he saw a sailing yacht heading for open sea. They were a couple in their thirties with three young children in tow. They had sold every possession they had to buy, outfit, and provision their boat. They intended to spend as many years as possible sailing wherever the winds happened to blow them. He remembered thinking about the great opportunity those young children had to learn about people and places in the world—experiences they'd never be able to learn in any classroom textbook. He wondered if he would have the courage to do something like that. He didn't believe so.

He was thinking about that now as he watched the large schooner crossing the bay. He was on the small pier he'd built the year before, resting his back against the sea wall honoring his morning ritual of sipping a cup of his special coffee. If anything could bring him to full wakefulness, it was his coffee, brewed with a small measure of cayenne pepper and cinnamon. It gave the coffee a definite and pleasant kick. Not a lot of friends ever showed up at his house to help drink it, though. He decided he'd been too heavy-handed with the cayenne this morning; his sinuses were protesting.

He hadn't slept well and was still feeling the drowsy aftermath from tossing and turning all night. The stock market was in a downslide, and whenever that occurred, day or night, his mind automatically began scrolling through client's spreadsheets looking for areas of vulnerability. He found it difficult to sleep on those nights with so much financial turmoil in the marketplace. He also hadn't seen Teri since their interrupted camping trip. There'd been little time to see her, or even talk to her during the past two days. All his spare time had been spent helping Guy search for his boat without any luck. He was finding that his thoughts got scattered when days stretched too far between spending time with Teri; it didn't help his sleep at all either. She was definitely becoming attached to his heart in a big way.

Bert was in the sand and coral at the base of the seawall, crouched low, her tail quivering in the air as she prepared to pounce on a crab. The crab had apparently made the certain fatal mistake of moving—Bert was always alert to the slightest movement of what she deemed to be *her food.*

Stone had rescued Bert, a gray-and-black-striped tabby, when it was barely a kitten. She had been cowering on the center-line of a busy highway south of Hilo, mindless of the pouring rain and presumably too petrified to move. He picked her up off the highway, wrapped her in a thick towel still warm from the Laundromat, stopped at a market to buy a container of cream, and then continued home. Stone was living on a fifteen-acre property in the rainforest south of Hilo at the time, and Bert soon became his constant shadow, tagging along behind him whenever he was home. Now, with the Bay as her playground, she'd stand on the beach, oblivious of the water lapping at her paws, watching whenever Stone paddled away in his kayak—as if she had full intention of swimming after him. Contrary to what the name implied, Bert was a female; Stone just hadn't bothered to investigate before bestowing the name.

The house phone rang and shook him from his daydream. His swift response caused Bert to jump six inches straight up off all fours as Stone rushed to answer in hopes it was Teri calling, although he knew it was too early in the morning to be her. Regardless, he felt a mild disappointment seeing Mike's name showing on the call identifier. He also noticed that he had splashed coffee on his new tank top with its large advertisement for The Chart House Restaurant and Bar emblazoned on the front. *Stuff invariably happens,* he thought. He could be very hard on his clothing.

It had been two days since Guy's boat disappeared, and because Mike was calling, Stone hoped it was to relay some good news. Today's plan was for Stone to go into his office for a few hours, and then he, Lloyd, and Guy were going to head out again to search the shoreline and private marinas just as they had done yesterday. Maybe Mike would tell him they didn't need to do that—it was wishful thinking at best on Stone's part.

After some small talk, which Mike cut short as quickly as he could—he was of the opinion that small talk wasted too much precious time—he asked, "Did you and the others find Guy's boat during your search yesterday?"

"No, Mike, we found nothing. As you can imagine, it's practically impossible to do a detailed search of the island in such a short time. We're going to go out again around noon, unless you have really good news." Stone was hopeful.

"None. Sorry, brother."

"Just hoping. We've divided all the marinas and sections of the island between us so we can be more efficient and cover a larger area. With so many private docks, small nooks and crannies around Kaneohe Bay, where Guy's boat could be hidden, it's going to be near impossible to do a thorough search."

"I put a bulletin out to all the precincts throughout the islands yesterday to be especially attentive, that should help some. There is one thing, though, you probably need to know." He hesitated briefly, tempted not to say any more but knew Stone wouldn't allow him to quit talking with words like that left hanging—and he was right.

"What's that, Mike?" Stone cautiously but firmly asked.

"There's been a rash of boats reported missing around Oahu over the past two weeks—six, to be exact. You'll read about it in Sunday's edition of the *Advertiser/Star Bulletin*. The article is warning boat owners to lock their trailers and take other protective steps. It's not going into a lot of detail—we've asked them to hold off on specifics.

All the missing boats are between fourteen and twenty feet in length, and we haven't found any of them yet. I looked at the missing boat report and noticed that Guy's boat was an eighteen-footer."

"Yeah, it was an eighteen-foot Chris Craft cabin cruiser with brand-new twin Johnson 55 horsepower engines. He and Deborah spent a year spit-shining it. Tell me, isn't it a bit unusual to have so many boats missing in such a short time?

"Your friend's boat fits into a specific group we've identified. You'd be surprised, Stone. There are a lot of boats reported missing each year, one or two a month at a minimum, but they are usually up on trailers and parked in front yards with no locks securing them. We often find most of these within a day or two. Usually turns out to be a family member or a friend who just happened to borrow it without bothering to ask for permission. The thing here is that the six boats reported missing over the past two weeks were floating, either tied-up at yacht clubs, at private piers or at anchor. The thefts appear to be organized, from what we have pieced together, but beyond that, I can't make much more comment, I know you understand my hesitation in saying too much more, having been a cop yourself once upon a time."

"So Guy's boat is number six in the past two weeks?"

"Yup," was Mike's only response.

"What could a thief do with six boats? They're not like cars; they can't be dismantled and sold for parts, except for the engines and some mechanical pieces. He or she would have to hide them in buildings, private yards, or in shipping containers," he said, more to himself. The container idea took instant shape in his imagination. "That's it, isn't it? They're being loaded into containers—the perfect hiding place." Being so remote Hawaii independent on shipping, for most of it needs resulting in a huge number of containers coming and going on a daily basis.

Mike was quiet, not adding anything to Stone's thinking.

"That's it, isn't it, Mike?" Stone repeated, prompting his friend. "Those missing boats are being loaded into shipping containers, aren't they?"

"We suspect so, but you've got to keep this strictly to yourself. If knowledge gets out that we may have found a weak spot in a theft ring, our leads could dry up, and we'd never be able to apprehend the ones responsible. The missing boats will stay missing.

"Just for your information and to add a deeper perspective, I've been told that similar thefts have begun to escalate around the Seattle, Portland area over the past three months. It appears to be well organized and none of the stolen boats are being found—they seem to vanish. All are between fourteen and twenty feet, just like here. Locally, we haven't been able to pinpoint an individual or a group yet since our involvement is still too fresh, but we're working on it. Two boats arrived in the islands by container yesterday, expertly refinished, but both carrying telltale similarities to two boats reported missing along the Seattle waterfront three weeks ago, but they haven't been positively identified yet. It appears that this could be a two-way theft ring. Pretty clever, actually. Smuggle them into a place where no one would recognize them, forge some documents, and simply sell them."

"I gather by what you're not saying, Mike, is that it's not an easy thing to go down and open a few containers at the Young Brothers container yard, find a boat and learn the shipper's name?"

"Think about it, Stone. With several thousand containers involved, heading for a hundred different ports in the world, we'd exhaust our manpower before the day was finished. Besides, we need probable cause to open a container, and we don't know enough to move in that direction yet, not to mention the horrendous liability that would be attached if we go around breaking seals on containers. Can you imagine what would happen, my friend, if we opened a container and found it filled with frozen lobster tails instead of stolen boats? The consignee would reject the shipment for fear his lobsters were contaminated, and HPD would be out hundreds of thousands of insurance dollars that we don't have, and we'd end up with way too many lobsters to dispose of."

"I could help you out with the lobsters, Mike," Stone joked. "In fact, a lot of friends would be more than happy to help eat a few." Then more seriously, "OK, I get the picture. But what am I to say to Guy and Lloyd? Just let them go on searching miles of coastline knowing it's probably a waste of their time and effort?"

"You have to, Stone. We're not a hundred percent sure Guy's boat is involved in this ring of boat thieves. You may discover that it actually drifted away from Kapapa and is bobbing up and down against a shoreline coconut tree right now waiting to be found."

"You've got a great imagination, Mike. Must be why they made you a sergeant."

"Yeah, that, my winning personality and my engaging smile," he quipped. "I'll let you know if anything turns up, and I'd like you to do the same for me."

After hanging up, Stone was left undecided about what to tell Guy and Lloyd and three friends of Guy's who'd volunteered to help in today's search. He finally decided everyone needed to know. If they were to discover the truth later on, which they would, he wouldn't be comfortable facing any of them having not told them. It'd have to be their own decisions whether they want to continue searching or not.

He went back to the seawall, where he'd left the remains of his now-cold coffee. He threw it out, barely missing Bert with the splash, before heading to the kitchen for a fresh cup. He needed to take a shower and get to his office for the morning, but he no longer felt the urge to rush. He grabbed the phone and hit Teri's quick-dial number.

Thirteen

TERI ANSWERED HER PHONE on the first ring.

"Hey stranger." Her voice sounded wide awake. "I was just thinking about you and was about to reach for my phone to call, but my warm blanket and soft pillow wouldn't let go of me. I must be telepathic. Aren't you impressed?"

"I'm always impressed with you no matter what you do."

"Oh, now that sounds like a 'just placate the woman' type of reply. I failed to hear an ounce of sincerity in that voice anywhere. What if I told you I was also psychic and could tell your fortune just by holding the strand of your hair I found this morning while snuggling up to *your* pillow? Would you be more impressed?"

"I probably shouldn't ask what color that hair is, should I?" he asked anyway with the best hint of accusation he could pull from his voice.

"Not if you had any visions of intimacy in the near or distant future you shouldn't. On the other hand, you could ask if it was just lying on the pillow or whether I intentionally pulled it out while you were sleeping the other night because I wanted one to practice some of my magic on."

"*Kahuna* magic? Did you actually do that, or are you conning me?"

"Did I do what?" She laughed at his seriousness. She was still feeling a little sleepy and decided she wasn't up to the task of teasing Stone any more this morning. "I must tell you I didn't sleep all that well last night. I think I need your head resting on the pillow beside me. What are you up to this morning?"

"You need my head on your pillow so you can fall asleep or so you can pull more of my hair out in order to practice your voodoo? I'm losing it fast enough on my own without your nighttime haircuts..." He paused for effect and to transition into a more serious topic, sensing her need for simple talk. "I didn't sleep well last night, either. With the market bouncing around, I was a jumble of turmoil most of the night."

"Is that all that was in your thoughts during the night, the stock market?" Her question was notably suggestive. "Apparently, I need more practice doing my magic. I think I'm going to need more of your hair. I better find my scissors, as this could be major."

"Well, I confess, there was a certain lady that kept floating in and out of all the turmoil."

"That certain lady had better be one that we both know and love or your time on earth and on my pillow may be limited."

"OK, beautiful man," she said with finality in a satisfied voice. "You've got me charged up and ready for the day. What's on your mind, if that's not being too presumptuous?"

"Only you and the weather, *kuuipo*," he answered, which was mostly true; he didn't want to bring his work into it right then.

A habit had developed between them over the last few months when too many days got between their being together. They loved to skirt the edge of taunting and teasing, taking turns to poke fun at each other's vulnerable spots. It was a game that had simply evolved and served to nurture their desire for each other. They had found, though, on infrequent occasions that it could get out of hand and end up way beyond simple teasing. They both tried to be aware of when that edge was looming too close.

She was still talking. "I'm due to be in the dean's office by nine, so I'd better be getting ready. What are you up to this morning?"

She had recently applied for and gained a supportive staff position in the Geology Department at the university. Her varied skills, having been a criminal psychologist for the police department and subsequently a practicing family counselor as well as a degree-holding geologist—all these attributes lent themselves to filling a position the geology department had created just for her. Two professors she'd done field work with and who knew her abilities were instrumental in its creation. Her job was to keep the students, professors, and the in-field geologists coordinated in their efforts, as well as making sure they all got along with each other for the betterment of the department and the university—a trying task at times, but one she was well qualified to handle. Stone was extremely proud and somewhat in awe of her abilities and people skills.

"I'll be in my office until noon," he replied. "Then the boys and I are going back out on the road to scout for Guy's boat, although honestly, my head really isn't in the search anymore." He told her about Mike's phone call and what he suspected was happening. "I don't feel good about not telling them and feigning to search as Mike suggested, so I think I'll tell them. I would feel like I'm lying to them by omission if I didn't. Got any thoughts on the subject?"

"Tell them, honey. If you don't and Guy finds out you knew something like that beforehand, it could seriously hurt your friendship. It would be perceived as, and actually would be a veiled lie. Tell Lloyd as well then the three of you can decide whether another day's search is warranted. See," she exclaimed, softness in her voice, "you really need me. I keep telling you that. Call me later at the office after you find your cell phone and let me know what you decide."

"I probably need you more than even I know, and how would you know I don't have my cell phone sitting right next to me as we speak?"

"I'm psychic, remember? I even know where your car keys are right now."

"You know where they are because I always hang them on the hook beside the door when I walk in, and you know that." It was a habit he'd picked up from Pops. For a quick moment, though, he had to think if he'd hung them up when he came in last—the eerie power of suggestion. "So how'd you know about my cell phone?" He realized he actually had no idea where it was.

"You mean you want me to divulge my secret? Let's just say that this early in the morning, while you're deep in thought, if you knew where your phone was, you'd be calling me from the seawall where your coffee now sits getting cold instead of being on your bedroom phone. Bert's probably out there right now lapping up your coffee while you're not there."

"You clearly know me too well. I'm going to wear a skull cap to protect what hair I have left next time we crawl in bed together. I think I also need to devise a new secret or two just to keep you on your toes. I may even have to start believing that 'psychic' bit. Tell me where Guy's boat is and save us all a lot of effort, and I'll cook shrimp scampi for you tonight in payment if you guess correctly."

The smile in her voice was evident. "Call me later. Scampi sounds wonderful, I always guess correctly. Load it with garlic."

"I always do—but then you know that too."

"By the way, I don't think Guy's boat is where you might envision it to be—it doesn't feel right. Bye." She sang the word as she hung up.

Stone sat holding the phone for a moment, reflecting on how God, luck, and Viane had brought this woman into his life. He looked over at the bedside clock and saw it was just past seven o'clock. *No time left for more seawall this morning. Bert will just have to guard the yard for the next few hours,* he thought as he headed for the shower. *And why did she say that thing about Guy's boat? She just likes playing with my head, that's why.*

But he hadn't really totally convinced himself.

Fourteen

E VEN KNOWING WHAT MIKE suspected, each of the guys felt compelled to spend a final afternoon scouring the island for *Lehua*. They really had no choice if they wanted to assure themselves that the boat wasn't resting on a beach somewhere concealed by an outgrowth of *hao* tree branches instead of sitting on blocks hidden inside a container. They proceeded with their original plan even though their enthusiasm was somewhat dampened by Mike's comments.

The three others that had volunteered to help in the search were all friends of Guy's, having worked with him at the fire station before his injury. The six men divided up the island and headed off in their varied directions. Stone volunteered to cover the coastline from Kaneohe north to Sunset Beach. Lloyd was going to drive the area from Kaneohe around the eastern tip of the island to Waikiki, leaving Guy to head toward the Waianae coastline and North Shore areas. The other three decided their best effort would be to walk all the larger marinas, pier by pier, affording the others time to cover additional ground. Everyone planned to meet back at Stone's house late in the afternoon.

STONE OPENED THE GATE that led through the moss-rock wall enclosing his yard and absently pulled a banana from a ripe bunch hanging from one of the trees lining the walkway. He walked through the house, used the bathroom on the lower floor next to his bedroom, and then continued out to the seawall to wait for the others. He had searched as thoroughly as he could but came up empty. He was beginning to suspect Mike was right about the theft ring but decided he'd reserve judgment until hearing from the others. Hopefully, one of them found it, clearing away the question and giving cause to celebrate.

Lloyd pulled up moments later and parked in front of the rock wall. He saw Stone's car in the carport, so he opened the gate and walked through. He could see his friend through the spaces between the banana leaves sitting by the water.

Lloyd always enjoyed coming to Stone's house. It seemed like a magical setting with the magnificent view out over Kaneohe Bay. There were so many banana trees lining the walkway inside the gate, Stone had placed a wooden box beside it, filled with plastic grocery bags for friends and visitors to use. He encouraged people to help themselves to bananas on their way in or out—something Lloyd always did. It was general consensus that nothing tasted better than dwarf apple bananas ripened on the tree, and Stone had a lot of trees.

Stone had been fortunate, if that can be said about the aftermath of a divorce, in finding his utopia in Kaneohe on windward Oahu. When he was finally able to drag himself into the daylight after the judge stamped it official, he began the arduous task of finding a new home. A real estate friend, Kim Liu, took him to look at a house she thought would be a perfect fit for him, and she'd been right. She knew Stone was handy with hammers and saws, and this house needed a lot of that kind of TLC. Stone had fallen in love with it as soon as he walked through the gate and had signed the paperwork the following day.

It was an older two-story, right-leaning A-Frame house sitting on the back edge of Kaneohe Bay. It had been designed and built by a neighbor, a local Japanese architect, who possessed an uncanny sense for bringing Nature indoors. Huge bay windows on the short side of the *A* overlooked Kaneohe Bay and Kaneohe Marine Corps Air Station on the distant side. There was a large open-sided but covered lanai off the living room on the second floor that looked down on a sea wall bordering the ocean side of the backyard, the pier, and a small private beach. He loved it and loved his life living in it.

Over the several years that he'd owned it, he'd done extensive repairs and renovations. Repairs were necessary because homes anchored next to the ocean, as he quickly discovered, were subjected to an enormous amount of punishment from the elements. And renovations were made simply because he felt compelled to make them. He found it difficult to own something like a house—especially a house—and not personalize it. He'd had his contractor friend, Gary, gut the kitchen and rebuild it using fine-quality marine-grade teakwood. Generous cabinets and cupboards embraced the space. The all-new black appliances added a rich dimension and finishing touch to the remodel.

The back half of the lower level of the house was the master bedroom with an exterior wall of glass barely twenty feet from the water buffered by the sea wall. Nothing but the sound of waves brushing against the wall of rocks filled the room. He had never slept better. The front portion on the lower level was a large office. A laundry room with a driftwood laundry table he'd built shortly after moving in bisected the two rooms. It was a house that would probably be featured in *House Beautiful* magazine if he ever wanted to pursue it.

Since buying it he'd thought a lot about divorces and how bitterly difficult they could be. He had to admit that in his case, regardless of the harsh words that came from both sides, it had worked out for both of them: it had afforded him the money to buy this house and money to his ex-wife to buy hers.

"Hey," Lloyd called out, drawing Stone's awareness as he walked toward the sea wall. He passed along the side of the house under the extended overhang of the roof. "No sign of the boat. What about you?" He sat down and gazed out over the bay while peeling back the skin of the banana.

"Me too. Nothing. Guy and the others should be here soon. Maybe one of them had more luck than we did. You want some coffee, tea, water—anything?"

"No, I'm good, but mahalo anyway." Bert had wandered over and was ru   bbing up against Lloyd's back.

"I've been thinking of what Mike told me, and it's bothering me a lot." Stone mindlessly tossed a pebble into the water. "I think the boat theft ring could be fully involved in this. What's your take, Lloyd?"

"If someone were to take a bunch of boats, shove them into a shipping container, and ship them off to the mainland or to China or Timbuktu, all of them could easily disappear forever. They'd get repainted, cabins built on or torn off, or they could be stripped of motors and gear and the carcass destroyed and nobody would ever know. Guy's boat is so unique in design it would be identified very quickly around here, but those two motors of his are worth a few thousand all by themselves. I'd venture a guess it's been stripped of its hardware, the motors sold and the carcass destroyed by now."

"Did either of you two find my boat? I'm counting on it," Guy's voice rolled across the yard. Stone and Lloyd both looked back toward the gate as Guy walked toward them, pushing a banana leaf out of his way.

"I guess that means you didn't find it either," said Lloyd. "We're just talking about it and starting to put a lot of weight behind Mike's words." He avoided offering his own viewpoint.

Almost on cue, Stone's bedroom phone rang. He got it on the fourth ring. The conversation was short, and he quickly rejoined the group.

"Surprise, surprise. That was Mike himself," he announced, a questioning expression spreading over his features. "He wanted us to know that two of the boats reported missing over the past week were stolen the same night as yours"—he was addressing Guy—"and in the same general area and of similar description. One from Heeia Kea Marina and the other from Kaneohe Yacht Club. He said he just read the reports that were filed. That means all three disappeared within a radius of about three miles, all during the same night. He feels pretty definite that the theft ring is involved, but he still has no concrete evidence. He said chances are that all three are already in a shipping container someplace and therefore as good as gone. I'm so sorry, Guy."

"Eh, brudda, me too," said Lloyd. "If Mike's hunch is right, it doesn't look like there's anything else we can do except wait and see."

"Mahalo, guys. I really appreciate all your help with this." Guy's voice carried obvious disappointment and the defeat he was feeling.

"One of the guys helping us search called to say they hadn't found anything either. They're on the other side of the island and don't feel like driving over here right now."

"Man, I guess that pretty well cinches it, doesn't it?" he said as he sat down beside Lloyd on the sea wall. He absently ran his hand down Bert's back. "I better get down to the police station and finish documenting the theft so my insurance company can take over. Is there anything we can do at this point according to Mike?"

"No. He said pretty much what you just affirmed, that you'd best get all the paperwork lined up. He'll keep us updated if anything new shows up."

Stone's cell phone rang, and a smile creased his face after pulling his recently found cell phone from his pocket and looking at the caller ID.

"Hi, *kuuipo.* I'm glad you called," he said, rising and moving away from the others. He had a dim view of people talking into cell phones while close to him, so he was keenly aware of others when he did so. "Are you making progress in your paperwork catch-up?"

"I see your cell phone reappeared," Teri joked, but Stone could tell it had been an effort to lighten whatever she had called for. "I was moving through paperwork like a small fish swimming in front of a big shark, honey, until I got a call from Pops. He's certain something bad has happened to Viane, and he's looking for help. Said he's been calling her phone every hour, leaving a message, but said the message box is full, so that's become a dead end. I'm really worried, Stone."

Pops was known by his family, close friends and anyone who spent any time in his company, for having an uncanny intuition when it involved family members and close friends. He often became annoyed when that innate intuitiveness he was blessed with sprang to life unannounced, as it often did. It was as if someone hit a switch to start a movie playing in his mind. He held great faith in it, though, having witnessed it being validated too many times for him not to believe in it.

"So what does he think may have happened to her?"

"You remember I mentioned that she was heading for the Big Island to hike and asked me to go along? Well, she went and, according to Pops, she was going to spend a day or two hiking out of Mauna Kea State Park. Pops, the eternal worrier when it comes to Viane, asked his police chief friend to have one of the patrol cars crossing over the Saddle Road stop in at the park and eyeball things for him. Well, not only was his pickup not there, but another police friend of his mentioned in a conversation that he saw Pops pickup heading south the day before yesterday." Hilo was a small community, and Pops so well known that his aging pickup was easily recognized on sight by most old-timers around town.

Teri continued, "That news got his intuitive awareness working and he's asked his son John to come help look around for her. He's out right now scouting out all the places his sister had ever mentioned enjoying."

"What would you like to do about this, *kuuipo*?"

"I thought I'd fly over tomorrow morning and see what I can do to help. Projects are at a standstill here in the geology department, so I can leave for a day or two without any problem. It'd be nice to see Pops again anyway. What about you? Could you leave your work and boat search for a day and come with me?"

He paused before answering to let his mind's eye run through the paperwork accumulating on his desk. He decided that his secretary—Loris Nashe, or Lori as she preferred— was quite capable of handling anything that came up. She was not only an attractive asset in his office, she was very efficient, a winning combination and one that Stone would never dare take for granted. Without kidding himself too much, he knew he could leave for a month and she'd probably double his business. In fact, he wondered if many of his clients wouldn't be just as happy talking only to her—he knew some that openly admitted that, but that was usually when she was standing within hearing distance.

He had planned to spend the evening catching up on some loose-end paperwork, having lost a lot of work hours over the past two days and was silently weighing everything that he needed to do when Teri spoke again.

"You're being a little slow in responding, buster" She was trying her best to sound threatening. She knew him well enough to know what he was wrestling with, but Pops's nervousness had had its impact on her, and she wanted Stone with her. She was also feeling a little selfish, that *enabler* part of her personality that she allowed to creep in to her psyche once in a while and was about to withdraw her request to ease him off the hook.

Stone spoke before she had a chance to say more. "I want to go with you, *kuuipo*. Viane means so much to the both of us, as does Pops, I want to help. My hesitation was mentally going through all the paperwork I need to catch up on versus time with you—you're the hands-down winner. I need to see you and help Pops much more than I need a stack of paper. Besides," he joked, "it'll give me a reason to give Lori the raise she's been hinting at. Let's make plans over dinner tonight." He went on and briefly explained the news about the two other boats missing the same night as Guy's and about not finding any sign of Guy's boat during their afternoon search.

"You made a very wise and noble choice," she said, feigning as threatening a voice as she could. She wasn't at all sure she succeeded when she heard Stone's brief attempt at laughter. Ever since he'd rescued Viane, he'd been inclined to think of her as a daughter—the one he'd always wanted but never had.

"What about Sonny? I wonder if he can get time off to help."

"Sonny told Pops he would be there in a flash except for the fact he's on the mainland right now working with a transportation company on something. Said he'd fly home as soon as he could."

After closing the connection, Stone looked at Guy and Lloyd. "Viane has apparently gone off Pops's radar, and he's getting worried." He saw the questioning expression on Guy's face. "One of these days, I'll have a chance to introduce you to Pops and his daughter Viane. One thing about Pops, and I know this for a fact, he can be eerily intuitive about things, especially when it involves the people surrounding his life. When he becomes concerned about someone, most of those who know him have learned to pay close attention. I guarantee you'll like him, Guy."

"Teri and I are flying over to Hilo tomorrow morning to see how we can help. Mike knows how to reach each of you, so if I get delayed for any length of time, he'll call you direct if something new comes along. Sorry we didn't find any sign of your boat today, Guy."

"Yeah, me too." He sounded depressed, and for good reason.

Hilo, Big Island of Hawaii

STONE HELD THE DOOR of the rental car open so Teri could slide in. They had just arrived at the Hilo airport and rented a car from Local Boy Car Rental—they would need one if they were to be of any help in looking for Viane. To Stone's pleasant surprise, it was a new off-white Ford Fusion, showing only 1,022 miles on the odometer. It still retained a new car smell. As an avid Ford supporter, Stone considered this a very good omen. They made their way out of the airport for the five-minute drive to Pops's house.

Hilo experiences a hundred-plus inches of rain each year, so there is generally a perpetual cloud hanging over the entire east side of the island north of the Ka'u Desert; but today it was crystal clear—the sort of day that makes you slow your pace in reverent recognition of God's nature at its finest— another good omen.

A blue car was just pulling away from the front of Pops' house as Stone and Teri turned into the driveway. A quick glance at the older woman behind the wheel left Stone with a fleeting impression that he knew her. It was a familiar face, but he was at a loss to know who it belonged to.

Pops and John were in the front yard waiting for them. They weren't waiting in the sense of standing in the yard looking at their watches but were sitting quite relaxed on lawn chairs as they might on any sunny morning, under the branches of a large *kamani* tree, the tree's umbrella of leaves shadowing a major portion of the front lawn. A third, now-empty lawn chair sat between the two, and Stone guessed it had probably been occupied by the woman who just drove away. There were three coffee cups left on a small nearby table. He was curious to ask Pops about her but decided to wait for a better opportunity.

The men waved as Stone and Teri drove up the long red-cinder driveway, neither making a move to rise until Stone got out and went around and opened Teri's door.

As warm hugs and alohas were exchanged, Pops led the way up well-worn cement steps to the front door and held it open for them. Teri immediately noticed the disturbed features woven deeply into the wrinkles of Pops's forehead and wondered if Stone had picked up on this as well. She knew he was pretty quick to notice things like that, but because of the situation, his attention may have been distracted. She decided he probably did, but not wanting to say anything, she took a different route to the same concern and asked Pops if there was news of Viane or her whereabouts—the woman in the car had been forgotten.

"I just don't understand why she doesn't call. Appears obvious she changed her plans." There was sadness in the way he hung his head and slowly shook it. "She's an independent woman," he continued, his voice nearly too soft to hear. "Maybe too much so. Just like her mother was, God rest her soul.

"Let's go sit on the lanai 'round back," Pops said, looking at Teri but ignoring her question. He led the group through the house and out through the large sliding glass doors. He was limping noticeably. Teri knew he'd always had a slight limp, but today it was much more noticeable.

She recalled Viane mentioning her dad's limp and how it was so oddly connected to his uncanny awareness into the lives of his family and friends. Almost, she had said, as if his mind could only work one thing at a time: either make his leg work well or concentrate on his family and friends' issues—one or the other, not both. When he was deeply troubled, his limp became pronounced.

Stone, knowing Teri's question remained unanswered and knowing she's been looking for a soft way to approach the subject of where her dear friend was and why Pops looked so disturbed, decided to step in. "Pops, I see you're limping quite a bit more than usual. Did you injure that leg again?" He was unaware of all the connections involved in Pops's cognitive abilities and their effect on him but figured the simple question would lead the older man into opening up.

Relieved the subject matter had shifted for a moment, Pops seemed to brighten. "Naw," he said, stopping to look down at his right leg as if he'd forgotten it was there. "Sometimes that old injury acts up more than a *pake* standing in front of a pay toilet." He shook his leg as if it was the answer to casting off any discomfort. "Depends on what's on my mind at the time. Direct connection to the stress I got myself under at any given moment." He looked over at Stone and half smiled. "You don't know the story, do you, Stone? Figured Teri might'a told you." He looked at Teri with a fond smile momentarily brightening his features but didn't wait for a reply. They had stopped inside the front door as Pops began to tell the story. "Years ago, I was at the Honokaa plantation selling my *patis* when this old man standing close by decided to swing the cane knife he was holding on to at some sugarcane stalks close at hand. Guess he had nothing better to do at the moment. Well, he missed them completely and let go of the knife at the same time. It ended up embedded in my thigh. Had about a hundred stitches that afternoon from a young plantation nurse." He paused in his story as fond memories flooded him, the smile absently responding to distant thoughts and his recent visitor. He brought himself back to the present and continued telling his story. "Luckily, it only cut into the meat, could'a been much worse. Still hurts sometimes, though. Was a good stroke of luck, as it turned out. That old man felt so bad he bought every bottle of *patis* I had to sell and wouldn't let me give him any discount. It also gave me a decent excuse to go back to Honokaa to visit the plantation nurse as often as I could. Leilani Davis was her name. Sweet young thing. I'd forgotten about her until recently." But he didn't explain what he meant by *recently*.

"You saw her during that time we were at Pearl Harbor Yacht Club when Viane got herself mixed up with those antique thieves. Maybe you'll meet her again. She's coming for dinner one of these nights after Viane's back home. Thought you might'a seen her drive away when you got here."

Teri and Stone looked at each other, silently acknowledging a connection they had suspected a year ago when they were at the yacht club: that Pops had some sort of history with the lady and her tiny dog but had trouble remembering where from.

They continued to follow Pops through a screen door onto the lanai at the back of the house. As they walked out through the screen door, a short but very wide policewoman stood up, looking somewhat uncomfortable as if she was now expected to launch into a tap dance.

"Everyone, this is Moku, a good friend," explained Pops. "Built like a fire hydrant and tough as a barrel of nails." He looked at her with a loving smile that she returned. "She's been helping track things for us, like driving up to Mauna Kea State Park to see if Viane and my truck might be there."

Plates laden with food rested on a table against the side of the house. It was a well-known fact that no one visiting Pops's house ever left feeling hungry, unless by either their own choice or if they held reservations about Pops's eclectic creation of Hawaiian and Filipino foods. If they did, they stood an excellent chance of not getting invited back for a second visit. Several bottles of *patis*, Pops's own label, were haphazardly placed among the food platters. Stone reached over the table as he walked toward a chair and picked up a piece of *haupia* cake. He loved *haupia*. The intense coconut flavor and soft consistency made it impossible to resist, and Pops was an expert at making it.

Stone was first to break the somewhat-solemn mood that prevailed after the alohas to Moku subsided.

"Have you any word on Viane's whereabouts, Pops?"

Stone felt Teri's hand tighten in anticipation of Pops's reply. They had hoped and prayed that their journey to Hilo would prove to be an unnecessary one, that Viane would be there ahead of them with wild, exciting stories to relay about her adventure.

The wrinkles across his forehead and a tired look in his eyes quickly returned. "Nothing. I'm even more certain something bad has happened. All we know for sure is she went into Hawaiian Acres to look at a caved-in lava tube on John's new property. We know she went 'cause a different police friend, not Moku here, said he saw my old pickup heading south and turning onto South Kulani Road leading into Hawaiian Acres the morning she left here. But she's not there now. John and I drove into the Acres all the way back to his new place to take a look.

"Moku here made a second stop at Mauna Kea State Park, where Viane told me she intended to be, but didn't see my truck. That's what she came over to tell me. I also called the park ranger at Hawaii Volcanoes National Park and asked him to check the trailhead at Bird Park next time one of his rangers went by to see if my truck was there, but he called back a while ago and said the parking lot was empty."

"Why Bird Park, Pops?" asked Stone.

"That mountain, Mauna Loa, has been a continual drawing card for Viane for as long as I can recall—like *honohono* grass or dandelions to a favorite corner in the yard. If she had just one choice in life, I believe she'd find a spot on the slopes of that mountain and settle down and live her life right there, studying the rocks beneath her feet and never give the rest of the world a wonder. The road through Bird Park ends close to the trailhead. I figure since Hawaiian Acres was halfway there, she'd find a reason to travel the other half. I'm puzzled, though, that she didn't call me. She's a reliable woman, just the way I raised her, and I know she'd call me with any change of plans 'cause she wouldn't want anyone to worry—like we're doing. But she can be an impulsive and strongly independent woman at the same time when she chooses to be and is subject to abrupt changes in plans. My intuition of something disconnected has kicked in big time."

John rested his hand on top of his father's shoulder. "She's going to be OK, Pops. She knows what she's doing, and she knows this island better'n anyone. She'll call. Probably got distracted and just forgot. You know how she is: great intentions, but a piece of rock will absorb her attention completely."

"I'm with John on that as well, Pops," voiced Teri.

Pops was about to reply when the phone inside the house rang. He jumped up almost before the second ring and rushed the best he could manage to answer it, mumbling something to himself about the pain in his leg all the way through the door.

John broke the silence that followed as they waited expectantly for Pops to return. "How's your new boat working out, Stone?"

Teri silently waited for Stone's verbal correction of John's reference to Stone's new yacht as a *boat*. He continually insisted it was a yacht, not a boat and had corrected her enough times that she was oversensitive to the word, but he didn't say anything. *This is the second time,* she recalled. *He didn't react when they were on the island either.* She'd have to ask him about that later—or tease him, more likely. Could it be that he was softening? She doubted that very much. She shook her head, unnoticeable to others, in answer to her own unspoken assessment.

"My yacht's doing great, John. It's everything I've wanted in an oceangoing craft, mahalo for asking. Let me ask you something, John. Are you aware of boat thefts around the islands lately?"

"I'm not, Stone, but Pops is very close to the boating community around here. You should ask him. Why you asking?"

"A friend had one stolen while a group of us were camping on a small island in Kaneohe Bay recently, and we've been searching all over Oahu trying to locate it. Two other similar boats were taken the same night relatively close by."

"I remember Pops losing a boat a few years back," John replied, "and we all thought it had been stolen, and maybe initially it had been, but to everyone's amazement, it washed up on a beach in the Philippines a year later, covered in barnacles with several *malolo* and one octopus rotting inside on the floorboards. The amazing thing was the outboard engine and the gas tanks were still in place. Strange, huh? The fish and the octopus that ended up inside probably thought it was a bit strange as well." He laughed at his own humor. "But that probably doesn't answer your question does it?"

Stone was about to respond when Pops came back into the room, still limping badly, his features were now a mix of puzzled concern with a hint of fear.

"Pops," John said, "I was just telling Stone about your boat floating all the way to the Philippines." John saw the look on his father's face and let the comment drop.

"Yeah, that was something, wasn't it," Pops politely replied, noticeably not interested in elaborating. He was vigorously rubbing his leg where the wound had been.

"What is it, Pops? What's happening?" John moved closer to his father in anticipation.

"That was Vic, my friend and the beat cop that covers the area around Keaau and Pahoa." He looked at Moku for collaboration and support and then rested a hand on his son's arm. He went on to fill in the details of the call. "Vic says my pickup's been found in the parking lot at Shipman Park up by Keaau." He looked from Stone to Teri and then came eye to eye with John. "It drips a little oil now'n then, as you know, and the guy who found it said there's a small puddle of oil underneath so figured it'd been there a while. Apparently, he has an old truck that leaks oil too, so he could relate and figured two days' worth. Told Vic that he saw some wires dangling from the ignition and figured it'd been hot-wired. Vic said he's going to drive out to Keaau and take a look and talk with the guy that found it and wants me to go with him. I've gotta go downtown to the station and meet up with him. While I'm there, I guess I'd better file a missing person report."

These last words came out with obvious difficulty as he slowly looked around the room but saw nothing but an absence.

Moku stood up and put a massive arm around Pops's shoulders. "I take you down, Pops. 'Bout time I go back on the job."

"Mahalo, Moku." Pops looked over at John solemnly standing behind a chair, using its back for support, both his arms ramrod straight against the wood. "You know, John, I got a bad feeling about our Viane."

Pops's psychic ability to see things affecting his family was never taken lightly. Moku tightened her arm on his shoulders, pulling him off balance and inadvertently forcing him hard against her ample bosom. The cap he'd just pulled on over his head rose up at an angle against her shoulder. It would have been comical if the moment had not been so strained.

Sixteen

Oahu to Hilo

THE ACTIVITY DIRECTOR FOR the Naniloa Hotel located on the ocean-side of Banyan Drive in Hilo was an older Hawaiian man, with dark, coarse hair showing signs of graying at their roots. He was a heavyset man with large, expressive features. A small brass plate fastened to a piece of richly polished wood in front of him proclaimed that he was David Naki. He sat behind a small koa wood desk, a welcoming smile spread easily across his face as he looked up expectantly at the tourist couple standing before him.

Chris and Sue Lund, hailing from Moses Lake in Washington State, had just arrived in Hilo and driven their rental car straight to the hotel. They were seeking advice on good hiking trails around the east side of the Big Island, anxious to explore the island. They told David they had reservations but were hesitant to check in before they had pieced together a schedule of their desired hiking and sightseeing adventures. Conveniently, as David Naki explained, check-in time was still several hours away.

They were outdoor enthusiasts and planned their Big Island trip specifically to hike some of the remote trails the island offered. A travel brochure they'd looked at during their six-hour flight from Seattle had suggested the trail to the summit of Mauna Loa. If they did this, they'd want to delay checking into the hotel, they explained to the man. If they stayed on the mountain for the three days the brochure suggested, they didn't want to pay for a room they wouldn't be using during that time.

As a convenience, David Naki explained, the hotel was willing to delay their reservations and would also hold their luggage, for a small fee, of course. To further convince them to leave their things at the hotel, David cautioned they really wouldn't want to chance leaving their belongings in a rental car while hiking. "Too much temptation for would-be thieves who might happen to pass by the parking lot," he explained. The hike to the summit appealed to both of them, so Chris declared their instant decision.

In a gravelly voice, the result of an eel bite to his throat while he was out reef diving on a past trip to Punaluu on Oahu, Chris asked and got directions for getting to the trailhead, which the brochure mentioned was a "scenic drive on Bird Park Road."

"Make sure you fill in the hiking notice before starting your hike," advised David. "There'll be a box of forms on a notice board close by the beginning of the trail. This lets the park rangers know how many people are on the trail and when they anticipate being back—it's a very remote trail." David's warm manner confirmed why the hotel had placed him where he was. "Eh," he said, breaking into a hint of pidgin, a part of his charm, "*bumby* if one eruption starts they like know they got everybody off the hill before lava starts running down."

It was decided. Chris and Sue left their luggage, took their backpack, and drove the thirty-odd miles south, turning off Mamalahoa Highway, Hawaii Belt Road, onto Bird Park Road and continued to the trailhead parking lot.

It was quite evident they would be the only hikers that were going to be on the trail, judging by the empty parking lot. This gave Sue an uncomfortable feeling, but also one to be savored from past experiences with overpopulated trails. They both loved the solitude of hiking, away from kids and too-loud adults, but the absence of others for the three-day hike meant they'd have few options if either of them sustained an injury.

The thought had crossed both their minds that maybe they needed to shorten the hike by a day and allow themselves more time to sight-see around the town of Hilo and the inviting water of Hilo Bay just outside the hotel's door. They planned to hike to a cabin at Red Hill their first day, spend the night, and then hike to the summit the following day. Another cabin at the summit would give them a place to sleep before heading back down on the third day.

IT WAS A BEAUTIFUL, clear day, and the trail well marked by an abundance of cairns, those carefully balanced piles of rock. The terrain consisted of nothing but black lava, some smooth, once-runny *pahoehoe* having cooled centuries before into imaginative shapes, swirls, and glistening colors. There was also a lot of the shoe-ripping *a'a* lava, an exploded air and molten rock mix with razor-sharp edges forming hazardous sole-cutting stepping-stones. Fortunately the path was walked by enough people over time that most of the sharp edges had been worn smooth. As long as you stayed on the path and didn't try to take short-cuts the soles of their shoes would survive.

After three hours of strenuous hiking they stopped for a water break and to rest their legs. At these higher altitudes dehydration becomes a large problem to hikers: altitude sickness brought on by dehydration makes it difficult for anyone to continue hiking. They were experienced enough to know all this and weren't going to take unnecessary risks.

They were simply enjoying being high up on the slope of the mountain.

When not vacationing Sue supervised a household of kids—she and Chris had four. She was secure, determined and very capable of handling the challenges of raising a family. To be away from it for a short time, though, in the peaceful solitude of the mountain was pure bliss.

Chris, too, breathed in the quietness as they took turns on the water bottle—he was in his element. His tall, lean and muscular frame handled the strain of difficult hikes with ease. He worked hard but also played with equal enthusiasm.

Sue was busy with her camera, zooming in on a formation of *pahoehoe* lava that had captured her attention. As soon as her camera focused on the sculpture, she saw a purple hat resting beside it and looking very much out of place.

"Look, Chris," she exclaimed, not taking her eye from the camera, "there's a hat beside that face-looking rock over there." She pointed in the general direction with her free hand still focused on the image the camera had picked up. "Someone must have rested there and forgotten to pick it up when they left. We should take it with us and turn it in at the ranger station's Lost and Found."

They walked—or better said, they climbed up and down over mounds of lava—to the hat. As Chris stooped to pick it up, he noticed a rope that was tied to a large bolder close by. The rope led toward a small opening in the ground, stopping short of the hole with its frayed end going no farther. To him, it appeared the sharp edge of the hole had been responsible for cutting the rope. Bending over and peering down into the abyss, he could see nothing distinguishable in the darkness. He thought that with the hat close by and the rope tied around a large rock but broken off at the hole's rim, someone may have used the rope to climb down into the void and become stranded when the rope was cut short.

Or, he reasoned, maybe a hiker suspended their food or beer supply for safekeeping from critters while exploring the area, but that didn't feel right to him. There was that hat. He bent close to the hole and called out, "Hey, anybody down there?" He listened for a few seconds but heard nothing but his echo bounding back as he stood up.

Sue took a turn and got down on her knees and called out, "Hello, is anyone down there? Hello...hello..." She heard no response either.

Chris was standing back appraising things when a smile slowly broke out across his face. "This almost looks too staged," he announced. "The hat, the rope...First of all, who would be wearing a floppy purple hat on a mountain hike?" He shook his head as if in answer to the absurdity of it.

Sue silently glanced up at the frayed lime-green baseball cap her husband was wearing but chose not to make a comment. "And that small hole," he continued. "It's hardly big enough for anybody to squeeze through." Chris judged the opening by his own dimension. "Just in case, though, take a picture of this and we'll drop the hat off with the rangers on our way out."

They spent the night in the cabin at Red Hill and started for the summit before six o'clock the next morning, the sun barely peeking up over the distant horizon. They arrived at the summit a little before eleven o'clock. They thoroughly enjoyed the ascent and the exhilaration of reaching fourteen thousand–plus feet above sea level, but both admitted they'd seen enough lava to last for a while. They spent an hour looking out over the gigantic Mokuaweoweo caldera that fanned out in front of them. They had already made the decision to spend only a short time looking around before heading back down instead of spending an additional night there. The heat on the way up had been intense, but now at the summit, it had turned unbelievably cold. The thought of swimming around Coconut Island in the warm water of

Hilo Bay and sitting in the shade of palm trees on the grass lawn of the Naniloa with a piña colada in hand was too compelling to resist. They had many more trails on the east side of the island to explore, snorkeling to do, and green sea turtles to marvel at before they had to board a plane for home.

UNKNOWN TO CHRIS OR Sue, standing less than forty feet above her, Viane became faintly aware of a man's voice—at least she thought she'd heard a voice, but she couldn't be certain. It was a low-pitched, strong, almost-demanding voice that echoed all around her, camouflaging its origin. She struggled to open her eyes in response and see if there was someone close by calling out to her. She went through the mechanics of opening them but found she couldn't be certain they were actually open—there was nothing around her but darkness.

Just moments before, her mind had surrendered to a surreal world and had begun a journey out of her injured body, leaving a sense of peace behind. She'd had the feeling of being in sunlight, her body warmed in its embrace, sitting on rocks edging the cavernous opening of her beloved Queen's Bath. She'd been dangling her feet in the crystal clear, cool, fresh water pool, amused by the way her feet appeared sticking down below the water's surface. The water made them appear strange in shape and color. The air around her was warm on her shoulders; no one else was there. This huge fissure in the lava, partway down the Chain of Craters Road in Hawaii Volcanoes National Park was rarely without at least a few others, families mostly, swimming and enjoying the absolute-clear deep fresh water so at odds with the stark surroundings; but her mind saw it now as deserted except for her. She was confused: the pool was so real in her mind, a place she'd gone to many times in her lifetime and which felt so real instead of the cold darkness and the strange voice her mind had returned to.

Searching for where she thought it originated, she suddenly saw movement in a small circle of light far above. Someone—something—moved in the light, and as the light was blanketed, a distinctive voice, now a woman's, reached down to her.

"Hello, is anyone down there? Hello...hello..."

As Viane watched and listened, she tried to respond but found her strength insufficient to project her voice beyond a whisper.

"I'm here," she responded weakly, giving as much strength to her voice as she could. "I'm here...I need help, please...help me."

The light above her had returned but began to grow faint again and disappear as her eyes once again began to close. She immediately felt the return of the sun's warmth on her skin. In illusion, she was back beside her pool, her feet freely splashing in the cool, fresh water; but she was no longer alone. Several shimmering images—people—moved quietly around her, with what she sensed as hands reaching out to her, beckoning her to take hold. She desperately wanted to move into their embrace, but something else—someone else—was pulling at her soul, keeping her from moving.

A vision of Pops crystalized in her mind, his arms enfolding her, pulling her back to the dark, cold place where voices searched the darkness for her. She felt her father's loving embrace but couldn't fathom why he would want to bring her back to that cold place when he knew one of her favorite spots on the island, and a place he frequently took her as a small girl, was right here by the edge of Queen's Bath.

She struggled from Pops's embrace, reaching out, trying to grasp one of the many hands outstretched before her, but she was not quite able to extend her arms far enough. They slowly began to fade and retreat from sight as her father's embrace tightened around her and his pull became stronger. She felt lost, adrift in a place of no dimension, no defining boundaries or substance.

She just *was*, and that was all.

Seventeen

"EH, RAYMOND, BORING SITTING here."

For the past two hours, Raymond and Vince had been sitting on a bench outside the entrance to Keaau Foodland Market that bordered on the parking lot. They were intent on watching for anything that might drop from someone's hand or pocket—loose change or, hopefully, a wallet—as streams of people poured out of the market pushing grocery carts and fumbling for keys, bulging plastic bags dangling from their hands.

They had spotted a dime under a bench when they first got there, which provided them with incentive to sit down in the first place. It seemed as good a reason as any to sit and spend profit-providing time.

They were about to get up when an elderly woman laden with shopping bags came out from the market and dropped her purse right in front of them. The contents immediately scattered across the pavement: keys, coins, and sundry other things. The boys sat and waited while she went about collecting her possessions. They were interested to see if she'd manage to miss anything, but she didn't, much to the boys' frustration. She had checked the area several times before leaving. They could have helped her retrieve her things but found it amusing to watch her scramble. More than that, though, they figured there was a strong possibility she might get hysterical if two strange boys began picking up her things. Her face didn't appear to be openly friendly; her features were crusty-looking.

They had abandoned the pickup the day before. Then after finding only the dime and an additional penny in the parking lot, they spent the afternoon at the movie theater before catching a bus ride into Hilo. They discussed driving their acquired truck into town instead of catching the bus since it was still sitting where they left it, but decided there were too many people around Hilo who might recognize the old truck, and that could only lead them to trouble. Somewhere in cloudy thought, even they thought the truck looked familiar but chalked that notion up to them being a little paranoid.

They had stayed the night around Hilo with friends hanging out under the aging Wailua River Bridge and then caught the bus back toward Keaau early the next morning. Hanging with their friends was cool, but one night of sleeping on the ground under the bridge was all they could handle. Besides, their friends were too inclined to get high and zone out, and that wasn't either of the boys' thing. They always wanted to be conscious of what they were doing. They didn't want to go home so soon, either, since they would only come face-to-face with parents who would stop at nothing to cause them grief for not showing up the night before. This early in the day, their parents would still be semi-sober, and that could be worse than if they were totally inebriated.

On the way out of Hilo toward Keaau, they thought about staying on the bus—just not getting off. If they did, they'd wind up in Kailua-Kona on the far west side of the island, which would be fun; but if they did that, they'd have to cough up additional bus fare, and that wasn't going to happen. They'd also have to eventually figure out a way to get home.

"Let's go to Pahoa, see if Eddie them stay around. There's bound to be some fun 'round his father's junk car lot."

"You rememba, last time we were in Pahoa, Eddie said they had to move. I think that new highway goes through his yard now."

They elected, instead, to get off at Shipman Park in Keeau, back within eyesight of "their" truck. They ran across the highway toward the mall at Towncenter, thinking they might find more loose change in the parking lot.

"Eh, I know," exclaimed Raymond, "let's go check out the steam vent, see if they got any naked *wahines* inside again. We can take the pickup since it's still there."

With this new direction in mind, they did an about-face and pressed the pedestrian button that would take them back to the bus stop and the adjacent parking lot where the pickup sat.

Their interest in the steam vent had escalated the last time they'd gone there. They had stumbled upon three naked women sitting around a bunch of candles inside the vent. They had only looked down into the vent for a few minutes, though. It had quickly become obvious the women were considerably older and large, their skin bunching up in rolls, sort of like the Dough Boy. They decided all three looked too much like their own mother to spend any more than a few seconds looking. They enjoyed seeing all the breasts, though, and might have stayed longer if one of the women hadn't started yelling and threatening them with bodily harm. Way too much like their mother.

Steam vents are quite common on the Big Island. They are direct openings into the depths of the earth, funneling rain down to the molten lava far below and then sending it exploding back as steam, much like a hole on the lid of a boiling pot of water.

This particular vent was in an area of lava formations a short distance off the highway. In centuries past, lava had bubbled up as air pockets of molten lava and hardened, as in this case, into a small room-like area big enough for six people sitting close together. There was a hole in its roof where the lava bubble burst, leaving a big-enough opening to climb through—or peer into, as circumstances were. Another, much smaller hole on the floor allowed the steam to rise and fill the small room. Over the years, people had built a rickety wooden ladder leading down into the room and some equally rickety wooden benches along the walls to sit on and enjoy the constant flow of hot, sulfur-infused steam. Remnants of many burned-down candles remained stuck to every available flat spot.

AS THE BOYS WALKED back across the Hawaii Belt Road to the parking lot, they talked excitedly about the prospects of what they would see, both remembering the naked women adventure. As they got farther into the parking lot, they happened to spot the beat cop for the area standing by the pickup's tailgate waving aloha to another policeman. The police officer just arriving was dressed much more formally, looking more like he was on his way to march in a parade than he was to drive around in the midmorning heat and humidity. He was accompanied by an older Filipino man who was in the process of getting out of the unmarked yet unmistakable police car, waving a return greeting to the beat cop. The boys stood a short distance away, partially hidden behind a parked car and watched, their thoughts of breasts temporarily evaporating. Raymond suddenly realized the Keaau cop was no longer looking at the new arrivals but was instead staring directly at them.

"Vince, let's go. Come, let's go," he urged, giving a sharp tug to the back of his brother's T-shirt. "We going get in trouble if we stay here."

AS SOON AS THE chief of police and Pops pulled into the parking area, they spotted Vic, the patrolman for the area, standing behind Pops truck signaling to them. At the sight of his pickup, Pops's heart sank lower than he thought it possible. The last time he saw his truck, Viane had been at the wheel, happily waving to him as she headed off on her adventure. Now his truck looked lost, void of life, an empty shell, its occupant gone.

Officer Vic Morro hastily greeted his boss; shook hands with Pops, whom he'd known since he was a kid growing up on Kinoole Street; and then quickly said, as he began moving away from them, "Excuse me, Chief, Pops, I see two boys that may know something about how this truck got here."

Vic moved quickly toward the retreating boys. He'd been patrolling the area long enough to know that trouble and the twins generally rowed together in the same boat. The twins were fresh in his mind since it had been less than a week since he'd been called to a home in Volcano Village by the owner of a large Rottweiler. According to the dog's owner, the dog had let out a loud yelp, and the owner had gone to investigate. When he saw his dog's snout bleeding and noticed several rocks lying close by in the dirt, he went back inside and called the police. The rocks had been easy to spot since his dog lived on the end of a ten-foot chain and the surrounding ground was bare dirt. There were several piles of dog-poop scattered about that the owner tried to ignore for as long as he could, along with several rocks that shouldn't have been there.

The man told Vic he had spotted Vince and Raymond laughing as they walked away. Vic, though, had difficulty fabricating much sympathy for the story. He certainly didn't like the dog's behavior but felt sorry for it. He especially didn't care for its owner. He knew the dog constantly barked and strained against its chain whenever anyone walked past. Vic's annoyance was aimed more toward the dog's owner than the boys. No one saw them throw any rocks as he did the obligatory canvassing. All the neighbors agreed that "if in fact the boys did throw the rocks," it was a good thing.

Apparently, they thought as Vic did, that the dog's barking and snarling was a constant neighborhood disturbance but placed direct blame on the owner for the deplorable conditions the dog had to suffer. Officer Morro, knowing the boys were more than likely the rock throwers, also knew there was little he could do about it except appease the owner and suggest, for the dog's sake, that maybe the owner needed to pay more attention to its comfort. He promised the man he'd speak to the boys about the rock throwing, but he hadn't done so yet.

He closed the distance on the boys and called out, "Vince, Raymond, I need to talk to you." They hesitated, wondering if they should run for it, but their better judgment prevailed, and they stopped, turning around to face the officer. Vince stayed partially hidden behind his brother's left shoulder. Total invisibility would have more to his liking.

"I saw you two boys checking out that pickup back there." He indicated the direction with a dip of his head. "What would either of you know about it or how it got there?"

"Eh," Vince quickly responded from behind his brother, surprising Vic as well as Raymond, since he was generally the last one to speak out about anything. "We don't know nothing. We never hot-wired—"

He was cut off quickly by Raymond talking louder than him.

"We don't know nothing 'bout that truck. Something wrong with it? Looks OK to me. Kinda old, but."

"What about you, Vince, did you want to tell me something more about it?"

Vince simply shook his head and said a quick no as his eyes played over everything except the officer standing directly in front of him as he retreated farther behind Raymond.

Vic sensed they knew a lot more than they were willing to admit, but he was unable to do anything about it right then. They would clamp up tighter than a turtle if he hauled them to the precinct—he'd also have to deal with the parents, and that pretty much made his decision for him.

"Let me tell you about that truck you were interested in checking out." He was going out on a limb with what he was about to tell them, knowing it could backfire. "A young local *wahine* was driving that pickup two days ago and is now missing, and no one knows where she might be, except the person, or persons"—he made a point of catching their eyes—"who drove it from where it was and parked it where it is now. If we knew where that truck had originally been, then we'd have a good chance of finding her before something bad happens to her."

He let the imprint of his words sink in as he stood looking from one to the other. He'd get called into the chief's office if the chief caught wind that he'd told the boys this. He waited for their reaction.

After a lengthy silence, Raymond, almost in a whisper, again volunteered, "We don't know nothing about it." He was smart enough to know that admitting to stealing the truck would be crossing into unknown territory, and he had no idea what his parents might do with that kind of serious turmoil hanging over them. He didn't even want to think about *that* possibility. Up to this point, any trouble they'd ever gotten into was comparatively benign.

The long silence that followed was finally broken when Vic said, "Think about the missing woman, boys. She could be seriously hurt and in need of our help," he said, intentionally throwing in the word *our*. He was certain he wouldn't get anything more from them, at least not at that moment. He held out hope that they weren't genetically bad kids; they just needed some strong positive guidance.

"Why you telling us all this?" asked Raymond.

Ignoring the question, Vic turned and walked back to where the chief and Pops stood, smiling to himself. He knew enough about kids like Vince and Raymond that leaving something like this on the table would eventually feed into their innate sense of things—at least he hoped it would. He would make it a point to drive by their home later in the day; they may notice him and want to talk. If not, he'd knock on their door; he really needed to know what they knew.

He thought it a good idea if he also managed to be in their neighborhood more often and put himself in a better position to help guide them, if that was possible.

Eighteen

SADLY, POPS WALKED IN the front door, reached up, and hung his truck keys on a driftwood hook he had mounted by the door. It was an unconscious habit cultivated over many years. Whenever he failed to put his keys on the hook—and there were times when he was in a rush or things were pressing on his mind that he did forget—it could often take him an hour or more to find where he'd put them. He continued through the house and out through the sliding glass doors onto the lanai, where he joined the others who were awaiting his return. Everyone looked up expectantly.

All the food that had been out on the tables had either been eaten, put away, or had lids put on to keep the cockroaches and flies away. A thin layer of water covered the *poi* remaining in the polished wood calabash bowl to keep it from spoiling. He suspected John or Teri, most likely both, had a hand in doing it; and he was pleased they'd taken the initiative.

"Tell us what happened, Pops. You've been gone a long time." John walked over and stood close to his father.

Gently laying his hand on John's shoulder, Pops looked around at all of them. "The old Beast was right where Officer Vic said it was. No sign of Viane's presence except for the absence of a length of rope that I kept behind the seat." He was obviously feeling depressed. "I guess it's actually her rope since she's the only one ever used it. A time ago, she asked me to keep it available so she wouldn't have to cart it on and off the airplane every time she came to hike. I think its absence means something if she was the one who took it, but we're not going to know until we figure out where she went or find the person who stole the truck.

As for the old girl, she was definitely stolen from wherever Viane parked her. The ignition wires were pulled down and used to start the motor. And if the thief was the one who took that rope, it won't help us none in finding our girl." He pulled a chair around facing the others and wearily eased himself into it.

"Took a lot of time," he continued relaying the events. "The chief insisted on calling his forensics team out to take a hard look at the Beast." *Beast* is what he'd named his truck many years before. "They didn't find anything," he added. "Actually, that's not true," he corrected himself. "They found too much—too much of my own history. They got hair from so many different people, a lot of dog's hair, and even some pigs. I had forgot helping my neighbor years ago take his pig out to a farmer in Puainako 'cause the pig was getting too messy to live inside his house. He insisted on carrying it in his lap all the way, darn sow squealing right in my ear the whole time. Seems he didn't like riding in my truck, probably thought she was going to be the guest of honor at an *imu*. They also found a few more fingerprints than they expected. There were so many they had wondered if I'd loaned the Beast out to the whole town of Hilo."

He chuckled at the thought. "They forget that truck's been around town for a long while. You know, kinda interesting."

Everyone was anxious to hear all the details.

"Vic, the cop from Keaau area, saw two boys hanging around the parking lot who he knew to be perpetual troublemakers—'mischief makers' is what he called them.

After talking to them, he's convinced they know more about my truck than they're willing to admit. Says they live up in Volcano Village, but the boys will show up anywhere from Akaka Falls down to Naalehu at South Point, so if they were involved, they could have grabbed it almost anywhere on the east side of the island. Said he's going to follow up with the boys this afternoon."

Teri broke the short silence that followed as each one assimilated Pops's story. "Stone and I were about to drive up to Mauna Kea State Park to look around and ask questions of anyone who might be there. I feel we need to cover as many areas she may have visited as we can."

"Yeah," added Stone, "we're feeling the need to do something constructive instead of sitting here eating all your *ono* food." Eyes unconsciously glanced around at the tables and the sparse quantity of food remaining. Pops saw this and just smiled. He was pleased they all enjoyed his cooking. "You or John want to tag along with us?" Stone asked. He looked from one to the other, but both gave a slight knowing shake of their heads in response. Their poorly concealed smiles silently acknowledged they knew Stone and Teri would want a little time alone.

"I'm going to go check out my property again," offered John, bringing a somber mood back. "I want to see if she happened to return there. After that, I think I'll take a drive through Volcano Village where these boys are from, then into Volcano Park and check around some of her favorite spots. What are you thinking of doing, Pops?"

"Someone needs to stay by the phone in case she calls, so I guess that's me." Pops continued to resist getting a cell phone, voicing the thought that he didn't feel he was important enough that someone couldn't leave a message on his house phone. *There is usually nobody that needs to talk to me that urgently that I care to listen to—except for right now.* His thoughts travelling to Viane's cell phone.

"Eh, Stone," he said, finally a humorous glint returning to his eyes, "I may have to follow in your footsteps." He was pointing to Stone's cell phone encased on his belt. "Sure would make things a lot easier right now." He knew of Stone's longstanding resistance to cell phones until Teri showed up in his life. She had told Pops all this soon after she'd met Stone. His smile faded as his gaze dropped to the floor, and he slowly shook his head in thought.

With a quick aloha, Stone and Teri followed John out the door.

Alone with his thoughts, Pops, who'd had a perpetual sadness written across his face since coming back with his pickup, felt the well of sadness being pushed away and a growing anger flowing in taking its place. He knew how to handle anger a lot better than he knew about handling sadness, and emotional anger provided him a path of action. He was never one to sit idly by and let bad things happen, especially when his family is involved, without trying to change the direction events were inclined to slowly move in.

He absently sat rubbing his old wound while he began formulating a plan. The only link to his daughter that he felt certain about was the two boys, and he was going to find them and convince them to tell him what they knew—maybe join forces with Vic. Unfortunately, with a loud sigh, that would have to wait until John got back.

"BIG CHANGE SINCE THE last time I drove up Saddle Road," exclaimed Stone as they made their way up the mountain to Mauna Kea State Park.

Over the years, Teri had heard stories of the infamous Saddle Road but had never found reason to use it. It was like a cartoon road made of ribbon: the ups and downs and constant turning made her stomach queasy as the car lurched up and over a rise and then quickly down the other side, only to bottom out before hitting the next incline.

Teri didn't say anything, but she was starting to feel very sick. She knew Stone was driving faster than he usually drove, simply because he thrilled at the roller-coaster effect so much, and she didn't want to spoil his fun in spite of the way she was feeling. She saw his smile and assumed it was being generated by past memories.

The old road bisected the Big Island running between Hilo on the east side and Waimea on the west. It used the saddle formed by the two magnificent volcanoes—the dormant Mauna Kea on one side and the not-so-dormant Mauna Loa on the other. The name developed after the army constructed it in order to gain access to their then-new training facility at Pohakuloa on the horn of the saddle.

"Can you believe that not too long ago this road was barely wide enough for one car and was so full of potholes and disintegrated asphalt on both sides that besides the ups and downs you had to swerve side to side to avoid a tire blowout? That's how it got its infamous image. The car rental companies used to have notices glued to dashboards that prohibited tourists from using the road."

He slowed down after noticing the ghostlike coloring showing on Teri's face. "You always had to anticipate other cars coming in the opposite direction over the next rise," he continued his narrative. "A lot of serious accidents took place up here. The state's done a lot of work widening and straightening it. In a way, it's too bad. That old road had a lot of charm—dangerous but charming."

"As well as thrills galore, I'm sure," she added, feeling better at the slowed pace.

They drove into Mauna Kea State Park and pulled up to the bathrooms—always a planned pit stop for travelers on this road. There were no other cars there, and it didn't appear anyone was currently renting one of the several cabins sitting silently alone. The place appeared to be deserted.

They walked around a portion of the park, breathing in the wonderful scent of fresh, clean mountain air, letting it wash over and engulf them. They quickly realized there were far too many trails Viane could have taken for them to know where to even begin to look. After an hour of aimless wandering searching for clues of Viane having been there, they left and drove up to the Mauna Kea Visitor Center. A ranger on duty checked the logbook and told them no one by the name of Viane Koa had signed in; nor did he remember anyone resembling the description Teri insisted on pressing on him. He was certain, though, that no one was hiking around the summit at the moment. They wondered how he could be so certain but didn't want to challenge him.

Feeling dejected, but at the same time satisfied they'd made the effort, they drove back down into Hilo and back to Pops's house.

JOHN COULD SEE WHAT he assumed were his sister's hand prints embossed in the grease on the D-9 Caterpillar as he used the massive machine to climb down into the open yawn of his newly exposed lava-encased chamber. Inwardly, he was thrilled with the prospects it presented. He was there to look for signs of his sister but couldn't keep from visualizing what he might do with this large new space. He envisioned building his home over the top of it with an inside staircase going down into its bowels. It was virtually an endless room stretching out in two directions. He was anxious to hear what his fiancée, Catherine, thought about it. He'd described it to her, but without seeing it in person, her imagination had been unable to grasp its enormity.

Finding no further sign of his sister having returned, he drove out of the Acres—the "Hawaiian Bushes," as someone had comically referred to the area because of the rainforest that encompassed it with near-impenetrable foliage. He continued on to the highway heading up the gentle rise to Volcano Village.

John was so absorbed in a multitude of thoughts about the future that he never realized his foot had come within mere inches of stepping on Viane's cell phone as he climbed the D-9 on his way out of the cavity.

As he drove toward Volcano Village, he decided that even if he saw two boys walking in the village he wouldn't know with any certainty that they were the ones he was looking for; nor would he know how to ask them if they were the ones who stole his father's truck. He decided that this was not going to work out the way he'd hoped, so he continued to drive the short distance to the national park, stopping at the guard shack at the park's entrance. The ranger there couldn't help him with any information about whether his sister had been there.

"Unless hikers come in and register to hike, we have no way of knowing who's on the mountain. If your sister was there, she didn't sign our book, so there's nothing we can do. If you find out for certain that she's here, we'll do what we can to help locate her." He turned a map around so John could see it and pointed to a spot. "You might want to drive up to this summit trailhead and see what you can see. In the meantime, we'll let all our people know there's a chance a young lady is lost somewhere on the trail. Sorry, son, that's the best we can do. Keep us in the loop, OK?"

As John drove up Bird Park Road toward the summit trailhead, thoughts consumed with finding his sister, he had no way to know the rental car approaching from the other direction held the clue to her whereabouts in the form of a purple hat and a broken piece of rope.

Nineteen

PLEASANTLY EXHAUSTED from their two-day hike to the summit cabin on Mauna Loa, Sue and Chris were anxious to return to Hilo and check into the Naniloa Beach Hotel. They'd taken the opportunity during the few moments they'd stopped to rest on the trail to make plans for the rest of their Big Island stay. They were anxious to move on to the next adventure.

Their immediate thoughts, though, dwelt on taking a refreshing swim in the crystal-clear water of Hilo Bay before doing anything else. The contrast between the hot dryness of their hike and the coolness of their coming swim was very persuading. The waters of the bay gently rose and fell against its centuries-old lava flow boundary where the Bay's water held fast against the lava. It was a dramatic yet beautiful edge of the hotel's waterfront setting.

Before that could happen, though, they had to complete their self-volunteered obligation to take the strange-looking purple hat they'd found to the park ranger's office. They weren't too sure what compelled them except knowing that if they themselves lost something along a trail, they would hope a fellow hiker would do the same for them. They passed a car on the way and joked about the possibility that the driver was on his way back up the mountain to retrieve a purple hat he'd left behind.

Inside the park main office, they referred to a map the ranger held up in front of them and indicated the spot, to the best of their ability, where they'd found the items. They had just turned over the hat and the piece of rope.

"That's about as accurate as we can be in pinpointing where we found it. We know it was a couple hours' hiking time from there to the Red Hill cabin. We stayed overnight, thankful for a place to lie down and rest our weary legs and feet."

The ranger wasn't too concerned with how accurate the hiker's report was—in fact, he wasn't concerned at all, which was very unlike him. Unfortunately, he had another pressing matter weighing on his mind involving a noticeable build-up of pressure inside the Kilauea crater. In his experience, hikers lost gear, and other hikers often showed up to add to the Lost and Found pile, but few ever showed up to claim any of it. He was tempted to throw both the hat and the rope away as soon as the people were gone, but he didn't. He did, though, throw the short length of rope in the trash bin next to him but tagged the hat with the information he'd been given, though much abbreviated and far from detailed. He dated it and threw it into a large box in the corner of his office, along with all the other paraphernalia that had been brought in from various areas of the park. Everything in the box—from binoculars, cameras and an abundance of cell phones—would be given to the thrift store in Volcano Village at the end of the month, provided no one showed up to claim any of it. He was usually much more attentive and detail-accurate; but barely five minutes before the people with the hat showed up, he'd received a call about pressure readings. He wasn't sure what he could do about it but knew he needed to go into the crater to see for himself. He'd know what he had to do by the time he got there. If Kilauea ever blew, it would be catastrophic, utterly unimaginable.

THE HAT NOW FORGOTTEN, Chris and Sue headed for their hotel and a cooling swim. They stopped briefly to pick a handful of white ginger stocks growing wild along both sides of the highway. The stocks were loaded with flowers, and Sue knew they would lend a pleasant scent to their hotel room over the next few nights.

Twenty

Kaneohe, Island of Oahu

ALL THE NEGATIVE ENERGY that had surrounded them ever since the boat theft simply had to change. He couldn't keep harboring the anger and allow the depression to consume him and affect his marriage. Guy knew Deborah felt as he did.

The theft of their boat left them with a sense of having been personally violated: a horrible emotion to cope with. It wasn't just the loss of their boat; it was mostly due to the fact that neither of them had any experience at being a victim. It was deeply emotional and was wearing on them like a damp blanket on a cold night. They found themselves unable to get out from beneath it. The depression was the worst and was causing them both sleepless nights.

In its simplest form, the loss was unfortunate, and their insurance reimbursement would allow them to buy another, perhaps better, boat so their future plans of enjoying the ocean surrounding them was still in place—nothing had changed except the vehicle they'd ride on. The depressing part, at least for Guy, was that he had become acutely attached to *Lehua* during the year he and Deborah had spent rebuilding her, and nothing could replace that loss. You can't recreate something the second time with the same enthusiasm. Somehow it symbolized more than just a boat—it was the basis of many dreams he and Deborah had interwoven into their lives.

Sitting in his backyard, massaging his emotions, his feet dangling in the clear blue water of the swimming pool they'd had installed shortly after buying the house, he realized all they'd been doing since the theft was reacting and allowing things to get to them, interfering with their lives, instead of taking charge—much more to both their natures. He decided a little physical activity was in order and may help bring about a shift in their mood; it couldn't make anything worse.

He'd been thinking of the Haiku staircase for a long time but had unthinkingly allowed other activities, busy work as some would say, to sidetrack his time away from his office: yard work when it didn't really need doing, ESPN that kept him indoors when an abundant world outside was calling, thinking of jobs that his print shop was working on that didn't really need his overview, boat repairs and all the dreams that endeavor brought to mind. He had yet, for the decades of his life, to climb the famous steps.

The name many local people had placed on this glorified ladder was the Staircase to Heaven. A different name voiced by many who'd experienced them was the Not-So-Quick Staircase to Heaven—or Hell, depending on the individual's outlook. He'd read recently that it may soon be closed to the public, and he wanted to experience the climb and share the experience with Deborah before it became just another part of Hawaii history—gone but for dreams left behind. Deborah had heard him talk about it and was excited at the prospect of climbing the El Capitan of Hawaii. He explained to her that it was essentially a very old and rickety iron ladder with equally old and rickety iron handrails. Wooden when it was first built in 1942, it clung to the sheer wall of the

Koolau cliff, snaking its way up the face of the rise behind the community of Haiku. It ended 2,800 feet above and better than 3,900 steps later. It was designed to provide access to the Coast Guard's Omega Navigation System transmitter, but Guy knew the transmitter had been decommissioned a long time ago.

Deborah trusted her husband explicitly but knew from past experience he could get them into situations that, in retrospect, she wished she'd had the sense to decline. She had read about this staircase in tourist publications and knew it would be a frightening experience climbing such a ladder, especially one that incorporated so few safety precautions. As fear generating as it was, a part of her really wanted to experience it regardless, so when Guy walked into the kitchen suggesting they use the day to do something crazy and mentioned the staircase, she quickly threw the dishtowel she'd been folding aside and said, "I'll get my shoes."

They packed the leftover spam *musubi* from last night's dinner and two bottles of water into a backpack and were out the door ten minutes later headed for Haiku and a climb to heaven, a fresh excitement claiming them both.

THEIR LEGS FELT LIKE wobbly rubber posts as they bent over, hands on their knees, taking deep breaths to replace the void of air in their lungs that the exertion had left them with; but they made it. They sat down on a broad cement foundation supporting a lofty transmission tower that reached skyward above their heads. From this vantage point, they could take in the vast top-of-the-world view that took form before them. They had a sweeping panorama view from Lanikai and Rabbit Island on the southeast all the way to Chinaman's Hat and Kanehoalani, the mountain that rose from the Kualoa Ranch area on the northwest; and in between, they could actually see the curve of the earth.

Deborah could just make out the old coral house built on the beach close to the remnants of the old mill sitting on the ranch property next to the highway. Guy had taken her for a beach walk one day, and they had stood admiring this unusual house and the intense labor it must have taken someone to build it so many years ago. It was built entirely of small, hand-sized pieces of coral cemented together to form the walls, window, and door openings with curving lines and rounded corners. Any structural support—and there had to be some—was visually obscured. It was an artisan's marvel. She'd love to know more about the person who built it.

From their height, Kapapa Island and all the surrounding coral-heads showed white against the azure-blue clear water of the bay. The coral heads they had carefully threaded between with their now-missing boat and the island that hardly looked big enough from this distance to stand on, let alone put up three tents and provide so much fun for at least the one night, appeared as a beautiful image. The unpleasantness they came away from the island with was still present, but seeing the island from this distance in context with the incredible beauty surrounding it helped dissolve some of the recent emotions.

Binoculars allowed her to enjoy all the intricate details in the sweeping panorama. She was caught up in the simplicity of people's lives as she looked at the collection of backyards far below and the profusion of colorful flowers tucked in along the base of the sheer walls of the Koolau Mountains. She looked and saw the parking lot where they had parked, their Explorer so distant it appeared as a miniature Matchbox toy. As she looked at the walls of the mountain and all the yards and houses, she couldn't help but think of the possible danger that existed for those people living beneath the shadow of the vegetation-covered sheer walls of this ancient volcano remnant rising virtually straight upward behind their yards.

As she idly scanned the view, she was suddenly jolted by a much too familiar vision: sitting in a yard filled with the skeletons of an old car, a forklift and various other indescribable pieces of machinery and old appliances were two boats. One of them, albeit quite tiny from her towering viewpoint, appeared to be too much like their missing boat to be coincidental. The coloring and shape was so familiar.

"Guy," she yelled, not wanting to lower the binoculars for fear of losing the image, her heart pounding wildly; but when he didn't answer, she hesitantly lowered them and looked around. He was nowhere to be seen, and a wave of panic gripped her before she spotted him behind a small shed a distance away from the tower looking out in the opposite direction toward the town of Kailua and Rabbit Island close offshore. She called his name again, a little louder, and finally caught his attention. He was smiling as he walked over to her.

"What are you yelling for? I was reliving some very fond old memories of all the places I can see and have walked a thousand times in the past. I was thinking," he relayed his story as he got closer, fully unaware of her impatient look, "of a night a group of us sat around a bonfire on a private beach down there playing ukuleles and singing and going through case after case of beer as the night progressed and the bonfire diminished to ashes. I had forgotten all about an old Waikiki beach boy named Duckie that was sitting beside me. He's the one responsible for my being on the beach when you came looking for a surf teacher."

Finally noticing her agitation, he asked, "What got you so excited all by yourself over here?" He could tell she was not the slightest bit interested in his reminiscing.

"Come and look at what I think I see." The obvious excitement shifted into her voice. "Follow my finger," she exclaimed, pointing as she quickly relocated the image. "The yard is hard against the sharp rise of the cliff. There's a deep crevasse in the cliff right behind the yard I'm pointing at. Do you see it?"

She pointed the best she could as Guy scanned the area through the binoculars, checking to see where her finger was aimed at. He abruptly stopped scanning and stood stock-still for several seconds.

"Well, I'll be darned," he exclaimed. "There's a naked lady with really big *attachments* sunbathing down there. Is that what you got so worked up about? I would have never suspected." He felt her slap his arm but knew it wasn't meant to hurt.

"Guy," she exclaimed, "don't you see what I was looking at?"

He raised the glasses to his eyes again and kept looking for what had gotten his wife so charged up. Suddenly his body tensed. "Son of a... that sure looks like ours, don't it? The motors are gone, but there's no mistaking that beer cooler I built into the rear bench seat."

He brought the glasses down, turned, and gave Deborah a death-grip hug before raising his hand as they high-fived each other, both grinning from ear to ear. He raised the glasses again, intent on looking. "Honey, you got your camera with you? Zoom in and take several close-ups of the area and that crevasse behind the yard. Then let's drive around and find it. That row of red bougainvillea along the roadway should help us zero in on the right yard when we get close. Take a picture of it as well. That's an easy area to get lost in. There are too many dirt roads leading nowhere and long jeep tracks that lead into private property."

An hour later, after a cautious yet somewhat hurried descent, they were on the ground and in their car. They sped off in search of the house but soon discovered that their ground-level view with all the bushes and tall coconut trees presented them with an entirely unfamiliar perspective from what they thought would be a straightforward hunt. Pinpointing the yard became frustrating.

He was about to call Mike but found there was no cell phone signal this far back against the mountain. He also realized he hadn't entered Mike's phone number into his contact list anyway, so the call would have to wait.

They drove slowly down each road that skirted along the rise of the mountain, determined to find that yard. They kept referring to the pictures Deborah had taken for any landmark that would lend direction.

Community of Haiku at the base of the Koolau Mountains

THE TWO MEN WERE concentrating on loading the carcasses of two boats onto a flatbed trailer—it was strenuous work. The fact that it was hot and they were sweating heavily added weight to their work, and they were becoming thirsty.

They were using a makeshift hoist they had welded together consisting of long chains holding both ends of two wide canvas straps, the chains looped around an electric winch. They had designed it so the straps could reach under the belly of the boat they were maneuvering, and while one of them toggled the switch up and down, the other kept the boat carcass level, pushing and shoving while it was raised high enough to drop down onto the trailer. They managed to get one boat loaded on the front of the trailer and then moved their contraption over top of the other—a labor-intensive job in itself, as they hadn't gotten around to putting the wheels on their invention yet. After much bending, shoving, and ample moaning, they raised the second boat into the air and backed the trailer under it, lowering the boat onto the rear end.

Using this apparatus was a hazard they faced when they had to get rid of boats. They had built the hoist to lift the boats, but they did so without regard to its safety, as the man called Alysdon discovered when a strap suddenly tightened as it took the boat's weight and smashed his finger against the trailer's edge. He muttered several words that could have easily been heard numerous backyards away if anyone had been paying attention. They would have used the old forklift that lingered in the yard, but it was only good for small boats; and even then, only when they could get the antique started. It would probably collapse like a tricycle bearing the weight of an elephant if they tried to use it on boats like the ones now resting on the trailer.

Exhausted and even more thirsty from their efforts, Alysdon and Bill, friends since they first began to crawl, sat down on a pair of lawn chairs under the cooling umbrella of a large *ulu* tree in the back corner of their yard.

Their friendship transcended time and circumstance. Both owned the house, which they had divided into a duplex arrangement. They had both been married and lived in the house with their respective wives, and both had subsequently been divorced, pretty much simultaneously as well. Somehow the men managed to hold on to the property during the dividing of assets. If truth were known, both ex-wives couldn't wait to get away from them and their house and would have paid in cash if they had to. They had often referred to their husbands as the Laurel and Hardy pair and wanted no part of what little they were leaving behind as they closed the front door and almost literally ran down the road. The men were certain it had been a coordinated effort on the part of both their exes, but they weren't certain—nor did they really care a great deal.

It was cool and relaxing under the tree. Alysdon reached into a cooler resting behind his chair and retrieved two chilled bottles of Primo beer. The icy water from the cooler ran down the outside of the bottles and dripped from his hand as he handed one over to Bill. The icy water felt good on his smashed finger, so he left it dangling in the cooler. They drank thirstily before absentmindedly reaching for another.

The last part of their job and the most important part was putting a tarp over top of the two boat carcasses and fastening it down—tight. They walked around the trailer, making sure their cargo was well hidden from view, and re-secured a portion of the tarp they thought might blow loose to allow prying eyes to see what they carried. Satisfied all was as it should be, they hoisted the cooler into the middle of the truck's front seat. Alysdon opened the heavy solid-wood gate while Bill got behind the wheel and drove out onto the dirt road fronting their house, the trailer rolling along nicely behind.

Guy's and Deborah's boat, or what was left of it, was pinned to the front end of the covered trailer by straps pulled achingly tight across its bow and stern. Someone else's missing boat rode the back end. They passed dangerously close to a Ford Explorer driving slowly past their property but paid little attention to the two people inside it.

The boats were destined to be destroyed. They had stripped each of them of everything of value, and since there was too great a chance of recognition with these two particular boats, they chose not to ship them to the mainland but instead take it to their friend, who would make them disappear. They'd done the same with a few other boats. The one named *Lehua*, as inscribed across the stern, was an old Chris Craft kit boat that had been modified enough to entirely personalize it, making it too difficult to simply repaint and ship to Oregon. Unfortunately, it had to be demolished—it and the other boat that was deemed to be equally too recognizable and too difficult to successfully face-lift. Their next stop, then, was Tim Giuseppe's place, a friend whose property was a few miles north in the seaside community of Kaaawa.

They were anxious to be rid of their load. No matter how careful they were in covering their cargo, traveling on a highway with stolen property presented enormous risk. Bill drove one step below the speed limit, not taking any chance of being stopped, seat belts fastened. Once they finished at Tim's place, they would head back home and spend the rest of the day celebrating their good fortune under the shade of their tree, a full cooler of beer, of course, within easy reach.

Before night,their inebriation would clarify their next location for acquiring boats. They both agreed their chosen line of work was getting very easy.

TIM GIUSEPPE WAS SEMI-confined to a wheelchair but managed, with great effort, to use a walker when he really had to.

Other than selling the hardware he salvaged from boats, he had no viable means other than his artwork to earn money sufficient enough to buy anything beyond basic necessities. He received a meager social security check, which barely covered utility bills. In exchange for making things like boats disappear, his two partners, Alysdon and Bill, provided him with fish, squid, a bag of rice now and then, some spare cash when they had any that they considered spare, and a case of Primo every so often. He enjoyed his Primo. He looked forward to the time of year when *ulu* were in season and his two friends, with that large *ulu* tree in their yard, gladly shared the breadfruit with him rather than letting the huge fruit splatter to the ground. The rest of his food supplies were supplemented from his own garden of vegetables and a small dry-land taro patch. He had difficulty harvesting vegetables and taro from his wheelchair, but some neighborhood kids would often show up to help. They'd frequently bring him *opai* from the nearby stream and some *poi* when there was some left over from their own dinner table.

Creating what he considered works of art was a passion, but he was good at scavenging usable boat parts before destroying the remains. It was all contingent, of course, on his two cohorts not bringing too many too often.

Clever at using pulleys and ropes to do his bidding, he had devised ways he could sit on a bench much like a swing, and using one rope or another, he could maneuver himself anywhere on or above a boat as he went about cutting it apart. He chopped wooden boats into small pieces and feed them into a firebox, rendering everything to charcoal, which he used to dry fish and squid. He was cautious, though, to let the fumes from paints and varnishes dissipate before transferring the coals to his drying boxes. He cut fiberglass boats into artistic shapes and used those pieces to fashion different items that he could sell on his once-a-week trek to Waikiki and the Art on the Zoo Fence Hawaii art sale. He was currently making tabletops out of larger pieces of fiberglass, laminating and resining them together when he could afford to buy laminate and resin.

He was actually pretty satisfied with his life. He lived simply and worked the best he could with the malformed legs that God had served him at birth. He was very fortunate to have a large property, a good house, and an extra big workshop that allowed him the space he needed for his craft.

Looking at the two newest arrivals, he noticed that one of the boats had the name *Lehua* painted across the transom, bordered with nicely painted red lehua blossoms. He decided to save that piece since it reminded him of an old girlfriend who had come through his life once upon a time. Why she'd shown up he'd never been able to figure out, and it was too many years ago to think about now, but she'd been able to convince him that lehua blossoms were one of God's most beautiful creations. He knew just where he'd hang the ornate piece of transom after he cut the boat apart and decided he would also create a painting of it to sell.

Twenty-Two

THEY DROVE SLOWLY ALONG the dirt road, their eyes scanning the neighborhood for anything that would help pinpoint the yard they saw their boat sitting in. The crevasse in the cliff wall they had photographed was the actual landmark they were looking for. The trouble was that most of the cliff features were hidden behind trees and tall hedges. It was a frustrating endeavor to see any details at ground level.

Finally, through a narrow portal that opened up among the tall coconut trees, the crevasse materialized—at least they hoped it was the right one. It appeared to be, but the differing perspective at ground level, which was somewhat obscured by tall bushes, made it difficult to be certain. As they slowly crept farther along the road, the foliage finally opened, giving them a clear view—it was exactly what they were looking for. Their excitement at being in the right place, however, was quickly shoved aside as a truck hauling a huge trailer suddenly came barreling out of a driveway right in front of them, a driveway that Guy hadn't noticed. The trailing dust cloud obliterated whatever view they had, and they were forced to stop momentarily.

As the dust slowly settled, they began to slowly move forward, their eyes focused through the clearing air. The side of the mountain came back into view directly behind the property the truck and trailer had come from. Just to be certain, Deborah pulled up the picture she'd taken to compare it to what they were looking at. There was no question about being in the right spot. Earlier, from her vantage point above the staircase, she'd noticed a tell-tale scar low on the cliff face, the result of a large piece of mountain letting go of its attachment; the stark brown of rock contrasted sharply with the lush green of the vegetation surrounding it. The disfigurement was quite a bit higher off the ground than it had appeared from up above, but it was the same scar—it retained its likeness to a huge bird in flight that had struck Deborah as being somehow meaningful at that moment.

Guy came to a stop again beside a wooden fence covered by a wall of brilliant, stunningly beautiful red bougainvillea that seemed to go on forever. It was the bougainvillea hedge they had noticed from the mountaintop, the one that showed up in the picture. They got out of their car and continued on foot.

Deborah leaned over close to Guy and, in whispered tones as she took on an almost humorous clandestine posture, asked, "How are we going to do this? We should have been discussing this before we found the place, not while we're sitting out in front of it. We can't just knock on the door and say we came to see if your backyard is harboring our stolen boat. Why don't we drive out to where cell phone coverage is decent and call Sergeant Mike and tell him where we are and what we suspect. Maybe he will tell us what to do and may even volunteer to join in."

"We don't know Mike's number," he said, somewhat disgustedly as if it were his own personal shortcoming. "Anyway, he'd probably tell us to leave it alone and go home. You know that he still leans heavily on the theory that all the boats being stolen are being shipped off to the mainland."

She shrugged, no longer whispering. "You're just rationalizing things. He can't argue with the picture we took and the identification of our own boat." She didn't push her point too hard, though. She had just tasted a level of excitement in what they were about to do that she'd not felt before and really wanted to continue on and definitely wanted Guy on board with her.

"You have to admit our view from way up top was far from perfect." Guy was beginning to entertain doubts in what they saw.

"Oh," was all Deborah replied in a *Don't be silly* tone. She played with the zoom feature on her camera, enlarging the picture to make the boat they saw fill the small screen. It was blurry, but she was satisfied with what she saw and held the camera up for her husband to look at once again. "The built-in beer cooler?" was all she said as she looked up at him.

"OK, OK. It's definitely our boat. Mahalo, sweetie." He put his arm over her shoulder and kissed her forehead. Keeping his arm in place, he took in more detail of the image. "Huh. I'd forgotten about that stain that came through the paint on the roof. It's kinda sad to look at it now remembering all the fun we had working on it. Why don't we take a casual walk past the house and see what we can see. Let's face it, a local boy and a *haole* chick—we'll fit right into this neighborhood." He gave her hand a playful squeeze. He enjoyed kidding her, but in the same breath, he was praying they wouldn't run into a group of local boys who leaned heavily toward island sovereignty. It could get nasty.

They discovered an empty property beside the yard and pushed their way through some bushes and weeds that skirted the edge. An opening in the *haole koa* toward the back gave them a view of the entire yard through a chain-link fence. They were shocked to see the yard empty of boats. Theirs and the other one that had been there were gone.

The old car, the forklift that looked ancient up close and sundry pieces of machinery was all that remained. Centered in the yard was an old washing machine with an extension cord running toward the house. "They probably use that to tenderize fresh octopus before smoking or drying it." At Deborah's questioning looks, he added, "Hey"—his body language suggested that everyone should know this—"it's a common practice. Beats sitting around pounding them tender with a rock."

"Our timing is rotten, isn't it?" Deborah voiced a mutual thought. "I bet that truck and trailer that whipped up all the dust was our boat going someplace else."

Guy grabbed the fence and started to climb over, but Deborah grabbed the seat of his pants and pulled him back down.

"What are you doing? Have you suddenly lost a few screws?"

"I'm climbing over so I can take a better look around. Don't worry, I can do this. I'm an ex-fireman, remember?" He grinned at his own humor.

"Yeah, but you're an injured ex-fireman, *remember!* Besides, we don't know if there's somebody there ready to take a pot shot at us or if a pit bull with hungry teeth is close by, ready to bite." They scanned the yard and house, and were satisfied they were alone: no people, no visible dogs, and no dog poop in the grass. "OK," she said, grabbing the fence and working her boot into a toehold, "you're right. We can do this."

"We?" exclaimed Guy. "Not going to happen," he said, getting a hold on one of her belt loops. "You're staying put right here on this side of the fence." He pointed at her feet with his index finger.

INSIDE THE YARD, THEY both hid behind a rusting powder-blue Buick convertible collapsed to the ground on four flat tires, the *honohono* grass gaining a camouflage hold on it.

"That's a '48," he exclaimed in a whisper, suddenly becoming aware of what they were hiding behind. He pulled a handful of *honohono* grass aside and leaned back to take a better look. "I used to own one just like this. Same color. It was stolen and never found." His eyebrows suddenly rose in a puzzled expression hearing his own words as he realized what they may have stumbled upon. A nudge from his partner brought him back to awareness.

Feeling a bit braver, they crept across the yard to where their boat had been.

"Look." Deborah held up a red square flotation cushion with white bunting and white canvas straps on both sides. She turned it over and felt a rush of sadness seeing the inscription she'd written across the face of it just a few weeks ago.

To protect the butt I love

She'd given the cushion to him on the morning he'd pronounced *Lehue* "ready to roll out and caress a few waves."

"Put it back exactly where it was and take a picture of it. Then let's get out of here while we still have *okole*s worth protecting." He took her hand and led the way back to the fence. "Take a picture of this car as well," he said. He lifted the engine hood against its noisy protests, took a hard look at the faded red paint that was still evident in the compartment, and then gently let it back down with a sad shake of his head. The rest of the unknown story of where the car from his university days disappeared to what was now evident— the car that had been stolen so many years ago. He was experiencing mixed emotions, unsure of what was more upsetting: his missing boat or finding his missing car—both in the same place.

Twenty-Three

MIKE KALAMA PULLED INTO the empty parking lot off Nimitz Highway on the Ewa side of downtown Honolulu. The dark of night was already settling in.

He knew this area like the inside of his house and had picked it specifically for this meeting place: it was close to Young Brothers, the inter-island barging company, and it was also deserted, most of the time anyway. Interestingly, too, it was almost directly beneath the towering pineapple-shaped water tower of the aging Dole Cannery. But best of all, it was rarely frequented anymore, and tonight it appeared that was the case.

He drove a hundred yards off the highway, coasting to a stop beside the dark silhouette of a building. The evening was eerily quiet, as if all the critters of the night suddenly stood still the moment he opened the door and got out. The distant soft drone of trucks and cars passing on the highway was the only audible giveaway that life continued. The highway had been the main connecting road between Waikiki and the airport before the H-1 freeway was built; however, it was still heavily used.

He walked a short distance between two large abandoned iron warehouse buildings, some of the sheet metal siding already letting go. The rodent population scurried for cover in the dim light, unaware their safe metal sanctuaries were due for destruction. The gossip was that a new Foodworld Supermarket and several upscale stores were in the planning stages for the area; and unfortunately, so also was word that Dole's iconic and much-loved water tower, humorously rumored to be filled with pineapple juice, was also slated to come down. Mike had little attachment to the old warehouse buildings and could easily let them go, but he felt that destroying the huge pineapple-shaped tower was a huge travesty. The only thing that could be any worse would be if some lame politician lobbied to dismantle the Aloha Tower—another piece of the magic that once was Hawaii that was disappearing a piece at a time at the hands of developers and bulging-pocketed politicians.

In years past, when Mike was new on the force walking a beat, this area of Honolulu known as Iwilei was part of his territory; he knew it well—including its infamous and long-forgotten history.

In the Roaring Twenties and decades before, this area had been the notorious red-light district of old Honolulu. Close to the spot he was standing on, there'd been a fifteen-foot-high wooden fence surrounding rows of small green with trim white cottages with small covered lanais in front. Skimpily clad ladies would sit on their lanais and wait for clients to walk past. The existence of this infamous community was something the elite ladies around town consistently refused to acknowledge. Their husbands staunchly refused to acknowledge its existence as well—but only until their wives were out of hearing range. It was common practice among many husbands in those days to secrete away portions of their earnings to be kept for rainy days—days that consistently came regardless of the weather. Politicians, local police, and regular everyday husbands alike continually kept the ladies of Iwilei active.

Mike walked toward two men standing in a shadowed doorway. The men gave the appearance they may have recently crawled out from beneath one of the doomed buildings. Both wore coveralls that were long past the point of needing a wash, as well as sweat-stained and dirt-grimed T-shirts that Mike suspected by their soiled appearance, would be able to stand up in a corner unassisted if the men ever took them off to find out. Both of them were several days past needing a shave, their hair held in place, one by a bandana tied around his head and the other hidden beneath a backwards-turned baseball cap.

The one with the bandana, the taller of the two, took a cigarette from between his lips and flicked it in Mike's direction, splashing on the gravel roadway and sending sparks showering around his feet as he briefly paused in his approach. Everyday citizens seeing one of these men walking toward them would surely turn and quickly find another direction in which to hurry off. Not Mike Kalama. These were his men, and he knew them well. He appreciated the characterizations they had cultivated and maintained even in the privacy of their meeting.

As he drew close, he briefly looked around to make certain there was no one else within earshot; it was purely by habit. He knew that as long as his men were present, the chances of anyone else being close by was remote.

"What did you find?" he asked the smoker. "The incoming call sheet at the station said you had something for me."

"We have a container just showed up this morning and is in line to ship out on Wednesday bound for Portland, Oregon. The shipper is listed as Wood Industries of Waimanalo, but a record check shows no such company, and the address given is a vegetable farm way back against the mountain. Sounds phony, you ask me." They had been checking background and content on every generic container entering the yard, generic in the sense the shipper's name was not emblazoned across its side in large brilliant lettering. If a container came in that appeared questionable, they would look up the shipper's name and address in police files to verify legitimacy—not a foolproof method by any means, but more of an *only* option.

"Did you crack it open and look inside?"

"Naw, we figured that was your *kuleana*. This is your show. You ought to be the one to have that fun. Besides, there's no way we could do that and chance getting our cover blown by some of the dockworkers." The two had been posing as homeless derelicts looking to do some work to earn cigarette and beer money. They were actually there to watch for illegal activity—anything shipping through illegally, not just boats. Mike had specifically instructed them to be especially watchful for stolen boats shipping in or out. They were undercover police officers—a duty assignment often given to a new recruit that had yet to become publicly identified with HPD. Mike knew the operations manager of the inter-island barging company well enough to request that he let his men work undercover around the yard for a few weeks.

"OK, good work. Hang around these buildings for a short time after I leave and then continue your surveillance back in the shipyard. We'll hold the stakeout for a while longer. I'll see about the container."

"We're so grateful, Mike," said tongue-in-cheek by the baseball cap. "Now we can crawl back into our cardboard hovels for another night under the stars." There was a faint smile attached to the words, but they were definitely not heartfelt. Mike understood the sentiment: he'd been undercover as a recruit and knew the hardships.

He got the bill of lading information from them, along with the container number before he left. Two days remained before it was scheduled to be loaded on a ship, but he didn't want to waste any time. He'd get some help and open it first thing in the morning. If it contained stolen boats as his men suspected, he at least hoped it was Stone's friend's boat that was inside—that would be a big plus.

EARLY THE NEXT MORNING, Mike drove onto the Young Brothers dock in his own unmarked car and parked in a spot designated for customers. He was dressed in civilian clothes—just another YB client there to check on his container. Investigations tend to become awkward when company employees find out HPD is snooping around. He didn't want to take that chance. He walked back along the pier to where the container had been relocated, thanks to the operations manager who had it moved to this more obscure place on the pier.

Leaning up against the container was a short, stout man neatly dressed in black slacks and a brilliant red aloha shirt—birds of paradise in profusion. He stood with one leg crossed over the other, arms folded across his chest— strong, muscular, hairy arms. Mike figured he was the Young Brothers' insurance adjuster, a man named Chauky O' Marle, whom Mike had called late the previous evening to arrange the time. The man had been waiting for Mike's arrival so they could proceed to break the seal on the container.

Once the doors were opened, they were confronted by a wall of boxes from floor to ceiling, side to side. The bill of lading listed the container's contents as four hundred boxes, weighing 48,000 and each box containing 250,000 pairs of chopsticks, all supposedly made in Waimanalo. Mike stood and took in the massive wall of future eating tools. *Bet the Chinese aren't too happy about the competition into their sacred territory*, he mused.

"That's a lot of chopsticks," voiced Chauky. "Of course, Seattle and Portland have large populations of Orientals," he continued, "so it makes sense they would need lots of chopsticks. I use the plastic kind myself, and so does my wife so we don't have to keep buying new ones all the time. Waste of good lumber, you ask me." Chauky had a propensity to drone on, so it seemed. "Of course, the plastic kinds are difficult to get used to using because the food slips out too easily, but after you know what you're doing, it's pretty simple. Wife and I don't use forks much anymore. Can't say it makes the food taste any better, but I find I don't eat as much as when I use a fork. I guess that makes sense, right, Officer?" He took a breath. "I think someone in your department made a mistake. This shipment looks legitimate." He finally ceased his chatter and busied himself looking up and down from the documents in his hands to the stacks in front of him as if waiting for a revelation to appear.

Unfazed by the uncontained stream of words and letting his instincts work instead, Mike motioned to Chauky. "Mind helping me unload a few rows of boxes? We need to look farther back into the container."

They worked for forty-five minutes unloading the top three rows, both quickly becoming drenched in sweat. The sun bearing down on the metal container turned the inside air into a baker's oven. As they pulled a carton off the fourth row, they were confronted by a wall of wood, obstructing further progress. As the remaining boxes were removed, they found the wall was floor to ceiling, side to side, and well secured in place.

"This is interesting." The amazement was evident in Chauky's voice. "I've never seen anything like this before. In all the years I've spent working multitudes of claims along the waterfront, I've seen a lot of very strange things. I remember once when a container came in, but it was so light it actually fell overboard into the harbor and floated. Imagine that—it *floated*. Someone on the other end had closed and locked it before loading any of the—"

Mike cut the insurance man short. He had a slim tolerance for social chatter, and he'd reached his limit. Robin, his girlfriend, was trying to help him overcome that shortcoming, but they both agreed a lot more work was needed. "You ought to be a little more sociable once in a while," she would quietly remind him when they were out with friends, and he would invariably begin to softly drum his fingers on any flat surface available. When working the radio at the Coast Guard station on Sand Island, Seaman Robin Jaffers was a stickler for military discipline but thoroughly enjoyed talking, needed to talk, about nothing consequential when she relaxed and deflated from long days of military presence. She needed Mike to supply conversation that didn't require brain cells to decipher. He appreciated her willingness to help him and felt it was paying off—most of the time anyway.

"I'll call for help to unload the rest of this container," he said to the insurance man. "I definitely want to see what's behind this wall. Our Young Brothers contact vouched for you as being trustworthy, Chaulky." He looked down at the shorter man, his face emotionless. "I require you to keep this quiet. Our investigation would be seriously compromised if anyone else was to find out that we're looking for something specific and innocently start to second-guess our motives in public."

"Eh, Officer Kalama," Chauky began in an atmosphere of camaraderie, reaching up to place a friendly hand on Mike's shoulder. "No worries about me. After all, we're both in a similar line of work as far as investigators go, right?"

Mike didn't bother to answer.

ALL THE BOXES WERE out and stacked helter-skelter around the open container.

A fork lift was brought over, and a rope was attached to the wooden wall that had been pressured into place. They put some back pressure on the rope and watched as the panel slowly released its hold on the container walls and fell out through the open doors. Behind it, tightly secured in place, were two boats neatly arranged to occupy minimal space. Both were securely strapped in place, holding them against any movement; but neither, he noted with some disappointment, appeared to be Guy's.

"And I thought I'd seen everything in this business," offered Chaulky. "Thirty years in marine insurance game and a lot of weird things witnessed, but this is a new one for me. I'm writing a book documenting all the odd..."

Mike, feeling the need to repeat his words, cut off Chauky's word stream once again and pulled him aside, hand on the shorter man's shoulder. "I may be repeating myself, but I've got to have your assurance that you'll keep quiet about this until we can find who's responsible."

Chaulky's assurance given, Mike faced the fact he'd simply have to trust the man. He'd learned through one of his foot patrol officers that Chaulky was in the habit of hanging out after work at O'Toole's Pub on Maunakea Street. That put any assurances he'd been given on questionable grounds; all Mike could do was hope.

Mike's men took as much information as they could discover on the two boats, checking the HA registration numbers on both for owners' names and addresses. They were able to match reports filed on the two missing boats. The owner and the person filing the report matched in both cases. Mike would take care of how and when notification would be made, but he needed to buy as much time as possible. The container wall was pushed back in place, and the arduous task of replacing the boxes began so the doors to the container could be closed and resealed. A vice president from the barging company came and officially resecured the doors and promised to watch for all containers coming in from Wood Industries of Waimanalo.

Mike planned to touch base with the Seattle and Portland PDs and request them to have the container followed when it docked. His job now was to find out who loaded it, and where they did it. His counterparts on the mainland would supply whatever information they could learn from their end on who took delivery of it. The boats in the container would eventually get shipped back to the islands. Their owners and respective insurance companies would take over from there— they just had to be patient.

Twenty-Four

BILL FOUND HIMSELF WANDERING along the main street in Kaneohe with nothing to do. Alysdon had an appointment at Kaiser Hospital to have his finger x-rayed; he was sure it was broken but had insisted on driving to the hospital himself. He was like that when pain was involved; he never wanted anyone's help. Bill had known that for a long time, so he asked if Alysdon would drop him off in town on his way to the hospital.

He walked past Harvey's Tavern and would have loved nothing more than to go in and have a few cold ones, but he had very little cash and didn't have a credit card, so that wasn't an option. He and Alysdon would come back when they got some money from their mainland boat connection. They always enjoyed spending time in Harvey's when they had a little extra cash. It was their kind of crowd. Harvey's Tavern was well known in Kaneohe, and throughout most of the island really, and drew a large number of the local drinking crowd. Many of those local regulars had been on hand to witness the beginning of the singing career of a now-well-known Hawaiian piano player and vocalist. It was quite a tribute to their local tavern.

The men had been expecting payments to begin arriving from their mainland partners, but nothing had shown up yet. They'd tied up all their available cash to containerize and ship several boats. Fortunately, they'd gotten a steal on their most recent shipment when they chanced on a damaged container full of chopsticks. They were perfect camouflage. They were beginning to think they were either being stiffed out of the money or something had gone wrong on the other end. Even the chopsticks were supposed to be selling in the local oriental districts when the container was unloaded for access to the two boats, but nothing was being returned. Whatever the hold-up was, they were coming up short.

Bill wandered into a fiberglass shop next door to the tavern and stood watching a tall, lanky young man work fiberglass resin onto what appeared to be a future surfboard.

"Can I do something for you?" asked the young man, obviously being pulled away from his work, irritation quite evident in his features.

"I'm a little short on cash at the moment. You have any you could loan me?" He had never come right out and asked like this before, but the draw to Harvey's had been a strong incentive; he figured it *couldn't* hurt.

The young man, Kawika, simply shook his head and went back to his resin, hoping the man would take the hint and leave. Too many barflies from next door ventured in looking for handouts after they'd used up all their money, but not their desire to have a few more.

If truth be known, Kawika would like nothing better than to be able to give them all something. It was his softhearted nature to help wherever he could. He believed in paying it forward as the mantra offers, but he wasn't about to do so and have to watch them walk out of his door and directly into the bar next door with his cash in hand.

Bill's thirst was compelling. "Listen, I don't mean to take your money and not give anything back. I got two Johnson 55hp outboards that're almost brand-new. I could let you have them for two grand, thousand bucks each. Some people at Kaneohe Yacht Club are hoping to buy them," Bill wasn't sure where he came up with that, but he liked it, so he continued, "You could save me a trip over there. I could deliver them later today or tomorrow if you'd like. You could pay me part up front and the rest when I bring them back."

He waited in silence for an answer, but none came. The young man simply expressed a withered *Get lost* look, along with a hand motion shooing him out the door.

Bill turned and walked out. He'd have to forget about Harvey's for today. Maybe he and Alysdon would come back later. He knew his friend would need something to soothe the pain in his finger, and what better than a cold beer?

He realized while he'd been making that offer to sell the motors that if Alysdon ever caught wind of what he'd done, they'd fight each other for the rest of the day and most of the night. He was becoming less proud of his actions. *Besides*, he told himself, unexpectedly feeling very contrite, *that's not the way you go about selling hot property.*

Twenty-Five

Hilo, Big Island of Hawaii

STONE SAT RESTING ON a swing that hung down from the roof of Pops's front lanai sipping coffee. He was gazing out over Hilo Bay and the distant breakwater as waves spilled over the rocks sparkling in the morning sunlight. The coffee was strong—close to being too strong. He was fairly certain that part of a branch off the coffee tree got mixed in with the beans; but then it *was* just Pops's way of making coffee.

Teri walked out through the front door cradling a cup of tea and sat down beside him. The swing responded to the additional weight and began gently swaying back and forth as if it were honoring its predestined purpose in relaxing two lovers. They sat close to each other in the quietness, arms and shoulders pressed tightly.

"How's Pops's coffee this morning, sweetness?" She'd recently started to call him sweetness. He wasn't sure how he felt about that—terms of endearment were new to him. He made use of them frequently but had rarely received any. He figured he'd let it ride for a while and see how it fit. The more he heard it, though, the more he was inclined to like it. This woman had a unique spirit-energy that he could feel flowing through her words.

That she had opted for tea instead of her usual coffee fix reminded him that he had been too deep in thought when he'd walked into the kitchen earlier and poured himself the cup of coffee he now sat holding. He actually knew better. He glanced at the cup in his hand and wondered if he would be able to drink any more of it.

In addition to his well-known *patis*, Pops was famous—perhaps infamous would be more apt—for making coffee so thick that a spoon could stand straight at attention and never lean one way or the other. Pops usually went out of his way to buy special Olaa coffee beans from a small grower in Pahala because of its strong yet uniquely pleasant, earthy flavor. It normally made an excellent brewed coffee that Stone always enjoyed; but in Pops's hands, and with an overused measuring spoon, the result was unique in a much different sense. Pops's motto was "The stronger the better." He generally claimed his good health was partly due to the "Olympic proportions" he used. You could almost see him chewing the coffee as he drank it.

Stone had been sitting in the swing for the past fifteen minutes reflecting on how quickly his day-to-day life had changed; how quickly Teri had become such an integral part of his well-being and how completely he had begun to think of Pops and Pops's family as being his own.

Seeing Teri's devilish smile, he sensed she knew he was thinking about the coffee among other things. She'd heard his comments on other occasions when he absentmindedly poured himself a cup. She knew him well enough to know he'd drink it all whether he liked it or not and would later thank Pops for his great coffee-making ability.

He rested his hand on her thigh, a gesture they could both count on for reconnecting their deeper feelings—plus a few other feelings when the timing was right. The gesture had become one they acknowledged as a bond between them—a centering gesture that left words unnecessary.

She covered his hand with hers and hiked them both a bit farther north, another gesture they both also recognized as carrying a totally different connotation—aiming for those other feelings. In a matter-of-fact voice, observing their hands resting warmly on her leg, she sighed. "I think I want to get Pops's recipe for that coffee. It appears to create nice thoughts."

They had arrived back from Mauna Kea State Park and their side trip to the Visitor Center high on the slopes of the volcano. On their way back, they had taken a circuitous route through Hilo along Banyan Drive, the beautiful and famous Hilo Walk of Fame. Most of the very old and large banyan trees that flourished along Banyan Drive had been planted by famous people in the 1930s and 1940s. They continued to flourish despite tsunamis that had destroyed much of the town over past decades. They formed a natural canopy of intertwined branches above the roadway that residents and tourists alike marveled at.

It was depressing to arrive back at Pops's, only to learn there had been no further word on Viane's disappearance. John told them about the drive to his property, his stop at Hawaii Volcanoes National Park and his quick trip to the trailhead for Mauna Loa's summit and not finding any sign of her presence.

"Teri and I are going back to Oahu this afternoon, John. We both need to catch up on work and be prepared to fly back here on a moment's notice as soon as something new shows up. We're doing no good just sitting here rehashing things and eating Pops's great food, hoping for the phone to ring." He thought of mentioning his concern for Bert but decided against it. He'd left Bert in the house with lots of food and water. There was a small pet door so she could come and go as she pleased, but he was anxious nonetheless.

His neighbor's young daughter loved Bert, so Stone had no doubt the young girl was spending every unused moment sitting on the lawn eating bananas while keeping Bert company.

Stone and Teri politely declined Pops's gracious offer of a late lunch or another cup of coffee and left to return the rental car and catch the next available flight back to Honolulu.

They were quiet on the fifty-minute flight, taking the time to do a checklist of their thoughts and insights. They were sitting close, having lifted the center armrest dividing them. Teri held Stone's hand tightly in her lap. They were feeling emotionally exhausted.

He dropped her off at her home and then headed up over the Pali Highway to Kaneohe, feeling a sense of disappoint at the complete lack of even basic clues to Viane's whereabouts. As they parted, they reluctantly acknowledged their need to take the rest of the evening and night to put things into prospective.

Stone promised he'd call her in the morning and check in. He also planned to call Mike and bring his friend up to speed on developments, or lack of developments, in finding Viane. He knew his friend would want to be filled in and figured Mike would do the same with regard to Guy's boat.

Bert was sitting on top of the rock wall overlooking the street, keeping watch as Stone pulled into the carport.

Twenty-Six

FINDING POPS'S PICKUP, SEEMINGLY abandoned, carried mixed blessings for everyone. They could no longer hold on to any hope of seeing Viane bounding up the driveway with wild stories to tell. With utter certainty, they knew she was in trouble.

Officer Vic Morro was feeling the strain as well, but with an added layer of responsibility to act but wasn't sure what he needed to be doing about it. He had grown up with Sonny. They were close friends throughout their school years and had spent many hours together at the Koa household singing and playing ukulele as Pops sat and listened, or often picked up his own ukulele to join in. He had always considered Viane his kid sister and knew she felt the closeness as well.

He was experiencing an inordinate level of obligation to do something both from friendship and from being a part of the law. He knew he was being called to act, and his instincts were pushing him toward the twins, Raymond and Vince.

As he'd sensed when he first saw the boys in the parking lot, he was even more convinced now that they had hot-wired Pops's truck and whether they realized it or not, which he suspected they didn't, they held the key to where she was and to eventually finding her.

Vic understood boys like them and knew they would opt for holding information inside rather than telling anyone. It was safer for them that way; it was how they viewed life. They lived the simple truth that once something was spoken, it was out there for anyone to use and react to. Too often, kids like Raymond and Vince learned early in life that those reactions could threaten a safe existence—their invisibility in society would be lost.

When Vic wasn't on duty, he managed a program for teen boys who found too much empty time on their hands. He had named his program the Warrior's Path, the name, hopefully, implying the learned personal strengths a warrior, on any path in life, had to ascend to. He wanted to help kids, like the twins, enrich their lives and teach male teens the value of living an honest, integrity-based, and fulfilling life— attributes most of those who came to his program weren't able to learn at home.

It was a new program he'd started during his off-duty hours, with his own money; but his program was now fully supported by his chief and several fellow officers. There were currently eight boys he met with at Shipman Park once a week for four hours every Sunday afternoon. During the three months he'd been running his program, he figured he'd learned just as much from the eight participants as he'd been able to impart to them. It was working both ways, and he was very pleased.

Raymond and Vince were not yet a part of it. He knew their of parents simply because of several late-night domestic violence calls he'd had to make and felt strongly about the many benefits the boys could gain if they were to join in. He also knew the parents would view it as an affront to their abilities in raising their own sons, so he would have to tread lightly.

He had already decided to drive through Volcano Village and talk to the boys and find out what they knew. On the fifteen-minute drive, he'd have time to decide whether to knock on the parents' door or simply hope he would have the fortune to spot the boys walking around. He prayed for the latter since he wasn't in the mood to confront the parents—he was *never* in that particular mood.

Thankfully, he didn't have a chance to choose between the two alternatives. Before he reached the turnoff for Volcano Village, he saw the twins standing by the highway thumbing a ride toward Keaau. He made a quick U-turn and stopped beside them and rolled his window down.

"Hop in the back seat, boys. I'll give you a lift."

A long moment of hesitation ensued, and Vic thought for sure they were about to take off running in the opposite direction. He was uncertain of what he'd do if they did, but the rear door finally opened, and Raymond climbed in followed closely by Vince. Their faces gave the appearance of being caught in a trap and unable to think of anything to do about it, but were thinking hard, nonetheless.

"You boys heading for Keaau or Hilo?"

"Ahh...we was think'n a going Keaau." Raymond's voice carried a nervous tremor; he did not offer anything further.

"Den, we was think'n a hitching down to Kalapana, maybe collect some *opihi* shells, maybe sit on the black sand beach. You going that far?" Vince felt an elbow jammed into his ribs. It was his brother's way of reminding him that volunteering information was never in their best interest, and especially not to a cop.

"I could do that, Vince, but I have to stop in Keaau first. Can I buy you and Raymond a soda while we're there?"

As the patrol car began moving, the automatic door locks slid into place. To the boys, it sounded like what they imagined iron bars sounded like slamming closed on a prison door; they knew they were trapped.

It was no comfort to either of them to discover that this cop knew their names so well—that was not a good sign.

It was a development that cast them out onto the ledge of a very deep crater of uncertainty—the kindness being shown served to put them farther out on the ledge. Nobody does nice things for you unless they expected something big in return. They looked at one another and instinctively knew silence was their key to safety, totally bewildered how their day of adventure had been so easily hijacked.

Officer Morro pulled into the parking lot of the Keaau police substation and parked.

"Wait in the car, boys. I'll bring us some sodas in a few minutes.

The minutes were hours to them, but the cop finally came back carrying three cans of guava-passion drink. As he passed the cold cans back to them, the twins heard the locks on the doors click into place, once again renewing their feeling of helplessness. They knew the real, up-to-this-minute hidden reason for all the friendly gestures was about to be set in motion. Unconsciously, they pushed their bodies back into the seat cushion, the scrunch of the soft leather of the seat giving testimony. The officer smiled to himself. He knew body language.

Instead of starting the car, he turned in his seat and faced them. "Don't be alarmed, Raymond, Vince. As soon as we drink our sodas and have a little chat, I'll drive you to Kalapana. I want to take a few moments to repeat a story I think I told you in Shipman Park parking lot when we found that pickup belonging to Pops Koa." He was certain the full impact of the story had been lost on them when he'd told them the first time. He wasn't positive that they'd even heard him.

He commenced to retell the story of a *wahine* going for a hike and becoming lost somewhere on the island with no one knowing where to begin looking. He told them the only possible clue to where she might be was where the pickup might originally have been parked before it was taken. He told the story with as much detail as he could, trying his best to elicit some sympathy from the boys.

In an effort to avoid their thinking about lying, he said, "Let's pretend the three of us want to hot-wire a car and go for a ride. I wonder what the best way would be to do something like that. Any ideas?"

He remained directly facing the boys, sipping his soda, slowly and silently looking from one set of eyes to the other. He could outwait and outstare the best of them.

It took more minutes than he figured it would, but Raymond finally spoke up. "That would not be a good thing to do."

More minutes of silence went by. Vince finally had to speak. Vic knew the twin couldn't withstand the strain of silence.

"No, it wouldn't," was all he said.

Vic drained his soda and took extra time to put the empty in a trash bag he kept on the passenger floor, then, still in the silence, resumed his eye contact with the two.

It again took longer than Vic anticipated. Vince was getting more and more fidgety. Both the twins sat looking solemnly down at the still-full soda can in their hands. Raymond was equally fidgety, but for a different reason: he knew his brother all too well and knew Vince was about to make Raymond's concern a reality—and he did.

"We only took it 'cause we didn't want to hitch. We never broke noth'n. That window was open, and we treated it real good, hardly used any gas." Even before he finished speaking, Vince felt his brother's elbow slam hard into his ribs. He winced in response and instantly knew he just dug a hole and fell in.

Officer Morro smiled at them. Not an *I knew it* smile but the smile of a friend. The twins' nervous flair smoothed out a fraction.

"You boys know about the Warrior's Path program at Shipman Park each Sunday afternoon?" The subject change had its desired effect, as he hoped it would—it opened an amenable avenue of interest. They immediately jumped onto the new subject matter as they would if they'd seen a twenty-dollar bill lying on the floor of the car. A partial smile accompanied their shaking heads as they finally relaxed enough to take a sip of their sodas.

He spent a few minutes telling them about his program, mentioning the first names of two of the boys who lived close to Volcano Village that he thought they might know. He volunteered to pick them up on Sunday when he came to get the other two boys. Their smiles had widened.

"So tell me, where was Pops's pickup when you so ingeniously hot-wired it?" The smiles evaporated instantly. Vic knew his push may have been too hard and too quick, but he had to try.

Seeing no way that a lie would be of any help to them at this point, Raymond told about finding it in the Bird Park parking lot.

The officer's friendly smile returned, and the twins let out an almost-inaudible sigh. "You both did real well in telling me. I guess that's all we need to say about the pickup. Let's keep this between us and not mention anything." Vic had always believed there was a boundary when kids like Raymond and Vince walked on a tightrope of society. They could be pushed the wrong way, and society would eat them up and spit them to the ground. However, they could be pulled off the rope in the right direction, and they could become good members of society and responsible adults. He knew these two had been dealt a rough hand in the parents they had been born to.

"Now," he said, turning to face the front, the muscles in his back thanking him after the cramped posture he'd been forced to hold, "let's get you two down to the black sand beach. I hear some *opihi* shells calling you boys." He pulled out onto the highway, anxious to drop them off so he could start wheels spinning in the search for Viane.

Before Raymond and Vince got out at Kalapana, Vic gave them a note with the date and time he'd pick them up the following Sunday. He signed it and told them to give it to their parents. The last thing he wanted was to have their parents accuse him or them of doing something behind their backs.

Port Townsend, WA

TEAK CUSSED TO HIMSELF, and not too quietly either; but he didn't really care. He was a boatswain working on a very large and expensive yacht. Contorted into an awkward position, he was in the final stage of fitting the piece of wood he'd been working on for the past three hours into a difficult place to reach on the starboard gunwale. The piece of wood slipped from his hand and fell into an impossible place to reach down in the bilge. On his hands and knees, he bowed his head and took a deep breath as he attempted to peer down the small opening that his wood disappeared down. Cussing didn't help the matter, but he thought it made him feel a little better just the same.

He needed a break before slithering into the damp, oily bilge to retrieve the wood. He climbed his ladder to the ground and walked to the edge of the marina looking out over all the various boats tied up there.

Teak was the head boatswain at the *Boat Haven*, Port Townsend's large marine facility sitting on the edge of Puget Sound. It was a marina as well as a major ship repair facility that he'd been associated with for more years than he cared to think about.

He bought himself a coffee from the Blue Goose Café and went and sat next to the boat ramp in the sunlight to enjoy a few moments. He watched as two men busily pulled a runabout out of the water onto a trailer. By their actions, Teak could tell they had no clue what they were doing. They were obviously a couple of city folks, probably Seattle, and improperly dressed for doing what they were attempting to do. *First time boaters?* he wondered.

Instead of watching the spectacle of the dance the men were doing as they tried to figure out what rope to pull and what part of the boat to push, his experienced eye took in the boat itself and immediately noticed it had been neutered. Someone had done a poor job of removing all its identity: the manufacturer's plaque had been removed, and the boat's name as well as its registration numbers had been painted over—but not too well. As the paint had dried, the words and the numbers had shadowed through.

He did notice that the men continually looked over at him as if appraising him and wondering what they needed to do about it. Teak wasn't worried. If they started over toward him, he had a few surprises up his sleeve, including a marlin spike he always carried hung from his belt.

He'd heard about the boat thefts that were occurring down in Seattle and Portland—people he associated with on the waterfront did a lot of talking. He wondered if these two were somehow connected but finally decided they were probably just novices. He figured one of them bought a boat and called a friend to come help him.

Not wanting to crawl into the bilge on the yacht he was working on but knowing he would have to, he downed the last drops of coffee and turned to go. At the last moment, he turned back and wrote down what he could see of the registration number, noting it was an HA number. He decided he would report what he saw. Boats were his life, and if people were going around stealing them, he wanted to be a part of putting a stop to it. The attempt to obliterate the registration numbers was making him suspicious.

Back at the yacht, he looked up the number for the police department in Honolulu and called. He was told that he needed to speak with a Sergeant Mike Kalama who was heading up that particular investigation, but he was instead connected to voice mail. He left all the information for the officer, along with his phone number, and then prepared himself for the bilge.

Before he got there, he got a call back, so he relayed the same information as he'd left on the officer's voice mail. He was told *mahalo*, thank you, and that the officer would take it from there.

In his office, Mike immediately noticed that the registration number, as much of it as Teak could identify, matched closely with a boat that had been stolen from Lanikai Beach a few weeks before. The description of the boat Teak gave him fit perfectly. He relayed the information to his counterparts in Seattle and gave them Teak's phone number. Seattle PD told him they'd work with the Port Townsend police and would keep him updated.

Twenty-Eight

Ongoing boat search, Oahu

THE BUILDING THE DOWNTOWN police precinct occupied on Maunakea Street wasn't old in comparison to many of the others that surrounded it, several of which had been in place for a hundred years or more. There were even a couple that dated back to the days of the Hawaiian monarchy, although these were mostly as fixtures from times gone by. The old police station had aged just enough to have acquired a palpable atmosphere of history both inside and out.

The smell of leather and polish permeating the air gave evidence to the growing complication of equipment the officers were required to strap around themselves in the name of occupational safety and health and staying alive. There were few contingencies that could confront an officer on the streets that couldn't be handled or eliminated by a piece of apparatus suspended from their belt, hung over their shoulder, or strapped to one of their legs. The officers squeaked as they walked the wooden hallway past the chief's office, leather rubbing against leather, the gear giving off the necessary leather and gun oil aroma befitting the aged building.

Together with that scent came the malodorous smell of cigarettes and cigars that had invaded the wooden walls and floors over past decades and hung heavily in the air. Most of the officers that thought of themselves as old-timers drew comfort in the familiar flavor and feel of the place and lamented the fact that they were required to go elsewhere to light up an old stogie or two. The newer officers, however, were heavily in favor of moving to a new building, or at least having professional cleaners come in to sterilize the old place, but money for either option wasn't available. Mike felt right at home. He figured that if the officers under him didn't like it, well...they should be out on patrol anyway, not hanging around complaining about the scent of nostalgia.

RETURNING TO THE STATION from the container inspection at Young Brothers, Mike had no sooner settled comfortably at his desk than a call came in from Guy Montana. It surprised him since he'd been about to place a call to Stone as well as to Guy to relay recent developments and to tell them about the contents of the container and the unfortunate absence of any sign of Guy's boat.

After the customary alohas, Guy told him about seeing what he was absolutely certain was his boat, or what was left of it anyway, sitting in the backyard of a house below the Haiku staircase and its subsequent disappearance.

"It was my boat, Mike. Deborah and I even found the flotation cushion in the yard that she'd given me that had been on my boat when it was taken. It was lying on the ground right where we'd seen the boat." He mentioned his suspicion about the trailer that nearly ran them off the road, coupled with the fact that both boats that were there had disappeared by the time they got there to look. He decided not to mention finding his car. He'd wait on that for a more opportune time.

"How do you know that was your boat you saw? From your perch on top of that staircase, it's a long way down for anyone to identify a particular boat clearly, especially looking down from that angle. I speak with experience of those broken old stairs." Guy's suspicions were difficult for Mike to accept since he was still convinced, even more so after his recent experience, that all the missing boats were being shipped off the island heading for the mainland; but he was also willing to listen to a good argument. The boat cushion was compelling evidence.

Guy told Mike the whole story: his and Deborah's journey up the stairs. Deborah spotting their boat through her binoculars and their search for the yard. "Unfortunately, it took us over two hours to climb down and begin hunting for the yard," he admitted, defeat evident in his voice.

"I know it was my boat, Mike, no question. I could see the icebox I had built into the rear bench seat—it stood out clear as day. I guarantee no other boat has anything like that."

"The cushion is pretty strong evidence, Guy, as is your visual identification, but it's not conclusive in the eyes of the law. It doesn't give us sufficient cause to go in and search the yard or the house. Besides, and this is a big one, you were trespassing on property you weren't invited to, and that's something the owners could nail you for if we were forced to bring that to their attention, and it would invalidate any evidence we found *if* we were to search the place."

Mike could see the possibility as well as the probability that not all of the stolen boats were being shipped out. He knew that if Guy was right about seeing his boat, and he was sure he was, then it was certainly proof that there were more avenues to the boat thefts than he first thought. From his past experience, he knew this was always a possibility that had to be taken into account, and he reminded himself that most criminals were anything but stupid when it came to covering their crimes or following too close to a pattern. The experienced smarter ones—up to a point anyway.

"Do you remember seeing your flotation cushion when you were out on Kapapa Island?"

"No, Mike, I don't recall seeing it. You know how you get used to seeing something in its place, and even if it's gone, your mind's eye still sees it. That's how the cushion was. Oh, and by the way, I didn't mention that Deborah took some great pictures looking straight down on the yard, did I?"

Mike was quiet for a moment replaying what he knew. He was his own witness at least that some of the boats were being shipped off the island. Now he had additional proof, if he put weight on Guy's observations, that some were being kept on the Island and probably stripped. But then what? The remaining carcass would have to be gotten rid of somewhere, somehow, and all the equipment and motors would have to be disposed of. The islands became quite small, if one was attempting to make things disappear. He needed to find that trailer Guy mentioned and determine where it had been going.

"Guy, could you e-mail the pictures to me or put them on a flash drive and bring them down to the station? With a picture in hand, we can pinpoint the property and then decide the path we need to take."

"Yeah, I'll forward a copy soon as I get back to my desk. Give me two minutes."

MIKE HAD CALLED STONE to fill him in. From the pictures Guy e-mailed to him, HPD was able to pinpoint the Haiku property and call up property records to ascertain the owners' names.

"So that's what we have so far, Stone." Mike didn't mention the mainland call; he wasn't in the habit of giving out too much information, even to close friends. "These two guys that own the property have become prime suspects. I had HPD do a fly-over with the chopper, but all they saw was an empty trailer, a small boat, an old car, and a forklift. It's a big yard. I sure wouldn't mind having a place like that. Big enough to set up a horseshoe pit and have space left over for a weekend *imu* just like old times. Now your turn. Have you had any luck finding leads to Viane?"

"We've heard nothing and found nothing, Mike, other than Pops's truck showing up in a parking lot outside Keaau without Viane in it." He told Mike of the hot-wired evidence and the search of Mauna Kea State Park as well as John's trip to the Volcano National Park but nothing turning up.

"Teri and I decided to come home this morning. There's nothing more we can do until some new information shows up. Besides, we both need to catch up on work and get prepared to return as soon as something new develops. I think Pops has the whole of Hilo's police department out in force scraping the ground for clues."

"Yeah, I heard. Things like this spread rapidly through the department, even though they concern the neighbor islands."

Stone continued to tell Mike about the two boys and their suspected involvement and his hope that when the boys surfaced again, they may be able to shed some light on things. At that point in time, Stone didn't know that an officer on the Big Island was in the process of turning that particular light on.

"Hey, Stone, not to change the subject, but to change it anyway, and since you're going to be in town, why don't you and Teri join me and Robin at Davy Jones Locker? You know that bar in the parking garage of the Reef Hotel? She and I are going to meet there after work tonight. Be a great time for you guys to finally meet Robin."

"I'll pass it by Teri, Mike. It sounds like a good plan. I haven't been in that place for a very long time. In fact,

I'd almost forgotten about it. I bet the entertainment hasn't changed." He had to laugh thinking about it.

"Yeah, the entertainment's probably still what you remember it was. I'll call the others as well. It's about time everyone had an opportunity to meet Robin."

Twenty-Nine

TAKING A BREAK FROM the arduous work of cleaning the engine compartment of a car he wanted to sell, Lloyd walked across the lush grass of his backyard to the beach that boarded a portion of his yard. He shook the sand off one of two lawn chairs and, with a sigh, sat down and leaned back. It was his favorite place to relax. From this vantage point, less than ten feet from the sand of Lanikai Beach, he had an unobstructed view of the Mokulua Islands less than a mile straight offshore. He could also see a fair stretch of beach in either direction furthering his relaxation.

The water off Lanikai Beach on Windward Oahu was crystal clear. The subtle color of the emerald green-blue water contrasted wonderfully with the white sand and coral that lay beneath. Lanikai was a beach community that had been off the tourists' radar until the recent years but had inevitably been discovered. For kayaking and outrigger canoe paddling and small-boat sailing, it was ideal. It was also a great fishing area, something Lloyd fully embraced and often took advantage of.

It had been an unanticipated twist of fortune when Lloyd and Pam found the place. Its previous owner, apparently tiring of island life and unable to accept its nature, had moved to Tulsa, Oklahoma, to be close to family. He had literally *given* the property away just to be rid of it—the price was that low. Whether he didn't know its value or just didn't care wasn't clear, and it didn't matter to Lloyd or Pam. It needed a lot of repair work and general TLC when they bought it, common hazards of homes that existed next to the ocean. That was fine with them as they both discovered pleasure in fixing, remodeling, and painting projects. There wasn't a value that could be placed on the panorama Lloyd enjoyed from his beach chair. Bikinis along the beach were numerous so he had little trouble indulging his favorite pastime of sipping iced tea and watching *people* pass by. The *people* part was the story he told Pam—the bikini part was left out for good reason.

"Eh, anything good out here today?"

Kawika, Lloyd's son, collapsed into a beach chair beside his father. He was tall and lanky, and his legs stretched out far in front as he leaned his chair back beside his father. He operated his own company that specialized in underwater diving projects, primarily contracting with boat owners to clean and maintain the submerged portion of their boat. Sea life and general grunge were hazards to salt water boating. Creatures could find their way onto boat hulls like young children find their way to mud puddles and sandboxes. Almost half the boats tied up in the Ala Wai Boat Harbor were under contract with Kawika. His best friend worked for him and did much of the labor-intensive cleaning, leaving Kawika to do the client relation and financial side of things. Word about how good his company was had quickly spread from the first day he opened the door and symbolically hung his shingle out. Since Hawaii has a large number of boats per capita, his company was growing rapidly. When not under a boat with air tanks, weight belt, and scrubbing gear, or shuffling invoices, he worked part-time, strictly for pleasure, in a fiberglass shop in Kaneohe that built kayaks, outrigger canoes, and surfboards.

"Someone came into the shop this morning looking to sell a pair of 55hp Johnson outboards for real cheap." He exaggerated his words in a tone of amazement. "Dad, you need to buy these. This guy was willing to take just a thousand for each, and I think he'd go for even less."

"Why would he do that?" exclaimed his father. "Those outboards are worth over ten grand each if you had to buy them new. And what boat am I going to put them on even if I did buy them?" He gave his son an amused but withered look. "You see a boat sitting around here that I don't know about?"

"Go buy one." It was an old discussion the two of them aired at least once a week. "Trade that junk car you been working on for an eighteen-foot Sea Ray. Then you and me can go fishing. You could keep it anchored right out here in front of the yard." Kawika knew his father's love of fishing was second only to bikini watching. Actually, his own pastime interests were pretty closely aligned to that was well.

The thought of a boat floating at anchor in front of his yard with twin 55hp Johnsons nested on the transom was a dream Lloyd could replay frequently while sitting beside the beach. Right then, though, it made him think about Guy's missing boat. He had looked on in envy at Guy's boat when Guy and Deborah were following Stone out to Kapapa Island and the twin 55hp Johnsons that looked so powerful. They had been brand-new and equally beautiful and menacing at the same time. Hearing of someone wanting to unload two engines like these, for the price being asked, he immediately guessed they were probably Guy's—it wasn't too big of a stretch to tie the two events together. He knew what Mike had told them about the mainland connection, but he still couldn't help but wonder at the synchronicity being presented. If some of the missing boats were being dismantled and sold right here, there'd be a lot of money to be made if they managed to get away with it. Avoiding the law, though, was not a winning proposition. Hawaii was a pretty small community in many ways and rumors often spread with intense speed, especially since half the people in the island were related to the other half in some fashion. Whoever approached Kawika apparently wasn't the sharpest knife in the drawer.

"Did this guy leave a card or phone number or anything?"

"Naw." Kawika had already lost interest in the subject as a colorful blue and minimally sized string bikini adorning an attractive older woman walked past their chairs. "Wouldn't leave his name either," continued Kawika, his head turned away from his father as he watched the receding view. "He did mention Kaneohe Yacht Club, but I had a batch of hot resin in front of me that was quickly getting hotter, so I couldn't pay much more attention to him. He was only looking for money. Harvey's Tavern seemed to be pulling at his feet."

After Kawika left, Lloyd called Mike at the police station but was told the sergeant was out of range of communications. It was difficult to understand how a policeman could be out of range of communications on an island, but he let it go. He had hoped to pass the information on and let Mike deal with it. He left a message to that effect and then decided it was time to go check out boats at Kaneohe Yacht Club and talk to the port captain and see if he knew anything about the motors.

LLOYD PULLED OFF KANEOHE Bay Drive and drove through the gate into the parking lot in front of the club's office. He knew the port captain, Kelvin Spencer, but hadn't seen him for almost a year. He wanted to see what Kelvin may know about someone trying to sell stolen outboards. It also gave him a good excuse to wander the piers and check out all the boats moored to see what might be for sale that could interest him. Kawika was right—he really wanted a boat. It was that additional avenue of freedom the ocean offered that was so appealing. He had an open invitation to use Stone's yacht anytime he wanted, but that wasn't the same as owning his own. Besides, taking Stone's big monster out would be anything but relaxing—more like a constant uneasiness.

As he walked into the office, he was immediately greeted by Wilma, the office manager. He'd met her a year earlier when he'd come looking for Kelvin on a different matter. He noticed she was still overflowing with enthusiasm, which she exhibited the last time he was here. Fortunately, he was able to halt her charge before she could get to the coffee machine and pour him a mugful. He enjoyed coffee, but just not right then. He was about to ask her where he could find Kelvin when the door on the opposite side of the office opened and Kelvin walked in.

Lloyd had forgotten how tall Kelvin was as he watched the man duck slightly to avoid the doorframe as he came into the room. He had an athletic build—wide, strong shoulders the result of his earlier career in construction. A generous hint of having a Hawaiian background that gave him his thick black hair, his broad muscular stature, and a generous white smile.

Kelvin remembered Lloyd immediately. The last time they had talked, there had been a discussion about a vague family connection between them through a second or third cousin. Lloyd still wasn't too convinced but marveled at the fact Kelvin could remember that.

It was apparent from his abrupt but apologetic actions that Kelvin was in a hurry, so Lloyd went immediately to his reason for being there. He told Kelvin what his son had said and the seller's reference to the yacht club.

"Twin 55's for two grand," he exclaimed. "Wow, where are they? I'll buy them myself right now." Lloyd was sure he didn't really mean it. Yacht clubs would be in a world of trouble if they started buying stolen boat supplies. "I haven't heard of anything like this being mentioned. I usually hang around the bar when I have a little extra time just to hear what the barflies are talking about. It's a good way to keep up on all the gossip." He gave Lloyd a wink and nudged him with his elbow. "Their hearts are gold, but they can be a very candid bunch when they're hoisting their sails over a beer. Since being in this job, I learned quickly that the good and the not-so-good things get discussed at length during happy hour. If there was a deal like this going around, it'd be thoroughly talked about, discussed, and hung out to dry."

"What about boat thefts, Kelvin? I've heard of one that was stolen from here recently. Any others?"

"We've actually had two that I know of. Both power boats, no sailing ones, both eighteen footers." This confirmed what Lloyd had heard Mike mention.

"I don't want to take a lot of your time, Kelvin. I can see you're in a hurry. If you hear anything about the two Johnsons, would you let me know? A friend's boat was taken from Kapapa Island that was powered by two such engines— new ones."

Both men had walked out onto the grass area overlooking the boat harbor.

"I heard that being talked about last week," Kelvin admitted. "It was a day before we discovered our two boats were missing. The barflies—" He didn't need to finish.

With an apology upon hearing a commotion on D pier and looking to see what was happening, Kelvin hastily excused himself and rushed out to resecure the lines on someone's yacht that had apparently worked loose from its mooring and was in the process of damaging a neighboring yacht. Lloyd hoped it wasn't Stone's *Wailana Sunrise* that was being bumped into.

He took a few moments to walk out to C pier and admire the yachts tied up there. All of them, he decided, were much bigger than the one he envisioned ever owning.

He was about to retreat to his car when someone behind him spoke up.

"Aloha kakahiaka. Beautiful morning, isn't she?"

Lloyd found himself two feet away from a roundish, balding man with glasses resting on the tip of his nose, wearing a tattered tank top. There were tufts of gray hair protruding from the arm and neck openings. He had a beer clutched in his hand as he stood on the bow of a beautiful sailboat leaning out over the pier, his elbows resting on the bow rail.

"Howzit," responded Lloyd, backing up a few paces to open distance between them. "That's a beautiful boat you're standing on," he offered.

"Mahalo nui loa. I try to keep her looking cherry. Name's Chuck, by the way," the man said, reaching out his hand. Without offering his name in return, Lloyd shook the hand that was extended, feeling the cold wet palm of the hand that had been holding the beer can. He decided it was a handshake that someone might give a two-year-old. Lloyd figured the halfhearted handshake couldn't have cost the man more than a calorie of effort.

Lloyd also noticed that the lenses on Chuck's glasses were unusually thick—and improperly fitted. He kept pushing the round wire rim's up on his nose, an unconscious action that he seemed to be prone to every few seconds as they continually gravitated back toward the tip of his nose with every motion of his head. He kept changing the hand that held the beer can in order to do so. It was enough to make Lloyd nervous.

"This is a yacht, by the way, not a boat. Saw you looking pretty carefully at all the yachts along the pier. You looking to buy?"

Lloyd had to smile thinking of Stone's frequent boat-yacht retort. "No, not really," he lied. "Just looking." Having been sober for going on twenty-four years, Lloyd chose not to spend any more time with someone putting away beer at eleven in the morning. "Interesting to have met you, Chuck." He held up his hand in a gesture of good-bye and continued down the pier toward his car.

He crossed the grassy area and walked out to D pier. Kelvin had apparently solved the crisis and was no longer there. He asked a few individuals in passing if they knew anything about two Johnson outboards being offered for sale, but no one did. He passed Stone's yacht as he walked to the far end of the pier and decided to check the lines while he was there. Satisfied that everything was in order, he walked back to his car, feeling it had been a waste of his time and effort to come to the club. He headed back home to his beach chair.

Thirty

Having hung up the phone following a brief conversation with Mike, Stone leaned back in one of the dining room chairs and let his thoughts drift and mingle with the view through the large windows his dining room table rested beside. He got pleasant vibes sitting next to this table with its magnificent view of the bay. He'd built it entirely from wood that had drifted onto his beach after an old wooden sailing vessel, the *Thess Parker*, which had burned to the waterline on Coconut Island years before following a party that obviously had gotten carried away. The energy of the wood seemed to impart an amazing energy of calm, sunny days.

The view of the bay could always open his mind to calmness and the present moment. It helped him sort his priorities not allowing his thoughts to get too tangled in short-term needs and desires. He watched a boat floating idly at anchor on the edge of the reef that surrounded Coconut Island. He assumed the small boat was either one from the University Marine Biology Laboratory close by or belonged to a spear fisherman swimming beneath it hunting among the coral for an elusive *ulua*, perhaps for his evening dinner.

His thoughts had settled on how uncomplicated his life had been the year before: he didn't know Teri back then; Guy and his boat were unknown; Viane, who he hadn't yet met was happily engrossed in her studies; and he was anxiously waiting for his new yacht to arrive on a Foss-Alaska barge that had sailed from the West Coast earlier in the week—the *Wailana Sunrise* as he named her even before seeing her, the name imparting the calming, quiet nature of a sunrise.

He worked out at the Clark Hatch Fitness Center early each morning, jogging for an hour with his friend Jimmy Nest, and then spending the remainder of the day standing guard over his clients' portfolios. Every Wednesday, he looked forward to having lunch with Lori, his secretary. It had been and still was their weekly time to regroup and support one another as a team. Then there was the anticipated enjoyment playing poker with his Hui O'Kainalu buddies each month. Yes, his days were uncomplicated a year ago. They were relaxed and predictable.

Today, though, was a hundred percent different, and he wouldn't trade any of the past. His current life was so much richer, and the prospect of life with Teri thrilled his heart. Meeting Viane during her rescue, then meeting her family, had allowed a depth of family involvement he'd not known before; he couldn't accept the thought of ever being without any of them.

The truth was that with Viane now missing and presumably in danger and his friend Guy experiencing the pain of losing something that he'd deemed precious, Stone's only recourse for getting life back on its proper track was, along with Teri, concentrating on finding Viane while supporting Guy in any way he could.

Guy's and Deborah's missing boat was something else. He felt an underlining responsibility for helping to bring them closure: either find it or find out what happened to it so they could get it back or get the insurance money and buy its replacement. Their joy had been so evident on that first day when they'd come out of Heeia Kea Marina to join in the adventure to Kapapa Island. They deserved to that joy again.

A RINGING PHONE INTERRUPTED his contemplation.

"Hi, sweetness, you doing OK? I felt my big toe itching, so I knew you had me included in your thoughts."

"I've always heard it was the ear that twitched when you thought someone was thinking about you. Never heard about the *toe* thing. And how would you know I had been thinking about you anyway?" It was a leading question to stir things around a little—things needed a little stirring from time to time. "What if I was thinking of someone else or was out in the garden planting a chili pepper tree and thinking about fertilizers?"

"Stone, you so easily forget about my psychic brain and the strand of hair I have beside the phone. Anyway, are you going to argue that my big toe doesn't know when things are happening?"

"I may have to examine that statement. Perhaps I need to take a closer look at that toe of yours very soon."

"Only if you think you're up to the task of where that may lead." There was a wicked smile in her voice, and he loved it.

"I spent some time this morning at the geology department, but my mind isn't letting me concentrate on anything except Viane." Her voice took on a serious note. "I'm so very worried about her, Stone. I feel sick to my stomach every time I think of her. The dean knows her and is fully sympathetic with the situation. He told me there's nothing important in the department at the moment and has suggested I go back to Hilo. He said I could stay as long as I need to."

The dean was Teri's direct boss, and from all Teri had mentioned about him, was a very compassionate man. Stone had yet to meet him but hoped that would soon be resolved.

"Does he warrant toe-twitching as well?"

"Only when it rains. Do I hear jealousy edging through your voice? That's sort of sweet, Stone."

"Who, me? Doesn't happen. No jealousy on this side of the phone. Just looking for background information, that's all."

"I've decided to fly back to Hilo and stay at Pops's place until she's found. Please tell me you're OK with this. It'll mean we'll be apart for as long as it takes—our first real separation since we met, but hopefully, it won't be more than a few days. I don't think my heart can bear more than that—the absence of you and my anguish for Viane."

"You know what they say, angel: Absence makes the heart grow fonder. We'll be just fine. Besides, I may leave the office work to Lori and follow you over in a couple days."

"I've also heard that they say, out of sight, out of mind. If you ever think about buying into that one, just remember there are always two ends to that string of thought," she cautioned, but he could hear the smile in her words.

"When do you plan on leaving?"

"I was thinking of tomorrow morning. I want to spend tonight with you before leaving."

"Ahhh, toe analysis on the horizon. Does that mean I'll have to check your bedside table for scissors first? Probably should, just to be on the safe side."

"Don't worry, I have all your hair I need. Let's have dinner later. My gloomy mood needs food."

"We haven't been to Irifune's for a while. Maybe it's time for seared ahi and tofu, how does that sound? I'll pick you up in an hour." He decided to wait to ask if she was up for a short get-together with Mike and Robin. He'd play that one by ear.

Belowground, Mauna Loa, Big Island of Hawaii

VIANE WAS ON A roll slipping in and out of consciousness. Her semilucid moments came in brief spurts, with barely a dull awareness defining the difference between being somewhat aware of her surroundings and that of floating though a kaleidoscope world of her past.

The moments of awareness were brief before she slipped back into some dark recess of her mind. At one moment, she was floating in her treasured Queen's Bath, swirling around in the clear, cool water; but the very next moment, she would find herself walking hand in hand with her parents, her father holding one hand while her mother held the other as they walked along the shoreline of Keaukaha. She was small and had to look up to see their faces. In a moment of awareness, a memory returned of hiking, feeling wonderful as she explored the depths of a lava tube, happily dangling on the end of a rope examining rocks. The abrupt awareness of that image left her empty and frightened. A dark, cold feeling coursed through her veins, imprisoning her will.

She immediately drifted back into a deeper unconsciousness as the loving presence of her mother appeared together with a host of others. Her mother and the others began to caress her and gently draw on her spirit, willing her to move deeper into an endless tunnel. She felt a wonderful, loving energy and willingly moved forward with them.

She couldn't see him but instinctively knew her father was behind her, reaching out to keep her from leaving—his presence growing stronger and more forceful, pulling her from the grasp of the others.

SITTING RESTLESSLY AT HOME gazing out of a large living room window toward Hilo Bay, Pops suddenly felt a cold chill blow across him. It made chicken-skin bumps and the hair on his arms stand up. He knew it was Viane. The cold air he felt didn't make sense, though. It was a hot, muggy day.

IN HER OFFICE MILES away, on a different island, Teri felt an uncomfortable *awareness* tug at her heart. She'd been feeling somewhat giddy having just got off the phone with Stone, with the planned evening together; but the strange emotion persisted. She knew it had something to do with Viane and a perceived danger her friend may be in, but that was as far as she could take it as the sensation settled in her belly, leaving behind an empty numbness.

Thirty-Two

Irifune Restaurant, Oahu

IT WAS A BEAUTIFUL evening to go out and enjoy. The full moon was low on the horizon, casting romantic shadows wherever they looked. Stone figured it couldn't get any better—mood-wise anyway—but it did.

They found a parking space on busy Kapahulu Avenue, mere steps from the restaurant's door, and walked in without a need to wait in line. To Teri's and Stone's delight, they discovered their favorite table was unoccupied. As simple as that sounds, it was an unusual occurrence, being that it was the favorite table among all the restaurant's regulars. The table was snuggled into a back corner overlooking a small flower-and-bamboo garden with a koi pond in the center, filled with enormous, slow-moving, and very colorful fish. An arched footbridge crossed over the pond.

Moss-covered rock walls sheltered the cozy table and the garden from the busy street beyond. The placement of the table and the surrounding ambience could only soften the darkest of moods and a person's hardest edge. The effect was obviously not lost on them as they settled into the soft chairs with a decisive sigh. They shuffled their chairs closer, their knees gently touching.

Irifune Restaurant was a small, neighborhood restaurant, drawing crowds from the entire island. A few wise neighbor islanders coveted it as well whenever they found reason to travel to Oahu. Limited to ten tables with a "No reservation" policy, the wait to be seated could extend to an hour or more with the line of patron's stretched out along the sidewalk.

As they relaxed into the tranquil atmosphere, Teri decided not to mention the uneasy feeling she'd had earlier. Her initial plan had been to solicit Stone's input, but the conversation didn't fit with their current mood. She refused to be the one responsible for placing a dark cloud over their evening, so she decided it could wait for the appropriate time and atmosphere. Besides, she wasn't entirely sure what to tell him about it anyway.

They talked gently about various things in their lives with a mutually unspoken intention of skirting the topics of Viane's absence and Guy's missing boat. They had agreed earlier to take a short break from both problems. They needed space to ease the tensions they both felt, and it was working—their tensions were indeed easing. Too much time had already been devoured in analyzing, strategizing, and agonizing. They needed this seventh-inning stretch.

The breaded tofu appetizer they ordered, one of Irifune's signature dishes, disappeared rapidly, what with both of them ravenous. Eating something so delicious proved to be the perfect ingredient to raising their cheerfulness, as did the Pinot Grigio that Stone ordered—everything went down easily. They shared an order of seared ahi, another culinary masterpiece done to perfection, and also shared a dessert of fried bananas and ice cream. Both were more than satisfied.

Irifune Restaurant had become one of their favorite places for an intimate get-away-from-it-all dinner, and they returned to it frequently when time permitted. They had introduced Guy and Deborah to the restaurant a few weeks before and would occasionally find them there; but on this particular evening, they were selfishly pleased not to recognize anyone.

"I'm hoping I can get the few hotspots on my desk cooled down to the point Lori can puppeteer things for a few days while I join you in Hilo," Stone intimated. "My clients know, in very general terms, that there's an emergency in my family, so most are content to hold off any changes they may have for a few days. Luckily, the markets are pretty flat, so nothing should come up that Lori can't handle. Besides"—Stone's features softened as he turned to look fully into Teri's face— "it's not as if we'll be so far away I can't fly back if I have to." She was absently nodding her head, thinking of the short separation they would experience before he arrived in Hilo.

"Your clients are lucky to have you, sweetie. I know I am. My life has taken on vivid colors from the black-and-white existence that was my world before we met." Her hand found Stone's thigh under the table, and she let it rest there. He reflexively moved his hand and folded it over hers. "How many days do you think you'll need before heading for Hilo?"

"The best scenario," Stone replied, "would be the day after tomorrow. I think one more day at the office will give me sufficient time to flatten any crinkles in the paperwork. Actually, the *very* best scenario"—he put emphasis on *very*— "would be to receive a surprise call from Pops or John and learn something significant about Viane's whereabouts before you leave in the morning." He momentarily lost concentration as he caught the sudden deepened look in her eyes and gently squeezing the hand still warm on his thigh. "If that happens, I'll trust Lori to do what I know she's capable of doing, and I'll either join you on your flight or catch one of the following ones. What time do you fly out?"

"I'm on the 9:00 a.m. John said he'd be at the airport to meet me, but I told him I planned to rent a car. I think we'll need the flexibility to come and go at will. What do you think, honey?"

"That sounds best, angel. That way, we won't have to rely on anyone to be our chauffeur."

They let thoughts float in the air and were quiet for a moment, both contemplating their time apart and grateful that it would be brief.

Stone broke the momentary silence and did a 180-degree change in the direction of their conversation, breaking into their agreed-upon off-limit topic. "Are you up for a Kahlua on the Rocks or a Tropical Breeze before we go back to your place for the night?"

When she didn't reply and simply stared at him, her forehead creased in question, he realized she was waiting to hear more. "Mike called before I left to pick you up and suggested a quick meeting so we could meet Robin and also be brought up to date on Guy's boat. I think he also wants us to bring him up to date on Viane because he expressly asked if we had anything new to report. I got the distinct impression he was holding something back, though, and that's got me on edge. He may not know her that well, but he wants to be in a position to lend a hand if and when help is needed. He called Lloyd as well and told him about us getting together, so hopefully, he and Pam will be there too."

"Absolutely, let's go." She flashed a bright smile in return. "It'd be fun to see everyone and find out what Mike has discovered about Guy's boat before we leave. Maybe he's found it and wants to surprise everyone. We won't have much to tell him about Viane that he doesn't already know."

"I'm betting he has some pretty good ideas about the boat thefts by now."

"Are we to meet him at the station in town? I like the energy in that old place."

"No, he mentioned meeting at Davy Jones Locker in the Reef Hotel. It's where he goes to meet Robin, his Coast

Guard girlfriend, whenever they can coordinate time off. From a few things he has mentioned, I get the impression they're getting quite serious about each other. I must admit I'm a little puzzled about this meeting, though, surprise or not. When he asked us to join him, his voice had an urgency that I found unusual for him."

The words brought back a chill as Teri's earlier uneasiness resurfaced again, but she still said nothing. She'd never been to Davy Jones Locker but had heard a lot of stories—some good, some not so good. She found herself with a mixed bag of emotions—from intrigue to hesitation.

They both knew it was time they met Robin, and had even mentioned it to each other just days before. This was a perfect opportunity to resolve that. They knew she was involved in the Coast Guard, but that was all they knew other than the fact that Mike was finally interested in someone for the first time in a long while, and that was a good thing.

"That would be wonderful, Stone," she finally agreed. I'd love to see the place and have been dying to meet Robin since Mike mentions her every time we see him. It'll be fun to see Lloyd and Pam again as well if they show up. Are Guy and Deborah going to be there?"

"When I talked to Mike, he said they would be, but he wasn't certain how quickly they could manage it. From what he told me, it appears Guy and Deborah were about to go back to Haiku and continue snooping. I think the idea of taking time to talk with Mike temporarily trumped the Haiku idea at least for a short time. I called them as well and got the same story. I also talked with Lloyd and told him approximately what time we'd be there. I was banking on you saying yes." He grinned sheepishly.

"I hope they show up. Playing amateur detective is not the best of ideas, if anyone were to ask me. I wouldn't want Deborah and Guy getting into a situation they couldn't get out of."

Thirty-Three

THEY NEEDED A FEW moments after walking into Davy Jones Locker for their eyes to adjust to the dim lighting in the bar, having entered from the brilliance of the Reef Hotel's parking lot.

Stone and Teri spotted Mike's recognizable silhouette sitting at a large table toward the back wall engrossed in conversation with a woman they could only assume was Robin. She wore a white Coast Guard uniform that was reflecting what little light there was like a beacon in a dark cave. It was very white.

Mike didn't notice them as they approached and received a not-so-gentle-yet-playful nudge on the shoulder from his companion. He followed her gaze over his shoulder and reactively reached his hand out in welcome when he saw Stone smiling down at him. Stone figured the conversation between the two must have been quite involved to have distracted Mike so completely. He was trained to instinctively react otherwise. Judging by the caught-in-the-headlights look they both wore the interrupted discussion must have been quite intimate.

Only two other tables were occupied—a rarity for this bar and a condition that wasn't likely to last too long. It was still early evening by Waikiki standards but rapidly closing in on happy hour. Patrons would soon start drifting in the door filling the room to its capacity. The bar's continuing popularity was attributed to the predominantly young male population that flowed in from the numerous military installations around the island. It was currently the *in* place for young military types, both male and female. It was also the only bar that offered perpetual entertainment of a very unique nature, day or night, which added measurably to its popularity. Interestingly, the entertainment went on regardless of whether the bar was open or closed.

Davy Jones Locker prided itself on at least this one uniqueness: it was the only bar in Waikiki, or anywhere else in the Islands, for that matter, that featured a wall—twenty feet in length and a good six feet up and down, stretching from one end of the bar to the other, made up entirely of two-inch-thick glass looking directly into the deep end of the hotel's outdoor swimming pool. The bar top and tables were all arranged in such a manner that the window behind the bartender became the central focal point from everywhere in the room. Despite the numerous advisory signs anchored topside around the pool's edge telling swimmers of the presence of the window, bar patrons could always count on seeing a show that ran the gamut of simply boring to startling X-rated—regardless of the signage. The stars of the show were hotel guests that either failed to read the signs or read them and were delighted to discover a waiting audience to show off their moves to as they swam past the window, treaded water in front of it, or did a number of other bizarre and at times gross things within viewing range of the glass portal and its beer-drinking audience.

Young kids with goggles would plug their faces tight to the glass, attempting to peer into the bar. Stone always wondered if that was possible but had no desire to personally go out and try. He assumed they could since many would suction up to the glass and wave to the captive audience.

Occasionally, rousing laughter would erupt among bar patrons when an unsuspecting swimmer let an explosion of gas loose from the back side of his bathing suit as bubbles cascaded to the surface and the swimmer went blissfully on his way, ignorant of having been a momentary star attraction.

"Where's Guy and Deborah?" asked Mike. "I didn't get a chance to call them. I'm hoping you did." He still held tight to Stone's hand.

"They're coming soon, and Lloyd said he'd be here before Teri and me. Apparently, I drove too fast."

Before the words could fade in the dim light, they realized Lloyd was standing directly behind them.

"I was following you," he said, looking at Stone before turning to take in a view of the pool. "You know, Stone," he said, still looking at the window, "I haven't been in this place since you and I skipped classes at UH and came in for a couple cold ones. That was a long time ago. Hasn't changed from what little I could see on the way in, and I see the entertainment hasn't changed a bit. In fact"—he pointed to a swimmer moving pas the glass—"isn't that the same girl we saw swimming here almost twenty-five years ago?" He smiled, temporarily lost in some distant memory.

In truth, Lloyd hadn't been inside *any* bar for the past twenty-plus years, ever since becoming sober. Coming in here was a milestone, and it would probably take him another twenty years before he ventured into another, if he ever did.

"Pam's involved in one of her many art projects and couldn't muster the will to leave it alone," he claimed as he pulled a chair over and sat down. "So I am here," he exclaimed, arms extended, hands clasped resting on the table, a smug look on his face.

Being the kind of guy not to waste time, Mike spoke, directing his words to everyone at the table in a fashion that gave them all the distinct impression they had stumbled into a company board meeting. The bar's waitress approached but quickly backed off, sensing her table was involved in something she didn't want to interrupt just then.

Mike walked a fine line between being a friend and being a policeman—something he found difficult to regulate. He had obviously made an unconscious shift into his police mode as he spoke. "Before we get too carried away with detecting lost boats and dear friends, I want you all to meet Robin Jaffers, a very special woman in my life."

As he said the words, he caught her eye and held her gaze for a long moment, affectionately rubbing her arm, his demeanor softening. "Robin operates the radio at the Coast Guard Station when she's not out with me, hiking ridge trails or hang gliding off the windward Koolaus. In her spare time, she polishes boats." He smiled at her as he covered her hand resting on the table beside him, and it disappeared beneath his. "She's due to rotate out in six months, and I'm doing my darndest to convince her to stay in the islands."

He told everyone about meeting Robin after responding to a called-in report of a broken security gate on the Coast Guard Station on Sand Island, across the harbor from downtown Honolulu. Robin had discovered the intrusion and placed a call to HPD. He told them about the immediate attraction that had been quite evident between them after responding to the call and said their attraction was continually growing stronger.

She was a woman whose presence was difficult not to be aware of—a natural beauty off the cover of a fitness magazine. Thick dark hair that looked like it might only require a few early-morning fingers ran through it to be good to go for the day. Slim, tall, and athletic and possessing an engaging yet quiet presence that might draw attention like honey-sweetened water draws hummingbirds. Her looks were classic; she possessed a charm that could have influenced Picasso.

She beamed, a shy delight evident in her features, as she acknowledged everyone and responded to the chorus of approving words in support of Mike's intention of keeping her in the islands. Mike reacted with a pleased smile.

As they relaxed comfortably at the table with the enjoyment of meeting Robin settling in, the energetically charged waitress bounded up to their table once again, carrying a tray laden with empty glasses haphazardly balanced on its too-small surface. "What can I get y'all?" Her Southern drawl was accompanied by a brilliant show of more white teeth than could possible fit into one's mouth. Even in the dim light, they sparkled. She was pointing at a drink card resting in the center of the table and stood waiting, pencil poised over a blank guest check that had found room on her tray.

Other than Lloyd who opted for tonic and a lemon slice, each of the others ordered the house specialty listed on the card as "the Water Tank." It was a rum-and-pineapple drink, the cheerful waitress explained in her melodic tones, with a host of other things mixed in and garnished with a deliciously juicy slice of pineapple. A stalk of sugarcane served as a swizzle stick. It all came in a very large glass with a cute paper umbrella sticking out of the pineapple. Her attitude of freshness appeared genuine despite the probable fact that she would describe this drink a minimum of thirty-nine more times before her shift was over—a hazard of the job. She emphasized the largeness of the glass the best she could using her arms without dumping the tray of empties into Lloyd's lap. Davy Jones Locker was essentially a hotel bar, and many of the tourists and hotel guests roaming Waikiki expected to find and consume such drinks. Stone was convinced the only reason they needed such oversized cocktail glasses was to house all the *extras* that were attached to the rim, floating on the surface or dangling off its edge—it was a contained meal instead of simply a drink.

Orders placed, the waitress, Nancy according to her name tag, literally bounded away to retrieve their order.

"Guy and Deborah should be here soon," Stone informed everyone. "Guy is anxious to hear news about the boat thieves." Before Stone could finish speaking, Mike's attention was pulled away from the conversation as he involuntarily looked to see what had caught Robin's attention. Everyone at the table followed their gaze like a yawn that couldn't be ignored. Centered in the viewing window was a heavyset man treading water. *That should be outlawed,* thought Stone, but he didn't want to voice it.

Conversation was proving difficult as eyes unconsciously turned whenever someone swam past the portal, causing a loss of concentration in the thread of what was being talked about. During one such interruption, Stone made the observation, with no malice intended, that the average body engaged in the act of swimming was not meant to be viewed from beneath the water's surface, at least not ordinary, everyday bodies—athletes and movie stars would probably get away with it, but not ordinary Joe Dokes. The average person had too many seemingly extra parts that rippled and shook in unnatural ways.

"While we're waiting for Guy and Deborah," suggested Stone, looking back at everyone at the table, "let's cover the details of Viane and the lack of any word on her whereabouts."

"What lack?"

Mike's words, spoken with a comedian's deadpan face, had the effect of bringing all surrounding sound to an abrupt silence. It wasn't solely his words that struck a chord, but it was the knowing expression that accompanied them as he looked from one to the next as if saying, *I know something good that none of you know.*

Teri was the first to jump on his startling declaration, barely able to constrain her reaction. "What's going on, Mike? What do you mean by what lack?"

"It's primarily why I wanted all of us to sit down together tonight, before your plans"— he was talking directly to Teri now—"are set and you fly off to Hilo tomorrow without knowing the latest." He paused to let this sink in. "Here's what I learned from a Big Island police friend." He took a deep breath, meeting the gaze of each of them as if to ratchet up suspense. Knowing what he knew, he was actually finding a small amount of humor in building up anticipation—just a bit anyway—although the subject matter remained very grave. "A cop beating the bushes around Keaau has come up with two young guys who claim they were the ones that hot-wired Pops's pickup and drove it to Shipman Park outside Keaau."

There was a collective gasp at the news as each put their own spin on what the news implied.

"I gather you haven't spoken to Pops in the past two hours?" he asked Teri. She slowly shook her head in response, her eyes not leaving his. She was waiting for more. "He probably knows all this by now. These two boys, according to the officer, took the pickup from the Bird Park trailhead on Mauna Loa. It looks like that's where Viane started out before disappearing. At a minimum, it gives everyone a lead as to where the search should begin. That's a good thing, right? The cop involved is positive the boys had nothing to do with her actual disappearance, only with taking her truck. Before this came out, no one knew where on the Big Island to start looking, right?" He looked around the table for confirmation. "That's a lot of island to think about searching. Now we know a place to start."

At that point, Guy and Deborah made their appearance beside the table. They said their alohas to everyone, pulled two more chairs up to the crowded table, and squeezed in.

Immediately sensing the exhilaration circling the table, Deborah asked, "What did we miss, and how many of those huge drinks has everyone had so far?" She was pointing at Stone's nearly empty glass sitting next to a pile of drink umbrellas. She looked over and saw Lloyd's smaller water glass and gave him an approving *shaka* sign. Guy gave the waitress, who was still showing a big toothy smile, a couple of hand signals, ordering himself and Deborah the big-glass drink without even asking what was in it. Stone wondered if the waitress was relieved at not having to recite the drink's pedigree once again. He decided that if asked, she would have done it without altering her smile. He also decided she knew exactly how to earn bigger tips.

Mike introduced Robin to the new arrivals and then proceeded to quickly repeat what he'd just told the others.

Stone looked at Teri. "This changes plans considerably. Looking around the table, he went on to explain, "Teri's flying over to Hilo first thing in the morning, and I was planning on going to the office and then catching an evening or next-morning flight." Addressing Teri again, he said, "I won't be able to concentrate on work knowing this new information." A better plan, he said, after hearing Mike's information, was to go to his office, get Lori squared away with what needed doing, and then catch the next flight following Teri's.

He was about to ask her to delay her plans and fly with him, but thought better of it, knowing that she would have left for the airport right then if it were possible.

From that point on, both Stone and Teri found it difficult to pay much attention to what others were saying. Their minds had shifted to Hilo and Viane; their quiet reverie of Irifune was lost in the dust of excitement. Through the jumble of his thoughts, Stone overheard Mike tell the story of the container he had opened and Guy's mentioning that he saw his boat in a yard in Haiku.

"Stone, with you and Teri heading for Hilo, I think I'll stay around here and help Guy." Lloyd took the opportunity to tell them about Kawika and his conversation regarding the two Johnson outboards.

"Why didn't you tell me this before, Lloyd?" Mike was visibly upset. "Did your son tell you the guy's name?"

"Just happened this afternoon, and his name is Bill, no last name. I was waiting until tonight to tell you so everybody else could hear it." He then told everyone of his unproductive trip to the yacht club.

Mike listened intently, absorbing the details before speaking up. "We need to find legal reason to search that house where your boat was, Guy. That name, Bill, could tie in with that of one of the owners, a William Jefferson, and he may be an important link to the boats being shipped to the mainland. That photo you took, Deborah, will be a big help, but I'll have to tell the judge that the boat is no longer there. That's going to jeopardize the issuance of a warrant. I won't bother to tell him the two of you jumped a fence and trespassed on the property. We need something that's compelling enough to convince a judge beyond any doubt."

Guy's face broke into a knowing look, and his smile widened. "Mike, let me tell you about a missing 1948 Buick convertible that's also in the photo." He told them about the theft of his car from the quarry on the grounds of the university a lot of years ago. "It was under a big banyan tree that used to be there—and may still be, I don't know. A buddy and I used a tree branch to hoist the engine and work on it before putting it back, in perfect working order, mind you." He paused at what was obviously a fond memory. "One day the car was sitting there in the shade, and the very next day, it was gone, never to be seen again—until yesterday."

"Was a police report filed at the time?"

"Yes, but the investigating officer told me there wasn't much they could do other than put it on report, which I already knew from past experience."

"That certainly adds some weight to the pile of evidence, but I think the judge is still going to see the time lapse since your car disappeared as a hurdle he can't easily jump, and my guess, Guy, is he won't budge on the warrant. My gut tells me we got the right individuals, but we need to pin things down a bit tighter."

Saying little else, Mike was already formulating a plan that he hoped would wrap things into a nice bundle. They had a boat in HPD's impound lot that had been sitting on a trailer for over two years. It fit nicely with the type of boats being stolen. The owner, a military draftee according to an old registration file, had parked it on a street close to Schofield Barracks but never returned to pick it up. Mike told them of his plan to set up a sting operation using that boat as a decoy and would set things in motion after Robin headed back to the Coast Guard Station.

At that moment, his planning was interrupted when Robin touched his arm as the noise level in the bar rose to a level that made hearing any conversation and strategy impossible. All of them turned in time to see a young couple treading water centered dead-on in the window, the man's right hand reaching up presumably holding on to the edge of the pool. The couple was engrossed in an intimate embrace, hands rubbing and probing. Both wore bathing suits covering very little and slowly becoming less with each motion of their legs.

The show abruptly ended as the couple broke apart, propelling themselves from view, leaving everyone in the bar to assume the warning signs on deck had finally caught their attention or someone poolside had given them a heads-up. The collective sigh of disappointment was audible.

Thirty-Four

LLOYD WAS THE FIRST to leave, offering the excuse of wanting to check on Pam. Stone silently accepted the fact that Lloyd's having been sober for twenty-four years could have been posing a hardship for him sitting in a bar he'd frequented so many times in non-sober days. Stone figured he'd probably been riding a roller-coaster of thoughts and feelings during the past hour.

Stone appreciated his friend showing up at all and his willingness to be a part of the group. He conveniently used Lloyd's exodus as a timely excuse for him and Teri to be on their way as well. Just as they got up and bid everyone *ahui hou*, another boisterous swell of voices rose up in response to the swimming pool entertainment. As they navigated through the accumulated bar crowd, Stone glanced at the window display, only to see a host of young people, too many to count, jostling each other and dunking heads. The dangling awkward movement of legs was hilarious.

With the knowledge of Viane's possible location greatly narrowed down and initial search plans more than likely already set in motion, they began feeling as though they were on a swing, their emotional limits being pushed in two different directions. The challenges that were being presented between boat thefts and Viane's absence were draining both their emotional reserves. Each of their compassion to help their friends was limitless, but nonetheless was being strained.

They drove up Nuuanu Avenue heading for Teri's place. Knowing Viane's general location was a huge relief to them and was reason enough to elevate their strained positive attitude. The question still remained, though, that even with this new information, would they be able to find her? Mauna Loa was massive and imposed infinite possibilities for getting lost, hurt, or both. And when they found her, remaining as positive as they could manage, would she be physically unharmed?

Teri was squeezing Stone's thigh so tightly as he drove he was tempted to ask her to ease off, or at least attempt to gently unclench her hand from his leg; but instead, he chose to let her endure the emotional ride she was experiencing— there wasn't much he could say to allay any of her apprehensions anyway as his own probably mirrored hers. He rested his hand over hers and felt it begin to relax in response.

GUY AND DEBORAH REMAINED seated in the bar talking with Mike and Robin. It wasn't too difficult to guess that they were looking for some time alone before the evening was gone; but in the same breath, Guy didn't want to waste any more precious minutes finding his boat. When he last saw it in the backyard of the house in Haiku, it looked to be in decent shape, although, he admitted, the distance had been almost too great to assess the possibility of physical damage. He could see the motors were missing and assumed the steering, gear, and throttle mechanisms had also been removed, along with the gas tanks and, he was certain, his favorite fishing pole and reel that he'd just purchased two days before their camping adventure. The depth finder he'd also recently bought and installed was surely gone as well. If they could find it quickly, their boat might still be in one piece.

Guy could sympathize with Mike's situation. The man was heading up the stolen boat investigation while simultaneously doing background work to help Stone in his search for their friend. On top of all this, there was everything else his job called on him to do. But Guy needed to move the search for his boat forward, and he was curious to know more about the sting operation being planned and what Mike hoped to discover from it and how the information would connect to finding his boat.

Mike could only tell Guy that he and Deborah would have to be patient, and he reassured them he and his fellow officers were doing everything they could to arrive at answers. He didn't want to tell Guy that his boat was more than likely already in a container.

"Please be patient, Guy. The investigation is moving forward. I know you and Deborah are anxious to find your boat, but please don't do anything further, like going back into that yard. We'll talk after the sting." His final words before turning his attention to Robin were, "Wait and see."

It was Mike's favorite new phrase that he had been using more and more frequently lately. He picked it up after he and Robin had watched a movie that made frequent use of the phrase—he liked the finality of it.

"Just a quick question, Mike, then Deborah and I will leave you two to enjoy the remainder of the evening. What time, and where should I meet you tomorrow assuming the search is still on?"

"We," interjected Deborah. The sideways glance she gave Guy, along with an intimidating sweet smile she used so well, left little doubt that he wasn't about to go on this adventure without her. *How the heck does she manage to do that?*

"I'm assuming we'll be ready around midday," responded Mike. "You'll need to remain flexible since most judges operate on a different time schedule than the rest of us, and I need to see where the sting operation takes us. You'll have at least an hour or two warning. If the judge stalls for whatever reason, it could be the next day after." Mike told them that his hands were tied as to exact timing. "Sorry, that's about as good as I can make it. Plan to meet me at L&L Drive-Inn in Kaneohe when the time comes. Pull around back in the parking lot and wait if I'm not there. If the search is held up for any reason, I'll give you a call."

They said their alohas, and Deborah and Guy headed for home.

Thirty-Five

The Sting

Dawn WAS STILL MANY hours away as two boats
stealthily made their way out past the breakwater of Heeia
Kea Boat Harbor and continued a short distance into
Kaneohe Bay—one towing the other. As the small procession
passed the harbor entrance, the towed boat's bow caught a
reflection from the light high atop the light pole standing
guard at the end of the pier. The boat had undergone a quick
makeover during the late evening, its deck and brightwork
were brought to a high polish—it had to look its best.

Its destiny was a fixed buoy floating two hundred yards
outside the harbor. As they came alongside the buoy, the
decoy boat was tied off and left. The other boat with its
crew of three glided quietly back into the harbor and a
preassigned slip. Mooring lines were made fast, and the crew
got off and walked away, two of the three going to a rusting
nondescript brown van backed into a stall in the parking lot.
They stepped in and closed the door behind them. The third
got into a car parked next to the van and drove out onto the
roadway and disappeared in the dark.

Anyone looking out over the water could have easily seen the buoyed boat in the peripheral of the strong pier light. The placement of the boat was specifically chosen just because of that light.

Inside the van, an overcrowded matrix of electronic gear and video monitors packed the confined space—HPD had spent a lot of money on the vanful of state-of-the-art equipment, but not a penny on the van that housed it all. The observation post, they figured, would have been too obvious to the wrong people, had it been new and shiny.

Andrew and Charlie, sitting in very close confines within the van, were used to this kind of stakeout. They had been partners for a very long time during their careers at HPD and got along as if they were brother and sister—usually quite compatible.

They began the familiar pattern of rotating turns watching a video monitor from a live feed camera mounted on the post below the pier light. The monitor showed four different magnified views of the decoy boat. Now it was a matter of watching and waiting, much like a shark hiding in the shadows of a rock anticipating its next meal.

AS WAS THEIR HABIT, Alysdon and Bill drove along Kamehameha Highway on their way into Kaneohe, headed home. It was a roundabout way to get there, but they both enjoyed driving down the old highway that skirted the water's edge of the bay, especially late night when the bay took on a serene, almost-mystical quality. Since boats had become their primary avenue of interest lately, this area of the bay was boat heaven to them. It had become their favorite location for finding and making boats disappear because of the general absence of people frequenting the area during the night.

On this particular drive-by, though, there was something new in the water. It hadn't been there yesterday when they passed by, and it immediately struck them both as an ideal specimen, the exact size and general condition they were on the lookout for—sufficiently generic in appearance to be shipped to and sold on the mainland without question. Both agreed a closer look was essential. Alysdon braked hard, made a sharp left hook into the harbor's parking lot, and drove as close as he could to the water's edge.

"Come on, Bill, let's walk out to the end of the pier for a better look at what's out there. Looks almost too good to be true."

They were both excited at the prospect of finding another boat they could *aihui*—and looking so easy to do. It may be too close on the heels of the other thefts, but they'd been known in the past to throw caution to the wind. As they got closer, they could see the various antennae and radar scopes mounted on its cabin roof, and that translated to a lot of dollars' worth of electronics mounted below. They stood stock-still, gaze intent, feeling their need to have what they saw growing stronger.

Through a window of the rusty van, Charlie saw the two men walk close to the pier camera and stand looking in the direction of the decoy. As they turned around to walk back, she took several pictures of them from the roof-mounted video camera. She thought it quite interesting that both subjects were smiling. She turned the camera, aiming it toward the vehicle the men had arrived in and snapped a picture of the truck and license plate. Her partner, Andrew, had his cell phone out and was calling their boss, Sergeant Mike Kalama, to let him know what they saw and the license number involved. Having done this, the officers returned to their view post.

It was Andrew's turn to monitor the video screen in case someone else showed up exhibiting interest; there was a lot of hours left before their shift ended. They spoke softly, reminiscing about past stakeouts they'd been on and some of the humorous events they'd shared, a topic of conversation they frequently gravitated to—it was the fun part of downtime as they waited for chaos to begin.

IT WAS NEARING DAYLIGH,T but still sufficiently dark, when Alysdon and Bill pulled back into the boat harbor with a trailer in tow, with a small boat strapped tight riding piggy-back. The trailer was huge compared to the small boat it carried—a horse with a fly on its back. The small boat was rigged with an electric motor designed for near-silent running—the kind often used by lake fishermen not wanting to scare their prey away with gas-powered motors. Alysdon and Bill were fairly confident the harbor would be devoid of people this early in the morning, but they did their due diligence and scouted it anyway prior to backing their trailer onto the boat ramp.

In very quick, well-rehearsed fashion, the two had the small boat in the water and, just as quickly and silently, moved out into the bay, pulling alongside the decoy boat. They cut its tether to the buoy, retied it to their small craft, and began dragging the decoy back to shore. They were prepared with what they hoped was a good cover story just in case they were confronted before they could make their getaway but were confident they wouldn't need to use it. Alysdon always wanted to cover any bases needing covering, but in this case, he suspected anyone who would anchor a boat out away from a pier was intent on leaving it there for a length of time and wouldn't be showing up to ask any questions. Since it just showed up overnight, they felt fairly safe the owner wouldn't be close by and would probably not realize it was missing for a long time.

THE THIEVES PULLED THE decoy boat onto their trailer, secured their small boat to the floating pier, and removed the electric motor. They didn't want to take a chance on having someone come along and steal it; they knew the world was full of dishonest people. They would come back later in the day for their boat. They finished their clandestine work and drove out onto the old highway, turned left, and disappeared in the dawn's light.

Unknown to either of them, though, their escapade was being captured on high-definition video. As the men drove onto Kamehameha Highway heading for home, the gleaming trophy of their night's work trailing along nicely behind them, an unmarked patrol car that had been signaled from the van pulled out of the roadway that led from Heeia State Park and began tailing them. The officer had been concealed behind a maka-orange hedge, quietly waiting for their quarry to pass.

The officer notified his boss, Mike Kalama, that the subjects appeared heading for Haiku. He told Mike he'd radio back soon to confirm the exact destination. The officer wasn't concerned about losing the subjects, so he stayed well back to avoid detection. The bug planted on the underside of the boat's deck was sending back a good signal.

The decoy eventually stopped moving at the very house everyone expected it to stop at.

Stone and Teri were late by the time they arrived at the drop-off area for Hawaiian Airlines—unplanned and mostly unavoidable.

Soon after leaving Teri's Nuuanu home, they wedged themselves into the muddle of the usually heavy morning rush hour on H-1 freeway and were instantly hemmed in by chaos the rest of the way to the airport—three lanes of wall-to-wall cars and trucks. It was obvious Oahu had finally become overpopulated.

Their delay in arriving probably had more to do with the news about Viane than with any highway chaos. They had been awake for a good part of the night, neither of them able to sleep. They started second-guessing everything they'd heard, thought about, or felt about their missing friend. And as if that wasn't enough, they had agonized over a few topics that had nothing to do with present circumstances—it was just one of those nights experienced at one time or another by most of us.

During part of the night's exchange Stone relayed his personal experience of the Mauna Loa summit trail. He told her about a time he and both his sons spent three days hiking from Bird Park to the summit many years prior. He described to her the ruggedness and desolation of the mountain trail, giving her a vision of how easily one could miss trail markers and become disoriented. He described the abundance of brittle *a'a* lava that presented a walking surface to challenge the most experienced hiker and its helter-skelter pattern that could easily lead to confusion about the correct path to follow. One would think it'd be a simple matter of walking uphill, he'd told her; but the mountain is so massive that *up* encompassed a hundred-eighty-degree view of a surface resembling a world tilted upward, the summit virtually hidden beyond the horizon.

As he relayed the story, he honestly thought knowing more of the detail about the trail they were about to hike would help Teri relax. That was wrong. Even before finishing telling her about his experience, he realized his mistaken thinking. Her horrified expression told it all, and he became annoyed with himself for having brought it up at all, realizing it was something she didn't need to know about until they were on the trail looking for clues. He decided too late she would have quickly discovered the harshness for herself. *Maybe I embellished the details too much.*

He knew he had a habit of doing just that. He knew Teri had probably experienced equal, and even more difficult, terrain during her years studying geology; they'd never talked much about that part of her life.

Their rolling conversation during the remainder of the night resurrected a memory of the older woman they saw driving away from Pops's house. Neither of them could remember her name but did recall her showing up at a critical time after Viane became entangled with kidnappers almost a year ago—the event that had brought Stone and Teri together. That discussion brought on more thoughts that only served to energize them additionally. They couldn't imagine why the woman was showing up at Pops's house at the very time Viane was in trouble—again.

The timing seemed to be a little too coincidental. They recalled that she lived in Ewa Beach outside the gate leading into Pearl Harbor Yacht Club. In order to bring their talking to an end, they concluded Pops would come up with a good story to explain it all. Their last wakeful words were agreeing that it will probably be a great story. They finally drifted into a shallow sleep.

TERI'S FLIGHT LEFT AT 9:00 a.m., which gave her fifteen minutes to purchase a ticket, get checked in, and navigate the security maze to Gate 52. She made it just as the ramp doors were being closed.

On landing in Hilo, she picked up her rental and drove the five-minute distance to Pops's house. He was sitting on the swing on his front lanai, ostensibly waiting for her to arrive as she drove up the long driveway. He had wanted to come to the airport with John to meet her flight, but she and Stone both agreed that they would need the flexibility of their own transportation.

Stone was going to fly in on the following flight arriving two hours later. This gave Teri time to gather any additional information Pops might have and then figure out how best she and Stone could fit themselves into the search.

SHE WAS AT THE bottom of the terminal escalator waving to him as Stone rode down to join her. He noticed she was no longer wearing the red muumuu she had on when he'd dropped her off at the airport earlier. Instead, she had on a pair of beige convertible cargo pants and a too-large white shirt, an ideal garment for reflecting the intense sun during their coming hike—the main reason she'd brought it along. She was carrying a plumeria lei in her hand and was wearing another draped around her neck.

"A lei for me?" he inquired. "We've been apart for all of two hours."

"Pops made them this morning and insisted I give one to you, so cool it with the remarks and let me give you the required kiss." She was smiling widely as she spoke and drew close. She draped the lei around his neck and gave him a very warm, lingering kiss.

When he caught his breath, he tightened his arms around her waist, softly asking, "Got another lei, or do I get to remove the one you have and re-lei you?" All he got was a teasing nudge with her shoulder. He'd settle for that for now.

Walking arm in arm to the parking lot, Teri brought him up to speed on what she'd managed to learn since arriving. "Pops is going to go to the ranger's office at the National Park and get a detailed map of the trail system. He doesn't want any of us getting lost while we're hiking. He was also going to see if they would be willing to help in the search, thinking they may have a helicopter at their disposal he could talk them into letting us use. He also called his friend, the police chief in Hilo, to see if any of his off-duty officers would like to join in the hunt. That's a lot of potential people that may show up at the trailhead."

"It'll be good having lots of help," replied Stone. "That's a big mountain, and we're going to want to spread out as we go. I doubt if the ranger or any of his people will be able to help us much, though. All national parks are operating shorthanded on a drastically skimmed budget. I also read somewhere about the Kilauea crater starting to inflate. They'll have their hands full."

"I didn't tell you about another group of potential helpers he's contacted." She couldn't help inwardly smiling at Pops's resilience and at the number of contacts he seemed to have around the island. "He called a guy named Randy, who heads up an outfit called BIVSAR, whatever that is—he didn't take time to explain. This Randy person is going to see if anyone in his organization is available to help on short notice." She looked at him, obviously pleased to share the information of the many people who might show up to help, but instead of seeing the expected reflection of her joy, she saw a far-off glimmer in his eyes as some distant memory apparently came flooding back.

"Big Island Volunteer Search and Rescue," responded Stone when he was sure she had finished her rushed recap of what was going to happen; he hadn't wanted to interrupt her excitement.

"What? Who or what are you talking about?" She looked puzzled.

"That's what the letters, *BIVSAR*, stand for. Big Island Volunteer Search and Rescue. I was a part of that group many years ago when I lived here. Randy Wellworth is who Pops probably called. He was the man with the brainstorm to put BIVSAR together. Your mentioning the name brought back a memory of a strange night he and I spent together when we were on a search for a lost tourist up around the volcano. I'll tell you the story, but I'd rather save it for a better time. You OK with that, angel?"

"You are a man of unseen talents and experiences, aren't you?" Her face showed surprise and admiration as she unlocked the passenger-side door and then threw the keys over the car's roof to Stone.

With index finger pointing toward his head as he got in, he proudly proclaimed, "There are many hidden talents and secret knowledge lying beneath this brain's outer cover that you so much admire. Stick with me, and I promise you a life of continual surprise."

Her responding "Hmph" wasn't the response he expected, but she looked happy.

He waited for more comment, but when none came, he continued to fill in the gap as they went along. "Tourists and hunters get lost on the island with great regularity, especially pig hunters," he explained. "The tourists just don't know where they're going. The pig hunters are so busy keeping up with where their dogs are going they often fail to pay attention to where they themselves are. The dogs will always show up back at the guy's truck, but in the meantime, he's gotten left behind and ends up lost in the thick growth of vegetation. BIVSAR is simply a group of people who volunteer to go out into the bushes and find them. The group can be out searching the trails a lot faster than the fire department's search team can get mobilized. Great bunch of people. What time are we to meet at the trailhead?"

It took a second for her to shift gears back to the task at hand. She was envisioning Stone heading through a curtain of vegetation with a compass in his hand. "Pops said eleven o'clock or soon after."

"In that case, let's grab something to eat. It may be a long time before food shows up again. Our meal at Irifune seems a long time ago, and I'm hungry."

"Me too. Let's go over to Empire Café and say aloha to Danny. I'd love some of his chicken adobo right about now."

They were quiet for a few minutes sitting at a table in the café while waiting for their food order. "It may be a late thought, but in our rush to leave this morning, did you remember to pack your boots along with your hiking clothes?" he asked.

In answer, Teri hoisted her left leg up almost level with the table and, with a proud smile, showed him the new Vasque Breeze hiking boots she'd bought the week before at REI. I wore them on the flight over. Not very observant this morning, were you? Muumuus are great for covering footwear, but how could you not see me grimacing as I walked? They're new and feel gigantic, and they hurt my feet."

"I'm very observant. I thought the grimace went with that new puffy white shirt you're wearing. Obviously, you're not going to expose anything to the sun or to me while we tramp around looking for Viane, are you?" That's probably a good thing."

"If I expose too much, we may not get to where we're going. Is the shirt too large, you think? On second thought, maybe I should undo a few buttons and let the sun shine on some open space—some valley landscape, so to speak. What would you do about that if I did, Mr. Excitement?" she teased.

"Whoa. Catching up on some taunting this morning, are we? What happened to the admiration of moments ago?"

"What admiration? No such thing happening on this side of the table." She could carry off a faultless straight face with ease.

It was Stone's turn to "Hmph," but the smile was reaching his eyes. He shifted his chair closer. "We'll talk more in depth about your valley landscape later. As for your boots, they appear to be about the right size, *kuuipo*. Didn't the salesclerk tell you about wearing two pair of socks while you break them in?"

"I recall him mentioning something about that, but I didn't really understand what he was talking about. I forgot to ask him to clarify that before I left. My mind was elsewhere at the time, more concerned with being on the mountain and not so much about what was covering my feet in order to be there. Tell me, why would I want to wear two pairs of socks, Keeper of Secrets?"

"It helps keep your feet from blistering. If you put on one pair of thin, tight-fitting socks, then put a thicker pair over the other, your feet will stay happy as your boots soften up. The socks will take all the rubbing, and your feet won't be affected. You hiked a lot when you were studying geology. Did no one ever tell you that pearl of wisdom before?"

"No one ever did. I was too busy suffering with blistered feet until my new boots got broken in. Then I wore them down to their nails. I'll put on an additional pair of socks before we hit the trail. Where were you when my feet needed advice, honey?"

The smell of food arriving brought a momentary halt to conversation as Danny placed heaping plates of chicken adobo, steamed rice, and a large scoop of macaroni salad in front of each of them. They simultaneously reached for the bottle of Pops's *patis* that was grouped among the many condiments on the table. The quantity of food was enormous: there'd be enough left on their plates for several more meals.

THEY PULLED INTO THE Bird Park parking lot a few minutes before eleven. Officer Vic Morro was standing beside his police cruiser looking up the slope of the mountain, lost in thought, while John was engrossed in a cell phone conversation. There was another man standing there wearing a large well-worn hat with lengthy brown-gray strands of hair hanging down around its edges. He was standing close to the policeman with his back toward them, talking animatedly with both arms obviously in support of whatever it was he had to say. They both stood apparently looking at the same spot on the slope. He was tall and wiry, dressed in a T-shirt, long baggy cargo pants, and hiking boots—all looking a bit like he'd been wearing them for the past month. It took a few moments for Stone to realize it was Randy Wellworth. He hadn't seen Randy for a very long time and so assumed Randy wouldn't remember who he was. Too many years and circumstances have elapsed. He decided to wait until later to talk with him. Looking around, they saw there weren't the hordes of helpers he and Teri figured there would be—and no Pops either.

"Pops not back from the park office yet, John?" queried Stone as John walked over to them. He had a mixed appearance of expectation and puzzlement evident on his face.

"Not yet, Stone. He'll be on his way back pretty soon. I was just talking with him. And guess what?" His excitement took over whatever inner puzzle he'd been working through. "He went to the office for maps and to get advice on how to proceed, but as soon as he walked into the ranger's office, he saw Viane's unmistakable purple hiking hat sticking out of their lost-item box." Viane's penchant for that hat had been a topic of fun conversation several times. "Apparently, some hikers found it on the slope and turned it in. The ranger didn't recall where on the trail they said they found it but did remember them mentioning staying at the Naniloa Beach Hotel. I was on the phone trying to locate the couple to see if they could help pinpoint where they'd found it, but without names to go by, it has become too difficult to discover who they are."

Officer Vic walked over to see what the excited talk was all about. Randy remained where he was, bent over a map spread out on the ground. When Vic heard what John had to say, he immediately went into action. All they heard him say as he rushed to his car was that he needed to get hold of Moku. He was back beside them a few moments later.

"I radioed in and was able to reach Moku. Her brother happens to be the concierge at Naniloa. If anyone knows where hotel guests might be, it'll be him. She was close to the hotel, so she's going to swing by and ask him. Said she'd call right back."

At the sound of his radio, he hurried over to his car. Moku's voice was broken by static, but the message was clear. Her brother knew exactly who the couple was and where they went because he had drawn a map for them. He said they'd left the hotel heading for Millionaire's Pond on Red Road less than an hour ago. He'd described Chris and Susan Lund to Moku, and she relayed it the best she could to Vic, who in turn relayed it again. Thirdhand information was notoriously anything but accurate, but they all hoped they'd get a chance to dispel that idea by finding them.

With this news, they began to feel more positive about their prospects of finding Viane. It was definitely a good omen. Now the only question remaining was whether she was simply lost, or would they find her injured—or worse? None wanted to carry that thought any farther.

"OK," voiced Stone, his actions quickly taking over, "Teri and I will drive to Millionaire's Pond and look for them to see if they can pinpoint where they found the hat. I've got an old trail map with me that'll work for what we need it for. We'll call as soon as we know anything. Let Pops know what we're up to."

They noticed Randy walking over to his old, beat-up Ford Bronco and get in. He yelled something to the effect of 'I'll be right back; time to go round up my crew" as he drove off.

As Stone and Teri also drove away, they saw Raymond and Vince walking into the parking lot and approaching John and Officer Vic. From what they'd heard Vic talking about, the boys had participated in his Warrior's Path program and were looking forward to the next gathering. As they walked across the parking lot, they appeared apprehensive yet determined. They had obviously made some sort of decision.

"What's up, Officer Vic?" Raymond was standing directly in front of him. "Mind if me and my brother hang around a bit?"

Thirty-Seven

IT WAS AN EVENT that couldn't possibly have had worse timing.

The sound began a long distance away but, like a truck rapidly accelerating on a bumpy road, it was growing closer by the second. It was also becoming quite loud, filling the air with sound as it approached like a huge wave on the ocean's surface, cresting and thundering down onto a helpless shoreline. As the encompassing sound grew near—there was no doubt of it passing directly under your feet—it was inescapable. Earthquakes are like that, and there's little you can do about them except pray.

To island residents, the rapidly approaching rumble was unmistakable. Earthquakes occurred with great regularity on the Big Island, where lava had been belching from the earth almost continually for thirty years, leaving huge voids far below the earth's surface as molten rock escaped its confines. Any armchair scientist will tell you that where such voids are created, matter will move to take its place, the movement often catastrophic to everyone and everything above it.

Thankfully, it wasn't a big quake. It only registered a magnitude of 3.5 on the Richter scale—more noise than shake as the earth settled.

In Hilo, it rattled windows and doors and several shelves in the local antique shop. It caused the barber's hand to jerk, accidentally trimming a large swatch out of his client's hair—he'd conveniently forget to mention it, though. If you had just set your cup of tea on a table to turn the page of your *Deep Green* novel, the cup may have taken the opportunity to walk off the edge and spill on the carpet. Fortunately, not a lot of other damage was inflicted other than in the minds of nervous people standing stock-still in a doorframe of their home for protection—something many island folks had gotten into the habit of doing, as it helped avoid things falling on their head.

LIKE THE TEACUP, though, the shaking that lasted for twenty-four seconds—a lifetime in earthquake lingo—was sufficient time to cause a larger object, like an unconscious human body, to slip dangerously toward the nearest edge of a rock shelf.

If Viane was conscious, the generated fear would have been incapacitating. Unfortunately, or fortunately as was the case, she was unconscious and didn't feel her body drift closer to the edge of the drop-off. She also didn't realize that a relatively substantial piece of the ledge beneath her and that had been supporting her, quite narrow to start with, had broken free and gone crashing to the depths far below. A few smaller chunks of rock also broke free from the walls above her, falling to the depths. One piece, fortunately a smaller one, managed to find her. Even for its size, a mere geological pebble, it hit her left cheek and quickly drew blood before bouncing away.

The vibrating earth had managed to gain a stronghold on Viane's body on the now-diminished ledge as it loosened the surface beneath her. As her drift toward the drop-off approached the point of no return, one of her backpack straps snagged a fingerhold ridge of rock and stubbornly held fast, arresting her movement fractions of an inch from a fatal plunge into the empty place below.

IN THE PARKING LOT somewhere above the few remaining individuals, waiting to begin the hike, they felt the old volcano rattle as the noise passed beyond them. It managed to trigger an avalanche of fear deep in their souls for their loved one.

Randy didn't feel the earth shake as he was still on the highway rounding up his men. Besides, he'd lived on the Big Island for so long he was immune to all but the very worst of them.

Pops was in his pickup after having left the park headquarters heading toward the trailhead parking lot, excited to begin searching. Like Randy, he felt nothing of the movement beneath him.

Stone and Teri were just passing Keaau turning toward Pahoa and Kalapana and Red Road, hoping to find the tourist couple. They felt nothing but a perceived bumpy road surface.

Only John, Officer Vic Morro, Raymond, and Vince, standing in the parking lot waiting for the others to return, felt the earth tremble and knew exactly what it was—and what it meant. It was a bad omen.

Viane, like most of those who would soon be searching for her, was ignorant of the escalated danger she was in and of the narrow canvas strap that was holding her life.

Thirty-Eight

"THIS ROAD MUST BE on the top of the list in the car rentals manual of roads to be very cautious driving on. It's probably number one on either that list or the list of roads that say stay off." Teri trusted Stone's driving completely— well, almost completely. What she didn't trust was Red Road and the other drivers that passed by. Thank God there was very little traffic to speak of as they made their way around another blind curve.

After leaving the others at the trailhead parking lot, they had driven to Keaau, turned right, passed Pahoa to Kalapana—the end of the highway and the beginning of the ocean. They'd turned left onto the narrow Kalapana-Kapoho Road, affectionately known by local residents as Red Road. It was paved for a few miles before changing back into its original hardpacked red cinder trail. It was wide enough for two cars to pass except for a few hair-raising spots that were anything but. It rose and fell on its way over small roller-coaster hills, turning sharply in places where the road builders had opted to deviate around a tree instead of cutting it down. The road had been in place for a very long time and followed an ancient path known as the King's Trail, a pathway from centuries past. Tourists drove Red Road with caution. It was the local drivers who seemingly drove with a vengeance—the ever-present tourists in their domain were not overly welcomed.

The tropical vegetation was lush and thick with a canopy of old-growth trees. It was a storybook picture of the Hawaiian landscape. There was a rich mixture of trees: kukui nut, ohia, hala, coconut palms and a sundry other non-native behemoths, their branches swaying over the roadway essentially blocking out most of the sun. A few homesteads appeared along the way when clearings in the forested land came into view. Some of the homes were architectural marvels, with beautifully kept lawns and gardens, frequently built next door to a house that appeared thrown together with scrounged sheet metal and driftwood, their yards unkempt. A proliferation of rusted-out vehicles, bikes, wheelbarrows, and a few washing machines well past their prime littering any available space. The only similarity between the two homes was their yards, which stretched from the roadway all the way to the pounding surf a few hundred feet away.

"It would be an interesting but very solitary existence living along here, wouldn't it?" voiced Teri, looking through an opening in the vegetation to a wide expanse of ocean. "You sure wouldn't want to forget to buy milk at the store before heading home. I don't think I could exist here," she admitted. "I'd feel too isolated from the rest of the world."

Stone admitted that neither could he unless his house had a helicopter pad, a hot tub beside the ocean, and a pier big enough for a large boat. "The isolation is probably the main reason many of these people live way out here in the first place. Just think, you could run around naked as a myna bird and only attract the attention of a few mosquitoes."

"Are you saying that's all I would attract...just a few mosquitoes?" Her eyebrow rose with an accusing question as she looked over at Stone, doing her best to suppress a smile.

All she got in return was a devilish expression that said more than she wanted to think about right then, so she let it go.

"Driving this road reminds me of something, as so many places in the islands do. When Viane is safely found and all has returned to normal, there's a place at the end of this road I'd like to show you. Along the coast a few miles ahead, behind the houses in Kapoho, is an amazing lagoon that borders the green lawns of many of the house lots. It's like a gigantic saltwater lagoon: clean, clear, and heated by volcanic vents. *And* you rarely see anyone there. It's a hidden warm-water oasis."

"Too bad we can't go now. I could use a hot pond right now, and then I could *probably* show you a couple things that would attract your attention more than just mosquitoes would." There was no fun in letting it go—completely.

They drove past the aging Opihikau Congregational Church before pulling into Mackenzie State Park to use the facilities there.

As they continued on, the red cinder parking lot for Ahalanui Park, better known by old-time residents as Millionaire's Pond, or just *warm pond*, came up on the right. It was empty but for three cars and a fire-engine-red pickup truck whose monstrous tires came level with the top of the car next to it. They walked around the large pavilion and house and out onto a lawn overlooking a large rectangular pond half the size of a football field, lofty coconut trees dotting the green grass and lining the ocean beyond. A few breakers were crashing over the lava rock barrier at the *makai* end, cascading into the pond. Two young children were sitting on a submerged concrete slab bursting with laughter with every wave that hit as the spray rained down over them.

The pond averaged only three and a half feet deep with warm, ninety-five-degree water. Several fissures on the floor of the pond opened to the depths far below where lava percolated, heating the water above. Three lifeguard stands stood empty as the lone life guard on duty went about picking up trash on the surrounding lawn. *I bet he's the one that owns the monster truck.* There were nine people in the pond or sitting at picnic tables on the grass around the perimeter enjoying the shade from the hot sun.

"I guess we'll just have to call out names until Chris and Susan respond." Several of the people in and around the pond appeared to be local people from the area. Moku had said the couple was Caucasian, which cut their choice to four individuals.

They targeted the couple closest to the pond's rock wall, a few feet away. The couple was floating on their backs over one of the hot water vents, arms stretched lazily to the side, seemingly lost to the world. An embroidered fishing reel was visible on the crown of a lime green hat the man wore. Amazing that it would stay on his head half buried in the water.

"Excuse me." Stone's voice came out louder than he had intended. Eyes opened immediately in response as they struggled to get their footing and stand up.

"Sorry to startle you," Stone went on. "You both looked so peaceful I hesitated to speak up, but this is an emergency. Would you happen to be Chris and Susan Lund?"

The man responded, voice not at all friendly, "That depends. Why are you asking?" His voice sounded like a gravel road.

The woman, realizing there didn't appear to be a threat, said, "Yes, we are, but how would you know that?" She made her way to the edge of the pond, her forehead crinkling in an attempt to understand how strangers would know their names. The man, Chris, remained where he was, a scowl prominent in his features.

"What's the emergency about? How do you two know our names?" she repeated her question, voice edging toward demand. By her questioning demeanor, her reasoning had settled on the fearful side of possibilities, expecting to hear the worst of news about their children, pet dog, or God knew what. Stone could understand all the emotions the couple were likely experiencing. He probably would have been just as suspicious had roles been reversed, and he knew he needed to put these people at ease, and sensing his and Teri's calmness were already beginning to do that.

Stone knelt on one knee beside the water so the man wouldn't have to strain his neck looking up as he waded over to stand beside his wife. "I apologize if we've startled both of you. My name is Stone, and this is Teri White. We understand you were hiking on Mauna Loa two days ago and found a purple hat."

Comprehension washed over them as they looked at each other with noticeable relief and puzzled humor. "Must be a pretty valuable hat for you to come looking for us," Chris replied. "How did you manage to find us way out here anyway? This isn't the most popular spot in the islands, as we found out."

"We found out via the island telegraph."

"What? I don't understand that." It was Susan's turn to speak up.

"The hotel's concierge, Don Nakiohana, has a sister who is a policewoman and a friend of the father of the woman who lost the hat. It's complicated—island residents are a pretty close-knit group. Family and friend connections here are like a spider's web—it runs through the fiber of the community. You apparently made a good impression on Don. He remembered you and remembered exactly where you were heading."

"Does that hat have anything to do with the broken piece of rope that we also found? It looked to lead directly into a hole." It was Chris.

Now it was Stone and Teri's turn to express surprise. "It certainly might. We weren't told anything about a piece of rope or a hole. Information about it apparently didn't filter down to us."

Susan spoke and explained what they saw and the subsequent lack of response to any of their calls down into the hole. They had simply assumed whoever lost the hat had used the rope to enter the opening. But from what they could discern from the lack of response, there was nobody down there anymore. They figured whoever it was forgot to pick up their hat as they left, although the broken rope remained a question mark.

"You don't suppose the missing woman has somehow gotten lost down that hole, do you? Does that sound like something this friend of yours might do?" Chris obviously possessed a questioning mind.

"Not necessarily, but stuff does happen," answered Teri. "This hole you mentioned is the first real clue we have as to where she might have gotten to and why she hasn't contacted any of us. Maybe this is the answer we're looking for."

"The opening really looked quite small for anyone to fall through." Susan climbed up the rock steps that edged the pond, dried her hands on a towel close by, and brought a camera over to show them something. Her husband remained in the water. She scrolled through an endless stream of pictures until she came to a shot of the hat, the rope, and an odd lava formation. The opening could be seen not far from it. It appeared as if the rope led right to it. Chris's observation was right. Stone took a picture of the picture on Susan's camera screen. He knew the picture of a picture wouldn't be very good, but he thought it'd do for reference when they were on the trail. Better than nothing.

"If we were to show you a map of the trail, could you point to where this was?" Stone inquired.

"I don't think whatever we could pinpoint for you would prove to be very accurate. It's a very long, monotonous trail, as we discovered. We could probably hike back up there and show you, though."

"Would you really be willing to do that? I must say I stand amazed." Stone was astonished these people who didn't know them from a long-dead tree stump would go to that extent to help.

"Of course—more adventure for us and a chance to give back," Chris offered. "But we'll have to see about extending our stay at the hotel for another day first, then check with the car rental people. We've already checked out and were planning to head for the airport and Honolulu after our swim."

"If you're willing to do this, I think we can arrange another night or two at the hotel, and even handle any charges Hawaiian Airlines wants to collect for making the changes." Stone was certain Pops and the others would support the idea and share in any costs.

"Give us a few moments to shower the salt off and collect our things, and we'll follow you back to the trail."

Thirty-Nine

STONE DROVE INTO THE trailhead parking lot just as Pops was emerging from his truck. Teri had mentioned seeing Pops's recognizable odd-colored brake lights a distance in front of them as they drove up Mauna Loa Road. They parked and got out, and saw him getting out of his pickup, clutching a sheaf of paper in his right hand, his face giving the appearance of being deeply troubled by something.

Viane would be an easy assumption, but there was something else going on. Stone knew he'd tell them about it if he thought whatever it was that was on his mind seemed important enough to share. Just as they started to group together, Chris and Susan pulled in. John, Vic, and the twins were sitting in the shade of a large *kiawe* tree, waiting for everyone to return and start preparations for finding Viane. They were still very shaken by the earthquake and wanted desperately to talk about it.

There was no sign of Randy and his group yet. They'd be along soon.

Stone had called John to alert him about the broken piece of rope found beside Viane's hat and the close proximity of the hat and rope to a vertical opening into what sounded like a lava tube based on Chris and Susan's description.

John had relayed that information to his father who, at that point, was still sitting in the ranger's office. He had explained what Stone had learned from the tourists about the rope and cave opening. Pops, who'd done a lot of spelunking in his life, hadn't taken the news well. He was familiar with all the scenarios this news presented. Most cave mishaps, thank God, ended wel,l but there was always that remaining small percentage that went the other way.

After hearing John mention the lava tube opening, Pops remembered Viane, excited with her find, telling him all about a lava tube on Mauna Loa that she'd discovered and planned to check out someday. He was upset with himself for not having thought of that earlier—they could have already been on the search, and maybe even found her by now. It was an obvious place for her to head for. Pops could only shake his head in dismay at himself, and at his distress with the ranger for not seeing fit to keep the broken length of rope. It would have told part of the story. The ranger, though, offered no apology, and Pops was OK with that because now they knew. He didn't put much stock in thinking about what-ifs.

A call from Moku to her brother was all it took to secure the visitors two additional nights' stay along with a dinner at Harrington's, the classic old restaurant on the east side of Hilo that sat on the edge of a large koi pond surrounded by coconut palms. Between Pops and Stone, all the charges would be taken care of. There was no guarantee that Viane was still on the mountain where her hat was found, much less down a hole; but Stone, Pops, and John figured it was the best they had and was something they needed to investigate. Right then, it was their *only* known course of action, and they were happy picking up a share of any costs incurred just for the possibility.

As for Chris and Susan, they couldn't be happier with their extended stay. They'd wanted to hike down to where the lava from the ongoing eruption was pouring into the ocean below the Chain of Craters Road, adding hundreds of acres to the island—something they'd read. They also wanted to drive to the southern tip of the island but had run out of time to do either. Now they would have the opportunity to do it all.

As everyone gathered in the shade of the *kiawe* tree, it became apparent that something quite traumatic had happened. John's and Vic's faces were pale and looked badly shaken.

"Didn't you feel the earthquake?" John exclaimed, looking from face to face for confirmation. Seeing nothing but surprised looks, he continued talking, arms waving excitedly, addressing most of his speech to his father. "After we talked, Pops, a quake hit. This mountain shook like it had a bug on its back. I could have sworn it wasn't going to stop. How could you not feel it?" Astonishment was evident in his voice and in the look on his face.

The implication of a quake rolling through was immediate to everyone. John's and Vic's concern was understandable. Having just learned that Viane may be stuck down a vertical lava tube, an earthquake would top the list of the worst-case scenario of possibilities. Quakes on the Big Island were the number one cause of many below-surface caves and lava tubes collapsing in on themselves. Bulldozer cave-ins were far down the list of causes and were considered inconsequential—except, perhaps, to the one driving the bulldozing. If Viane was indeed at the bottom of a cave, her chance of getting hit by falling hunks of rock was enormous.

The six quickly outfitted themselves with everything they thought they needed, including a collapsible stretcher, just in case: Pops had adamantly insisted on it. There was a new urgency in everyone's actions as they stepped out onto the trail in single file. Randy and his crew were nowhere to be seen, and they could wait no longer.

It was overcast and a chilly fifty-eight degrees—good hiking weather. They would soon be above the cloud line where the sun's glare would intensify and could cook an egg still in its shell, but the air would get cooler. Temperatures at the summit in September could hover in the forties during the day and drop to the high twenties by nightfall—always a contradiction considering it was Hawaii. December and January would often see the summit slumbering beneath a blanket of snow—more contradiction.

Chris and Susan were strong hikers and led the way. Stone and Teri were content to follow, with Pops and John not far behind. Pops's leg was giving him problems, but he wasn't about to stop or complain. Teri had been worried about him but quickly changed her mind when he came up to walk beside them, still limping but breathing as if he were in a forested park while she was beginning to draw labored breaths from the thinning oxygen.

Officer Vic had to return to duty. He was disappointed at not being able to join the search. Before leaving, though, he asked Raymond and Vince if they needed a ride home. They had declined and instead asked if they could tag along with the others. They trailed well behind. Vince wasn't able to hike too fast, but both were eager to be a part of the adventure. If truth were known, both of them would have taken an opportunity to dig a ditch through solid rock if it had been offered instead of being taken home in a police car. Following at a distance behind the others, interestingly for both of them, they were feeling the edges of guilt about what may have happened because of what they'd done. The feeling was something new to both of them, and they weren't sure how to handle it except to keep trailing silently along.

THREE HOURS INTO THE hike, the thought began to prod at all of them that it was past the middle of the afternoon and the inevitability of dusk was approaching.

They had been so anxious to find Viane that none had thought too clearly about the time. Various ideas were being tossed around as they trekked up the trail, but no one was willing to take the lead on doing anything but keep going. What was the alternative?

Without warning, Susan exclaimed, "There!" She was pointing to a spot a long way off the trail and immediately quickened her pace in the direction she was pointing. The others followed, but none other than Chris could yet see the unusual rock formation that had prompted Susan's outburst. No one was sure of exactly where they should be looking. The excitement grew, nonetheless; they didn't have to see it.

As Stone approached the formation that Susan rushed up beside, he felt his heart suddenly drop like one of the rocks he'd been stepping over as he moved closer. Teri, feeling much the same, squeezed Stone's hand so tightly he frowned but he kept hold as they walked closer. There was nothing to be seen but the rock formation. As notable as it was, the surrounding monotonous landscape looked no different from what they had been hiking on for endless hours: no cave opening was visible, and the thought of the quake closing it immediately brought an element of panic careening through his thoughts.

As he and Teri came up beside Susan, Chris moved past them and knelt down over a hole a few feet beyond that at first looked to be about the size a mongoose would make—but it was still there. As they walked close, they noticed it had been partially hidden from their view by the uneven terrain—that's why they had failed to see it in the first place. They now noticed that it was actually big enough for a *normal-sized* body to fit through. Stone silently voiced a prayer of thanks. He knew he wasn't the only one feeling a sense of relief. He felt Teri's arm snake around his waist and squeeze tightly; they were connected even in their perception of events. They could feel the cool air wafting up out of the hole as they bent closer.

Susan opened Stone's backpack and extracted the flashlight, and together they tied a cord around the end of it and secured the other end to a large rock. She wasn't about to take a chance losing their only light. She bent close to the opening and turned the flashlight on as everyone crowded close in an attempt to see down into the darkness.

"Oh my God." Susan's passionate outburst froze everyone in mid-movement.

Forty

The sting's aftermath

MIKE WAS BEGINNING TO accept and appreciate the reality that the boat thieves roaming around the island were actually making a choice with the boats they stole: some shipped to the mainland while others kept in the islands. The criterion for that distinction was not obvious, but Mike knew the information would be extremely helpful when he eventually figured it out.

With the success of the sting operation, he would watch to see which way the thieves handled the decoy boat. He wasn't entirely convinced that even knowing what they eventually did with it would help him gain a clear picture of *why*. It could end up being as simple as a toss of a coin or the twist of a beer cap. The one thing he *was* certain about was that the thefts were confined to Oahu; none of the neighbor islands were being affected. He'd called the other island police departments and gotten negative responses in return.

He now suspected the owners of the Haiku property were acting on their own with threads of connection to mainland operators. From the video of the sting that he'd watched more times than he cared to think about, they didn't give any indication of being very sophisticated—in fact, they were close to the opposite.

The registered owners, according to records, were Alysdon Lau and Bill Jefferson. He'd already shared this information with Guy, trusting Guy would do as asked and not say anything. Mike had asked him to be patient and wait for HPD for the outcome.

The Haiku property was owned jointly by the men, and both carried rap sheets for minor theft and B&E; but neither had served time in OCCC (the Oahu Community Correctional Center). Hard evidence was needed before that could happen, and Mike hoped ample evidence would be found when they did the physical search of the house and property.

Knowing the boat involved in the sting remained in the suspect's backyard helped tremendously. He knew judges were skeptical when looking at evidence gathered from sting operations since anything staged often led to too many gray areas in the validity of evidence. He was confident, though, that the case could move forward quickly now; his people had documented everything they had done perfectly.

With the video he possessed, he knew he could persuade a judge to issue a search warrant—hopefully, first thing in the morning. His instinct told him the two thieves would be more than willing to open up and fill in some of the blanks about the details once he confronted them with the evidence. His physical size alone could intimidate thieves and often had in the past. According to their rap sheets, they were two-bit crooks with two strikes against them. The real threat of OCCC jail time was sure to make them shake in their slippers. He would definitely call their attention to that possibility.

EARLY THE NEXT MORNING, on the windward side of the island in the community of Kaaawa, Tim Giuseppe was slowly loading various pieces of his precious artwork into the back of a worn-out, rusting-red, balding-tired pickup. Working from a wheelchair presented certain difficulties, but he'd done it enough times in his life that he was well practiced and had long ago found ways to overcome most of his limitations.

Most of his art pieces were large, so he'd devised ways to handle them as he went about loading the bed of the truck. Taking his time, he eventually managed to maneuver a tarp over the pile and snug it down tightly. He'd made so many trips over the Pali highway he could win bets that some form of moisture, rain, or mist, would show up before he got to the tunnels that divided the windward from the leeward side of the island. He didn't want any of his artwork to get damp and perhaps ruined, and therefore unsellable.

Art on the Zoo Fence Hawaii, located on Monsarrat Avenue across from Kapiolani Park and the Waikiki Shell, was a regular weekend event that he counted on to make a little money. Artists from all over Oahu brought their work to hang on the chain-link fence that bordered the zoo. It drew a lot of attention, resulting in a constant stream of tourists, as well as local people strolling past. Families brought their kids to see the animals in the zoo or just to sit in the grass in the area around the zoo and feed the cloud of pigeons and to wander around to look at the artwork.

Tim's journey getting there, though, was always a strain for both him and his aging truck. The drive up the highway to the tunnels just about pushed them both to their limits. His legs, with limited muscle use, tired quickly when he drove any stretch of time over thirty minutes, while his truck's water temperature rapidly rose to the red overheating line on the dashboard's gauge. He tolerated the discomfort and effort because he counted on making a few sales, which made the effort of getting there unavoidable; he had little else to trade for money.

Tim was very proud of his artistic ability. He could glue together parts of boats that he had cut into small pieces in such a unique fashion it never failed to attract attention; and he set his prices low enough to encourage buying. His style was rustic: his *canvas* was simply a piece of boat siding cut to size; the frames were salvaged deck or railing wood. He was an inventive artist as well as frugal in his artistic pursuit.

He arrived at the zoo's fence early enough to capture the primo spot closest to the corner of Monsarrat and Kalakaua. He pulled to the curb to begin unloading. It took some effort to get his handicapped body extricated from the truck's cab and positioned to get into his wheelchair. His truck had a difficult time as well—it kept on rumbling and shaking even after Tim removed the key, like a nervous sprinter at the starting line of a race. He'd had the truck for so many years he took no notice of its lingering rumbling. It would quit on its own when it was ready; it didn't bother him. He had no idea what to do about it anyway.

An inventor by necessity, Tim had fashioned a unique method of *hanging* his collapsed wheelchair on the side of the truck. When he opened the door to get out, all he had to do was carefully slide his butt off the seat straight into the chair and then hydraulic himself to the ground. He thought he'd be smart to patent the idea but had never quite gotten around to doing so yet.

Settled comfortably, he rolled to the back of the truck bed, pleased he'd gotten here so early. The end spot was the best on the fence because of the visibility from both streets as well as being out from beneath the overhanging branches of the too-numerous banyan trees and the resultant multitude of pigeons and myna birds that congregated there. To Tim, the birds were a constant menace to his customers, to his truck, to himself, and to his fine artwork, not that the latter would ever be considered *fine*; he was wise to the reality of things.

GUY AND DEBORAH WERE up early, pacing around their kitchen, a second cup of coffee already in hand and half gone. They were both nervous about the coming search, but also quite anxious to get on with it and see what turned up. If nothing else, Guy would gain an opportunity to examine his old Buick and see if it was worth hauling home—*if* he was allowed to haul it home. He wasn't sure about the statute of limitations and how it applied to stolen property that turned up in this fashion. Also at issue, and perhaps most crucial, was how Deborah would feel about having it sitting in their driveway up on blocks taking up precious space.

"Let's grab an early lunch at Canoes and then walk to Kapiolani Park. It'll make waiting for Mike's call a lot more pleasant," Guy offered. "While we're there, we can walk the beach and check out who's teaching surfing these days. I'd like to see if any of the old-timers I once knew are still hanging around."

On rare occasions, Guy wished it was possible to return to that carefree and immensely enjoyable life that he had experienced as a Waikiki beach boy—with Deborah by his side, of course—a lifestyle that he'd once thought would never come to an end.

After a delicious lunch of *mahimahi* cannelloni at Canoes, spending relaxed moments watching body surfers ride the waves off Kuhio Beach, they strolled through Waikiki and wandered along the beach. Guy noticed all the beach boys were young, and he didn't recognize anyone: all the old-timers like him, were gone. He and Deborah turned toward the park and the artists displaying their work there. They had no intention of buying anything but were always curious to see what was there.

As they came close, though, they spotted something much too familiar. Their breath caught as they tried to take in what they saw.

Hanging from the fence confronting them was a five-foot-wide painting, an exact reproduction of their boat's transom complete with the colorful lehua blossoms bordering the name *Lehua*. An older man in a wheelchair noticed their interest and rolled toward them, a bud of a smile beginning to form on his lips.

"Don't that picture just grab your fancy?" he asked innocently, hoping to encourage conversation that would lead to a sale.

Deborah's initial instinct was to accost the man with a broom handle and demand he tell them where he saw their boat; but instead, she repressed the impulse and instead politely asked, her teeth partially clenched, "Did you paint this?" She thought it was a logical question since the man had an easel set up beside a cash box. He hadn't wet any brushes yet, though.

"Yes, madam, all the things you see here, I either painted or glued together. All things considered," he humbly admitted, "I don't usually go to this sort of work"—he pointed at the picture—"but I know it'd sell quick. If you want it, I can make you a real special deal. Let's say, a hundred dollars."

"We really like it," claimed Guy, also holding back aroused emotions. "But if we bought it now, we'd have no way to take it with us." They actually didn't have sufficient cash with them and didn't want to carry it the long distance to their car anyway—it was simply too hot for that. At the same time, though, Guy didn't want to miss out and take the chance of someone else buying it. "What if we gave you 50 percent—fifty dollars in cash right now and you hold it for us? We can arrange to get it later and pay you the rest. I'll even add 10 percent just for your troubles? What time do you leave here?" Guy was hoping to stall and gain time so he could think of what he should do, hoping the old man wouldn't get suspicious. He wanted to contact Mike and get advice on the best way to proceed but they'd have to walk a distance away in order to use their cell phone for that.

Tim unknowingly resolved Guy's dilemma. "I can do that, but you'd have to get here before four o'clock o'clock, as I godda pack up and head over the hill. Kaaawa's a far drive, especially for me and my old truck," he said, tapping his leg with a long-handled paintbrush he'd been holding the entire time, indicating his leg was wholly responsible for the distance he had to drive.

"You want a hundred dollars for it, just as it is, with frame and all?" Deborah asked the man again. She was also stalling, not knowing exactly what Guy was thinking, but she had her suspicions.

Deborah was well acquainted with boats from the hours spent working beside Guy. She knew that the wood of the picture's frame looked very much like old deck wood, perhaps from someone else's missing boat. Regardless of whether this represented a dead-end to finding answers to their missing boat, she wanted the picture. The artist may have innocently taken a camera photo of their boat and painted its likeness, but she couldn't imagine when or where that could have happened. She reached into her purse for her wallet; no further thought was needed. She knew Guy was right there with her on this. She was also sensing a definite connection between Haiku, Kaaawa, boat parts, and paintings, and that puzzled her. The fact was plain that all the art surrounding this man was either a painting of a boat or what appeared to be boat pieces glued together to form bird baths, small tables, and a few other things that defied explanation. Everything added conviction to her observation. The only thing not in context was that the man seemed to be so genuine.

"In case our timing gets tight, where's your truck parked? We could meet you there." Guy's plan was to get the license plate number and have Mike come up with an address. The artist had already told them his name. Mike would have no trouble verifying that.

"That's my truck right there behind you," he was pointing with the paint brush. "I'll be curbside here around three-thirty loading up."

Guy had noticed the old pickup when they first approached the fence but thought it was an abandoned vehicle, not a viable operating machine.

"Tell you what," the man continued, "I'll load it last, and if you don't get back in time, it'll most likely be right here next weekend. And if you don't show up, then that'd be OK too 'cause I got part of your money." He feigned a look of innocence that Deborah thought was almost sincere. He seemed a little *kolohe*, a rascal with a twinkle in his eyes that gave him away. In the same breath, though, she suspected he'd have no qualms about keeping the money, sell the picture again, and never look back.

She was still tempted to threaten him with something tangible and demand he tell her where he saw their boat but decided she didn't want to take the chance of rousing his suspicion and perhaps chase him into hiding.

Forty-One

LEAVING TIM AND THEIR partially-acquired painting hanging on the fence, Guy called Mike and filled him in on the surprise they had discovered. He wanted Mike's advice on how to proceed but was equally curious to find out how the search warrant was progressing. He'd expected to have heard from Mike already. Mike put him on hold and didn't return for a full five minutes. His voice immediately fell into a routine, long-learned monotone as he rattled off the information he'd been able to find.

"Your artist's name is indeed Tim. Born Timothy Lane Giuseppe on April 20th nineteen hundred thirty-eight at Kapiolani Hospital. His address is a house in Kaaawa on Makua Village Road. It appears he has no priors, so we have no further record on him. Either a clean life or a well-hidden one. His driver's license detail shows he's physically challenged and must use either a wheelchair or crutches." Mike's voice softened as he explained it was easy information to obtain when you have a vehicle license number matched with a reference sheet put together by a detail-oriented promoter of the art show. They have a special category for wheelchair-bound artist. Not too many artists fall into that particular category. In telling Guy all this, Mike knew he was stepping over a line of police ethics as the law and good police policy dictate he shouldn't be divulging any information. He liked both Guy and Deborah and wanted to help bring a conclusion to the mystery of where their boat ended up.

"As for the warrant, we expect to have it in hand in an hour's time, just as soon as the judge returns from the court room. Let's hold off thinking about Mr. Giuseppe until after our Haiku search. It may dictate how we need to proceed, including what we'll need to do about Tim. I'll go ahead and add his property to the warrant so we have it if we need it. Don't pick up the painting," he advised Guy. "Let him take it home. It could help us knowing it's on his property if we have to pull his place into our search parameter. Since you've paid for a part of it, let's bank on your initial thinking that Tim appears somewhat honest and will hold onto it until next weekend. I'll see you at L&L in Kaneohe. Let's plan to meet there in two hours. I'll call if the timing changes."

"I DISLIKE WALKING AWAY from it." Guy looked quite distraught. "It's like turning our backs on the boat we poured so many dreams into and put in so much effort fixing."

Deborah moved closer and took hold of Guy's arm as they approached their car. They planned to drive over the Likelike Highway to Kaneohe and L & L Drive-Inn as Mike instructed, and wait there for the search team to arrive. They would have to trust that their newly acquired piece of artwork would be on hold for them at the artist's house. The thought of getting a small order of *limu poke* from the drive-in erased some of her concerns as they drove toward Kaneohe.

As they pulled into the small parking lot Mike and two other uniforms had somehow already arrived. *There goes my limu poke,* thought a disappointed Guy.

Mike got out of his patrol car when he saw them arrive. He drove a midnight blue Ford Mustang, a very recognizable unmarked police cruiser to anyone who had an interest, hidden or otherwise, in such things. The other officers Mike brought with him remained sitting in a separate car. He approached them and leaned over, looking in through Guy's open window. Mike explained, in answer to an unvoiced question on both their faces, that the department was stretched thin at the moment, as any extra officers along with those currently off-duty had been pulled in to watch over the activities surrounding the Trans-Pacific Yacht Race that was in progress. Honolulu was the termination of the bi-annual race, one that stretches from San Pedro, California to Waikiki. The first yacht had crossed the Diamond Head lighthouse finish line at 1:37 a.m. morning, a fact that both Deborah and Guy were well aware of having volunteered to help out in the past. They knew the parties were already beginning around the Ala Wai Yacht Harbor and Waikiki Yacht Club and there was no question the celebrants would overflow like the incoming tide onto the streets of Waikiki. HPD was needed to show a solid presence in order to keep celebrants out of trouble—an impossible task. He assured Guy that they were well manned for this search. He considered it a simple and straightforward process.

"When we get to the house, you two remain in your car until I let you know it's OK to join us inside," he instructed the two civilians. "You both OK with all that?"

They both agreed.

It was a short five-minute drive from the drive-in. They pulled to a stop in front of the Haiku house. Guy and Deborah felt an odd sensation being back here again—like returning to the scene of a sinister crime unfolding in one of the movies they'd recently watched but now they were playing an integral part of.

MIKE AND HIS MEN had obviously choreographed their plan or had done similar searches to where their actions had become routine. No sooner had they stopped in front of the house than Mike and one officer went up to the front door while the third pushed his way through the vegetation toward the backyard, the same place Deborah and Guy had been short days before.

As the officer made his way as quietly as possible through the brush toward the chain-link fence, not an easy task, he heard Mike ring the front door chime. At the same moment the chime sounded, he caught a glimpse of two men rapidly exiting the yard through a gate in the fence on the opposite side from where he stood. By the empty bottles scattered on the grass between two lawn chairs under a large ulu tree, he had to assume the men had either heard him or the very-audible doorbell and took off. He radioed Mike through his lapel transmitter and told him what happened and quickly mentioned the decoy boat was right in the middle of the yard still on the trailer, seemingly untouched.

"Stay there, Moss, they may come back," instructed Mike. "The front door is unlocked, so we're going in."

THE SIGHT OF A uniform pushing through the bushes beside their fence simultaneously hearing their doorbell sound convinced the duo it was time to end their comfortable beer break and quickly leave. It was definitely time to figure out what to do next and begin planning some damage control. They had thought their crime spree was 99 percent fool-proof, but it appeared that the 1 percent negative chance was suddenly being played out.

When they had the fence built years before they had added a gate in the side of their yard for convenience. It gave them access into their neighbor's unfenced yard, a route they often took when they went to visit their drinking buddy who lived several houses away. They knew their buddy wasn't home at this time of the day but knew where he kept the spare house key and went straight to it. They just hoped their buddy's wife wasn't home—she could be a real screamer, especially when it involved the two of them and an uninvited intrusion through the back door. Any fondness they could find in themselves for her was purely wasted effort. They could receive a kinder response from a road grader with no working brakes.

AS MIKE OPENED THE front door and went in, he called out, "Anyone here? This is the Honolulu Police Department. We have a search warrant for this house and property."

His words were met with silence. He repeated the words, louder, and then waited for a response; but still none came— he hadn't really expected to hear one, but he had to be sure.

Deborah and Guy remained in their car as Mike had asked them to. Through the car's open windows, they could just barely hear the cop in the backyard talking loudly into his lapel transmitter. They couldn't distinguish his words, though.

ALL ALYSDON AND BILL could do was guess at what was currently taking place in their house and why. The only thing they could figure out in their beer-soggy minds was the police came because of the boat thefts—their most recent endeavor. They both thought of the boat in their yard with dismay but at the same time couldn't believe it had been reported missing so soon.

Their crime wave, actually more of a ripple as they liked to refer to it, had gone through growth phases, beginning with taking whatever they could get their hands on. They had moved on to cars before finally refocusing their efforts on boats. Cars had proved too hard to get rid of, as evidenced by the old Buick, the first car they ever stole, that sat in their yard growing weeds, so they had abandoned that effort. The boat thing, though, was way different and more lucrative. It had come about through a chance meeting with a fellow bar patron late one night while they sat nursing a beer in Biggies Lounge in Kailua. It sounded simple enough and virtually detection proof. Their stream of successful experiences stealing boats along with all their other exploits had left them with a feeling of invincibility. They had learned to steal with impunity, and often in broad daylight. They reasoned that if they stole with unbridled contempt, no sideways glances or looking over their shoulders—*authoritatively* as Alysdon called it—they could usually get away clean without raising any eyebrows. Alysdon equated their actions with stealing a wheelbarrow full of sawdust. Casual observers would simply wonder why anyone would want to steal sawdust. No one would think to wonder about the wheelbarrow.

"Tim must'a done something stupid that tipped the cops. What else could it be that tipped them off?" Bill was feeling guilty about trying to sell the outboards and was thinking his actions may have tipped off someone but decided to keep that to himself.

Their thinking was a bit fuzzy. They'd just opened their fifth beer when they had to drop them and run. They proceeded to help themselves to their friend's abundant supply, positive it would help them think of a plan of action much quicker. Their friend had a really old "beer" refrigerator missing its handle but they had the secret of opening it and relished the fact it kept beer perfectly chilled, just the way they liked it.

Comfortably sitting in their friend's living room out of sight and very happy that their friend's wife was not at home, they quickly downed a beer and were ready to open another. They preferred Primo Beer instead of the Oly their friend insisted on buying, so they were drinking slower than they normally would have. On the following beer, they realized their best course of action was to be aggressive—to act like they were the injured party; and oddly enough, they were beginning to feel they actually were. They decided that being aggressive would get the cops out of their house faster with less argument.

Explaining the roomful of stolen property was a stumbling block in their aggression plan, and they really hoped there would be no need to explain it, just as long as they got there fast enough. They were just sober enough to know they had waited too long to get rid of the evidence. They came up with the plausible story that they'd gotten a great deal at the swap meet at the old Kailua Drive-In. As for the old car and forklift that sat in their backyard for so many years, they figured there wasn't any need to invent a cover story to cover them. They were stuck on how to explain the boat but knew they'd come up with a good reason if asked.

AFTER THIRTY MINUTES, MIKE came out and motioned Deborah and Guy to come inside with instructions to not touch anything, not even a door handle or a light switch.

"Follow me," he said and proceeded down a short hallway, turning right into a room that, by appearance, had once been a garage but had been remodeled to become part of the living area. It had large sliding glass doors facing the front street, as well as another set of glass doors facing the back. Both had blackout curtains pulled closed. The other two walls held two-foot-deep metal shelves and were covered with an assortment of boat-related items. Lying on a gray indoor-outdoor carpet in the center of the room were two Johnson 55 house-power outboard motors that appeared to be almost new.

Deborah and Guy squeezed each other's hand in anticipation as Guy bent down to look at the underside of the engine cowlings. On advice from friends, he'd engraved his social security number into the hard casing on each of them as well as on all the various removable parts of their boat. Not wanting to make the number obvious to anyone that it was a social security number he'd omitted the hyphens and reversed the nine-digit sequence. As anticipated, numbers were there, and they were his.

Over the next half hour, he was able to identify all the electronics and steering mechanism that were once a part of *Lehua*. It was bittersweet to see the bits and pieces that he had sweated over installing and not know if their boat even existed anymore.

Just as Mike finished his note taking and was about to radio in an APB on the two men, they all heard the front door burst open with a loud clatter before violently banging shut, sending a vibration rattling through the house.

A demanding, threatening, and somewhat slurred voice came in with the opened door and boomed down the hallway, "Who's in here? Who's in our house?"

Forty-Two

On Mauna Loa

Susan's alarming outburst upon peering down into the lava tube sent a shockwave coursing through everyone around her, halting them in mid-movement. No one could understand what had happened or what horrifying sight she'd witnessed. It was a quick shriek.Then dead silence. She remained transfixed, not moving, ostensibly fixated by what she was seeing.

Whether everyone had been subconsciously expecting to look down and see Viane standing waving up at them, waiting to be hauled out, or, worse, not see her at all, wasn't clear. Up to this point, no one had been willing to voice their expectations. An eerie stillness on the subject had unintentionally reigned.

Surprisingly, neither Stone nor Teri had mentioned their thoughts either on what they expected to find, if or when Viane was found. They had talked in vague generalities, almost as if discussing detailed thoughts would end up creating those negative omens and setting the stage for what they would ultimately discover. *Self-fulfilling prophecies can be a scary situation.*

Pops and John had remained quiet since beginning the hike from the parking lot, completely lost in their own thoughts and emotions. What neither of them, nor any of the others, would have ever imagined in the faintest reaches of their expectations was to be shaken to their core by a vocal eruption from a woman they barely knew.

At the sudden outburst, Pops responded swiftly, unthinkingly. With little hesitation, he took command of the flashlight from Susan's hand and knelt down to peer into the void. He knew in his hasty reaction that he'd physically shouldered Susan aside; he would apologize to her later. Right then, his sole attention needed to be on Viane.

During the hike up the trail, he had reinforced his own perception that he had successfully steeled his mind against any unforeseen expectations and was prepared for the worst eventuality. He had already witnessed the most devastating events one could ever imagine many years prior and had since honed his internal controls so sharply he knew he could face whatever harsh reality that turned up ever again. What could possibly be worse, he would often reminded himself, than seeing old friends that only moments before he'd been laughing and making plans with be suddenly washed off the face of the earth by a tidal wave that came roaring up Waianuenue Avenue, nipping at his heels—that was in 1946. Now, he was discovering he wasn't prepared at all seeing his daughter hurt and helpless and far out of his reach and not even knowing whether she was still alive. He had been determined from the beginning that everything was going to work out for the best; but now, seeing his daughter as she was, it shattered all of his hardened nerves.

There, thirty feet below, his baby girl lay unmoving and deathly still in the beam of the flashlight. He shuddered violently, seeing what he knew to be a mass of blood matted on the top and on the exposed side of her head.

As he looked down, unable to move, he got the impression his eyes were playing tricks, and he shook his head to bring a clearer vision but the image remained. The way his daughter's body was positioned gave the impression she was lying in space, hovering in the dark, cold air, with nothing visible supporting her. All the hidden emotions he had ignored and had allowed to build up finally came crashing to the surface. He hadn't experienced such an emotional upheaval for a loved one since he saw his wife, Etta, lying unresponsive, gone forever from his life, after giving birth to Viane's youngest brother John. His body started to shake violently, his convulsions coming close to causing him to lose his grip on the flashlight. Teri snagged it just as he let it go and fell back on his haunches. He could do nothing but sit in stunned silence, reminding himself that he was of little use to anybody, especially his daughter, if he didn't manage to regain some semblance of control. Her rescue was all there was; he just needed a few more moments, though.

Each of the others took turns holding the flashlight, calling out to Viane in hopes of gaining a response. The reality of seeing a body, the body of a loved one and friend, in the contrasting, hostile embrace of raw nature was startling—seemingly so out of place with life.

Everyone began milling about in a haunting quietness, unable to direct their focus toward Viane's rescue. Almost inaudibly, each arrived at rescue scenarios they voiced but without conviction and weren't pushing because of serious impracticality.

Pops quickly regained some of the determined strength his friends knew him for as he got to his feet and pulled in a lungful of chilly air in order to center himself. He began rummaging through the backpacks they'd carried with them, trying to piece together strings of a plan.

Stone looked over at Raymond and Vince and judged by their expression and the way they'd been holding back away from the others that they may be experiencing their first taste of guilt—their faces gave the story away. He called to them, motioning them over to take a look. When they cautiously took hold of the flashlight and peered down into the hole, they remained transfixed in silence, like the others, unable to draw their attention away until Stone gently took the flashlight from Raymond as they both slowly backed away from the opening.

Returning to the hole and calling out several times, almost pleading with his daughter to respond, it was clear to Pops that he needed to turn the faltering actions he'd been experiencing into resolution if he was going to be of any use to her—she had to be brought up to the surface, and fast.

Quickly going over to one of the backpacks that he'd rifled through, he pulled out a length of rope and proceeded to fasten one end around himself. He called Stone and John over to take a few turns with the other end around a rock he pointed at and told them to be ready to play the line out slowly and to stop when he yelled for them to do so. It was obvious he was preparing to drop down into the abyss.

From an observers point of view, it didn't appear to be a very sound plan—there were just too many *ifs* involved. Both John and Stone began expressing their cautions, but Pops waved them off like he would a pesky fly. He wasn't about to listen to anything but his own renewed determination to save Viane—that was his sole focus. Besides, he thought, no one else was coming up with any better ideas. His only uncertainty, as he cinched the rope tighter around his waist, was in response to a comment Chris made that his daughter appeared to be caught on something that no one could clearly see and suggested that the slightest wrong move on Pops's part could send her plummeting to unfathomable depths.

Pops had two legs dangling down the opening, caught up in indecision, thinking more about what Chris had said. He was about to slide off the hole's lip anyway just as Randy and two others walked up beside him. Randy reached out and put a hand on Pops' shoulder.

"Hold on, Pops. Whatever's about to take place, gimme a second to size things up so I'll be in position to offer help, eh. Sorry we're so late getting here," he offered in explanation, "but it took time for these two characters to make up their minds to come help, eh." His face showed appreciation as he looked at each of them, his thumb gesturing in their direction. "They were both about to tear into some *kalua* pig and a bowl of *poi*. Was real tempted to sit down with them." Turning back to the group he asked, "What's the story? I just caught the gist of things earlier when Pops Koa called for our help, eh." He singled out Pops with a nod of his head.

John brought him up to speed while Randy busily pulled a huge flashlight off his belt. Pops remained sitting on the edge of the hole, all the while silently gazing down at Viane.

Pops said, "Before you go down there, I'd like to see what the situation looks like, eh. I hope that's all right with you?" He possessed a strong, commanding voice. "Scoot back a ways from the *puka*, will you, Pops."

Pops reluctantly moved back from the opening as Randy bent over, illuminating the depths with his light.

Obviously a man accustomed to being involved in rescues and quick in decisions, he stood up after a few moments and looked around, taking inventory of available equipment. His face showed a pleasant surprise at seeing the folding stretcher they'd brought along. Pulling a radio off the other side of his belt, he called the fire department's search and rescue division, walking a short distance away to talk. Pops remained sitting weighing thoughts on what he should be doing, still not convinced he shouldn't be heading down the hole trying to reach his daughter.

Returning to the group, Randy informed them the fire department's search and rescue team was sending a chopper but the only place they could set down was up at the Red Hill cabin. The rest of the terrain, he said and everyone readily agreed after having walked it for three hours, was too unstable for landing.

"Any help we can expect from them is at least two hours away by the time anyone is able to hike up from the parking lot or hike down from the chopper, if they used Red Hill as a set-down point. It'll be dark by then, so we need to do this now."

It was very apparent, considering his actions, that he was a take-charge guy, and the others were more than happy to give way. Even Pops uncharacteristically deferred action to him, for the moment anyway. He kept the rope tied around his middle. Randy didn't seem at all fazed by the approaching night even as the rest of them were becoming anxious. He briefly got back on his radio and issued some instructions to someone, presumably the chopper pilot.

"Our task is to bring her up to ground level. The chopper jockeys will take over from there, eh." He motioned for everyone to quickly gather. "Let me suggest how this might be best accomplished."

They listened to Randy's plan and willingly agreed—anything to keep Pops from doing this on his own. "Suspending someone on a rope like you were planning, Pops, would be very difficult and extremely dangerous, eh. Once down there, how would you hold on to your daughter, and how would anyone be able to pull you both out supposing you figured a way of getting her close to the top? That rope around your middle would'a tightened up and squished you like a tube a toothpaste, or it could'a got cut by the sharp *a'a* on the lip." He was pointing at the razor-sharp pieces of lava as he talked. "And if all went well, you'd have to pull her through the opening by her arms and we don't know yet how badly she's broken, eh. Coulda ended up sustaining severe damage."

Randy was attempting to be as gentle with his words as possible but, as was his habit. He was actually voicing concerns about his own plan, letting them reflect back as he spoke. It was a learned habit he'd developed—nothing was ever a hundred percent sure in rescues. Too often he'd arrived at a crisis, only to have to clean up a problem made worse by the best-intentioned people—lessons he himself continually learned.

Everyone was nodding at his logic, even Pops.

Without saying much more, he proceeded to put his plan in motion, with everyone helping prepare the necessary items under his guidance. Three spikes were driven into the ground nearby and two ropes and pulleys stretched out and clipped to the spikes. Any loose lava rocks close to the opening were tossed aside to eliminate the possibility of one of them being accidentally kicked into the hole. He emptied one of his canvas backpacks and laid it on the rim of the hole to act as a rope guard.

Raymond and Vince saw a chance to help and began clearing more loose rocks that lay close with an enthusiasm that even surprised them—it was something they could do, and it seemed like the right thing.

Darkness was taking hold when they finalized preparations and heard the distant thumping of helicopter blades cutting through the thin air, moving toward them. Its underbelly floodlights were dancing across the uneven ground as the pilot followed the visual markings of the trail to arrive overhead. Randy made radio contact once again and guided it into position with arm signals and his flashlight, its high-pitched turbines drowning out conversation as it came near.

Stone, Teri, Pops, John, Chris, and Susan, along with Raymond and Vince, grouped together to the side allowing Randy and his men to begin the rescue. They had insisted on being the ones to go below to assist Viane and no one saw any reason to voice an objection.

"Helicopter floodlights or not," observed Stone, speaking in a tone barely audible to Teri as they stood leaning on each other. "Night is coming and even with a couple of flashlights, it's going to be very difficult to see what to do down there or up here."

As if in answer, Randy suddenly lit up like a roman candle and reached to clip one of the ropes to his harness. He was wearing a hard-hat with bright headlights attached to each side over his ears, and he wore iridescent-yellow arm bands around each bicep that were also equipped with several small lights. All three were walking, brightly lit bill boards as both Joe and Kala, the two men accompanying Randy, were similarly outfitted. It was like being in the middle of a football field with floodlights illuminating the world and three aliens roaming the field. He was glad he hadn't mentioned the *light* thing he'd been thinking about. There was now more light in their small section of the world than in the center ring of a Barnum and Bailey circus tent. The helicopter had gained some altitude and was hovering high enough overhead to lessen the sever downdrafts and accompanying bits of flying rock and the high-pitched noise. Its belly light shone down like a personal full moon.

"Joe and I will go down with the stretcher," announced Randy, having to yell. "Kala will keep an eye on things up here, eh. I want all you to help him by keeping an eye on each of the ropes and pulleys to make sure they play out evenly and don't tangle on anything. When we have Viane secured in the stretcher you'll all need to help pull her up; Kala will show you which rope to pull, eh. The stretcher will need to be collapsed a bit to make both it and her fit through the hole; but no worries 'cause she'll be well secured to it. Just listen to Kala. Joe and I will be pulling ourselves up trying to stay even with the stretcher—just in case.

"Once she's above ground, the chopper will drop lines and take over securing her safely on board. Help my guy get the stretcher attached and then stand back, eh.

"Above all, don't knock any loose rocks down the hole. Pay attention. Any questions?" He scanned the area around the opening and then looked over at Raymond and Vince, giving them two thumbs up. "Great job, men."

With the confidence he exuded he must have been an army drill sergeant in one of his past lives or a wannabe *for the next one.*

Forty-Three

As RANDY AND JOE slowly descended through the opening into the lava tube's depths, both tightly secured by rope harnesses, the interior walls suddenly came to life as a million green diamonds of light lit up in response to the array of lights each man was costumed in. The tiny chips of olivine that had fascinated Viane just days before and had drawn her through the opening were now helping to illuminate the cave well beyond where she lay unconscious. It presented the viewers above ground with an eerie, almost surrealistic glow as they watched the progress of the rescue efforts.

Pops and John had authoritatively taken command of the view as Randy and Joe disappeared belowground, each taking turns watching the events unfold, giving way only when Kala placed a hand on their shoulders, indicating his need to keep watch over his co-rescuers. All the others were intent to watch the ropes safely play out until they came to a stop as the two men belowground reached Viane and cleated their lines tightly to avoid dropping further. *It was show time.*

The rescue moved slowly but smoothly as Randy and Joe methodically went about preparing Viane to be moved onto the unfolded stretcher. There was still no visible sign of life evident, but Randy had felt Viane's skin and was relieved to feel relative warmth radiating back—her skin remained supple; she was still there. Each step in the rescue had to be calculated and coordinated as if it were a slow motion film clip of astronauts moving around on the moon. The men had learned to work well together from their years of friendship and the many past search and rescue missions they had been together on, so their coordinated efforts flowed smoothly.

Unexpectedly, without any warning as Joe was in the process of shifting Viane's left leg off the ledge onto the stretcher, he all of a sudden let out a frightening yell and dropped out of sight. It was a blessing that the ledge caught his end of the stretcher as he lost his hold. If it hadn't, it and Viane would have plummeted beyond reach.

Randy slowly let out his breath with audible relief when he saw Joe's head just below the ledge and saw his friend's raised arm with thumb extended. It had been Randy's split-second of eternity and an unusual moment of indecision for him.

The sudden move left Viane hanging precariously half on and half off the stretcher. She was listing dangerously to one side as Randy struggled to hold her from falling between the stretcher and the ledge while at the same time trying to keep it as level as possible and himself secured. He'd rarely felt so tense. It was a decision close to being strictly a reflective action—but not. It was instead something he'd never before had to face: either let go of the one being rescued in order to grab hold of his friend or pray for his friend and maintain grip on the one being rescued.

Joe, his breath returning to normal as well, remained as stationary as he could manage as he looked up at the bottom of the stretcher. It was swaying slightly as Randy struggled to maintain his hold. He'd given Randy a thumbs-up sign, along with a huge, uncertain grin that all appeared to be OK.

The combination of his face drained of color from the experience and the already eerie reflection of lime-green light made him look almost alien. Randy, feeling an overwhelming relief, would be sure to tell him that when they were safely back on the ground above.

As Joe worked his ropes bringing himself back up toward where he had been, he puzzled over what must have happened to make him drop so unexpectedly. The uncertainty and mystery of it was actually causing him an unaccustomed and uncomfortable level of nervousness. He could only assume it had something to do with his ropes' anchor. The main thing was he was OK and the ropes once again felt secure enough to bear his weight. He rose back up over the ledge even with Randy, his startled expression beginning to fade.

Aboveground, there had been a moment of sheer chaos of motion. No one had noticed that the place chosen for the spike that Joe's line was secured to was too unstable to remain in place and, without warning, had given ground under Joe's weight and went careening forward. The abrupt but brief noise was deafening as it glanced off several rocks. It came within a fraction of an inch of smashing into Vince's leg before slamming to a stop between two large boulders, halting it from following Joe down through the opening.

The sudden motion and sharp noise had been enough to make a falling tree in the forest stand back up straight in fear. It had a comparable effect on everyone milling around the opening: it stopped hearts as well as thoughts.

Pops, who had taken a breather from the intensity and was standing stretching his shoulders, immediately dropped down beside Kala as if his legs had stopped working. Both men crowded the opening as they peered down to see what may have happened, fear very evident in both faces.

With everyone's attention so keenly riveted on Viane's rescue, the commotion had taken a few moments for full understanding to wash over everyone and the dust to settle; but by then, it was over, leaving behind little more than startled expressions and a few chips of lava flying through the air.

Belowground Randy watched, relieved, as Joe slowly, shakily pulled himself back level with the stretcher. Kala, with Pops's face crowded next to his, both looking like a pair of Siamese twins, peered down as Kala gave them the thumbs-up signal, indicating that all was OK on his end, Joe's lifeline was once again secure.

Joe and Randy caught each other's eyes and held contact for a long, silent moment, both knowing that the rescues they volunteered for could one day lead to personal disaster, both thankful that today was not that particular day. They gladly, though more methodical in their movements, resumed their task.

During what felt like an interminable length of time, everyone above started to nervously mill about again, waiting for the next step. Kala was keeping a constant watch on the proceedings, keeping up a running commentary for everyone's benefit, and reaching over to test the rope anchors firmness every few seconds. He was feeling responsible for what happened but knew there was nothing that he could have foreseen—the anchor bars had all felt totally *paa*, immovable. He silently thanked God the young boy had escaped injury as well; he would never have forgiven himself had it been otherwise.

Down below, Viane was being gently rolled onto the stretcher and tightly secured for the ride up. It was not a simple, straightforward effort: she had to be secured in such a fashion her body could withstand the pressure as she and the stretcher were turned vertical so they could be pulled up through the hole. Randy and Joe went about fashioning a platform out of rope under her feet so her weight would be borne by those ropes while she was temporarily upright. Her arms and legs were individually fastened against movement and a strap was placed over her forehead and made fast to keep it and her neck immobile.

Satisfied they'd done everything they needed to or could do, Randy signaled Kala to get them out.

Kala quickly instructed everyone into their preassigned positions on each of the two ropes that attached to the head and foot of the stretcher. Relief was evident on everyone's face as they began to slowly but steadily pull Viane to the surface.

Pops wasn't on a rope. He insisted that he needed to be at the opening as the stretcher was pulled through. His fatherly protection was asserting itself—nothing more was going to happen to Viane if he could help it.

Luckily, the rope mishap had taken place so suddenly that Vince was still somewhat oblivious to the ramifications of what might have happened to him. He and his brother were now eagerly a part of the events unfolding, wearing huge grins, glancing at each other as they helped pull, one on each of the ropes.

Earlier, before the rescue efforts began, when Raymond and Vince were standing off by themselves, Randy had quietly told the others that he'd been given permission from the chopper crew that Pops and John, as well as the boys, were going to be lifted into the chopper for the ride to the hospital. Pops and John were a *given* for the ride as they accompanied Viane, but Raymond and Vince...

All were astonished but pleased to learn the boys were being included. In the relative short time they'd been on the mountain, Raymond and Vince had unintentionally endeared themselves to the others simply by their willingness to be there and to help with their young, energetic enthusiasm.

When asked why the boys were being included, Randy explained that Vic Morro, the cop who was working with the boys, had a brother who happened to be a chopper pilot with the fire department's search and rescue crew and who also just happened to be hovering overhead.

"Apparently, Vic has high hopes for these two boys," Randy explained, "and he wants to reward them for coming forward to help. And in case you're wondering, he did clear it first with his chief. Vic will be at the hospital when the chopper lands and will make sure the boys get back home. Their parents have already been notified."

Stone, Chris, and John, with ample instruction from Kala on what to do, were all that could fit over the lava tube opening as the stretcher, with Viane tightly strapped to it, was carefully collapsed enough to allow both she and it to fit through the opening to the surface. Teri and Susan were close by, ready to assist in any way possible.

As Viane's face appeared aboveground, Pops, tears overflowing, reached out and gently stroked her injured cheek. Her eyes were closed as if asleep; her skin drained of color and cold to his touch, like a strip of leather left flapping in the wind too long—but she was back among them, and Pops's heart was telling him she'd be all right.

Viane was pulled the remainder of the way up and laid flat on the ground. Her arms had been folded and strapped in place over top of her backpack that rested on her chest. Stone was impressed Randy would think to do that. When Viane was back to normal, she would be grateful to still have all the equipment it surely contained.

In the torrent of activity and keyed-up emotions embracing the group, no one took particular notice that the chopper had dropped down and was hovering quite close overhead. Its belly lights were blazing through the outward-flowing dust and rock storm that was again being created. A sling came down through the cloud of dust with lines attached. Stone, John, Pops, and Kala went about clipping them to the four corners of the stretcher before standing back and watching as Viane was hoisted aloft. Then Pops and

John were hoisted up next, followed by Raymond and Vince, whose very obvious excitement was bigger than anything they'd ever experienced, their faces giving testament to just how big that was.

As the chopper quickly rose and flew off toward Hilo, the mountain suddenly became eerily silent and dark as Randy and his men took off their light displays. Flashlights immediately came on.

With the impenetrable darkness surrounding them, it was apparent they were destined to spend the night right where they stood. It was much too dangerous to attempt hiking back to the parking lot. Even if Randy and his men were to illuminate the trail with their mass of lights, the dark shadows created would only serve to hide huge holes that would snap an ankle like a twig if one were to get their foot caught.

The chopper pilot said he was willing to come back for them, but the cost was high, and none were willing to foot that particular bill.

The worst was over; there was nothing left for them to do but to pray for Viane's safe delivery to the hospital and her quick recovery. They could do all that from here just as well as at the hospital.

The chopper had dropped seven down-filled sleeping bags for them at Randy's request before flying off. No one had been thinking far enough ahead to bring one with them since their sole thought at that time had been on finding Viane, not on where they might end up spending the night. Now they were equipped for it. It was going to be a rough, mostly sleepless nights, though. The ground was little more than unending mounds of loose sharp *a'a* lava, but at least they would be warm as they waited for sunrise to come, secure in the feeling they'd done everything they could for Viane. Just having found her would provide them with the warmth and peace of mind they'd need for the night.

Haiku, Oahu

AT THE DISRUPTIVE AND sudden intrusion by the home's owners as they barged in through the front door, Mike and his partner responded instantaneously. The sound of the new arrivals rushing through the front door was obviously threatening. Mike had his revolver in hand, motioning with hand signals and whispers to Guy and Deborah to stand close against the wall and not make a sound, and absolutely no sudden moves. He was quickly realizing, albeit too late, that inviting them in to view the stolen merchandise had been a huge mistake—it was forcing a more aggressive response than he would normally have taken. He wouldn't let that happen again.

A rush of movement accompanied by loud voices greeted Mike as he quickly moved through the door into the short hallway. Moments passed in the ensuing muffled undertones of grunts, subdued voices, and physical scuffling. Deborah and Guy huddled close, not wanting to admit to any of the fear they were both contending with.

The sound of the front door being opened again was accompanied by a surge of loud voices before it banged shut, followed by complete silence. Whatever had taken place was apparently over and had moved outside, its outcome uncertain. Just as Guy's and Deborah's curiosity got the better of them and they tentatively began moving toward the door, Mike came back into the room, his gun back where it belonged riding on his right hip. He wasn't smiling, but his face carried his normal calm and back-in-control demeanor.

"Eh," he said, "having you in here was a misjudgment on my part. I'm sorry. Hope you're both OK."

Almost laughing, he explained that, fortunately, the two men, the owners of the house who had charged in through the front door, were all voice and no action. "Drunker than mongoose in a boatload of beer." They had been easily handcuffed and were now on their way to a holding cell in downtown Honolulu.

"With that roomful of stolen merchandise and a stolen boat sitting in their yard," he explained, "there is sufficient evidence to charge them with grand larceny theft. They could spend a lot of years in OCCC sewing Tutu Annie Hawaiian-Kine bags." It was a common practice for the warden at OCCC to contract piecemeal work to keep inmates busy and teach them a trade they could take with them when they were released from custody. Sewing for Tutu Annie was the current prison endeavor; they'd already gone through the license plates and cooking classes.

"That Buick back there in the yard is still considered yours, Guy, unless the insurance company has already paid you for your loss. If that's the case, I guess it's theirs. We checked the VIN number and found the stolen-car report you made. Its inactive but remains on file. It showed up in the Never Solved basket. Wonder if it still runs?"

"Guess it's still mine, then, Mike. I couldn't afford insurance back then, and I'll find out if it still runs or not." The prospect of getting his old, long-forgotten car back was intriguing. He had loved owning it back then and spent a lot of effort working on it. He was more than curious to see if the engine block was still painted red and orange as he'd done on a whim. He wasn't sure what he'd end up doing with the car once he got it back, however. He didn't know how Deborah would enjoy crowding the driveway in front of their home with another boat and two cars.

Sporting a broad smile, Mike told them about checking the forklift that was in the backyard and his surprise at discovering it had been reported stolen twenty-five years earlier from Dole Cannery's warehouse and obviously never found. "About the same time as your car, Guy," he added. It was another file that Mike could remove from the Never Solved basket. "It'll be interesting to hear the story of how they managed to steal it and smuggle it home. "In their mumbling, those two boat thieves inadvertently mentioned Tim's name, so when they sober up, we'll have some good opening questions for them on their exploits in crime and who else is involved. It also gives us clear reason to search Giuseppe's place in Kaaawa. But," he warned, "you two won't be there. This lesson was clear enough."

Mike actually didn't need to explain that. Both Deborah and Guy had already decided they weren't up for any more cloak-and-dagger stuff. The past half hour of uncertainty was enough for this lifetime. "That picture you bought," Mike continued, "which I hope Tim still has, will give us a good starting point for the search."

"When can we expect to get the outboards and other equipment back? I don't suppose we can start loading up the car now?"

"It'll take a while. Sorry, Guy. There's a lot here that has to be inventoried, photographed, and catalogued. Then it's up to the courts to decide if and when they can release any of it. In the meantime, you should be getting all your paperwork lined up. They'll want bills of sale, personal photos, whatever you've got that proves it's yours."

"My social security number is on everything, shouldn't that be enough?"

"Oh yeah, sorry, I forgot. That'll probably do the trick, but other proof would still be a good idea in case we have to persuade a judge. I'll see if I can't get my friend Judge DaSilva involved—it'll make everything run a lot smoother. He's more compassionate toward victims than a lot of other judges." He added this because he didn't want them to think he was ragging on judges in general. He felt very sympathetic to what all of them had to go through sitting on the bench and wouldn't trade jobs with them for all the pineapple in Haleiwa.

"Now, I gotta go. I'll call you later with the outcome of our search in Kaaawa. I'll see if I can't put your painting in a squad car for you if it's still there, after it's photographed and catalogued. You'll still need to pay Tim the balance you owe on it. I suspect you won't have a hard time finding him when the time comes." He chuckled. "There'll probably be a lot of iron bars surrounding him."

He was still smiling as they all walked out the front door.

THE SEARCH OF GIUSEPPE'S property proved Mike's suspicions well founded but held several totally unexpected surprises as well.

The painting of *Lehua*'s stern that Deborah and Guy had bought was resting against a wall beside the front door on a lanai that encircled the house. It hadn't gotten very far from where Tim's old pickup was parked, or perhaps *resting* would be a closer reality, less than ten feet away.

The man seemed almost relieved that HPD was there. Tim met Mike at the door, accepting the search warrant with a veiled smile before rolling his wheelchair out of the way onto the front lanai, where he remained as though it was an everyday occurrence—a minor disturbance he could care less about.

On face value, the interior of the house yielded nothing incriminating, although nobody could be certain of that because of the massive amount of clutter.

The first room Mike's men entered was probably a living room, although that was just a guess, and if correct, it was in name only. The place was nothing but stacks of old newspapers and magazines piled as high as Tim was apparently able to reach from his wheelchair. Trails led through the maze toward four different doorways. They found that three of the other rooms were similar to the first, with the exception that each room appeared dedicated to just one thing: one was floor-to-ceiling paintings; another was odd-looking sculptures; and the third was filled with murals of various sizes and subjects, mostly maritime. The fourth room, the kitchen, was surprisingly neat and tidy, as was the adjoining bedroom and bath.

Many of the murals and sculptures in the house defied description. On close inspection, however, Mike noticed they were all made up of accumulated boat fragments. Tim obviously used boat pieces as the main components for his art. He was evidently quite a talented artist as well as a genius at making boats disappear.

"You've got to admire this guy," Mike said to one of his men close by. "He's developed a very unique way of getting rid of evidence and in plain sight. We're going to be hard-pressed to tie any of this to particular boats."

The yard around the house was large, appearing to be five or six acres—Mike hadn't taken the time to note the exact size. The records he'd pulled up indicated the house and property had been handed down to Tim by his father, who traced his lineage back many generations to the time of Kamehameha. Royal Governor Kekuanaoa, according to records, albeit sketchy, gifted Tim's many-times-over great-grandfather with the entire *ahupuaa*, the land mass encompassing everything from the ocean to the breathtaking top of the adjacent Koolau Mountains following formed valley ridges on both sides—a huge gift of land comprising several hundred acres. All but the remaining five or six had been sold off over the years or acquired by the state to satisfy owed taxes and set aside as watershed land.

Walking around the yard to the rear of the house, Mike discovered an old barn-looking building a hundred yards back, a dirt-and-grass jeep trail led to a large sliding door centered on the front of the building. It was apparent the barn had been in place for a very long time judging by the graying color and warped nature of the buildings siding and the moss-covered roof. There was an overgrowth of grass and weeds along its edges, and a *pikake* vine entangled with wood rose vine obliterated a huge part of one side. The whole structure had a slight list and was being held stable by numerous wood braces, like a tired old man leaning on his cane.

The inside, though, was a well-designed and maintained workspace, a total contradiction to the outside of the barn and the inside of Tim's house. Sliding barn-styled doors were centered on both ends with steel shelves rising up the walls, piled high with bits and pieces of fiberglass of various colors ostensibly taken from cut-up boats. There was a stack of deck, hull-siding, and railing wood as well. The interesting part for Mike was a deep pit in the center of the floor with a hoist built over top. When questioning Tim later, Mike would learn that the hoist could suspend boats at any level, allowing Tim to work on them from his wheelchair. He'd claim he could also hoist himself up and work over top of them when necessary.

Walking around the barn to see what lay beyond, Mike came to an abrupt standstill. He found himself not wanting to move farther as if to do so would subconsciously change the outcome and what he saw. The amazed expression that defined his facial features slowly eased into a grin.

A flat-bed trailer sat next to the rear sliding door. A tarp partially covered its contents, but the transom of *Lehua* sat exposed directly in front of him. Lying beneath the tarp hidden from view was a second boat. With a quick look at the HA registration numbers, Mike knew it was one of the other stolen boats. Both appeared to be in relatively undamaged condition. He was anxious to inform Guy of what he'd found and planned to call him as soon as he got back to headquarters. He figured he'd give Stone a call as well. It was obviously a day for making people happy—except, of course, for the three men involved in the scheme.

The grass trail behind the barn led to a pit—a large natural depression in the ground. It was partially filled with household refuse and beer bottles, but also held cut-up sections of boats: keels that had no purpose along with rusted boat railings, steering wheels, and damaged instruments.

Mike liked Tim for some reason he couldn't comprehend, but he still had to arrest him and have one of his men haul him and his chair to Halawa jail. He'd be joining Alysdon and Bill who were already on their way.

Forty-Five

KNOWING STONE WOULD PROBABLY like to hear the news, Mike called him from outside Giuseppe's front gate and told him about the results of the search.

"That's incredible, Mike. Guy and Deborah will be overjoyed when they hear that."

"I'm going to call them in just a second, but I want to hear how Viane's doing." Mike told Stone about Hilo PD channeling the word down that she'd been located and airlifted to Hilo General. "What's happening with her?"

When they finally broke connection ten minutes later, Mike called the Montanas.

"Your painting is in the back of my cruiser, Deborah. I'll bring it over later today or tomorrow morning." Mike suspected both Deborah and Guy had been practically sitting on their telephone in anticipation of his call—it had only rung once before Deborah picked it up.

She and Guy knew the search was taking place and were relieved to be home—excluded from the search. They had been as patient as possible waiting for Mike's call. She mentioned that Guy, only moments before, had to leave and go down to his print shop to cope with a problem, much to his displeasure. She was anxious to call and tell him the news.

Mike was just pulling away from Tim's property as
they talked. He was feeling good about the search and all
the evidence they'd found. He was feeling especially good
because he'd found the Montanas' boat, all in one piece, but
intentionally was not mentioning his find to Deborah. He
was going to save that bit of surprise for when they were face-
to-face. He wanted to feel as well as see their excitement and
wanted Guy to be there.

Deborah immediately began experiencing an odd
emotional swing listening to Mike talk. She was pleased the
painting of *Lehua*'s transom was going to be hers. It meant
always having a part of their boat. But it was a bittersweet
sentiment at the same time, having the memories of their
boat but not the boat itself. She knew Guy would feel the
same when he heard the results of the search. They'd already
agreed to look for another boat as soon as the insurance
money was available, but she was still holding on to a prayer
their *Lehue* would somehow show up.

"We've been wondering how the search of Tim's place
went," Deborah went on, still feeling at odds with the
conversation. She'd come to value Mike both as a friend and
as a very capable police officer. "Did everything go as easily
as you hoped? Were you able to get enough evidence to make
a case against the three of them?"

"I have to tell you, Deborah, in all my years with HPD
and the hundreds of houses I've been involved in raiding
or searching, I thought I knew all there was to know about
hoarders. But this house has the best of them beat hands
down. Never saw so much stuff collected in one spot. I'm
not sure how anyone lives like that, especially someone in
a wheelchair. One thing I have to admit, though, this guy is
sure talented when it comes to cutting up boats and using
the pieces. It's amazing what he could put together out of old
decking, wood siding, and bits of fiberglass. It's a talent that's

going to go to waste in jail. And to answer your question, yes, we found all the evidence we'll need."

Deborah felt a biting disappointment listening to the part about someone's *talent* at cutting boats into pieces. She could only envision *Lehua* cut up and rearranged into a piece of contemporary artwork that someone would buy and place in their yard among their rosebushes, only to forget it was there or really not care if it wasn't.

"When you bring the painting, I hope you'll have some time to stay for dinner, or breakfast, if it's going to be tomorrow. I'll cook us up something special to celebrate the end of your investigation, maybe my ono-licious loco moco, whether it's dinner or otherwise." She laughed to herself, remembering Guy say that very thing shortly after they were married. She told Mike, and then added, "I wasn't sure whether I should laugh or haul off and hit him when he said that. He saved himself from getting bruised by quickly telling me it was a local way of saying my cooking was absolutely delicious. It's my secret recipe, you know." She was obviously pleased.

"I may come right this minute if that's on the menu," he laughed. "I'll be there in the morning, Deborah. I have way too much to do here, and it's going to take the rest of the day to get everything sorted out and all the paperwork lined up in a row. By the way, have you figured out where you'll put that old Buick yet? Make sure there's also lots of space for easy access to your boat."

"We'll find room for the car. Guy really wants to get it running again and then completely recondition it. It'll be a fun project for the two of us to work on. He tells me there is nobody else, anywhere on the island, driving a 1948 Buick Convertible. As for the new boat"—she sighed—"that hasn't been decided yet. We plan to go next week and look at a couple that are being advertised, but we're both finding that a hard next step to take. Brings too much final closure with it."

"Maybe you'd better hold off on that last part until you figure out where you'll put *Lehua*." He could no longer resist telling her. Letting her keep disappointment alive seemed the wrong thing to do. "It was found on Giuseppe's property still on the trailer that almost ran you over."

"Our boat? Our *Lehua*?" Deborah's heart skipped over the next few beats along with most of what Mike said following that.

They talked briefly about Viane as well—so much good news it was difficult to contain it all. Deborah quickly broke off the connection—she couldn't wait to tell Guy the news.

THE NEXT MORNING SITTING at Deborah and Guy's kitchen table, launched over admittedly the best loco moco he'd tasted, Mike was describing Tim's place and how the search had gone in response to Guy's questions.

"A strange fellow, our Tim. He's *kamaaina*, going back several generations. The inside of his *hale*, which is a huge old plantation-style house, is a literal garbage dump of every collectable you can imagine, all separated into designated rooms: newspapers that appeared to go back ten years or more; paintings and sculptures galore. His old barn, though quite a distance away from his house, is immaculate, a well-set-up workshop. I was actually very impressed, and for me that's a rare thing. Inside this barn workshop is a hoist built over a cement pit. He could suspend boats and large pieces of art and raise or lower them in order to work so he could work from his wheelchair, or he could hoist himself up and work over top of them. Apparently, he was a boatswain in his younger days and did boat repair work in that barn until falling in with Alysdon and Bill and was talked into a different path. I got a feeling he's almost happy this is happening so he can eventually return to what his life used to be before meeting those two crooks. Whatever it is about the man, I can't help but like him. I'll ask Judge DaSilva to help mitigate his sentence.

"He has a dirt road leading out the rear of the barn ending at the edge of a huge depression in the far end of his property. The depression looks to have been a sunken area of an ancient lava flow. It's where he's been dumping boat parts he couldn't use and art pieces that perhaps went wrong or that he didn't like, which, judging from everything else around there, I can't imagine. It's going to take weeks and a village full of man-hours to sort through legitimate garbage and unused boat parts separating out his days of boat repair and then document all the parts from stolen boats."

"What about Alysdon and Bill?" asked Guy. "You find enough evidence to close them down?"

Swallowing a mouthful of eggs and pouring additional shoyu on his rice, Mike looked up and smiled. "Interesting, those two. They kept complete records of the HA registration numbers from all the boats they stole and what they did with them, either send them to the mainland or trailer them to Tim's place. They also kept the same info on boats coming into the Islands from their connections over there. Turns out they aren't very good crooks, after all. Those records they kept so accurately are all we'll need to close this up. We'll have enough evidence to close down the mainland operation as well as the local one. Not too *akamai* these two—couple loose bulbs without switches attached," he said, pointing his fork toward his head.

"By the way, Judge DaSilva said your boat has to be secured as evidence until all the legal stuff is *pau,* which could take months. But"—obviously pleased with himself as he scooped up the remaining forkful of rice—"I talked him into letting us keep it in your driveway. Told him it'd be safer here than sitting in an open evidence yard in Iwilei." Looking at Deborah and holding out his now-empty plate, he asked, "Any more rice and gravy over there in the pan?"

Mauna Loa trail

THE MORNING BROUGHT MUCH-needed warmth to the slopes of Mauna Loa, and the seven people haphazardly scattered amidst the lava. None looked like they had much rest—in fact, they looked quite the opposite. Most had been awake and huddled in their sleeping bags simply waiting for daylight so they could get up without stumbling over the rock-strewn surface. A hangover of euphoria still existed in their thoughts from the previous night's rescue, but it was being overshadowed by sore, aching muscles. It was agreed that even a pile of gravel would have been a preferable bed platform.

Humor was noticeably absent from everyone's face until becoming aware of feathers covering the surrounding lava, thousands of them—everywhere—with Kala, displaying an odd grin, sitting in the middle of them all. It was quite apparent he had not chosen a very good spot to place his sleeping bag the evening before. Instead of the billowy down-filled bag he and everyone started the night with, it now looked as if he were sitting on a flat sheet, in the middle of a field of down feathers that giving the impression a feather factory had recently gone haywire.

The spot he chose to sleep obviously contained a few sharp pieces of lava that he failed to notice in the dark. Sitting partially buried in feathers, he relayed the events of the night in such a humorous way it immediately raised everyone's spirits—he was a born storyteller. He claimed to have found a relatively comfortable-looking spot amongst the chunks of lava—hard to believe. And fell asleep.

He woke in the early hours when his warm and cozy sleeping bag made a sound like a muffled balloon popping and wispy down feathers blew out as far as they could float. He told everyone that he'd spent the remainder of the night swatting feathers away from his nose every time he took a breath.

It had been an unforgettable night's sleep for everyone as the lava-strewn mountain left little space to lie down without feeling sharp rocks digging deeply into already-tired muscles. Stone and Teri had put their sleeping bags together, one on top of the other, in an attempt to soften the jagged surface as much as was possible. They weren't sure it helped especially, but it did allow them an opportunity to snuggle close and keep each other warm as they lightly dozed through the night.

Susan was quite happy and volunteered that she and Chris had gained an adventure they hadn't anticipated. She admitted, though, that there were places on her body that may not ever forgive her.

The cool morning air that had initially greeted them was quickly dissipating as the sun began bearing down on the mountainside. The black lava they were surrounded by and the faintly sulphur-tainted air that engulfed them was heating up, dictating time to pack up and begin their descent to the parking lot.

As Stone and Teri busied themselves gathering their belongings in readiness for the hike down and doing their best to re-roll their sleeping bags and make them fit into the always-too-small sleeves they came in, Randy came walking over, his hand reaching out as he drew near.

"I haven't had time until now to say anything, Stone. It took me a while in the morning light to see your face clearly and realize you were part of this crew, eh. I guess you know I was a bit pressed last night to pay a lot of attention to who else was around and then it got too late and too dark to worry much about it, eh. I don't think any of us felt too sociable after getting Pops' daughter helicoptered off." He could be very loquacious.

"It's good to see you as well, Randy, and no apology is needed. I noticed you were a part of the rescue team last night and wanted to say something but figured I'd wait for morning light. You keeping yourself busy?"

"Between being a volunteer fire chief, a forest service employee, searching for missing pig hunters and keeping a house full of kids in line I don't have much time to get out of shape, eh. And if I did, the missus would give me the boot."

"You know, Randy, I'm a little surprised you recognized me at all. Our time together in BIVSAR was brief, a long time ago and was spent mostly tramping through wet forests up to our knees in mud and in the middle of rainy nights."

They talked a bit longer catching up on their lives, but it was apparent the time to leave had arrived. They were all anxious to get moving.

Putting his hand gently on Teri's back and drawing Randy's attention, Stone said, "Randy, this is Teri—sorry I'm a little slow at introductions this morning. She's probably the most important person in my life. Last night we were rescuing the second most important."

Teri, letting go of the partially rolled sleeping bag, letting it fall to the ground, stepped closer and, with a generous smile, shook Randy's outstretched hand before looking up at Stone with an accusing stare. "What do you mean *probably* the most important? I may have to rethink our sleeping arrangements if that word isn't immediately withdrawn." It brought a relaxed laugh to the threesome as she quickly gave Randy a wink and released his hand.

She could see the ruggedness of the man, with his old beat-up bush hat draping over his ears. She guessed he'd likely be an interesting person to talk to and become friends with—his eyes held a deep intensity that showed the wisdom of an old soul.

"Has he told you our story yet, Teri?" At the shake of her head and confused look, he went on. "Hope I'm not letting a wet cat jump out of the wash basin.

"Neither of us could forget that night, eh?" she said, looking at Stone. "We got lost searching for a *pupule* tourist walking around in the forest wearing nothing but shorts and slippers, carrying a pint of water in his hand?" He turned his attention to Teri to explain. "We were supposed to be the rescue team, eh," he laughed again before placing a hand on Stone's shoulder. "Didn't that guy come out of the woods all on his own the next morning long before you and me figured out where we were?

"No, I haven't heard that story yet, Randy, and I'm all ears waiting to hear the rest." She looked up at Stone's face, expecting to hear the story.

"I won't spoil it by telling you then, eh," said Randy. "I'll let Stone tell you so he can embellish it and spin it in his own light. Besides, I think we all need to get down off this hill and move on to other things before the sun bakes us, eh. I'm supposed to be helping the forest service put up fences to keep all them feral pigs out of the native-growth forest areas.

"I hope you won't mind my checking in with you sometime, Stone. I'd like to hear about your friend's welfare and recovery and what your life has gotten you into lately. Remember, if you ever decide to move back to Hilo, I could sure use your help again hunt'n for lost tourists and hunters, eh. Tell Pops when you see him that I'll be calling."

"Randy, when this crisis has taken its course let's plan to get together over a cold one so we can catch up. I'd love to hear what you've been up to since our adventures together."

Stone pulled a business card out of his wallet and handed it to Randy.

"Great. I can tell you all about becoming the volunteer fire chief in Fern Forest. Maybe it'll convince you and this pretty lady of yours to move back here, eh. There's still lots of great property around want'n a buyer to come along and take an interest, eh. Pops has all the numbers where I can be reached. See you at the bottom of this hill unless you dawdle and we godda leave."

With a final wave, Randy led for the next two and a half hours as they made their way down the trail to the parking lot. Joe and Kala, his two buddies, were close behind. It was a cautious pace after their sleepless night.

Chris and Sue were behind the three busily talking over plans for using the remaining bonus time they had for further exploring. They were looking forward to driving down to South Point, the southernmost tip of the whole country. Dan, the concierge at their hotel had told them about the unique style of fishing the local fishermen employed. He suggested they go and see for themselves after Chris mentioned being an avid fisherman. He told them that because of the water's quick drop to 2,000 feet off a short cliff, the locals employed either balloons or kites in the constant off-shore wind to carry their baited lines out several hundred feet before dropping them into the blue water that was frequented by big game fish like mahi-mahi, ono, and an occasional ahi. He said it could be quite entertaining to watch the battle that took place when a bull *mahi-mahi* took hold of someone's hook. He also told them there were stories of inattentive and hapless fishermen being yanked right off the cliff only to fall harmlessly but embarrassingly into the deep water below. Chris and Sue were anxious to see it all.

Stone and Teri were hanging well back behind the others. They were in a hurry to get to the hospital but at the same time were not anxious to hear what might be devastating news. Pops had reached them by phone shortly before they began walking down the trail and filled them in on her continued precarious situation. He'd sounded spent, his energy level reaching zero. Thank goodness John was with him.

The profound optimism that Stone carried secreted in his being had affected Teri as well, and both were feeling confident about Viane's recovery. Still they were profoundly concerned and prayed she'd have a full recovery. They planned to drive directly to the hospital but hoped that if enough time lapsed in their getting there, Viane would have miraculously regained consciousness and everyone would be sitting around her bed listening to her tale of adventure. If it was to be anything other than full recovery; their rushing to get there would only serve to prolong their anguish. It was a fool's paradox, but there it was. Stone was never in a rush to enter a hospital environment anyway, and Teri was doing her best to honor her partners' reluctance. It was a mixed bag of reasoning.

"I'd forgotten about Randy's habit of tacking on the word 'eh' to the end of a few sentences. Seems he mentioned once that he came from Canada. He told me when we were together on a long trek through the brush that his family used to farm a large spread somewhere around the small town of Sovereign in central Saskatchewan."

"I continue to be amazed with you, Stone. You still have a great memory, and with that, be warned"—she smiled sheepishly—"that should you ever forget my birthday you'd better plan on sleeping at your office on that couch of yours for a great length of time, keeping out of harm's way."

"Maybe I could talk Lori into staying late at the office if that should ever happen."

She gave his butt a not-too-soft slap in response, accompanied by a loud *hmph*. "So what's this story of adventure you and Randy shared? We've got a long hike down. Does two hours give you enough time to fully exaggerate everything?" Teri hoped that the timing of this story would allow them to settle their thoughts on something besides Viane—at least for a short time.

"Only, if you promise not to laugh."

"That may be asking too much of me. I need a good laugh right now so I might laugh even if it's not funny. Promise withheld until the end of the story."

"OK, I'll take that. It was late on a Saturday night and pouring rain as only Hilo can do when Randy and I went into the forest looking for a tourist who had apparently become lost. He hadn't returned to his car after heading off through the forest toward the active volcano vent on Kilauea. Randy and I were the only ones of our group to go. Well, we ended up tramping through mud in a circle all night and only realized it when we kept passing a particular log that was becoming much too familiar in the beam of our flashlights. Discovering we were hopelessly lost, we made beds out of *hapu* tree fern fronds beside that log, slept for two hours until daybreak, only to realize we had tramped through mud for seven hours, slept on the soggy ground, and all that time we were less than a hundred yards from where we had parked our cars.

The fire department was preparing to mount a search for us when we walked out of the forest next to their truck. Meanwhile, the tourist had found his own way out an hour before Randy and I did and had already driven away, never knowing the chaos he left behind. That's the abbreviated version. I'll embellish the details at a later date over a glass of wine."

Her laughter erupted. She didn't even try to stifle it. Stone was certain that even Randy, who was far in front, could hear her eh!

Reaching the parking lot they quickly said their alohas to everyone and headed for the hospital.

Forty-Seven

HAPPY ENDINGS DON'T NECESSARILY come in threes, as some old clichés suggest; sometimes even two in a row can be elusive.

Deborah and Guy's euphoria was practically contagious at having their boat returned and in easily reparable condition. Although it was going to require effort and some expense remounting the engines and reinstalling the electronic gear that had been taken off rather carelessly, it was also questionable whether they could reuse the steering and throttle mechanisms—both appeared to have been simply yanked from the console with callous disregard, causing major cosmetic damage and bent cables. Overall, though, they were very happy just to have it back. Guy considered the work necessary to rebuild things as inconsequently, a minor inconvenience in comparison to the joy he felt.

THAT HAPPY, SILVER-LINED cloud stopped at the shores of Big Island, where heavy emotions cast shadows over any silver-lined miracles, leaving a subtle quietness in Viane's room.

She lay unresponsive in intensive care. Tubes and IV lines too numerous to count filled the space surrounding her. By the appearance, they could have been forage for someone's nightmare—so many plastic lines hanging over the bed gave the impression of a strange being in the process of attacking the inert form lying beneath.

The hum of activity, murmuring voices, and the constant *beep* of machines watching over sick and injured patients echoed down the old wooden hall of the hospital.

Private rooms were rare, but Viane had been fortunate to have been placed in an extraordinarily large room by most hospital standards, with an empty bed next to her. This providential privacy, in effect until another patient showed up, allowed Viane's visitors to focus their full attention on her without the frequent congestion of strangers coming to visit or worry over the *other* patient. It was a sad blessing since the *other patient* that had recently occupied the now-empty bed had been rolled out on a gurney veiled under the cover of a white sheet moments before Viane was rolled in. It was a grave omen and everyone felt it, but none chose to validate it with words. The room privacy would, no doubt, be short-lived if the cacophony of sounds filtering down the hall from the admittance desk were any indication.

Thankfully, it was a bright, sunny room, providing a degree of lift to one's spirit despite where they found themselves. A large transparent-curtained window allowed the blue sky and gentle sway of coconut palms in the distance to render a calming element to anxious family and friends.

Viane's bed was close to the wall farthest from the door, leaving sufficient space for the two visitors' chairs, currently occupied by John and his father, to be placed close to the bed. Viane's eyes remained closed, but were she to open them and gaze out the window, she would see a magnificent view extending down over the older part of Hilo to the shoreline of Hilo Bay. The distant breakwater sheltering the bay, waves crashing over its top, was picturesque and would have been a very calming and nurturing view if it happened to be someone's lanai and they were able to sit with their morning coffee and enjoy it—it would be Viane's delight when or if she opened her eyes.

According to the doctor, Viane was in hemorrhagic shock, and had lapsed into a coma. He wasn't able to tell them the depth or severity of the coma, but added, "Her vitals are good."

The paramedics had done all they could during the short helicopter flight to stabilize her. It was a difficult task under the limited conditions of the aircraft, but nothing they did, though, could forestall the inevitable unconsciousness. For Pops, as well as John, the flight had been the longest twenty minutes either had ever experienced and hoped never to experience again.

They both sat in silence, one on each side of the bed, each resting a hand over one of Viane's, cautiously avoiding all the lines and tubes.

With pained hearts, they watched their daughter and sister lying deathly still like a warmed-over ghost. Her long black hair lay haphazardly splashed over the pillow, matted and filled with small bits of rock and dust that no one had seen any immediate need to comb away. Every so often, one of them would unconsciously straighten a strand or two of her hair or pick an imagined piece of debris from her forehead—busy work to keep them from sinking further into a well of anguish.

Pops' good friend, Dr. Matsuura, had just left the room with the promise to return as quickly as he could. Both knew there was little the doctor could do until a change in her condition dictated further action—it was all up to Viane.

The doctor said he'd arrange to have a small cot rolled into the room so family, speaking mostly to Pops and John, could take turns getting a little rest. This wasn't a common or encouraged hospital practice, but this was Hilo after all, where people looked out for their friends.

Raymond and Vince sat in the waiting room unsure of what to do. They were still feeling the euphoria of their adventure in the helicopter and knew they'd cherish that piece of adventure for a very long time. It was late night and both were exhausted.

Officer Morro, as promised, finally appeared at the door and motioned for them to follow him out to his patrol car for the thirty-mile ride up the hill to Volcano Village. None of them, Office Morro included, looked forward to the end of the ride and the emotional drama that may lie in wait for them when they reached home. He hoped upon prayer the kids' parents would be passed-out drunk so the boys could get to their bedroom without a confrontation and he could leave without rousing their ire and having to defend his actions—he was somewhat ashamed of his un-policeman-like thinking, but that was exactly what was going through his mind whether he liked it or not.

Pulling up in front of the boys' house, Vic found his prayers had been answered—at least he suspected they had been. The house was dark and quiet. Even the neighbor's dog was quiet. He guessed the parents had drunk themselves into a stupor and gone to bed probably assuming the boys were asleep in their own bedroom, having forgotten all about their son's helicopter adventure they had been told about. The house was closed down for the night.

"Good night, boys," he said. "It was a good day, wasn't it?"

He found it interesting that the unfortunate incident with Viane had served to bring these two young men to his attention—he'd known of *them* but hadn't *known* them. Universal energy, God in many minds, knew what It was doing by pulling the various puppet strings that set the course for events to unfold. Vic's instinct about the twins was proving to be a bona fide validation—there was a genuine caring slumbering inside them waiting to come out and show the world their value. He looked forward to watching their growth through his Warrior's Path program.

He carried a desire to find a solution to the boys home life—all the boys in his program. If he could find the proverbial magic bullet for the parents and make the kids' home life the nurturing place it should be, he would know he was doing his job.

He told the boys that if they wanted to, he would arrange to bring them back to the hospital to visit Viane whenever they asked—assuming, naturally, that she'd pull through. If she didn't...well, he didn't want to dwell on that possibility— life would change in so many directions for so many people if she didn't. During his career, he'd witnessed too much of the harsh side of life. For longer than he cared to remember, he had believed in the saying, *Where your thoughts go, so also goes the way of events*. He wasn't about to let his thoughts dwell on anything negative, especially when it involved Viane and her family.

Forty-Eight

Hɪʟᴏ ᴍᴇᴅɪᴄᴀʟ ᴄᴇɴᴛᴇʀ ᴡᴀs in a full-blown state of chaos as Stone and Teri walked through the front door, an unusual occurrence for this community hospital.

Nurses in crisp white uniforms moved with hurried efficiency among the small groups of people huddled in the confines of the reception area. They were standing close talking softly among themselves. Some were openly sobbing, either overcome from emotions of what they had experienced or from worry about loved ones who had been involved. Others were standing off by themselves staring at the floor as if expecting a pool of answers to appear—the eight ball that has all the ripostes. The lot of them looked anxious and dispirited as the hospital staff attempted to go about the many tasks being called for with as much efficiency as they could muster.

As they walked past one of the small huddled groups Teri overheard an older gentleman, being interviewed by a reporter for the *Hilo Tribune*, according to a tag hanging from the reporter's shirt lapel, mention a chartered helicopter on a circle-island tour carrying twenty passengers that had been caught in a sudden downdraft as it flew over the town of Waimea and had been forced into a too-hard landing. Waimea Hospital in Kamuela, essentially a small clinic by hospital standards, apparently couldn't handle the sudden rush of injuries (so many of the more severe cases were Medevac'd to Hilo Medical Center. Cuts, bruises and limbs in slings were evidentiary as Stone and Teri wove their way through the area to room 203, the room number Pops had given them.

Entering Viane's room, both Pops and John, as if synchronized by an invisible puppeteer, looked up and acknowledged their presence: Pops with a simple raise of his hand hardly above shoulder height, and John with a bit more enthusiasm with an abbreviated *shaka* sign before both men returned to their vigil. They had taken up positions, one on each side of Viane's bed, their chairs pulled tightly beside it.

An older, sweet-looking woman, the same woman Stone recognized from the car that had pulled out of Pops' driveway, was standing close behind Pops, her right hand resting easily on his left shoulder. She wore a gray-blue flower-print muumuu, a white *kukui nut lei* tied with a bright red ribbon lay draped gently over her shoulders and around her neck. A large collection of *plumeria* blossoms adorning her left ear gave off a beautiful scent that had permeated the room. Her thick silver-gray hair was pulled up and efficiently piled atop her head, giving the impression there was too much of it to do anything else with.

Teri walked over beside John, briefly touching his back in a gesture of mutual sympathy. She left her hand resting there for a moment, aware of the tension in his shoulders. Stone went around to the other side, since there was more space, and moved close to Pops and the woman.

A large vase of flowers—birds of paradise with stalks of lehua blossoms and white ginger—rested on the bedside table. Stone couldn't help but wonder how those managed to show up in such a brief amount of time since Viane had arrived but imagined that Pops or the woman was responsible. Stone decided he'd go and buy an arrangement a little later when time permitted. The room actually carried a festive mood but for the solemn looks on all its occupants and the drained-of-color appearance of the figure in the bed. He let his thought of the flowers go for right now; they were incidental at best, and there would be ample time later to truly appreciate them. He noticed a large piece of lava rock placed next to the flower vase and recalled Randy saying he'd carried a piece up with him from the ledge where Viane had landed. He said something about being a good souvenir that he was certain she'd want after her recovery.

Stone figured he was right and silently appreciated his thoughtfulness.

"Any change, Pops?" The stillness in the room was such that Stone had been hesitant to break it by asking questions; but he, and Teri as well, wanted—needed—to know. Neither had received any word since beginning their hike back to the car earlier in the morning. Stone hadn't wanted to call Pops or John and chance disturbing something that shouldn't be disturbed.

"Nothing." Pops's abbreviated, absent-of-thought response brought a soft shoulder squeeze from the woman behind him as she looked up at Stone and then over at Teri. She lowered her head slightly peering at Stone over the top of her metal-framed glasses—they looked like they were barely hanging on to the tip of her nose. A silver chain draped loosely from each stem and travelled around her neck.

"My name's Leilani Davis," she announced, a gentle smile creasing the edges of her lips. She held her left hand out sideways toward Stone in a gesture of connection, her right remaining attached to Pops's shoulder. Stone reached over and took her offered hand. "I believe we met over a year ago at Pearl Harbor Yacht Club," she offered. Her voice was soft and sweet, almost melodic as if a humorous story was about to follow.

"I remember distinctly, Leilani." *Sometimes it just seems more chivalrous to lie.* He did remember her face, though, now that she'd put things into context. "My name's Stone and this,"—he turned and cast a smile at her across the bed, "is Teri, my partner."

"If I remember correctly," added Teri, stepping into the conversation, "you were very instrumental in helping steer us in the direction we needed to be looking when Viane was missing at that time." Teri smiled warmly, lovingly as she took in Viane's peaceful face. She gestured with her hand at the spot beside the bed where Leilani was standing. "Can I get a chair for you, Leilani? I'm sure there must be a loose one close by in the hallway."

"Oh, mahalo nui loa, my dear. I appreciate your offering, but I'm perfectly fine for now.

"The doctor just left," she went on, seeing the concerned expressions looking back at her. Apparently, she had voluntarily taken on the position of spokesperson since it was evident neither Pops nor John was about to say much. "Viane is in something the doctor called a mild form of hemorrhagic shock, and her body's gone into a coma—hopefully just for a short time while it goes about repairing its internal damage. Isn't the body marvelous?" she exclaimed, almost in reverence, returning her gaze to Viane.

Stone assumed Viane's condition might be more severe than what Leilani implied, but he admired this woman's simplified explanation and was pleased she hadn't gone into a long assessment of medical terminology describing the injuries. He wasn't ready to hear all that yet.

"She has a severe head wound and broken femur in her right forearm, plus several very deep bruises," she went on. "The doctor's not willing to predict anything for now but mentioned her physical shape would be a huge asset in her recovery. The head wound has him worried, I suspect, and from my years as a nurse, I tend to agree." Pops absently reached his hand up and squeezed the hand resting on his shoulder—he had apparently been listening, which hadn't been evident.

Leilani's head remained tilted forward as her lips parted in a sweet, amazingly calm smile as she recounted the story of their meeting, seemingly satisfied for now with the information she'd supplied on Viane's current condition. "I remember you were all busy searching for Viane's kidnappers as I was walking my dog, Ichi, through the yacht club's park. My, but doesn't she get herself into pickles." She giggled softly into a closed fist as she looked at Viane, as if expecting agreement.

Her voice was soft, grandmotherly. Stone remembered noticing that the year before, when she had made her appearance at the yacht club by Pearl Harbor. He noticed her eyes belied her age: they were alert, taking in every moment almost as if in fear one would slip past without her knowing. The twinkle emanating from her eyes betrayed an inner secret that seemed to imply that under normal circumstances, she would prefer to be laughing and acting silly. Her lightness of the situation gave Stone a sense of relief and suspected Teri felt as he did.

There was a lull in conversation before she asked, "How is that handsome Sergeant Mike?" She giggled again. She had become slightly infatuated with Mike when they all met at the yacht club at that time. Being a tall, handsome Hawaiian in uniform it wasn't difficult to imagine *why*.

Pops pulled his attention from Viane and answered the unspoken question that was hanging in the air. "Leilani and I are friends from many years ago." Knowing he still needed to tell more, he added, "I called her from the helicopter and asked that she come. My daughter's kidnapping last year inadvertently rekindled a friendship between us that had been lost." He looked up at her as he said this, and then looked from Stone to Teri. "I'll tell you both the whole story sometime when Viane is there to listen as well."

It was apparent he didn't want to talk further right then as he turned his attention back to his daughter. John, during the brief conversation, had remained motionless, in deep meditation and prayer, having not spoken since Stone and Teri arrived.

"When are you two planning to return to Oahu?" It was evident Leilani was attempting to ease the tensions in the room. One could guess she'd been standing there with Pops and John for a good length of time already.

"That's something we haven't decided yet, Leilani," Teri looked over at her partner for confirmation. "I think we're here until Viane's prognosis is known and her condition greatly improved." Stone nodded at no one in particular; he was gazing at Viane, thinking about the strange way events can pull people together—or back together in some instances, like now.

Stone abruptly excused himself, explaining the need to make a phone call, and left, but not before going around the bed and kissing the back of Teri's neck. He knew his friend Mike would be expecting an update on Vianes' condition, something Stone had promised to do in order to keep his friend in the loop—besides, making the phone call was an ideal excuse. He really didn't like being in hospital rooms regardless of how much he loved the person bedded there— he wasn't fond of being in hospitals, period. For as long as he could remember, he'd been uncomfortable within such confines and their sterile antiseptic atmosphere. He'd given up fighting the emotion long ago, taking small breaks seemed to help him get through the unavoidable. Teri knew what he went through and supported him although she completely failed to understand it. She figured it was left-over baggage from childhood, one of those things that could remain in the minds of people, hidden in the recesses of the past.

Mike remembered Leilani and gently laughed when Stone told him she asked about him. When he closed his cell phone after their conversation, he called Guy. Mike had told him there was news of Guy's boat but had deliberately avoided saying what that news was—*Ask Guy,* was all he would say. Deborah answered the phone saying that Guy wasn't there but would be back soon. Stone noticed her voice carried an as-yet-unexplained tone of excitement. *What the heck was going on?*

"It's still in good shape, Stone," she blurted the words out, shifting the conversation away from Viane. Stone was inwardly pleased she didn't want to prolong the discussion of Vianes' condition—there would be time enough later on.

"Are you talking about your boat, Deborah? *Lehua?*" His voice was skeptical.

"It's amazing, Stone. Mike found it when they searched the property out in Kaaawa. He told Guy it appeared to still be structurally sound.

"The insurance company," she continued, "is arguing about paying the cost to have it towed to our house so I persuaded them that the very least they could do was hauling it to the Heeia Kea boat ramp and put it back in the water. Seems I was able to convince them they were getting off cheap. This'll actually make it easier for Guy and me to pull it back up on its trailer and haul it home."

"I'm surprised Mike's letting you do that," Stone replied. "Isn't it a crucial piece of evidence?"

"Mike's a good guy, as you've continually told us, Stone. He said it's still evidence but he's letting us keep it here instead of in some out-of-the-way impound lot getting all dusty and dirty. I'm so excited and Guy's beyond ecstatic."

"Are you going to get the motors and all the other gear back as well?"

"Mike hasn't mentioned that yet, but we're getting Guy's old car back. Did he ever tell you about that?" She didn't wait for Stone's response—she was so excited. "Not sure where we'll keep both of them, though, our yard is so small.

It's got us talking about selling this place and moving to a house with a bigger yard."

"But you just bought that house, Deborah. Surely, there's a way you can fit them all in your yard."

"Yeah, maybe, but we sat down with paper and pencil and figured we can make a little money selling the house now. You know, 'buy—fix-up—sell'. It's kind of like having a second job, don't you think?"

"If you're set on moving why not look for a place close to where I live. I'd love having you and Guy close by." He was serious. If his friends were going to move, why wouldn't they move into his neighborhood, provided they could find the right house to buy.

"You just want to have access to our small boat to play with in the Bay since your yacht is so big. Am I right?" She was having fun.

"Well," replied Stone, "there is that," he laughed.

"I'll let Guy fill you in more but guess what?" She sounded even more enthusiastic, if that was possible. "We *are* looking at a house that's on Mahalani Circle just a few doors down from your Bayside Place house. How about that? It's even got a small dock, a boat-launch ramp dredged back into the yard and a view looking directly at Coconut Island. It's fantastic, Stone."

"I know the house, Deborah. In fact, I walked through it when it first went on the market. I like what they did using part of that huge yard to create an in-yard boat ramp with a large area of deck beside it. The water in that part of the bay is a perfect depth for it."

He would have liked to continue talking about it but knew he needed to return to Viane's room. He'd been gone too long already. "I'm anxious to hear more, but right now, I need to get back to Viane." He let the conversation stand, said *ahui hou* before reluctantly walking back into Viane's room.

Forty-Nine

IT WAS GETTING LATE in the day, and weariness was beginning to show on everyone's face. The nursing staff had been vigilant and caring, the doctor had made frequent visits to tweak this or tap that, but Viane remained unmoving. She had yet to show any signs that life was even attempting to make an effort at returning. The machinery around her kept up a constant rhythm of blinking and beeping, indicating that all was well but a machine hooked up to a bicycle wheel would beep just as well if the wind blew hard enough—it meant little to those sitting and standing around the bedside. Through everyone's weary eyes Viane didn't appear to exist, only a body lying amongst a battery of medical paraphernalia; a body that simply resembled the daughter; the sister; the friend they all loved.

Everything to say had been said, the room subdued when the door opened and Wendy, the head nurse, the one who'd been so attentive throughout the day, came in with the obvious intention of making an announcement.

"The doctor doesn't think there'll be any changes in Ms. Koa's condition for a while," she informed them. "Perhaps everyone would like to take a break. And"—she smiled sincerely at each one individually—"we'd prefer not having a large number of visitors hovering over the patient during the night hours. We'll be short-staffed, and if any emergency should happen, well..." She let the unspoken words fall where they may. Communicating with visitors was one of the most difficult parts of her job and the part she least relished. Visitors were a valuable asset in the healing process, but in the same breath could impede instantaneous action when it was called for.

"The visitors' wait area is available and is much more comfortable than these chairs," she indicated the ones beside the bed. "There are a few people in there right now waiting for the last of the helicopter crash victims to be released, and that will happen quite soon. Maybe you could set up a shift arrangement among yourselves so someone is always here with Ms. Koa while the rest are down the hall."

"I'm stay'n right here if you're OK with that," a determined voice spoke up. "The chairs fin'e." Pops, not looking up, was still holding Viane's left hand much as he had done throughout the day. He felt there was no reason to leave unless it became obvious he was in the way, and then he would simply move back a few feet.

"Well, I'm going to go stretch my legs for a bit, Pops. Then I'll be back." John gently squeezed his sister's hand, patted the top of it, and then stood, stretching his back before heading out the door.

Leilani bent and kissed the top of Pops head—as short as she was, she didn't need to bend too far. "Sweety, I left Hawi so quickly this morning when you called that I left many things undone, like feeding poor little Ichi and taking him for his walk—he'll be waiting to do his *necessary*. Must be thinking I got lost." She giggled softly—a nervous reflex, something she couldn't help. "I'll be back early in the morning." She gently held Pops face and turned it to face her. "You call me immediately if there's any change." She held on to his gaze.

In an open act of affection, something Pops generally regarded as private, he placed two fingers to his lips and extracted a kiss and placed it on Leilani's, his fingers lingering on her lips. The soul connection they had was obvious.

Leilani's mentioning Ichi reminded Stone that Bert was at home alone as well—again. He wasn't too concerned, though—cats afforded that comfort. With her food tray overflowing and a water-on-demand bowl providing a constant fresh supply he knew she'd be fine. She had her own door to escape to the outdoors through or run back in if perceived threats appeared and a beach full of interesting and tasty things to keep her entertained. She probably didn't even realize Stone was gone except for the evenings when it was time to curl up in a warm lap. In truth, though, she always gave the impression she did know and would often show contempt, if an animal can show contempt, when he returned by taking two or three swats at Stone's ankle whenever he passed too close during the first few hours of being home. Sometimes her claws would be out if she was really put out— but then, perhaps that was just his guilt seeping through. A bowl of milk always seemed to be a good pacifier.

"I think, since we didn't sleep much last night," volunteered Stone, "Teri and I will head for your house and the guest room for a short rest-break, Pops, if that's al lright with you. We'll return quickly so you and John can take a break."

Pops nodded and reached for Stone's hand. "I'm glad you and Teri are here, Stone. Mahalo nui loa for being the people you both are. Enjoy my home and sleep well, ahui hou. John or I will call if there's any change."

TIRED OR NOT, THE need for food was making itself known, and both Stone and Teri felt it when they walked out through the hospital door leading to the parking lot.

"Let's stop by Café Pesto for a quick pizza and a glass of wine. We'll be ready to crash as soon as we get to Pops's place."

The Greek pizza was perfect as was Café Pesto's special Crème Brule with *poha* berries drizzled on top—so they'd indulged themselves. It did the trick in easing the day's emotional turmoil but did nothing to alleviate their deep concern and serious doubt about Vianes' well-being. They had both fully expected a more positive prognosis.

By the time they fell into bed in the guestroom both were quickly asleep.

Fifty

IT WAS 6:30 a.m. by the time Stone and Teri managed to get back into their car and leave for the hospital. Stone had hoped they would have been up and gone by this time, but after their sleepless night on the slopes of Mauna Loa the previous night, their bodies were obviously rebelling at the disrupted time schedule. Teri still had an uncomfortable spot on her left hip as a result of their night on the rocks and had woken her several times during the night, extending their bedtime.

There had been no calls during the night, and for which they were thankful. Had anything gone wrong, they knew Pops would have called before the nurses had time to even grab their charts and find a pencil.

Viane appeared unmoved as they walked into the room, much as she had been last night. Both Stone and Teri had hoped there would be some noticeable change from when they left the night before.

Pops and John were just as they had been, each sitting on opposite sides of Viane, each holding her hand. Their wrinkled clothing, however, gave clear indication they'd both been willing to take time to rest during the night. The second bed in the room remained un-occupied and unused but the rollaway cot had noticeable use if the crumpled blankets were any indication. *Even with the cot close by I bet neither of them got a whole lot of rest,* thought Stone. They looked weary and well-worn on the edges. The stress they exuded was palpable. Leilani wasn't there but Pops mentioned she was on her way. Hawi was an hour and a half drive from Hilo and longer depending on the speed of the driver in front, especially if she were coming over the Saddle Road.

They were in Viane's room just a few moments before Stone realized he'd meant to stop by the restroom on his way in—he really needed to get there quickly. He and Teri had tried to cut too much out of their prep time at Pops's place in order to get to the hospital as quickly as they could and certain things, important things, got pushed aside. He excused himself as he pulled the door open.

On his way back, he stopped at a vending machine and bought four coffees. He loaded a tray with packaged sugars and creams along with the short cups of coffee wedged into their designated holes and carefully walked back through the relatively quiet hallway. Balancing the tray against his chest, he was cautiously reaching to push the door open when John came bursting out past him, a look of apprehension frozen across his face as he rushed past yelling for a nurse. His hasty exit came precariously close to causing the entire tray of coffees to tumble from Stone's hands. Quickly backstepping like a circus juggler, he managed to adjust his grip at the last second as sugar and cream packets along with a few stir-sticks cascaded to the floor. John was "heading toward the nurses'] station a short distance down the hall calling for a doctor or nurse the whole distance. Stone watched to see where he was going. *He was curious as well as very startled.*

Holding tightly to the reloaded tray Stone quickly went into the room, not at all sure what he would encounter having witnessed the excited but unreadable look on John's face. He steeled himself for the worst but being an eternal optimist, he held high hopes for the best.

The mood of the room was much different than it was when he'd left less than ten minutes before to find a bathroom. Teri motioned him closer. After setting the tray down on a side table, quite apparent no one was interested in coffee he moved close to her and immediately felt both her arms encircle him. Her face brushed his cheek, and he felt the wetness of tears as she buried her face against his neck.

Glancing at Viane, he could discern no change from before—her eyes were still closed; tubes dangled and machines quietly sounded the life they were there to protect. But when he looked over at Pops, he saw all the previous tension he'd been wearing like a glove since Viane was brought in to the hospital was now replaced with calmness, a discernable happiness had broken through the hard façade of his features; smile lines appeared bordering his eyes.

When Stone looked back at Viane, he was startled to see her briefly open her eyes, look up at him or at least look in his direction for a brief moment before closing them again. Teri's excitement went overboard as she further tightened her hold around his waist.

"She's waking up, Stone! Just minutes before you came back into the room she moved her right hand and her eyes fluttered open. John went to find the doctor. Apparently, the doctor told Pops that it could either be a sudden and quick recovery, or it could go on indefinitely. Appears like his first prediction was a good one." They were all virtually holding their breath waiting for the next indication of Viane's returning consciousness.

The doctor came in swiftly with John close on his heels and head nurse Wendy rushing in close behind the other two. Pops quickly moved aside. The doctor put a stethoscope to Viane's heart, checked her pupils, her pulse, and the warmth of her feet, her arms and forehead before turning to everyone. "What you saw was Viane's beginning attempts to return to consciousness. You might say there's an epic battle raging inside her body right now as she struggles to return from wherever she's been. We don't know if she sees anyone when she briefly opens her eyes or not. We'll just have to wait and ask her." With that, he smiled and gripped Pops' arm with both hands in a gesture of the deep friendship that existed between the two men.

It was first positive thing spoken. With a smile Stone couldn't help connecting the doctor's words with how Leilani had described Viane's predicament the previous day. He marveled at her sense of intuitiveness.

"From this junction forward," the doctor explained, "and for the next hour or two, we need to ask that you voluntarily rotate yourselves so only one or at most two of you are in the room at any one time. If I or one of my nurses needs to jump in for any reason, we'll need full and *instantaneous* access." He had stressed the word.

Stone knew neither Pops nor John were about to leave Viane's bedside—not now, not with her returning consciousness just hoovering around the corner. He grasped Teri's hand as they headed for the waiting room, grabbing two of the coffees on their way out.

VIANE'S RECOVERY CAME QUICKLY after that. By the third day, she was sitting up in bed begging the doctor, almost demanding in her sweet way, to let her get dressed and leave and quietly begging her father to smuggle in some of his Spam broccoli and rice, his specialty, or even a little *kalua pig* and *poi*—the hospital food was good but came nowhere near what Pops could whip-up in an instant.

The first two days of those three, though, had been very unsettling for everyone. Viane's highs and lows triggered without warning. One moment she'd be talking and laughing and acting silly as she'd always done when stress was present, then without warning she'd suddenly sink into nonresponsiveness, by all appearances returning to her previous state of unconsciousness.

The doctor and nurses had cautioned them that this may happen; that everyone needed to steel themselves against overreacting during the low times.

During one of these times, Leilani commented that Viane's body wasn't finished repairing itself yet, that she needed to go into her silence and fine-tune the gears a bit. Leilani's lighthearted view was a godsend to all of them during those times, and it helped Pops handle the multitude of uncertainties that he apparently hid so well from everyone except her. She gave the impression she had a second sense into the way Pops's mind was handling things. It was surprising to witness the relationship they appeared to share, as though they had spent an eternity together—and in their minds, perhaps they had.

Leilani was doing her best to be available as well. She brought Ichi from Hawi to Pops's house so she didn't have to travel so far and be gone from his side for long hours of time.

The uncertainty and long waiting was difficult for everyone to handle. Neither Pops nor John had a clear idea of when, or even if they should take a rest break—what if something were to happen during that time?—but they did, they had to. They took turns going home to sleep for a couple of hours at a time.

Teri and Stone were also taking turns catching some rest at Pops's place, although Stone's breaks became longer each time he left. He used the excuse of needing to contact Lori, his office manager, and soothe the odd client's nervousness when their portfolio dipped for reasons that needed a detailed explanation. But in truth, the hospital atmosphere was beginning to play on his mind and the client contacts gave him a blessed break.

By the end of the second day, Viane's periods of normalcy were lengthening quickly, and by early morning of the third day, she was sitting up in bed and smiling at everything and everybody. The doctor cautiously claimed she was now out of the danger zone. He told them she would be released the following day if all the tests remained positive.

VIANE HELD THE PIECE of olivine- saturated lava that had started her frightening journey, turning it over and over in her hands holding it out for all to see.

Though feeling good about her recovery and returning strength, her emotions remained confused on what that piece of rock she continually picked up and put down represented to her. *Even if it ends up being a paperweight, It's OK—it's the tale of love and caring that came with it, the emotions she felt being on the cusp of life. Encased within were the lessons she learned that carried its value; the nurturing presence that showed up to guide her way; of Pops' emotional struggles to bring her back.*

WHEN EVERYONE WAS PRESENT in the room the fourth morning as they waited for Viane's formal release, she finally told her story of how she'd come to be on the ledge. Everyone had been anxious to know the details, but none had been willing to push her for the story. They all knew she'd get to it when she was ready. She told them how she came to be on Mauna Loa in the first place, of her climb; her fall; the miracle of actually landing on the ledge instead of falling past it. She also told them of her experience floating somewhere between life and death, of floating in Queen's Bath, a treasure of Nature that had long ago succumbed to a lava flow and been erased from existence, of knowing her soul was present but feeling as if she was existing in a void of fully present nothingness; of being pulled in opposite directions: forward into a saturation of loving presence by unknown beings and backward into the life she'd left—her life; back into the loving environ of family.

"Pops, you were the one on the other end of a forceful magnetism that was unrelenting in pulling me back to this life. I love you so much, Pops."

Judge DaSilva's courtroom

IT WAS THE KIND of sentencing Sgt. Mike Kalama could appreciate. Actually, he thought it was ideal and well thought out and fit the judge's style perfectly. Deborah and Guy, sitting in the front row of the court room, liked the verdict and sentencing as well and would have told Mike had they been sufficiently close to communicate. They would have a chance to talk with him after the proceedings were over and were anxious to hear his take on it although his tranquil look was telltale.

Mike admired Judge DaSilva's ability to plow through the mundane and attack the heart of issues while keeping a solid humanitarian outlook for the individuals standing before him.

DaSilva had elected to try all three men as a group—a bit unorthodox, but he wasn't one to worry about what other judges thought of him. He also swept all the charges under one heading instead of dealing with the separate issues of stealing, selling stolen property, transportation of stolen property across state lines, and destroying evidence. That last one gave him a good laugh when he first read the police report: destroying evidence by cutting it into pieces then creating artwork from them and having the brass to turn around and openly sell it—he'd never heard of anyone ever doing that. He planned to document it and include it in a book he intended on writing when he finally retired. The tentative title he'd already chosen was, *Don't Always Judge.* He thought that had a good feel to it. He anticipated every judge in the country would want to buy one.

The consolidated charge against the three was grand theft. He believed punishment was punishment no matter how many laws were broken. The city's appointed lawyer apparently agreed since he didn't voice any objections and actually looked pleased—an unusual experience and completely out of character for the man from DaSilva's observation. The judge reasoned that this trial didn't represent crimes of violence or sex, nor were they life-threatening in any way and unless the three were completely incorrigible, the judge knew he could ferret out the *good* that was somewhere present in each of them. Besides, making it all one charge saved the city a pile of money—he was, after all, a social conservative.

The lawyer did a respectable job in keeping the three men's rights protected and all the facts pertinent. He knew, by the men's own admission, they were guilty as charged—there was nothing he could do about that. His efforts were, therefore, to make certain the men's *better natures* were well displayed for the court and attempt to parley the shortest possible sentence.

ALYSDON LAU AND BILL JEFFERSON were sentenced to ten years in the Oahu Community Correctional Center. If they served their time well, they'd be out earlier—it was totally up to them.

The issue of what to do with their house and property just so happened to present an unexpected opportunity for Judge DaSilva—and he was going to use that to his advantage. The mortgage was paid in full, a fact the judge noted as something favorable for the two defendants—part of the *good* he was looking for—and it made it much easier to arrive at a decision.

He'd had a family come through his court the previous day, and the judge had made a promise to himself to do something to help them. The arsonist who, just for *kicks*, lit the family's house on fire had done an excellent job—it was totally destroyed, burned right to the ground. The family of four, a couple and their two young girls, were left stranded and totally dependent on the state to provide aide as they had recently allowed their homeowners insurance to lapse in an attempt to cut costs. Adding to their plight, the man had recently been laid off from Oahu Poi Factory and was filing to draw unemployment while he looked for work. Judge DaSilva knew that kind of paperwork took time to go through the system, and in the meantime, they would have to be housed at the State's expense.

As a conditional part of the men's sentence, they had agreed with the judge's recommendation to temporarily sign over their house to the family, to be theirs for the duration of the time the men were incarcerated. The men, being three-time losers, had a lot to gain by doing as the judge suggested, and the family in turn agreed to care for the house as if it were their own—in fact, they had to sign several sheets of paper saying they would. It was agreed they would pay a nominal monthly rent for the house. This money, in turn, was to be split between court costs and the insurance companies covering the lost boats.

The old forklift would be donated to a charity group since the original insuring company had written off the loss years before and Dole Cannery didn't want it back—it was outdated and in need of extensive repairs. Just getting it back to the cannery would be a major task they chose not to accept.

Guy's car was a no-brainer according to the judge. Guy could come and haul it away whenever he was ready, as long as he was ready within seventy-two hours. Everyone seemed happy with this arrangement.

Tim Giuseppe was another matter entirely. It was obvious that Judge DaSilva, as with Mike, liked the man. He was truthful and contrite and claimed to be extremely regretful that he'd ever got mixed up with the other two in the first place. He was handed a sentence of five years, to be served on probation, a house arrest of sorts according to the judge, with the understanding he mentor students from the high schools in Kaneohe and Kahuku, schools that served the kids from his community of Kaaawa. His mentoring was to be aimed at boatbuilding and artwork. The judge figured the man had dismantled enough of boats he should have the expertise to put a few simple ones together in a class setting. A man of his natural talent and physical awareness and abilities would make a good mentor for young adults.

Mike walked out of the court room smiling. All was well, and he felt good about the part he had been involved in. The mainland operation was shut down, and the trial of four men and a woman had been concluded. They were all awaiting sentencing. There had been enough evidence in all the detailed paperwork Alysdon had kept, along with the eyewitness testimony from Teak, to seal the verdict. The quick action from Port Townsend's police in apprehending the two men and confiscating the boat they'd somehow managed to get onto the trailer went a long way to discovering the names of everyone involved, and it had snowballed from there.

The old Japanese farmer and his wife in Waimanalo were exonerated—they knew absolutely nothing about any of it. They just happened to live at the address Alysdon wrote down one day to use for this express purpose.

A trucker, an independent driver with a CDL license, who had delivered the container and picked it up after it was loaded claimed to have delivered it to the empty lot next to the defendant's house with instructions to come back in three days, pick it up, and haul it to the Young Brothers. It was a normal drop-off/pick-up job so he had not given it further thought. The paperwork, he testified, claimed a load of chopsticks so that's what he assumed he was hauling.

Mike knew he and his department had done their job well, and he was quite pleased. Underlying it all, though, was the knowing that Viane was home and surrounded by love and Mike was pleased to have played a small but important role.

Hilo—Pops's house—two weeks after Viane's release.

LLOYD AND PAM WERE the last to arrive.

It was shortly past eleven in the morning when they walked into Pops's kitchen, Stone and Teri were close on their heels. Stone had agreed to pick his friends up at the airport after Lloyd told him earlier that morning that he and Pam planned on being there for just a few hours before returning home. Apparently, their daughter Annie was performing in a play at Diamond Head Theatre in Honolulu, and they didn't want to miss it. It made little sense for them to rent a car for the short time and Stone was more than pleased to be able to accommodate.

Walking into the kitchen the foursome was immediately confronted by the irresistible scent of baked sweet bread rolls fresh from the oven still steaming on the counter. It seemed Leilani was very adept at baking. There was no aroma on earth that could pull Stone into a state of gastrointestinal euphoria as quickly as fresh, warm bread.

Pops, Viane, Leilani, John, and Kaitlyn, John's fiancé, were thoroughly engrossed putting together the celebratory breakfast. Kaitlyn, who had pulled in the driveway a few minutes after Stone and Teri left for the airport, was already hovering over a wok filled with sizzling Portuguese sausage, onion, garlic, and a delicious hint of sesame oil. The mixture of smells was wonderful. It was a very active kitchen and easy to see that if any more cooks tried to vie for counter space the approaching feast would be seriously lost in the chaos.

Stone and Teri had arrived on the Big Island two days before and had been using the time for a much-needed minivacation. Everything was finally at ease with their closely held world of friendships: Viane was once again her normal self except for a few residual aches and pains and Guy and Deborah had already re-launched *Lehua* and had even expanded their horizon by navigating the distance to Haleolono Harbor on Molokai, a days' journey across the Kaiwi Channel.

The university was glad to have Teri back but were equally willing to give her a few more days off before the fall semester work load began to escalate; and Lori had done such a marvelous job with Stone's clients and experienced such a rewarding time handling it all, she virtually insisted Stone take more time off. Stone had no doubt that a pay raise was imminent and, he would be the first to admit, well deserved.

Over the past two days, Stone and Teri had driven around the south end of the island and on to Kailua-Kona, where they found a comfortable room waiting for them at Uncle Billy's Hotel. They spent the following time doing nothing but walking the waterfront, swimming off the stone breakwater or sitting reading in lawn chairs on the lush, green grass of Hulihee Palace. They enjoyed breakfast each morning, along with seemingly half the town, at the historic Waterfront Café.

The gathering of their group of family and friends in the process of being prepared was a celebration from stress—a reason for everyone to throw cares away for the moment and just be together as a family.

Pops, though, had a secondary reason for celebrating, but he wasn't saying a word to anyone about what it was. His features were telltale, though, silently telling everyone that he was harboring something that pleased him well beyond simply having his little girl safely home.

Having everyone in his house made Pops happy but as genuinely happy as he was he still held on to his secret, not yet ready to disclose any details. Unfortunately, he didn't have a poker face to hide behind, so they all suspected he was keeping something from them—and that was OK for now. Leilani was party to it, and that was the important point for Pops.

Stone suspected Pops's secret had to do with Leilani. Teri had mentioned she saw both of them stealing looks at each other when they thought no one noticed and appeared to go out of their way to be situated in the right place to brush against the other—*like teenagers in heat,* she thought and then immediately blushed, realizing how she'd acted when Stone was fresh in her life—and still did. Someone probably had the same thought about her when they'd observed her blatant actions.

The only missing links to the celebration were Viane's older brother Sonny who was currently away from the Islands; Mike; and Deborah and Guy. All had been given an invitation, along with encouragement, to be there. Mike, unfortunately, had to work. He mentioned that taking time off for personal reasons right then didn't sit well with his captain or his workload. He explained there had already been a lot of explosive situations arising in the aftermath of the Trans Pacific Yacht Race that required police attention. It seems yachtsmen, and yachtswomen alike, could easily and quickly get into trouble after having been confined to a listing, swaying, dipping, and damp-throughout rolling boat for several weeks.

Deborah had declined as well, saying she and Guy had planned their own celebration and were taking *Lehua* and going out to the sand bar for the weekend. She said it seemed like a fitting place to go since Kapapa Island, where their adventure started, was within easy sight. The popular island of sand in the middle of Kaneohe Bay could stretch from being nonexistent to several acres in size, depending on the level of the tide. And when it rose into the sunshine as the tide went out, it became the place to go for people with boats looking for something different to do with their time. It wasn't unusual to see lawn chairs and tables set up in a foot of crystal-clear water on the low edges of the sand before the sand bar gave way to the depths of the bay. Deborah did say, though, they'd make a special toast to Viane and to all of them. *Okolemaluna! Bottoms up!*

Danny, the owner and chief cook of Empire Café in downtown Hilo, dropped off a platter of adobo chicken and pork midmorning to add to the celebration. He and Pops had been close friends for a long time, and he'd known Viane and the boys since they were born. When encouraged to stay he could only say, and mean, he'd love to but the café was about to open and he was needed there. He asked for and got two bottles of Pops' *patis* to take with him saying his customers literally demanded that it be readily available.

AS THEY LOUNGED ON the lanai, empty platters and paper plates piled helter-skelter on the table waiting for someone to clear them away, Lloyd asked the question they were all eager to learn the answer to but hadn't specifically voiced—perhaps it was the secret Pops held. "Tell us about you and Leilani, Pops. How come you know each other so well and in such a short time, if that questions' not being too personal?"

Settling himself a little deeper into his favorite chair, the depressions and folds in the chairs leather matching Pops backside perfectly, he let out a sigh and smiled at Leilani sitting next to him. He squeezed her hand in a symbol of encouragement before he spoke. "OK, Lloyd, everyone, it's a good time for all of you to know this," and he started his story: "We were very young. It was when I was going from plantation to plantation selling my *patis*. You already know about that *pupule* old man who buried his cane knife in my leg. Well, that's when I met Lei and she met me." He smiled into her eyes; hers had never left his. "You see, she was the young nurse who took care of me. Didn't have to have a degree back then to do nursing, least wise not on the plantations—just had to know what you needed to do, and she did.

"She looked to be my age," he continued, "and that had me worried some. What could she know about doctoring?" Leilani, nervous, giggled at the memory distracting them for a moment. This was obviously a story they both had held on to for a very long time. "I found lots of reasons to go back to Honokaa plantation after that so she could check on my wounded leg. Once I even went back just to steal a kiss—and a little bit more." He absently smiled to himself with the memory then leaned over and met Leilani's lips. A hush had descended in the room and remained until Pops continued. "We became very close—we were in love. Probably woulda got married, but then that big tidal wave in '46 washed through Hilo, and it was over a year before I got back to Honokaa. Getting there was difficult because of all the resulting destruction, there was just so much that had to be done in Hilo, helping family and friends who'd had loved ones swept away." His voice sounded as if it was reaching for some personal justification. The room remained silent—waiting.

"The possibility hadn't occurred to me, but Lei had left the plantation to go to Oahu to Tripler Army Hospital in order to help injured soldiers coming back from the war.

We never saw each other again until last year, when Viane was kidnapped and needed our help." Wonder crossed his expression at that revelation, the coincidence evident. Lei mirrored his expression as they both glanced over at Viane, who shrugged her shoulders in response. *Things happen.*

"My life took a different direction after I left the plantation." Leilani continued Pops's story, her voice soft, as if the retelling was a secret even to her. "Plantation life had become routine and with the war coming to an end, I desperately wanted to help in any way I could, so I went and volunteered. They really needed help, so no one ask too many questions about what I knew or didn't know. And that's where I stayed, for the next forty years. Never did get a degree. I guess I was always needed there, so they sort of let the degree thing slide." She giggled, mostly to herself, her eyes sparkling as she looked at Pops. "Or I just became a fixture around the place, and nobody thought to check further. Pops was always in the recesses of my thoughts, but life catches hold of you and time evaporates.

"When I wasn't working, I devoted my time to my daughter and rescued animals. Ichi always enjoyed having new company to share her food bowl with, and that has been my life."

Surprised looks appeared on everyone's face at the mention of a daughter. No one had given any thought to that possibility—except for Pops. By the look on his face, he knew she had a daughter although he had yet to meet her. Viane's accident, he said, had interrupted plans for doing so.

"Where are your daughter and her father now?" It was the first time Viane had spoken for a long while; she'd been simply sitting there, absorbing the moment. She was thrilled that her father was finally showing interest in someone. He'd only had memories of Viane's mom to encase the past decades of his life. She watched as Lei leaned over and whispered at length into Pops's ear before leaning back, but they maintained eye contact for even longer. It was obvious to everyone that something very intimate had been passed on. He nodded his head as if agreeing it was OK with him that she proceed.

"Lokomaikai, my daughter, lives in Hawi," Leilani picked up once again. "I've been staying at her place since your accident, Viane. She moved there recently from Oahu. I don't have a husband and never got married—I sort of lost interest." She was gazing at Pops, any trace of giggling had ceased.

"How old is she? John spoke the thought that was on the other's minds as they unconsciously did the math, the possibilities running rampant.

"I have pictures of her," she said, pulling her purse off the floor into her lap, rummaging through things. She was relieved this was coming out in the open—at least part of it was—the other part was about to come out into the open as well. She held her breath as she offered the picture of her daughter.

A noticeable hush descended on the lanai as each took the picture in hand and gazed at an almost-too-familiar face and smile.

Stone was the first to speak up. "She looks like she could be Viane's twin sister!"

As he reached to pass the picture back to Leilani, Pops intercepted it and held it tightly in both hands, looking hard and long at it before allowing a broad smile to breach his face.

"This is so perfect I can hardly believe it," he finally said. "We're celebrating the whole family today: being together, having Viane safely home." He gestured at everyone around the room. "If Sonny were here, we'd be *almost* complete." His emphasis on *almost* wasn't lost. "We are also celebrating something I want to tell all of you, something that only two of us know about. Now"—his gaze fell to the picture again—"it seems we have something else to celebrate, something that even I didn't know anything about." He paused and took a couple of deep breaths, still looking intently at the picture of Lokomaikai.

"Viane, John, I pray you will love Leilani as much as I love her 'cause she and I are getting married. I loved your mother, and there's no doubt I always will, but our lives must move on."

He paused again, looking back at the picture he couldn't seem to put down, and then raised it up in front of him as if paying homage to a deity as everyone's attention riveted to it. "Lloyd, Pam, sorry you're not sticking around 'cause tomorrow morning we're going to celebrate again when Lokomaikai drives over from Hawi. Stay if you can. There's plenty room here for you both. In the morning, it appears we'll all get to meet your new sister," he said, looking at Viane and John with a big sheepish grin, "and a daughter I never knew I had."

If some of the italicized words used in my story are unfamiliar perhaps this inventory will be of help.

a'a lava. Its size defies its light weight. Essentially exploded lava rock; sharp and jagged, the edges of which are quite capable of cutting through the soles of your shoes.

ahupua'a. A land division that extended from the uplands to the sea, so called because the boundary in bygone times was marked by a heap (*ahu*) of stones surmounted by a pig (*pua'a*). The pig was a form of tax paid to the chief.

aihue. To take what's not yours. Stealing.

akamai. Smart or clever.

Auwe. An exclamation. Oh! Oh dear! Alas! Too bad! (Used to express wonder, fear, scorn, pity, or affection.)

Bumby. "I'll get around to it soon."

calabash. A relationship that often defies description. A brother-in-law, but not really; a sort-of cousin, etc. Also refers to a bowl holding food—a poi bowl for everyone to dip into while eating at a luau.

haole koa. Shrubby, arid climate tree, originally brought into Hawaii as cattle feed and for decoration.

hale. House.

hanai. A foster child. In old tradition, a family with several children may 'hanai' one or more, give, to a couple without children, usually done within a village. The child then gained an additional set of parents who loved and cared for them.

haole. A foreigner. Pidgin slang for Caucasian. (See note under *pake*.)

haupia cake. A dessert of chilled sweet coconut cream custard.

heiau. A shrine or altar. In ancient times, it was constructed of lava rock often hand-carried for miles, built to honor a particular god, and could be over an acre in size. One of the largest and most well-known is the heiau built by Kamehameha I, situated close to the town of Hawi on the Big Island of Hawaii.

honohono grass. If you think dandelions are a nuisance, honohono grass grows rapidly and snakes across the ground putting down roots, thereby extending its reach. It has been used for animal food.

imu. An underground oven generally used to roast pig for a luau.

kamani tree. A large tree. Its wood is hard and formally used to make calabashes.

kama'aina. A local person of non-Hawaiian blood.

kiawe. Noted to be the most important tree ever introduced to Hawaii. The tree was excellent honey bee forage and the pods are good for animal food, particularly cattle. The wood is part of the mesquite family.

kuleana. Right, title, responsibility, jurisdiction, authority.

ku'uipo. Sweetheart, an endearment.

makai. A word used in referring to a direction: "toward the sea." (see Mauka.)

malie. Calm, quiet, still.

malolo. A flying fish.

mauka. A word used in referring to a direction, 'toward the mountains'. (see Makai.)

musubi. Local family's convenience food. A Hawaiian style finger food made from sticky white rice, grilled Spam, or shoyu chicken all wrapped in nori seaweed.

okolemaluna. A toast when drinking. Literally, "Bottoms up."

ono. Delicious, tasty, savory; to crave.

pa'a. A very common and broadly used word. Its simplest meaning is "firm," "solid," "fixed," "stuck," and "secure." It's not going anywhere!

pahoehoe lava. Smooth, ropey lava.

pake. Pidgin slang for Chinese people. It should be noted that Hawaii has Pidgin terms for all races. Since the islands are populated by a hybrid of cultures, Pidgin terms grew for ease in conversations when referring to individuals. *Generally* used with total respect.

pau. Finished, the end.

pikake. Hawaii's jasmine flower often strung into leis and given to your ku'uipo as a token of love.

poke. Raw fish cut into bite-sized pieces, mixed with a varying assortment of seaweed, shoyu, green onion, roasted kukui nut. Goes really well with beer!

pupule. Crazy, insane.

shoyu. A local term used for *soy sauce*.

the United States
nasters

Print
By B

Printed in the United States
By Bookmasters